PATRICIA CRUMPLER

This is a work of fiction. Names, characters, places, and incidents are products of the author's imagination or are used fictitiously and are not to be construed as real. Any resemblance to actual events, locations, organizations, or persons, living or dead, is entirely coincidental.

World Castle Publishing, LLC
Pensacola, Florida

Paperback ISBN: 9781955086752
eBook ISBN: 9781955086769
First Edition World Castle Publishing, LLC, September 6, 2021
http://www.worldcastlepublishing.com

Cover: Karen Fuller
Editor: Maxine Bringenberg

Dedication

This book is dedicated to all of my writer friends who helped me along the process, especially Janet Little, Roxanne Smolen, Elayne Cox, and Susan Kite.

Thank you to my dear Welsh Friends, Lin and Keith Davies who took me to Eversham England. The lush beauty of the area gave me the background for Apple Valley.

Endorsements

Fate's Sweet Passion delivers everything readers love about historical romance, and more, transcending the genre with freshness and depth. Steep some chamomile, pull up your lap blanket, and prepare to be stunned. Lovers Alexina and Peyton await. —**Chris Coward, Royal Palm Literary Awards chairperson and former president of the Florida Writers Association**

Fate's Sweet Passion is a book that grabs you from the first moment. The characters are real, major and minor alike. The reader could not be more immersed in the action if they had a time machine taking them to the Victorian past. There are twists and turns that will keep you riveted until the last satisfying moment. No matter what your favorite genre might be, this is a novel you can't miss! —**Susan Kite, author of the *Mendel Experiment* series, *Mooncrusher, Realm of the Cat,* and more.**

If you love a historical romance with a hint of magic set in Victorian England, Fate's Sweet Passion will check off all the boxes with its rich setting and characters filled with depth and passion.—**Janet Franks Little, Author of Contemporary Romances**

As an action-adventure writer, I wasn't sure I would enjoy an historical romance. To my very pleasant surprise, the story's twists and turns held me right to the end. The author did a magnificent job of developing the character arc of her heroine.—**Dick Berman, Author: *The Collector, The Machalniks, The Hacker***

Fate's Sweet Passion is one of the best historical romances I have ever read. The first chapter held me captive. Within those pages I smelled the bread, tasted the brandy, and relished the first thrill of new love. A delight for the senses.— **A.E. Easterlin, Author of *Winds Across the Prairie, Sonata by Moonlight,* and *A Necessary Woman.***

Chapter One

Alexina Poole's heart lurched when the thick oak door of her classroom groaned open. *This is it.*

The school girls gazed at the young woman entering the room holding a folded paper. Without words, the woman gave Alexina the paper. *Come to the office immediately. Miss Nixon will take over your class.*

Shaken, Alexina put her finger on a page of an opened book. "I stopped here." When Miss Nixon began reading aloud, Alexina headed to the office.

That brat has placed me in trouble again. Another go-round with the headmistress. She will relieve me of my duties. There was nothing she could do to restrain Bernice, that nasty little demon.

"Miss Poole!" The words echoed in the hallway. "Are you looking for me?"

Bernice.

"Come with me to the office." She kept her voice level. In her deportment class, she coached the girls in maintaining grace under fire, and the teacher must practice what she taught. Bernice skipped to her side and took Alexina's hand like a perfectly behaved child.

In the wood paneled hallway, Bernice paused for a moment to observe three workmen as they struggled to hang a large painting.

"That's the likeness of Her Highness, Queen Victoria," Alexina said.

The girl took a long look. "She looks like you, Miss Poole, pretty."

"Thank you." Alexina wouldn't be taken in by the compliment.

Bernice wrinkled her nose. "That picture stinks."

"That's the smell of the oil in the paint. Victoria is no longer a princess, so we have new paintings showing us how she looked at her coronation."

Bernice touched her own head as if she were looking for her crown. Alexina took the girl by her shoulders and steered her around the workmen. Bernice broke free and ran away to the nearest door. Letting out a long breath, one of many regarding Bernice, Alexina looked out the door, but there was no trace of the young menace. She picked up speed down the shiny planked floor of the hall nearing the school's office, the place where Miss Poole—art, reading, deportment, and life skills teacher at the Greenfield School for Young Girls—had been called. It took a swallow and a self-push to enter. Katherine, the clerk, a sweet soul, indicated with her head toward the headmistress's door.

Once again, Alexina's heart mis-beat. She knocked, and as usual, the stern voice said, "Enter."

"You called me out of class?"

Narrowing her eyes, the headmistress held up a calling card. "Your attorney claimed his visit is of the most importance. He waits for you in the lobby. When you have finished with your business, find Bernice and bring her here."

"Thank you, Headmistress." Alexina took the card announcing Ignace Smith, Esq., her solicitor. *Well, who else visits me here?*

In the lobby, a familiar balding man with mutton-chop whiskers and dressed in a dark silk suit waited. "Good day, dear Alexina," Ignace Smith said as he took her hand.

"Good day," she returned. "I didn't expect you. No problems, I hope."

"None, dear cousin. In fact, I have something that will not only surprise you it may gratify you exceedingly. Pray, sit and listen."

"Please tell me you discovered a mistake in my yearly stipend that will allow me to quit teaching at this horrid school."

"Oh, Alexina, how hard it was to appoint you here. You cut my heart."

"And you haven't found me another? All of those letters you said you wrote? I have three years' experience. Surely, some other school—"

"Now, now, my valued cousin, you know my ethics and how I feel about being dependable. You cannot doubt I sent those letters on your behalf."

She did doubt. Four years before, at her mother's death, Ignace Smith had appeared, offering his help. Grandfather Geoffrey sent the man packing. The inherited assets, such as furniture, jewelry, clothes, and dishes, were to be kept with Geoffrey, but her financials were overseen by Ignace. In addition, to keep her away from her grandfather's influence, Ignace secured her the position as a teacher at the Greenfield School. At that time, Ignace read her mother's will describing Alexina's assets and her small yearly stipend. He pointed out that Alexina had two choices—stay with her cranky and sometimes mad grandfather, or work. Smith advised her that the only employment for which she qualified would be governess or tutor. She often thought of marriage and having her own family, but no man had presented himself as a suitable husband. She accepted the position as a teacher, fully knowing she would meet no eligible men while working at this school. Since then, Smith had only visited her for business matters.

"Ahem, Alexina?"

"I beg your pardon. You were saying?"

"I have good news."

Alexina gathered her long skirt and took a seat on the red velvet couch meant to impress the visitors.

Ignace moved a bowl of apples aside to make room on the small table in front of her. He took a paper from his leather valise and laid it down. The title of the page said in fancy script, *Marriage Contract*.

"What is this?"

"Oh, my dear. Listen carefully. Today is your twenty-first birthday."

Alexina nodded. "So it is."

"As of today, your grandfather has no further hold over you. Look." Ignace ran his finger along the bottom of the document, indicating the signatures. "Both your mother and your father signed this when you were three."

Alexina picked up the certificate. "My parents? I see they signed, but who are Clive and Bertha Woodleigh? And their son, Peyton? I do not know these people."

"Your parents did and thought enough of them to betroth you to their son. You do not have to abide by this, but allow me to say it was your mother's final wish. She whispered to me to give you this on your day of maturity. And so, I am."

Alexina read the record carefully. "I do not know what to say."

"Have you other prospects? I speak of work or marriage.

You should know that I believe the gentleman will acquiesce to the arrangement."

Alexina bit her lip and looked away. *A husband. A home. Children.* She pictured what it would be like teaching here at this school for years to come. In a nearby office, the headmistress's voice echoed sharp notes as she reprimanded an unfortunate teacher.

Alexina turned and caught the man's gaze. "I have no other prospects. You are sure the gentleman, Peyton Woodleigh, will accept the bargain?"

"Quite sure."

Alexina reread the contract. The signatures in her mother's fine script left no doubt of its authenticity. She remembered little of her father, but she recognized the sure strokes of his masculine hand. *A marriage contract? A serendipitous birthday present?*

Another sharp reproach emanating from the executive quarters forced her decision. "I am interested."

"Excellent," Ignace said, rummaging through his case for a pen. He brought forth a sharpened quill and small cut glass inkwell. "Sign here, and," he produced another document, "this will take care of moving your belongings."

"To where?" Alexina did not take the pen.

"Northern England, where your betrothed lives on his estate."

She couldn't suppress the wave of delight rippling through her. "A landed gentleman?"

"No great wealth, but he does come from a highly regarded family."

That caught Alexina's attention. She had heard about Ignace's deceptive devices. Her grandfather, Geoffrey Downing, had complained about Smith's devious ways, including untruths disguised in twisted words. Edwina had put her trust in her first cousin and allowed him to handle all her legal matters. But that didn't mean Alexina would allow him, or anyone else, to expect her to blindly accept direction without reason.

"Sir, I need more information."

Ignace smiled.

Grandfather said that was when the man was most dangerous.

"Of course, you do. I shall tell you as much as I know."

Alexina read the marriage contract for the third time. "You say Peyton Woodleigh has an estate in Northern England. He will abide by the contract our parents made over seventeen years ago. I am to bring my worldly goods as my dowry."

Ignace stared into her eyes. His face became rigid, and he pointed at her. "All of your assets. Your furniture, dishes, silver, linens, and personal items left by your mother."

"Does the man have no furnishings? You said there was an estate—doesn't that include a home?"

He relaxed.

There's that smile again.

He steepled his fingers. "Needing a woman's touch, my dear, which you can provide. I have a contract ready for Davis and Sons Removing Company. I will arrange everything. Once you have signed, that irrational grandfather of yours can't stop you from taking your goods from his house."

"Grandfather doesn't use the items Mother left. He stores them in vacant rooms. Although I'll admit, he won't like anyone violating his peace, as he calls it."

Ignace snarled. "His peace. That man needs to be put down like a mad dog."

"Even though you are my mother's first cousin, I cannot let you besmirch my grandfather. Please do not say anything more. He is a good man, even if he can be cranky or unpredictable."

Ignace mumbled unintelligible words. "Sign here. I'll have Davis start the move. Oh, and I will arrange for a maid to accompany you on your journey."

Alexina picked up the pen, but as she lowered it to the document, a howl echoed from the courtyard outside. She recognized that howl.

"Bernice!"

Alexina ran from the lobby, down the hallway, and out into the courtyard. Bernice and another girl rolled on the grass, screaming obscenities and pulling each other's hair. Before she could get to her charge, Bernice took a bite from the arm of her combatant. As Alexina pulled her from the bleeding child, the girl broke free and kicked the unfortunate opponent several times with her dainty black patent leather shoes.

Alexina gave Bernice a good shaking. If Alexina hadn't pulled her arm from the vicious bared teeth, she, too, would have donated her blood to the rich grass of the Greenfield School for Young Girls.

Alexina turned to see the headmistress, her hands upon her hips and her lips pulled together like a tight purse. "I'll see *you* in my office," the headmistress said, "just as soon as you take Bernice to her room and calm her down."

Her freedom from the school existed in the contract she had yet to sign. Moving close to the headmistress and trying to keep control, Alexina modulated her voice. "I should come to your office to hear of my discharge?"

The headmistress sputtered, obviously unable to gather her words at this indignation. "Uhm, er, why—"

"Don't bother. I'm leaving. I'll be gone this afternoon."

Alexina held her head high and forcefully glided her steps toward the lobby. She strode in and without words and signed the marriage contract.

"Now the contract for the removing," Ignace said.

"Later. I have to tell Grandfather I will be married. I will tell him about the furniture later."

"But my dear—"

Buoyed by her performance with the headmistress, she put her hand on her hip and stared at the balding man. Unhappily, he shoved the paperwork into his valise. She stood for a few moments reviewing the last fifteen minutes and how her life was about to change. Could she even imagine what would unfold?

Alexina ambled down the hall, past the new queen's portrait.

It took her less than an hour to pack, and within two hours, she stood outside the wall of the school waiting for the cab she'd ordered. Weeks ago, she wouldn't have been able to catch a cab with all the visitors jamming the city, but now the hoopla of the coronation had settled, and transportation had returned to normal. Would the small amount of money in her reticule be enough to get her to her grandfather's house? Once she took her seat in the cab, she wondered how Grandfather Geoffrey would react to her quitting her position at the school, signing the marriage contract, and moving to northern England to marry a man she had never met.

Chapter Two

The little boy with blond curls flying ran into the barn. He pointed at the open barn door. "Bad man here."

"Hold on a minute, Jim." Aligning the final nail with the shoe's hole, Peyton Woodleigh drove it at an angle through the hoof of his favorite horse, Dragon. Peyton rose from his crouched position and tussled the child's hair. "Now then, what is it you want to tell me?"

"Big-house bad-man. Said important."

Casting his glare in the direction of the gravel road near the house, Peyton scowled. "The mean man?"

The boy nodded.

"I figured it was him when I heard the coach on the pass."

All visitors to Peyton's land were announced by the gravel road. Horses and wheels made grating sounds as they crunched on the stony lane of the pass, the southern entrance into the valley. His valley. He could have made the road smoother, but the grating served as an alarm, the sound alerting him that his protected world had been invaded.

Peyton flexed his arms and stretched his back, then led Dragon to the rear, where Dragon trotted to the meadow. He walked to the wide doorway of the building, cupped his hands into a bucket of clean water, and splashed his face. Using the towel hanging on a peg, he dried. In no hurry to see his guest, he took his time brushing back his dark hair with his fingers.

"Woodleigh!" a smallish young man in the finely appointed carriage yelled. "I know you are in there. I can see you."

Peyton removed his leather apron and strode to the buggy.

"Get off my property."

Smith pushed his head through the opening of the buggy door. The midday sun shone on patches where his wispy brown hair thinned. "If you don't see me right now, you will not *have* any property, you ruffian."

Enjoying the ability to annoy Rufus Smith, Peyton stroked the neck on one of the fine white horses harnessed to the luxurious conveyance. The driver hopped from his perch and opened the door for his employer.

"You kept me waiting. I'm an impatient fellow," Smith said, smoothing his embroidered satin waistcoat.

Peyton, being a head taller than the slight-bodied interloper, stepped close to the man and stared down. "State your business." He moved even closer, catching the man's attention with a threatening glare.

"One day, you will go too far." Smith backed up a few inches, enough to proclaim his cowardice.

"Then what?" Peyton asked.

"I'll call you out, and you'll—"

"Say what you have come for and be quick about it."

Rufus Smith flinched. He snapped his fingers at his man, who handed him a crocodile skin valise. Making a show of the gaudy case, he unsnapped the top, brought forth two documents, and held up the first. "You recognize this, of course."

The top of the document said *Deed* in large letters. Peyton took the paper. "Why do you have a copy?"

Rufus pointed to the bottom. "Listen, and you'll find out. See where it says addendum?"

"There's no addendum on my deed."

"But there is. That is why it says addendum on the bottom." Rufus held up a second sheet and twirled it in the air. "If you had bothered to read it."

Peyton snatched the sheet. "I know every word on my deed, and there is but one page. The word *addendum* is nowhere on it. What are you up to?"

"Perhaps, not being educated in the law, you don't know that when a document says addendum, it means there are additional clauses. As it does here, on your deed."

Peyton's nostrils flared. "This is outrageous."

"It is no fault of mine if you lost your addendum. As a matter of fact, you are indebted to me for bringing this matter to your attention."

"The only thing I could possibly owe you is a sound thrashing."

Rufus waved his arm in a wide arc, indicating the vast valley. "Oh, yes, how like a man who willingly works in the dirt to threaten physical violence."

"Get out of my valley," Peyton snarled.

"Your property *now*. Not in the future if you don't abide by the terms of the deed."

Peyton read the second page, then balled the parchment and threw it on the ground. Smith's driver picked up the ball and straightened the wrinkles.

Smirking, Rufus Smith, Esquire, pulled a third document from his valise. "Your marriage contract. Take a long look. If you do not comply with the terms of the deed's addendum, this estate shall be forfeited by you and sold, the proceeds to be distributed equally to you and your heirs."

"I have no heirs."

"Your mother and two stepbrothers would be considered suitable heirs."

"My *mother?*" His face grew hot. "And those two reprobates? What do they have to do with this?"

"I was under the impression you retained some of your education. The information contained in the addendum should be clear to even the most casual of readers. However, I shall spell it out for you. Slowly, if you need it to be so. Therefore, understand; if you are not wed in three months' time, by your twenty-fifth birthday, you will lose possession of this...well, whatever this place is. And the document I hold here," Smith rattled the paper with the heading *Marriage Contract,* "is the answer to the problem. Furthermore, if you notice the signatures and the dates, you will see your parents signed this when you were seven."

Peyton scowled. "I don't remember any of that."

"You do not need to remember. That is why we have official documents. Your parents contracted with Alexander and Edwina Poole to marry you to their daughter, Alexina. You have a short time left. I suggest you sign and hope the lady agrees."

"The lady? Alexina Poole?"

"Yes. She has reached the age of maturity and no longer has to abide by this contract." Rufus pulled a pen and inkwell from his valise and extended them toward Peyton.

Peyton's jaw moved as he clenched his teeth. He jerked the pen from the solicitor's hand, dipped the point into the ink, and signed.

Chapter Three

Later that afternoon, Alexina rested her carpet bag on the step and rapped the lion's head knocker on the door of her grandfather's house. It had been a long day, and the temptation to lean against the doorjamb grew stronger as she waited. When no one answered her knock, she tried the handle. The door opened to a dark and musty-smelling house. Dropping her bag on the step, Alexina entered the parlor one slow step at a time. With her eyes unaccustomed to the dark interior, the drawn draperies offered no assistance to her movements.

In front of the low flames of the fireplace sat her gray-haired grandfather, head back and mouth open.

"Grandfather, are you all right?"

He snorted and sputtered. "Uh, what? Who are you? I'll take a poker to you, intruder."

She moved closer to him and brushed his gnarled hair back with her hand. "I'm Alexina, your granddaughter."

"You've come for my money. You can't have it."

Alexina pulled a burgundy damask silk wing chair closer to the old man. "I haven't come for your money, Grandfather. I've come for—" She broke off her explanation. With Geoffrey Downing, her cantankerous grandfather, one must carefully plan one's words. She moved to the windows and opened each set of draperies, allowing light into the room.

Grandfather Geoffrey shielded his eyes. "Don't do that."

"Sitting in the dark is not good for you. When did you last eat? Wash?"

He waved his hand in the air to dismiss the questions. Alexina retrieved a towel and a washbasin from his bedroom and put water into the bowl, warmed in a metal pitcher by the fire. She dabbed his face until he sat still and allowed her to finish his head and hands.

Taking his coat and hat from the pegs by the door, she brought them to him. "We're going out for a walk. The fresh air will do you good."

Geoffrey offered little resistance and even produced a key to lock the door behind them. They strolled for a quarter hour. When they reached the park, Geoffrey pointed to a restaurant overlooking a small duck pond. Alexina hoped the purse that had contained the key also held money. The host led them to a table, and they ordered. Even though it was still light, a candle flickered on the table.

Geoffrey's eyes seem to clear, and his face took on a bright expression. "Oh, my darling, how lovely you look. I shall propose to you all over again. Isn't this the place we made our promise to each other?"

Alexina winced from a tug on her heart. "Oh, Grandfather, I am not your darling Abigail, but her granddaughter."

Geoffrey's face fell. "Yes, I see. Where is Abigail?"

"In Heaven, Grandfather, with her daughter, my beloved mother."

He put his hands on the table and then fidgeted with his watch chain. "I remember now. You're Alexina."

"Yes, Grandfather. You'll feel better when you've dined. Here comes our tea now."

When the roast beef came, Alexina's complaining stomach reminded her of the last time she ate, hours before—breakfast at the school. She had taught deportment and employed manners to overcome her hungry inclinations, even though on the plate lay the finest Yorkshire pudding she had ever tasted. Grandfather Geoffrey labored under no restrictions and wolfed his food.

During the after-meal coffee, Alexina observed her grandfather's face. She could ask questions now.

"Where is your housekeeper? Your cook?"

"I fired the cook. She was stealing from me. The housekeeper comes once a week."

"Do you still visit your club?"

"Of course. Why wouldn't I keep my membership?"

"You feel a membership to your gentleman's club is more important than a clean house?"

Geoffrey mulled the question for a few moments. "Yes. I take my evening meals there."

"Oh, good. At least you get a proper meal every once in a while."

"I go most every day."

"Truly? Do you still have your carriage and driver?"

"No. I don't remember what happened to the horse. The buggy needed repair, and the driver stole from me. I take a cab to the club."

By the expression on his face, she knew Grandfather had reached his limit for questions. Later, when they arrived home, with his nightly glass of port, he would be amenable to answer further queries and to hear her news. After consuming a wonderful treacle, Geoffrey put money on the table and pulled the chair for his granddaughter. Alexina was pleased he associated this meal with the proper etiquette. He took her arm inside of his bent elbow on the walk home.

In the house, Alexina bade him sit while she assembled his evening nip. His liquor cabinet fairly bulged with assorted ports, sherries, and fine vintages. She sat a tray with a cut-glass decanter and a clean tumbler on the small table near the old man's chair. He tasted the drink, and with an audible breath, proclaimed it satisfactory.

"How lovely you look in the firelight, my precious Abby."

At first, Alexina thought Grandfather was drifting again, but he was looking over the fireplace to the magnificent portrait of a lovely woman, brown hair curling on one side of her alabaster face, green eyes smiling, revealing her true, sweet nature. Geoffrey held his glass high in the painting's direction.

"How much like them you appear," he said.

A miniature of her mother sat on the mantle. Alexina agreed; she did resemble Abigail and Edwina.

"I am to be married, Grandfather."

He jerked with a quick movement and glared. "I doubt you truly understand what that means, young lady."

She understood. After the death of her father, her mother, Edwina, had clung to Alexina, keeping her home sheltered and adored. Hired tutors provided much of her education. However, the cultured necessities—French lessons, piano, embroidery—had been accomplished by Edwina herself. The poor woman had bouts of uncontrollable sadness, but occasionally she had moments of absolute joy as she remembered the love she shared with her husband, Alexander. When Alexina was fifteen, in uncommon action between mother and daughter, Edwina disclosed a few details of the physical love she had shared with her husband. She recalled her mother's reference to the joy and pleasure of *becoming as one*. Alexina knew what it meant, but not the details of achieving this union. The knowledge of this act had taken root in Alexina's mind, and she longed for the same intimacy.

"Grandfather, I am twenty-one today. I have reached the age of maturity."

Geoffrey put down his glass with a clink on the tray. "What do you want from me? Why are you here?"

"I do not wish anything from you. I am here to tell you of my engagement and to arrange to move my belongings."

"You'll get no dowry from me. I'll not give you anything."

"Grandfather!" She took a breath and calmed her voice. "I wish to move the items I inherited from my mother's will to my new residence." She scowled. "I'm not so sure where that is, however. I will have to ask Ignace for the location. I believe he has arranged for a remover."

"Ignace Smith! That charlatan, that robber, thief, degenerate—"

"He is my solicitor, my mother's cousin. He looks after my business."

"Fire him immediately. I'm sure he has stolen from you because he stole from Abigail. She was the only one of the Smiths that came to good. I could not say no to her, and she insisted on having that malefactor run her business. She convinced your mother to use him as well, and so on down to you. I tell you, he is a criminal. My dear girl, your sainted mother was the only one of my children who gained the sweet nature of my Abigail. Those others may have my name, but they are Smiths through and through."

"Your own children, Grandfather? Shame on you for saying that."

"Shame? It is true. Even a crazy man knows truth once in a while."

Alexina laughed. Geoffrey Downing could be amusing at times. "My aunts and uncles—"

"Are miscreants, just like Ignace and that wily son of his. Ignace married my good friend's daughter and abused her terribly. I jumped at the chance to help her flee that monster. She was a good soul. It broke her heart to leave that boy. And he turned out like his sire. You must not allow that man to control your property."

"But, Grandfather. I need to have my possessions removed."

"I have an associate at the club who owns a transportation

company. I'll speak to him. You can trust him."

"I don't know…."

Geoffrey turned his head toward the painting. "What, my dearest Abby?" he said. "Of course." He nodded his head and turned to Alexina. "Dear Granddaughter, allow me this favor to assist you." He pointed to the portrait and then to the miniature. "For them."

His words and the feeling her mother and grandmother would wish it so gave Alexina a kind of comfort as if through the old man, her departed loved ones desired to help her.

"All right, Grandfather. Let us strike a bargain. I will agree to your help if you hire your housekeeper for three times a week and give her an extra fee to keep your pantry stocked."

Geoffrey Downing shot a glance toward the mantel and looked once more at the portrait. "I'll think about it." He rose and headed toward the front door.

"Grandfather?"

He took his hat, coat, and walking stick from the oak hall tree. "I'm off to my club."

"Tonight?"

"I shall speak to the owner of the transportation company. Yes, in all things, it is who you know." Then he added, "And, who you can trust."

She nodded. "That is quite so." Alexina sighed. "I wonder whom I *can* trust."

Chapter Four

Peyton moved through the northern apple orchard marking the date, the trees' location, blossoming capacity, and progress of the fruit in his leather-bound book. As he had for the past eight years, each evening, he compared the current conditions to past years' records. After his confrontation with Rufus Smith, Peyton found it difficult to concentrate on his work. He hadn't considered marriage. In fact, he seldom thought about women, much less a permanent female relationship. He treasured his land, the thousand acres and deep lake surrounded by the ring of high hills, his valley, his "Applewood." This estate and its animals headed his list of loved ones.

Marriage. According to the addendum of the deed, unfamiliar to him before a few days earlier, if he didn't wed, he would lose this, the only place on earth he wished to be. *Why wasn't the contract invoked before now? What if the woman doesn't agree? Smith said she had reached her maturity. If she refuses, I could marry one of the Wagon Girls. I like the Wagon Girls when I visit, but so do a lot of men in Applewood and in the nearby villages, as well.* Although Peyton had removed himself from proper society, his upbringing wouldn't allow him to swear his vows with one of the friendly girls who lived in the wagons parked near the northern pass. He thought he had left the chaos of city rigors when he left Harrow. *I must forget Harrow.*

He checked the color of the cords circling the trees. In this section, yellow cords marked the trees that blossomed early. Small buds tucked behind leaves assured him apples would ripen in the summer. He moved to the grove with the red cords. These trees had the largest fruit when he first arrived after he left Harrow. Peyton picked up a thin branch that tapered to a point. He whisked it through the air like a sword, making the sound of a whip. The memory of Antony Sutledge came to mind. *I should have finished the fight and not let the other boys pull me from him.* The event played over in his memory as if it had happened the week before.

The problem with Sutledge had started on the cricket field and spilled over to fencing practice. When he opposed Sutledge in fencing, the boy removed his tip guard, but Peyton saw it and dodged the cut. Later, on the squash court, Peyton had come to the end of his tolerance. The fight immediately became one-sided when Sutledge cried foul. Both young men were brought before the dean, and both participants were sentenced to five strikes. Sutledge's father, a well-known judge, tried to bargain with the dean, but to the dean's credit, he wouldn't budge. The judge pulled his boy out of Harrow. Peyton, not a coward, submitted to the punishment, willing himself to make no sound. Afterward, he walked, head high, to his room. That night he threw his hat into the fireplace. He left school, and at sixteen, struck out on his own. Without a ha'pence, he made his way to London to the office of his family's solicitor, Ignace Smith.

When Peyton came into Smith's office demanding to see the deed he knew his father had drawn, the solicitor tried to dismiss him, but Peyton stood his ground.

"My father left me his estate, a large parcel. I want to go there now."

"Come back in a few days. I'll locate the original and draw up the new deed in your name. I'll have it registered for you."

"I'll have to pay you later for your service," Peyton said.

A broad smile came over Ignace's face. "No charge, in honor of your father." Peyton stayed in a stable, trading grooming for his board and bed, his bed being a bale of sweet hay. It was two days before Smith produced the new deed. Peyton accepted the document and memorized the directions on how to get to his father's, now his own, estate. He worked his way north until he found the valley.

Chapter Five

The next morning, when Alexina awoke, her grandfather had already left the house. Mrs. Pribble, a plump, older woman who served as the housekeeper and cook, worked in the kitchen.

"Morning," Mrs. Pribble said.

"Hello. Is this your day to work for my grandfather?"

"No. Strange thing. He visited me early this morning and asked if I would come today and then increased my work to three days a week. I'll bet you had something to do with that."

Alexina smiled. "I hope so."

Mrs. Pribble resumed dusting. "Life would be easier if you could, perhaps, have a good influence over Mr. Downing." She paused, seeming to search for words.

"I understand what you mean. I know he can be difficult, but he doesn't mean anyone ill."

The woman made a face. "I'm not sure about that. When I was here last week, a Mr. Smith came round, and the old man took up his walking stick screaming, 'Thief, charlatan, swindler!' That man ran for his life, I can tell you."

Alexina nodded. "I do not know how Mr. Smith crossed Grandfather, but it must have been something serious." She went to the front window and opened the drapery. "Light. That alone will be a good influence on Grandfather."

"I agree," Mrs. Pribble said. "I've kept the porridge and sausage warm for your breakfast, Miss."

"Thank you," Alexina pulled out a chair. After breakfast, she answered a knock on the door.

"Miss Poole?" A gray-haired man in a dark business suit tipped his hat. "I am Ralph Anderson, a friend of Geoffrey's. He said you needed my services." He handed her an engraved business card.

"Oh, the remover."

"Geoff saw me last night and told me to put your needs at the top of my list."

"Come in, sir."

The man walked with a slight limp. Alexina led him to the parlor and offered him a seat.

"There are so many articles, I don't know how you will go about it. You will have to see my solicitor for the payment. Actually, I don't know exactly where my things will go, just that it's North England."

Anderson patted Alexina's hand. "You are not to worry about anything other than providing an address. I have large vans, and we go to far places. We guarantee the safety of your goods. There will be armed guards riding with the wagon."

"Armed?"

"Absolutely. My record is perfect. Not one loss. Further, you must not consider payment, for I am so indebted to Geoffrey, I can never repay him. I am exceedingly joyous to have this opportunity to serve him."

"My grandfather?"

"Perhaps you don't know," Anderson said. "When Geoff and I were young, we bought shares in a transport ship, and for a lark, we sailed on it to the Caribbean. Being summer, the weather was beastly, and I decided to swim. I jumped off the deck into the harbor of San Juan, Puerto Rico. Almost immediately, I felt a jolt and saw the water turn red with my own blood. A huge shark had taken my leg as his lunch. Of all the men on deck, only Geoff dove into the water to save me. He hauled me up the side ropes and made a tourniquet with his shirt to stop the bleeding." Anderson tapped his right leg with his walking stick, causing hollow wood to sound. "I live because of Geoffrey Downing. Due to my near-death experience, I appreciate every day and have worked hard, leading to remarkable success in the transporting business. Geoff has asked for so little over the years, and now I can do something for him by helping his granddaughter. Yes, Miss, Geoffrey is a hero and a gentleman. Like none other." He rose and walked with Alexina to the front door. "Pray supply me with an address. I'll have my men come tomorrow, and your goods will be on their way."

"Tomorrow? Oh, kind sir. It's all happening so fast."

"Ah, yes, many important things happen fast." He tapped his wooden leg again. "Like this." He donned his hat. "Good day, Miss Poole. My best wishes to you."

Alexina returned to the room that had once served as her bedroom and rummaged through the dark mahogany desk, her *escritoire.* "I must write a few letters." Selecting a sheet of paper, she dipped her pen into the inkwell. *Dear Hester….*

Her only friend at the Greenfield School had been the music teacher, Hester Langley, who offered a glimmer of light in a dark world. Hester, with her talents and charming sense of humor, was also skilled at the cello, multiple violins, and the mandolin. She provided Alexina with hours of enjoyment. The school presented frequent concerts, where Hester played the strings and Alexina accompanied on the piano. On a few occasions, Alexina and Hester had taken a dozen or so girls to matinee concerts and ballets in London.

Rumors of Alexina's hasty departure must be flying around the school by now, and she intended to set it straight, at least with Hester, the only one whose opinion mattered. Hester, three years older than Alexina, was tall and ungainly, *long-boned* by her own description, and understood how unlikely it was that she would meet a gentleman who would whisk her away from the world of education to a family of her own.

After completing that and other correspondence, Alexina opened the two wardrobes in her room and studied the dresses hanging inside. She and her mother had the designer from Paris visit them with sketches and materials. Edwina had been keen for fashionable clothes and had ordered many for herself and her daughter. The clothes remained untouched because for the last three years, the school uniform, dull brown dresses topped with tan pinafores, had been Alexina's only apparel. She had all but forgotten the pleasure of fine fabric and sleek designs and stared at the dresses. *Which ones would suit my new life on the estate in North England?* What she needed right now was an audience with Ignace Smith.

Ready to take her hat from the peg in the foyer, the door knocker sounded. A young woman stood outside, dressed in a flowered cotton dress and an impractical straw hat.

"May I speak with Miss Poole?" the girl asked.

"I am Alexina Poole. Who are you?"

The young woman entered without invitation. A hole in her

glove exposed a dirty fingernail. She pulled off the hat, allowing greasy blonde hair to hang in locks. Pink ears peeked through the uncombed mane. "I'm Daisy Bently, your personal maid."

Alexina took a reflexive step back. "My maid?"

"Yes'em. Mr. Smith sent me. I'm to travel with you and take care of you."

Mrs. Pribble peered out from the corner she'd cleaned.

Alexina looked the girl up and down. "You are trained as a lady's maid?"

"Yes'em."

"Ha!" the housekeeper said from afar.

"I see." Alexina tried to keep the doubting look from her face. "How old are you?"

"Eighteen, Miss."

The housekeeper put down her duster. "Ha!" she repeated, and with hands on her ample hips, approached the girl.

Alexina shook her head. "Although I will require a traveling companion, I won't need a lady's maid."

Daisy's bottom lip trembled. Her eyes watered, and she put her hands together in supplication. "Oh, Miss, I must have this job. My old dad owes Mr. Smith money, and he can't pay. I work for you, and that man writes off the debt. If that debt ain't satisfied, my old dad will surely beat me. Please."

The housekeeper's throat-clearing punctuated the quiet.

Alexina sighed. "We can't have that. I am off to see Mr. Smith and post these letters. You stay here." She shot a glance to the housekeeper. "Have some tea. When I return, we'll talk." Alexina pulled Mrs. Pribble into the butler's pantry. "I'll give you a pound note if you'll clean that girl up," she said in a whisper.

The woman gave a long look at the challenge. "I'll be earning my pound, all right. I have control?" She pulled at her chin. "She might not like it and run away."

Permitting a smile to form, Alexina said, "I might have to pay you more for that!"

The housekeeper nodded. "Right then. We'll see you later this afternoon."

Chapter Six

With only one bedroom in the house, Peyton needed to supply private quarters for the woman. Two walls, one butting against his room and another angled at the outside wall, would provide another bedroom. He reached for the bellows to ignite the waning flame in the forge. *Fire.* His shoulders sagged. That woman would need heat, too.

"Little Jim," Peyton said. "Find Simon."

The boy grinned, his usual response to things, and skipped from the barn. The lad usually kept quiet, but like a shadow, remained near Peyton on most days. He appreciated the child's company. Simple or not, the boy kept the silence Peyton needed to think. And Little Jim often served as messenger, as long as the message wasn't too complicated.

After giving Simon directions to build a small fireplace in the room, Peyton motioned to Little Jim to follow him to the edge of the lake. Peyton threw a canvas bag into a small boat and pushed it to the water's edge. He jerked his head, and without a word, invited the boy into the boat.

"Fish?" Little Jim asked.

"Maybe." Peyton sent them toward the other side with a swift stroke of the oar.

When they reached the far shore, he guided the boat into a groove between the sand and the high bank, where the craft barely floated over rugged rocks. Coming out of the narrows, the boat drifted. He banged the side of the wooden craft, and three fish jumped nearby. Again, he banged, and more fish jumped. Handing Little Jim a long-handled net, Peyton nodded. "Ready?"

Grinning, the boy stood.

Peyton banged on the boat sides and shouted, "Hoo-hoo!"

Five fish jumped, and Little Jim leaned outward, holding the net. He caught one of the fish midair. Peyton grabbed the handle because the fish was so large poor Jim had started to lean too far.

"Well done, Jim," Peyton said, hauling the net to the boat floor. "We'll eat good tonight."

The sides of a ghoulish silver-pink fish moved as the gills pulsed. Keeping his smile, Little Jim made a face at the creature beside his feet.

"I know," Peyton said. "Ugliest fish I ever saw, but tastiest, too."

Little Jim nodded and rubbed his stomach.

Peyton patted the boy's back. "We shall have a feast because you are such a good *catcherman*."

Little Jim beamed. The pride and affection in the boy's face grabbed Peyton. His vow to not have children caught in his throat. Jim, in spite of his imperfection, was a glorious example of a child Peyton would cherish. He chided himself. *Why in hell am I thinking about having children?* Clearing his mind, he pushed the boat away from the rocks and caught the light current that took them to the home side of the lake.

The next day at the forge, Peyton struck the chisel with the hammer forcefully on the metal sheet. It pinged, and the sound echoed against the stone walls. He threw the cut piece, now a nail, into a leather pouch sitting on the workbench.

A man dressed in kneeless, tattered work clothes approached. "Master Peyton, you want the lumber brought into the house?"

Peyton nodded at his workmen and cut another nail. "I've marked the lines. You and Tony erect the walls. "Here." He handed the man the leather pouch full of nails.

"Ah," Phillip said, "is this going to be a guest room?"

Peyton lost the grip on the chisel as he looked up.

Phillip grinned. "Later, it can be a nursery."

The barn became silent. Peyton frowned. "Bad news travels fast, I see."

Phillip shrugged. "No secrets in the valley." He took the batch of nails and left.

How did Phillip know about the woman? Peyton let out a long breath and reflected on the day Rufus Smith came. What difference did it make, anyway? Everyone in the valley would know sooner or later. Peyton would honor the bargain and wed the woman to keep his land.

When she had had enough of the austere country ways, she would leave. He wanted no part of city traditions or city people. The harsh realities of living in this area would wear thin on a woman accustomed to the finer things of life.

The quicker she departs, the faster I can get back to normal.

Chapter Seven

Alexina began her long walk to Smith's office but didn't mind the distance. It gave her time to think. Her whole life had changed in less than forty-eight hours. She had signed a marriage contract. *Am I engaged? What is the man like? What do I know of him?* He was four years older, lived on a large estate to the north, and came from a good family. *He must come from a fine heritage, or Mother would not have aligned with them.*

The name Woodleigh sounded vaguely familiar. *Lovely name.* It rolled off her tongue. She said it aloud. "Alexina Woodleigh." A soft sound, pleasant. During one of her grandfather's lucid moments at supper the night before, she'd asked about the name. Grandfather said he knew of Bertha Woodleigh, once Lady Dunforth, but their food came, and the conversation ended.

She reviewed the past few years working at the Greenfield School and her decision to leave. Her thoughts jumbled with questions and doubts. *What does he look like? Is he kind? Why would he marry a woman he hasn't met?* She didn't know enough. *Was I too hasty?* Mr. Smith would give her the details. After all, Ignace had her best interests at heart, didn't he? Certainly, Mr. Woodleigh would give her time to know him. He needed to acclimate as well.

When she arrived at the office, the clerk offered her a seat in front of Smith's desk. As she placed her basket on the floor, two letters slipped from its confines. Smith retrieved them and began to hand them to her but stopped. He read the address of one, set in on the blotter, and read the other.

"I see you have a letter to the Woodleigh Family."

"I wrote it this morning. I'd like to meet them, but if that's not possible, I have introduced myself. I hope some of his family can come to the wedding."

Ignace smiled. He put the envelopes together on his desktop. "His father is deceased, leaving a mother and two stepbrothers. The stepbrothers live abroad, and his mother travels frequently. I doubt she will return in time for your wedding. I will post these letters for you. Mrs. Woodleigh will get hers when she returns. Let's talk about moving your dowry."

"My dowry? My grandfather won't—"

"Your yearly stipend, my dear. And, oh yes, your furniture and other items inherited from your mother's estate. I understand you have some jewelry. You still have it, don't you?"

"My jewelry?" She fingered the chain hidden by her blouse. She had worn that fine gold chain for as long as she could remember, along with a pendant, a small flower comprised of rubies and diamonds. Although she didn't recall the event, she knew her father had given her the pendant. When her mother died, Alexina added Edwina's slim gold wedding band. Wearing the two items together on the chain made her feel like her parents were with her.

"Alexina?"

"Oh, forgive me."

"You haven't sold your jewelry…or given it to your mad grandfather?"

"You mean my mother's jewelry?"

"It's *yours*. You still have it?"

"I suppose I do."

"Good," he said, forming a steeple with his fingers. "Now, as for the removers—"

"Please, don't bother. I have already spoken with Mr. Anderson about that."

The mutton chop whiskers in his jaw moved as he clenched his teeth. "What?" Smith's face turned red. In a moment, he regained his color and smiled. "I see. Mr. Anderson is a member of your grandfather's club?"

"Yes. He'll need the address. Therefore, please tell me the exact location where I shall be traveling. I should like to go to the library and see it on a map."

Smith grabbed a sheet of paper and filled his pen from an ink bottle. He scratched the pen on the paper, blew it, and slid it toward her.

Alexina read it and looked at him. "Eversham?"

He nodded. "West of."

Alexina read the directions aloud. "To Eversham, west to Stowston, south to Ravenswood, west to Kerrstead, on to Turnersfield.... This is accurate?"

Smith frowned. "It is."

"But, shouldn't you consult *something*? You wrote it without a reference." She had always accepted her solicitor's business acumen, but this didn't feel right. She needed an exact map for Mr. Anderson.

"Why do you question me?" His lips formed a thin line. Then he smiled. Reaching into the bookcase behind him, he pulled out an atlas. "Here." He flipped through the pages and stopped his finger at Eversham. "You might want this, as well." He handed her a printed map of the stage routes.

Alexina examined the map, matching it to the routes, noting the many stops and carriage changes. According to Smith's handwritten directions, the last change occurred at Turnersfield, where the instructions directed the traveler to take the western road toward the pass, but first, see the dry goods merchant in town to arrange for a guide into the valley.

"How do you know the way?

"Trust me."

"Have you been there?"

Smith looked at her as if he had been caught in a guilty act, then smiled. "Uhm, yes...some years ago."

Alexina thought of Grandfather Geoffrey's warning regarding Smith. *The wider the smile, the more grievous the lie.*

Smith cleared his throat as if clearing away the subject. He stood, indicating her time with him had come to an end. "Since you have used little of your stipend for this year, here is the remainder. Next year I will send you the amount in full in January." He handed her an envelope. "I have booked your passage for three days hence. You will be met at Turnersfield, for no cab goes beyond the hills there. All is arranged, dear little Alexina. Ah, so much like Edwina, you are."

Alexina had noted a long time before the soft tone Mr. Smith used when he referred to her mother.

He stretched out his hand, an extra gesture to end the audience. "Your lady's maid will call today. You should be there to receive her." Smith placed his hand on her back as a gentle escort out of the office.

Alexina didn't like his touch and stopped in the doorway. "Daisy. She's already called." Her words left no question to the annoyance produced by the young woman.

Smith's eyebrows rose. "Oh, she'll be fine, if perhaps a little rough around the edges. You can train her. Think of what a boon that will be to the poor girl. After being with you, the girl can be employed in service. You wouldn't deny that favor, would you?"

I've been manipulated. Yes, she would take Daisy and, using her experience gained at the Greenfield School, help the girl. At that minute, she couldn't get out of his office fast enough, repelled by his practiced charm. Unlike her previous dealings, his manner gave her a turn of unease.

When she returned to Grandfather's house, a cleaner, pinker, and unhappier Daisy waited. The girl's ill humor diminished when Alexina gave her two dresses, one a pale-yellow linen and the other a blue and green paisley cotton.

"There's no time to alter them. Perhaps we can put some weight on you," Alexina said.

"Thank you, Miss. I like them just fine."

"Since we will leave in a few days, we only have time to get you a few new things."

"New things, Miss?"

They spent the next day shopping, which netted Daisy a new felt hat, white leather shoes, and a traveling smock. As they spent time together, Alexina did her best to show Daisy proper behavior and etiquette.

Later that evening, Grandfather Geoffrey complained that someone had stolen half a bottle of port.

"Grandfather, there is no one here to steal your port. You drank it and forgot about it."

He huffed and thought for a bit. "No. My port is half gone. I'm certain."

"Good night, Grandfather." She kissed his cheek. "Sleep well. Have some more port."

He eyed the dark liquid level in the cut glass decanter and reached for a tumbler. "Good night, Granddaughter."

The following morning the removers were scheduled to arrive. Geoffrey ordered the housekeeper to provide a substantial breakfast. Daisy sat, picking at the plate.

"Your eyes are red. Are you ill?" Alexina asked.

"I didn't sleep well," Daisy said and moved a bit of sausage around.

"Girl," Geoffrey said to Daisy. "You need to eat."

Daisy whined and left the table.

"She's probably not hungry because she drank my port."

"Grandfather, please." Alexina waited a moment, hoping he wouldn't speak further of petty thievery. "I wish to leave a few things here if you don't mind. I won't have a need for ball gowns or the jewelry. I can always get them later. Are you sure I should take the bedroom furniture?"

"Yes, yes, girl. Why do I need a guest room? You are leaving me, and you are the only one worth having about."

"Grandfather! I don't know what to say."

"You could say you changed your mind. Contracts can be broken, especially foolish ones. You should marry for love, girl."

She sighed, bringing her shoulders up, then down. "This is the first time in my life I have a real future. He must be a good man. I trust my parents' choice."

Geoffrey pushed his hand into his vest pocket and withdrew a small leather wallet sewn shut. "This is your getaway fund. If you realize you have made a mistake, open this and leave. There's enough here to get you back. Back to your home…to someone who loves you."

"Grandfather." She bit her lip and squeezed her eyes shut. "I—"

"Tut, tut. Don't go all sentimental on me. Allow an old man to bestow his wisdom." His lips turned up at the corners. "While he's in charge of it!"

"Thank you."

The old fellow's eyes glazed over. She sighed again, wondering if that loving bit of humanity had just passed.

Geoffrey's pointer finger went up. "Keep that wallet hidden from everyone. People will steal from you."

Within the hour, the removers arrived. A dozen brawny men, each with thick quilted blankets, wrapped the items and stowed the pieces in a large covered van. Neighbors watched as the draft horses stomped and whinnied, appearing to be impatient to get on their way. When the last pair of removers took the trunks out, the house seemed different. None of the rooms seen from the foyer had changed, but Alexina felt the emptiness around her.

That evening Geoffrey did not go to his club. "My dear granddaughter, dine with me tonight. We'll choose an elegant place and toast your new life."

"Thank you. Daisy, get your new hat."

Geoffrey grabbed Alexina's elbow and guided her into the pantry. "Just you. Not that silly goose. Leave it to Smith to scheme something like this. I wouldn't allow such a girl to be your maid, but you can't travel alone."

"Grandfather, she needs to learn how to behave in social situations. We have to start sometime."

"Ah, how wise. You take after my side of the family. Have I ever told you that?"

"Yes," she said and touched the tip of his nose. "When you weren't accusing me of wanting something from you."

He shook his head. "I never thought that of you."

"Good." She kissed his forehead. "Shall we go?"

Daisy appeared with her new felt hat, tied on the side, and looked amazingly appropriate.

They dined at a refined restaurant, where under the glare of a haughty waiter Alexina whispered proper etiquette to her grandfather and Daisy. Geoffrey eventually summoned his manners from a proper upbringing, but Daisy became frustrated while trying to acquire the use of multiple forks. Even the girls at the Greenfield School did not require as much overseeing as her companions at this table. Alexina enjoyed her dinner despite the whispers and eye movements in her quest to tame these two wild animals.

In the morning, a cabbie rapped sharply on the door, asking for the two ladies he was to take to the coach station. The housekeeper hugged Alexina and would have hugged Daisy, but the girl had whisked out the door and jumped into the cab.

Geoffrey kissed Alexina's cheek. "Remember, you have a get-away clause in your contract."

"No, I don't, Grandfather."

"Money always trumps contracts." He wiped his eyes and cleared his throat. "But, love trumps everything."

"I love *you,* dear Grandfather."

"I know," he said, and walked her to the door.

At the station, Alexina and Daisy boarded a large coach, taking a seat inside the crowded interior. Lesser paying customers sat on the top of the coach. The buzz of conversation lulled to quiet as they reached the northern boundary of London. It wasn't long before the uniform clop-clop of the horses put many of the passengers into a slumber. The city gave way to the countryside.

Chapter Eight

Within the quiet of the coach, Alexina reached into her handbasket and retrieved a small red-covered book. She remembered another red-covered book from her recent past. Hester, the music teacher, had accepted her single status as permanent, but she hadn't given up speculating on the amusements enjoyed by married ladies. Many evenings she and Alexina, under the guise of composing cello music, hypothesized about what actually took place in the nuptial bed. Hester had a small red book left to her by the previous deportment teacher, Alexina's predecessor.

"Claire Dermott left this in her room." Hester handed over the soiled and well-used book and explained that Claire had been expelled from teaching. "She told me she was going to have a child."

Alexina shook her head at this notion. "A child? Married ladies aren't hired at the school. You can't have children until you're married."

"Apparently, you can," Hester said. "Claire told me she became one with the groundskeeper. I'm uncertain what that means."

Became one. The term my mother used. "The groundskeeper?"

"Handsome, he was, but unfortunately quite poor. He married her. Before she left, she said it was worth it—that is, losing her job. I wanted to know more but didn't have time to ask." Hester touched the red book. "It once had many drawings, but there are pages missing. It's written in French. How are your translation skills?"

"My French is adequate. But you speak French. It is a prerequisite of employment."

"You'd think so, wouldn't you? However, my skills are greatly lacking. When I sat for my hiring consultation, the headmistress asked me to translate a page in French. I just said what I thought it meant. She didn't question my translation, so I tried an experiment and told her I had a problem with one of the words. Would she be so kind to tell me its meaning? She snatched the paper from me and said she'd heard enough. I was hired. The look on her face told me she didn't know French at all."

"The headmistress is a fraud!" Alexina clapped her hands.

"True, but so am I, and I *don't know* what's written in this book."

Alexina flipped open to the first page. As she read, her French did not live up to her claim, for many words stumped her. According to the text, gentlemen possessed stovepipes, chimneys, and one-eyed dragons, as close as she could reckon. The females used their furry little pets, black foxes, red kittens, and honey pots to please the gentlemen. The book did not inform as much as frustrate. They needed a more detailed book.

Shortly thereafter, when Alexina and Hester took a dozen girls to a ballet in London, Hester pulled a pair of dark spectacles from her purse.

"I need to use your hooded cape," she told Alexina. Hester donned the cape, pulled the hood around her face, and wore the glasses.

"What are you doing?"

"See that bookstore? It's the same as the label on that one we tried to read. And today, we are blessed not to have the headmistress with us. Watch the girls and give me but a minute."

Before Alexina could protest, Hester had rushed into the small bookstore. She returned with two books, one red and one blue.

"Put this," she handed Alexina the blue book, "in your purse, and for heaven's sake, don't touch it until we're back in our rooms. Oh, Lexy! There are pictures!"

Alexina could hardly wait until the girls were shuffled off to bed so she and Hester could dive into their reading material. Opening the red book, she translated the title: *The Naughty Menu at Corrine's Table.*

Hester flipped past the words and found the first picture, a beautiful little watercolor of a Marie Antoinette-like lady, Corrine, sitting on a festooned swing, wearing only a bustier. Her legs were wide open, exposing a dark cavernous area. A gentleman stood in front of her, his trousers puddled at his feet, knees bent, waiting for Corrine to swing his way. The translated caption said: *First course, Swinging Sausage.*

"I can't see his front!" Hester took the book and pretended to peer at the edge of the page for a closer look. They both fell on the bed in peals of laughter. But then they heard footfalls on the wooden hallway and knew instantly who would be making them. Hester sat on the book and handed Alexina the cello. As the headmistress barged in, Alexina pulled a long squeaking note with the bow.

"You are making too much noise," the headmistress said. "I thought I heard laughter."

Hester shook her head. "Of course, you did. Miss Poole is trying to play my cello."

The woman pointed her finger. "Desist immediately."

"Mai oui, madame." Alexina smiled sweetly and added a sentence in French.

"Hmm, yes, of course," the headmistress said.

The two young ladies could hardly keep a straight face long enough to let the woman slam the door.

"I got the first part," Hester said. "But what else did you say?"

"I called her a fat ugly cow."

"And right you are, but on to important matters." Hester quickly retrieved the book and flipped to the next picture leaf, a set of four vignettes occupying a single page. The top scene depicted Corrine draped over a man's lap, receiving a paddling, making her buttocks bright red. Corrine's face radiated pleasure. The caption: *Entre, Red Meat served rare.* The next in sequence had Corrine, *sans* clothes, positioned on her side, buttocks still reddened, exposing the dark cavern between her parted legs, and the back of the gentleman, *sans* his pants, moving toward her. That caption: *Delicious side dishes.* The third drawing showed him kneeling, his face between her legs, captioned: *Don't forget dessert, Sweet Honey Cakes.* The fourth picture showed the man on his knees, his groin connected to Corrine's groin, the couple kissing in an embrace. Caption: *Second helping – Moist stuffing makes for a satisfying meal.*

Hester thumped the drawings. "Why didn't the artist show the man? We know what the ladies look like!"

"Find the next picture," Alexina demanded.

The last picture puzzled them further. The man, naked, buttocks three quarters to the viewer, stood in front of Corrine, who kneeled and pressed her face against his groin.

"What is she doing?"

"I don't know," Hester whined. "I don't know! Open the blue

one."

Racing through the second book, Alexina flipped past the text, viewing pictures just as maddening. Putting their limited knowledge together, it was clear that a man put his male organ into a woman, and it gave enjoyment to both. She understood what *becomes one* meant. But since neither young woman had ever seen a man's organ, they did not know how a couple achieved this wondrous feat of pleasure. They made a pact. Whoever first learned the secret would surely inform the other via a letter.

Riding in the coach that day, Alexina was still none the wiser about the marriage bed. She let the book slip to the floor as she thought about what may await her in the weeks ahead. Alexina very much wished to write Hester after she had firsthand knowledge of *becoming one* with her new husband.

Chapter Nine

Alexina was glad to find the first day's journey ended at a fine inn. She and Daisy enjoyed a tasty supper and retired to a room with a large, comfortable bed.

The second day of travel involved rain and mud, slowing their progress. They reached their day's destination late. The inn was crowded, and they were forced to share their room, three ladies crammed into a less-than-adequate bed.

As they headed north, they made more connections, changing coaches, and at the bustling city of Eversham, a six-seater coach accommodated the two travelers heading west. After more towns and a four-seater, they finally arrived at the village of Turnersfield and waited with their bags on a bench in front of the general store.

Within an hour, a richly-fashioned white carriage pulled by a pair of dapple grays stopped, and the driver jumped down and opened the door. A young man dressed in silk, his thin hair pulled back with a jeweled ribbon, emerged.

"Miss Alexina Poole?"

Alexina stood. *Oh, no. Is this overdressed dandy Peyton Woodleigh?* Suddenly the image of the gentleman in *Corrine's Naughty Table* came to mind. Even though she hadn't seen the man's face in full view, she had seen enough to think this fop looked like Corrine's lover. *Will he expect me to do the things I saw in the book? I still don't really know what I saw in that book. Whatever I saw, I don't want to do it with him!*

He bowed at the waist. "Allow me to present myself. I'm Rufus—"

A crow, cawing loudly, swooped by, obliterating his

introduction. Having heard his first name, she knew this man was not her fiancé. She put her hand to her mouth while she followed the black bird's trajectory and suppressed her grin as the dandy dodged a splash emanating from the diving crow.

She blanked her face. "I'm Alexina Poole. May I present Miss Daisy Bently, my personal maid."

The man cast a quick, contemptuous glance at Daisy and turned back to Alexina. The bird made another pass, and this time a plop landed on his head. Daisy giggled behind a gloved hand.

Alexina smiled inwardly at the justice. *The thin spot on his head must have looked like a target.*

He wiped the debris from the balding spot with his handkerchief, then pitched the soiled cloth to the ground. "As I was saying. I am Rufus Smith, Esquire."

The bird's insult did not dissuade him. He leaned forward quickly and took Alexina's hand, pressing it to his lips before she could react. She pulled her hand away with his lips still hovering. His brow furrowed, and his shoulders dropped for a moment. Then he snapped his fingers, summoning the coachman. The driver picked up the carpetbags and stowed them in the boot. The foppish young man opened the door and assisted Alexina into the luxurious chaise. He stepped in and left Daisy to fend for herself.

Daisy is just a maid, but still a woman. How rude.

Once Daisy took her seat, Rufus rapped his walking stick on the red velvet ceiling. The cab dipped on soft leather springs as the driver remounted, and with the snap of the whip, they jolted to a start.

"I am your guide, Miss Poole." Then with a discernible disgust to his tone, he added, "To the valley known as Applewood."

"Applewood! How charming. My fiancé's estate?"

Rufus cleared his throat. "Er, yes, his…estate."

Alexina squirmed as the man's gaze examined her.

"I hope you've had a good journey, Miss Poole."

Alexina dreaded the tedium of small talk sure to follow. A cart rumbling on the cobbled road offered a needed distraction, but a brief one. She winced when the man began his idle chatter again, coupled with his constant stare.

"Forgive me, Mr…," Alexina said, embarrassed that she had forgotten his name.

He dug into his vest pocket, retrieved a card on cream stock, and handed it to her.

She read the card. "Rufus Smith?" She put the card in her reticule. "Pardon me, sir, but I am tired from my journey. I will close my eyes for a moment to relax."

"Of course, my dear."

My dear! So forward. "Thank you," she said, and leaned back on the crimson velvet. She took a relaxing breath, but as she closed her eyes, his steadfast gaze upon her allowed little ease.

She gave up trying to nap, even though the fine leather springs of the exquisite buggy made the ride smooth in spite of the ever-increasing roughness of the gravel road. Opening her eyes, she turned her head, hoping he wouldn't see. Rufus stayed quiet, giving her a chance to see the countryside. As they progressed, the hills became more pronounced. The rolling land became ridges that led to mounded foothills. Emerald trees bordered the road, and the far hillocks were dotted with variegated greens looking like the chenille fabric her mother had once ordered from France. The beauty of the countryside was overwhelmed by a commanding house situated on the top of a hill, a Tudor style in bright white stucco punctuated with dark batten beams.

"Oh! How lovely." Her heart raced. Could it be Applewood, her intended's estate?

"Ah, you like it," Rufus said.

"I'm without words."

His eyes glossed over. "You'll make an exquisite mistress of that home."

She sucked in a breath.

He leaned close to her ear. "That which you behold is mine, and I offer it to you. Forget Woodleigh. Be *my* wife."

"Mr. Smith!" She pulled back. "You forget your manners."

"I have not, but this being an emergency, I must declare my feelings."

"Emergency?"

"Truly. You do not know what awaits you, fair angel."

A wave of ice in her blood made her shiver. "You may not speak to me in this fashion."

Rufus put his hand on his chest. "Against my heart, I shall not plead with you further. But know, if you change your mind, I await the slightest summons." The man's eyes became flints with an unrelenting stare.

Again she turned her head to the window, this time to break the gaze between them. *What do I know about this man who has me prisoner in his carriage? What do I know about the man who waits at the end of the journey? What have I done?*

The tension in the carriage felt like a curtain ready to fall. Then the crunching of gravel, so brutal against the fine spring mechanism, revealed that they had reached rough country. The hills came together except for a narrow corridor of land open on each side. Closer to the gap between the ridge, large ruts in the elevated road made the carriage dip down and up again. Pebbles dislodged and hit the steep sides of the pass. When the coach reached the break in the ridge and passed into the valley, orchards, fields, and a beautiful sparkling lake appeared like a mirage.

The coach slowed as the road changed from gravel to packed dirt, and a substantial stone structure came into view. The carriage stopped at that building. Off in the distance, small thatched buildings looked like workers' quarters, but she had expected a country manor like many of the wealthy Londoners retreated to during the hunting season. Several buildings, including a large thatch-roof barn, dotted a cleared area. Grass grew up to the stones of one-story walls of the stone building that the carriage waited at. A heavy door bisected the front, but no steps led to it. Surprisingly, many sizable windows pierced the rectangular hardscaped walls. The thatched roof of the building had a massive break in the thatching.

Along with the barking dogs, people came running, smiling, appearing happy to greet the carriage. A tall, fair man with curly light hair sprinted to the buggy and came around to Alexina's side.

Such a handsome face! Her heart fluttered. Her hand crept to her breast. *Will this be my husband, my love?*

He smiled. Alexina twitched in surprise at the absence of a few front teeth.

Chapter Ten

The sounds of horses on the coarse roadway of his pass alerted Peyton of a coach's arrival. He had left the path severe and harsh for that reason, and no one ever came or left without alerting the residents of Applewood. Rising from his stool where he had been making fine adjustments to the wooden screw of the fruit press, he silently scorned, disliking being interrupted from the delicate work, but he had been expecting visitors…a wife. The crunch of the gravel turned to soft thudding on the packed dirt driveway. He removed his apron. Pausing at the basin by the cask-barn door, he washed his face and glanced at the spotty mirror hanging over the basin. He pulled at the string holding his hair back, retied it with a tighter knot, and reluctantly headed for the buggy, which had come to a stop. From a distance, he recognized Smith's opulent coach.

Of course. That bastard is delighted to stick his nose in this business. For a moment, Peyton wished he hadn't agreed to let the loathsome busybody transport the woman, Alexina Poole, the lady he was being forced to wed. But he didn't want to seem eager to greet her—all the more reason for the lady to leave after the ceremony.

Many of the workers in his valley had stopped their labor to welcome the visitors. Peyton grudgingly joined the stream of people curious to greet the newcomers. One of the men in the crowd grabbed the leathers of the harness to steady the horses. People surrounded the carriage in twos and threes, and another man opened the door. As Peyton drew nearer, he stopped while Smith exited and helped a thin, blonde woman, pale, sullen, and exceedingly unattractive.

Peyton swallowed hard. *Lord help me!* How lovely those Wagon girls seemed. What did he expect? What kind of woman would choose to travel all the way from London to wed an unknown, and in all probability, an ill-considered man? He breathed in a long, cleansing breath. What choice did he have? *Worse things have happened to me. If that pasty face is the means to keeping my property, she'll do. I'll not invest a speck of emotion into this relationship, and I'll have no children.* He shuddered. No issue from his loins would suffer a mother's rejection, like his childhood.

But the carriage held another passenger. Peyton stepped forward and quickened his pace. Smith extended his hand to the remaining occupant and whispered to her. By the time she set foot down, Peyton had reached the carriage. Breathless, he saw no one but the beauty with the wheat-colored hair and the crisp blue eyes.

"Woodleigh, this is Alexina Poole," Smith said, touching the lady's wrist with too much tenderness. "My dear...."

Peyton's hands clenched into fists.

"This is," Smith continued with a harsh change in his voice, "Peyton Woodleigh."

Will that man ever shut up? Peyton wrenched his attention from the light-haired perfection standing before him and listened to the drone of Smith's dialogue.

"This is Miss Poole's maid, Miss Daisy Bently."

Daisy, who had been visually searching the area, increased her scowling, and the red rims of her eyes blurred from the tears starting to form.

Smith, his lips flapping and eyes staring at Alexina, had used up the allotted time of Peyton's endurance. "Get back in your carriage and get off my property."

The lips stopped moving, and Smith's mouth dropped. Anger, irritation, and confusion played on his face. Clearly, he did not want to go.

His mouth turned into a thin line. After a loud sniff, he said, "No thank you for my service? No time to spend in pleasant chatter with my new neighbor?"

Peyton's balled fists pressed against his worn breeches. "I won't tell you again."

Chapter Eleven

Huffing, Smith reached for Alexina's hand, which she quickly pulled behind her back.

In a cool voice, Alexina said, "Thank you for your escort, Mr. Smith."

He bent toward the lady, and in a softer voice, said, "Remember, when you need to be rescued, I will come, ever at your service." Then he took a few steps backward toward his coach. Inside and with his gaze fixed on Alexina, he tapped the ceiling on his carriage. The driver cracked the whip, and the horses sprinted away. The quiet lasted until the retreating carriage wheels made their crunching sound on the gravel.

The man stood unmoving, watching her.

She took a quick breath because she knew him. Alexina had seen him in her dreams and knew the dark hair, flashing coal eyes, his jawline, his physique.

A woman pushed through the crowd toward her. She had thick brown hair that curled around her smiling face. The woman wore a long-sleeve white blouse gathered at the neck and a white apron over her tan linen skirt. Moving in quick motions, she radiated a sense of confidence. Her broad smile warmed Alexina and helped her relax.

"Welcome. I'm Molly." Then she turned to Daisy.

Two other women joined Molly, and the group of three formed a circle around Alexina and Daisy.

"Hello. I'm Alexina Poole." She smiled at the ladies. "I'm pleased to meet you."

Molly cocked her head and shot Peyton a narrow-eyed look.

He responded by shoving his hands into the pockets of his leather breeches.

Molly took Alexina by the elbow and walked her closer to Peyton. "Oh, happy day. Our new mistress. How grand!" She paused, staring at Peyton. "I think our new lady needs a tour, don't you, Master Peyton?"

"Mmmm," Peyton said. "Show her around and explain what she needs to know. Answer her questions." He left, heading toward the barn path.

"Don't you mind him," Molly said. "He's overwhelmed by your beauty, that's all. You're sure not what he expected. How about some tea? You must be ready for something to wet your throat."

"Tea," Alexina said with relief. "I'd love some. Daisy?"

Daisy barely moved her head in a nod.

"Dutch," Molly said.

One of the three women, a heavyset ash-blonde woman, attempted a curtsy. "Yah?"

"Would you make tea for the ladies, please? And some of that bread you just took out of the oven. We have honey on the shelf."

"Yah, so be," Dutch said.

"Right then. We'll be along in a few minutes. Miss Poole and...."

"Daisy," Alexina said, grabbing the girl by her thin wrist.

Molly swept her arm toward the large stone building. "Come on, then, see your new home. We call it Stone House. When my people came to the valley, this was just a shell."

Molly swung the heavy arched door open. Alexina had never seen a house like this. No paneling, no plank flooring, only the same rock walls as on the outside, and an uninterrupted flagstone floor. The rectangular shell was divided into thirds. One of the sections contained bedrooms, and the middle third of the building was empty. The final third had become the kitchen, spacious with shelves and open cabinets filled with cannisters, bottles, and jars. The entire house was well-lit by the large windows and further illuminated by the oval of sunlight shining through the huge hole in the roof a few feet from the entry. Small puddles of water from an earlier rain lay in depressions in the flagging. Dirt had caked on the edges of pools, forming patches of mud.

"We don't use this part of the house much or this door," Molly said, closing it.

Alexina examined the roof, constructed with thin reeds woven together and supported by a complex wooden frame.

"When our Good Lad arrived, we put that roof on the frame.

Standing under the opening, Alexina pointed upward. "What about that hole?"

"A bad storm lifted a wagon and threw it right onto the roof."

Molly led past the empty area, took Alexina's arm, and headed for the wooden partition on the right side.

Alexina stepped over a mud patch and stopped. "This will be a good place to store my furniture until we decide where to put it. Of course, that opening will have to be fixed. Daisy, it looks like you and I will have a lot of cleaning to do to get this floor ready for the movers."

Daisy froze. The only movement occurred in her eyes as they ratcheted from side to side, seeing the puddled floor about them. She choked with a muted wail and crumpled into the dirt.

Alexina bent down to her. "Daisy!"

"Tad!" Molly called.

The good-looking man with the missing front teeth ran in through the door.

Molly pointed to the right. "Put her in the guest room."

They followed Tad, who carried Daisy, limp, arms dangling like a rag doll.

The room was small, with a cot on one side and a mat on the floor. *The guest room?* From the experiences of their trip, Alexina knew Daisy would not be happy to sleep on that mat. Now she lay whimpering on the cot.

Dutch rushed in with a slim bottle filled with red liquid. She poured a bit of the liquid into a glass and held it to Daisy's mouth. "More," Daisy croaked. She swallowed, opened her eyes, and licked her lips. Dutch poured. Daisy sat up and grabbed the glass, slurping large sips over and over.

"Has she fainted before? Molly asked.

"Once during the trip here. Luckily a gentleman had a flask and revived her with its contents."

"I see," Molly said. "Come with me. Dutch will keep an eye on that one."

They left the two women and passed through the next door in the long wall. The massive room had a fireplace built into the side wall of the house. A few feet from the fireplace, a waist-high counter had a sink with a pump over it. The sparse hand-fashioned furniture consisted of a small wardrobe, a bedside table with a mirror shard hanging over it, and a rough frame holding a lumpy mattress.

Alexina studied the pipes leading to pots on a track near the fireplace.

"Ah," Molly said. "I'll show you how brilliant Our Young Man can be." She turned a crank that made the ewers move, ending their trek on a shelf overhead. With the pull of a rope, water came down like a rainfall. Molly's face glowed with pride. "This is Master Peyton's shower-bath. He's shed most of his city ways but has a need to be clean. We keep the ewers filled."

Alexina had seen shower-baths in manor houses, but they needed to be filled by servants bearing buckets of hot water. This device was crude but effective.

Molly pointed to the drain. "That goes to our herb garden. Hie! Hie! There's so much to tell you about this place."

Alexina scanned the room. The lumpy bed made her shudder. "My furniture should arrive soon."

Molly nodded. "Right it 'tis, too. Our young master needs some better pieces. You'll be so good for him, Miss. Very good, indeed."

"You call him Master. Are you head housekeeper?" All the ones Alexina had met always had the title of Mrs.

Molly laughed. "We're not paid servants. My people call him that out of respect. You'll understand when you know more."

The woman held the door for Alexina and returned to the small room still occupied by Daisy. Dutch sat on a chair holding the bottle of red liquid. When Daisy saw them, she sat up and whimpered.

"Shush, you," Molly said. She turned to Alexina. "Our Young Man added this guest room only last week."

Alexina bit her lip. *Guest room? For what? Visiting sheep?*

"Maybe it's not as refined as you wish, but we keep it clean and warm. Come see the kitchen," Molly said, and shot an evil eye toward Daisy, who moaned and turned to the wall. "That one is pure trouble. Make no mistake of it, Miss."

"She's ill. The trip was hard on her."

"Hmph," Molly snorted. "We'll see about that. There's no idlers in our valley. That doesn't include you, of course. You're the new mistress, or soon to be. We'll take care of you."

"I wish to do my part, Molly."

"Aye, that you will. Your part is to make Our Young Man happy. And by the looks of you, what man wouldn't be happy?" Molly motioned to Dutch to follow them, then closed the door with one more glare at Daisy, who had pulled her knees to her chest and whined pitifully.

They passed the great empty area, avoiding the puddles. Dutch went on to the kitchen.

On the opposite side of the house, Molly showed Alexina a small room, the study, similar in size and placement to the guest room. Next to that, the large kitchen had the same pump and fireplace as the big bedroom but also had a built-in oven. Shelves and cabinets proclaimed the room as the place for cooking, and under the pump sat a soapstone basin.

Molly pointed to the drain. "Goes to the herb garden, like the shower-bath." She pumped water into the basin. "Can you imagine? We can wash dishes here. Young Master had our men make this kitchen after we put the roof on."

"Your men built the roof?"

Molly nodded. "The original roof must have been made of glass because we found pieces all over the floor and nothing left but a frame. My mister, Rene, had been a thatcher in France before he…left."

"Tell me about your people."

"Ramblers we are. Traveled in our wagons from town to town, country to country."

"Where are you from?"

"Everywhere and nowhere." Molly smiled. "Many of us are from Ireland, but we have a few from Scotland, France, Spain, and Holland. Townspeople welcome us…at first. Our men can do almost everything, and there are always jobs needing done. And then there's the Wagon Girls."

"Wagon Girls?"

Molly made a thinking face. "You being a city girl, all brought up proper, won't know about them. Best I tell you later. As for the townsfolk, once the jobs are done, we're not so welcome. We know when the time comes to move on. The same happened in Garry, north of here. But we didn't quite move fast enough, and the women of the town got up in their arses—oh, excuse me, Miss—about them girls, and we had to move really fast. As we headed out, we saw a pass and thought we could hide in there until things died down, see. We found this valley, like Eden! Fish in the lake, game in the woods, roots and vegetables and everything we needed. And no one to send us out. We decided we'd stay until we had to leave."

"And you're still here," Alexina said.

"Aye, we are. Thanks to Master Peyton. And it's worked out for eight years."

"That long?"

"He came to us when he was practically a boy. That's why we call him Our Lad. He wanted to live in this house, so a few of our men cut bundles of lake reeds and helped Rene build this roof."

"What about the hole?"

Molly sighed. "See, this valley has its own weather, usually very good. But sometimes whirlwinds form, and they can't get out unless they find the passes. They twist and destroy until they wear out. One day a whirlwind formed and threw a wagon onto the roof." She cast her gaze to the floor. The silence was punctuated by a drop of water from the ceiling. She returned her attention to Alexina. "When my Rene climbed the roof to fix it, he slipped. He hit his head on the stone floor, and that was it for him."

"Molly, I'm so sorry."

"Thank you," she whispered. "It's a torment to lose the man you love, Miss. Master Peyton said to get the wagon parts out and leave the roof that way. He didn't want anyone else to get hurt."

Alexina wished she hadn't made comments about repairing the roof.

"Don't worry, Miss. We all deal with losses." Molly pulled out a chair from the table. "Why don't you rest a spell? Here, take a seat. Have some tea."

Alexina eagerly accepted the lunch of tea and bread. Although not a complicated meal, the rich, nutty flavor of the fresh bread was enhanced with butter, so dark yellow it could be called orange, which tasted like no other butter she had experienced.

Molly offered a pot of honey. "The butter gets its taste and color from the grain the cows eat. There are lots of things in this valley we've never encountered before, and my tribe has traveled far and wide. Herbs, and grasses, and unknown roots...all tasty and healthy. Our animals thrive on the shrubs and wild plants."

"Your people...."

"We call ourselves Wanderers, but I know what you're thinking, what other people call us. You can say it."

Alexina looked down at her hands. "You mean Gypsies?"

"Yes. Gitanos, Vagabonds. There are rhymes about us used to frighten children."

"Molly, I mean no offense. I—"

"I know you don't, but we need to be honest with each other.

Some of our tribes have bad reputations, and I'm not claiming they don't deserve them."

Alexina shook her head. "Not your tribe of Wanderers. I know you are good people. I can feel it."

"Thank you, Miss. We knew about you the moment you stepped from that man's coach."

"You did?"

"Like I said, we know things."

"Your…tribe? It has a leader?"

Molly thought for a moment. "Not really. I reckon Granny Doctor could come close to a leader. We always do what she says."

"Granny Doctor? Your herbalist?"

"Aye, that she is, and more. Them city trained physicians could use some lessons from our Granny. You'll be meeting her soon." Molly pointed to the herb garden outside the window. "Our Young Man had this garden planted just for Granny. He ordered a catalogue, and from the pictures, Granny selected what she wanted. Sent away for seeds, he did. Rode all the way to the postal office in Turnersfield to get Granny her perfect garden."

"Mr. Woodleigh has just elevated in my esteem," Alexina said.

"Our Boy appreciates Granny because when he first came, he had an accident. While exploring the overhanging rocks of the lake, where we now keep the boats, he fell and broke his leg. Had the bone sticking right out of—"

Alexina felt faint with the picture in her mind.

"Oh, excuse me, Miss. We took him to Granny's wagon. She put him to sleep with her potions. While he slept, she set his leg, sewed up the wound, and bandaged him with poultices made from moldy fruit."

"That doesn't sound healthy."

"We trust Granny, Miss. Why, in a few weeks, Our Boy was walking around, and in a few months, you'd never know he'd been hurt. He gives Granny her due. You'll see."

Injuries and sicknesses took on a new meaning here, so far away from the city. "I think I should check on Daisy." She left the kitchen and peeked her head into the small room. "You're feeling better?"

Daisy nodded and took another sip from the glass. "This medicine helps, but I'm not recovered, Miss."

"I understand." Alexina shut the door and returned to the kitchen.

"Here," Molly said. "Make yourself at home. Take a look

around. We've plenty of room for your furniture. Maybe you can get some ideas of where you want things to be."

Oh, yes. My fine furniture in this fine country manor. Silk purses and sows' ears. She strolled around the large building, noting the cold floors and unpaneled walls. Avoiding the puddles in the great room, she imagined drapes over the large windows and carpets on the floors.

She entered the room Molly called the study. The spartan chamber contained a desk, more of a box than a table, and a rough chair. On top of the desk, smaller boxes stacked one upon the other with openings made a pigeonhole effect. Papers were jammed into the openings. The one elegant piece was a leather and flannel pad on the desktop, with a matching rolling blotter. An ink bottle sat open, with two pens disappearing into the black depths. Stacks of books made shoulder-high columns in each corner. She knew exactly where she would put her beautiful writing desk, her Louis XIV *escritoire*, and chair. The mahogany bookcase would benefit the room, too. Adding a leather wing chair and a table could make this room into a proper study. She looked forward to changing this austere chamber into a cozy, useful place to work.

After seeing the house one more time, including a peek at Daisy, she returned to the kitchen where Dutch, Molly, and another younger lady named Sissy worked.

Molly wiped her hands on her apron. "Our Good Lad will be here for supper." She placed six large fish fillets in an elongated copper pan.

"Shall I help? I can set the table."

"No, ma'am. That's our work."

"Would you mind explaining the dining arrangements?"

"I'm not sure what you're asking, Miss, but I'll tell you we don't have any. Those of us who work at Stone House eat here at suppertime."

"Together?" she asked without trying to sound snooty.

"Servants and Master. We sup together. Does that suit you?"

"Well, I...."

"Don't fret on it, Miss. Our ways are different here. We expect some changes. You should, too."

"I see. I did expect some changes to my life. The residents of Stone House should keep their routine consistent."

"Somehow, I reckoned you wouldn't mind."

Alexina fiddled with her small ruby pendant, allowing what she heard to sink in. *Oh, how I wish I didn't mind.* She looked around at the house she now knew would be her home. This was Peyton Woodleigh's world, a dreary house with servants who dined with their masters. She took a long breath and let it out. Still, she would have him, the man she saw in her dreams. After all, didn't Ignace Smith say this place needed a woman's touch? *I'm ready to touch it.*

Alexina's brain had reached its saturation point. "I believe I'll take a little walk."

She strolled outside Stone House, admiring Granny's herb garden, amply watered by the drains. She looked over the valley. In the distance, fields of waving plants looked like grain. In another area, corn flourished in neat rows. Cattle grazed in a fenced area, and in the far-off hills, sheep appeared as white specks against green. Near the lake, multiple lines of trees, an orchard showed their green heads. A ring of low mountains surrounded the estate. *Estate. It's a farm. My new home is an oddly-built stone structure with a roof made of river reed thatch.*

She sat on a fat tree stump and pondered the last few weeks and the weeks to come. She would have to write Hester with an address. When would she hear from her new mother-in-law? How long before the removers arrived? Ignace hadn't told her the details she needed. Yet he *knew* because he'd been here before. The word "fate" came into her mind.

She didn't know how long she'd been sitting on the stump. The faint sound of a bell brought her to attention. Dutch gestured to her from across the yard. Alexina answered the summons.

"Supper soon, Miss. Molly said to tell you so you could…uh, um…freshen. Yah, that's it, freshen."

"Thank you, Dutch."

Alexina returned to the guest room, where Daisy refused dinner but asked for more medicine. Alexina washed and changed into her dinner outfit, a mauve cotton and alternating silk striped dress with horizontal pleats at the bodice. She fluffed the sleeves trimmed with darker mauve ribbons and matching ribbons on the hem. The dress had been one of her favorites. She hadn't worn it since before she left to teach school. The bodice seemed a bit tighter than the last time she had it on, making her cleavage noticeable. Tugging at the bodice did not eliminate the shadow. She brushed her hair and pinned it into a bun in the back.

"Daisy, can you help me put this ribbon around my hair?"

Daisy moaned and turned her face to the wall. Alexina gritted her teeth, tied the ribbon herself, and left the room.

In the kitchen, the table had no cloth and was set with unmatched dishes for five. A combination of wooden and metal cutlery flanked the plates. Clean rags of differing sizes served as napkins. The table setting faded in importance when Dutch took the pan of fish from the oven. The smell wafted around the room, delighting Alexina's senses.

"Have a seat," Molly said. "Where's your maid?"

"Not well. She won't be joining us."

Dutch brought bread to the table and then sat down. "Yah, that one might be in bed for days."

Molly sat at the table. "That bed ain't for her. That mat's where she sleeps."

Alexina shook her head. "We can't do that. She's ill. I'll sleep on the mat."

"A kind heart can work against you, Miss."

Peyton came in, freshly showered, his hair still moist. He sat. "Mat? Aren't there two beds in that room?"

"Nay," Molly said. "We didn't know she'd bring a maid."

Peyton looked at his hands. He had not given the workers enough information.

"It's no matter," Alexina said. "The mat seems to be soft."

He shook his head. "You'll sleep in my bed."

"I can't deprive you of your bed."

"I'll sleep in the barn," he added quickly.

"But I don't mind—"

"Silence. I'll not have it. You will occupy my bed."

"Thank you, Mr. Woodleigh. How kind."

"Hmmm," Peyton said in acknowledgement.

The room went quiet for a time when the dining began.

"This is the finest fish I've ever tasted," Alexina said. "What kind is it?"

They looked around the table. Molly shook her head. "Don't think it has a name. Master Peyton?"

He shrugged and continued eating.

"Ugly, though," Molly said. "God's sense of humor, such an ugly creature giving such a good taste."

After dinner, Peyton excused himself and left the house.

Molly patted Alexina's shoulder. "He'll come around. Give him some time."

Sighing, she hoped it wouldn't take too long for him to adjust. The time was right for her. She was ready to be married.

That evening Alexina moved a few of her things into the huge bedchamber. She used the shower-bath and greatly appreciated its relaxing warm water. The mattress looked like a landscape of hills and valleys. *I'll be glad when my furniture arrives, especially my mattress.* She lay down on the bed, and, to her surprise, it felt blissfully soft. A thick sheepskin under the sheet had made the lumps and bumps, and Alexina felt like she'd fallen onto a cloud. Cuddled in the softness, the comfort made all the travel, the introductions, and commotions of the day fade away, and she drifted off to sleep.

The burlap hanging on the window did not completely block the light of the morning, and the roosters crowing under the sills conspired to awaken her. She stretched her arms, then her back, feeling better than she could ever remember feeling. She got up, pulled aside the remnants of burlap serving as curtains, and looked out the window. The stone floor chilled her feet. She dressed quickly and, consulting her watch pin, found it was eight o'clock.

She rushed into the kitchen.

"Good morning," Molly said. "Tea?"

"Coffee, if you have it. I like that in the morning."

"Sorry, we don't have any. Rarely do, but like I said, we expect changes. We'll put it on the list."

"Tea, then. Two lumps."

Molly made a puzzled face. "Lumps?"

"Sugar," Alexina said.

"Ain't never had that. Sissy, you ever taste sugar?"

"Nay. I heered of it."

"Oh, dear," Alexina said. "Best put that on the list, too."

Dutch pulled a pot from the shelf. "I know sugar. Honey? This do?"

"Thank you." Alexina spooned out the golden thickness and stirred it in her cup. "Is Mr. Woodleigh about?"

"The master and three of our men went hunting early," Molly said. "We've had our fish, now 'tis time for game."

"Time?"

"Yes, Miss. Master Peyton wants the fish to multiply, so the men only angle a few days a month. Of course, that doesn't include the jumpers. You should hear of our jumping fish."

"Do tell."

"These big ugly fish are easy-caught, loving the fat worms what live in our gardens. But some of them get nervous at sounds and jump high out of the water. Some jump into the boat, and our men have nets just ready to catch them. Our Bright Fellow says the jumpers ain't right—uhm, *anomalies,* he calls them—and says we can keep all the ones what jump so they don't breed so much as the regular ones. They taste the same, though, and we love eating the jumpers just like the normal ones."

No sugar, a dismal house, servants who mingle with the master, and now jumping fish. How many changes could she tolerate? She sighed and reckoned she would find out.

Chapter Twelve

Later that morning, Alexina stood in the doorway of the guest room. Daisy refused the meal Sissy offered. In fact, Daisy sobbed with a staccato breath and proclaimed her looming death. When Sissy brought forth another bottle of Granny's tonic from her pocket, Daisy consumed it without taking a breath. "More," she croaked.

Alexina turned to Dutch. "Should she have more?"

Dutch shook her head as Daisy fell back on the pillow and closed her eyes. "Nay. She's had enough." She gently took Alexina's arm. "Come, Mistress, let that one sleep it off."

"I need to unpack some of my things." Alexina turned toward the bedroom she had slept in the night before. She'd taken a few steps when prodigious snoring came from the guest room. Sleeping in Peyton's room had offered her not only a bed but a quiet night's rest.

She bit back a smile, but the amusement wore off in a moment. It was enough that a mistress had diverted the normal routine. Daisy had made the disruption worse.

As Daisy produced her slumber sonata, Alexina unpacked the bags they had brought with them. Through the open door, she could hear male voices echoing from the other end of the house. She left the unpacking and returned to the kitchen with the hope of encountering the master.

Her arrival coincided with Peyton's, who brought in two great hunks of meat. His hair hung free. He was shirtless, dirty, and had smears of blood on his breeches. The image reminded Alexina of the ads in the newspapers for the circus. The Wildman of somewhere—Borneo? This wild man wasn't from an exotic country; he came from civilized England. Soiled but attractive, he would be hers.

Molly held up her hands in praise. "Ah, venison! Thank you, Dear Lad."

Alexina stared at his tanned, sweaty torso, and her heart fluttered. Her betrothed was pleasant to gaze upon.

She forced her attention away from him by straightening a fold in the cutwork of her pink linen dress. When she looked up, she caught Peyton staring at her, and her hands flew to her face to hide her embarrassment.

He nodded at her as a parting gesture and walked toward the bedchamber.

Molly tracked his departure, then winked at Alexina. "I'd best get on this stew."

"Can I help?" Alexina said.

"You can watch. As mistress, you supervise. When Sissy brings in the carrots, see how she cuts them. Would that do?"

Alexina was grateful for the distraction. She couldn't do much until her furniture arrived and had already mentally arranged the guest room with some of the pieces. As soon as she could get a bed set up there, she could share it with Daisy. It wasn't fitting to be sleeping in Peyton's room until they were married, and she wasn't sure when that would happen. She was torn between allowing him to get to know her better and becoming his wife. Thus far, he had granted her the barest of communications. A husband and a family, the epitome of her dreams, needed to be overshadowed by good sense. She should know more about him and this unfamiliar world.

Supervising felt like idling to her, but maybe it was a good idea to observe. In London and at the manor houses she had visited, she never considered the work that took place behind the scenes. Like many of the nobility and gentry, she expected a set table and food to just appear.

Alexina observed Dutch, Molly, and Sissy as they worked in harmony. The ingredients—meat, tubers, fresh herbs, and unrecognizable bits—went into a large pot hanging on metal links shaped like S's over the fire in the hearth. Dutch adjusted the length of the chain by removing some of the links. The work fascinated Alexina but gave her a guilty feeling for taking the hard labor of others for granted in her privileged life. Perhaps if more gentry and nobility spent time in the back rooms of their wealthy estates, they would know how servants toiled for their masters' pleasures. When the lid rattled on the pot, she had acquired a new kind of education.

Later that afternoon, Alexina checked on Daisy. The girl rolled over and batted her eyes open. She struggled to sit up. "Oh, Miss. I can't stay here. I hate it so. Let's go back to London. I can be your maid there instead."

"Instead? You haven't been my maid yet. But we're not going back. As soon as you feel better, take a walk around and get acquainted with the place. You best make peace with it."

Daisy started to cry, uttering unintelligible complaints. She fell back on the cot and turned to the wall.

When Alexina returned to the kitchen, Molly removed the heavy pot lid. The gamey, earthy smell from the stew turned Alexina's stomach. Holding in a gag, she put her hand to her mouth.

Molly stirred the pot with a large metal spoon. "Don't care for venison?"

"I think not," Alexina barely answered through tightly pursed lips. "Although, I've not had it before."

"Here," Molly held out the loaded spoon. "Try."

The smell from the steaming spoon made her choke. She shook her head and stepped back into Peyton, who had entered with three other men.

"Pardon me," Alexina said, and turned, surprised to be face to face with Peyton, who was clean with his hair pulled back, fastened in a leather strip.

They locked gazes, his eyes soft. "My fault," he whispered. "Sorry."

She smiled. *So, he does have a tender side.*

One of the men inspected her, running his eyes up and down. He glared, then crossed his arms over his barrel chest. His ruddy face did not reflect a welcome. "I'm Boyce. I'm in charge around here."

Molly moved behind Boyce, caught Alexina's attention, and put her thumb to her nose.

"I'm Steve-O," said a shorter man.

A tall man with an unruly lock of reddish hair curled over his forehead smiled. "I'm Seaton, called Seat. Pleased to meet you, Miss."

Peyton took his place at the head of the table, then the other men sat. Dutch, Molly, and Sissy sat, leaving an empty seat next to Peyton. Alexina waited, but as no one pulled out her chair, she pulled it herself and took her place in the empty space. Did that wrinkled brow on Peyton show a sign of regret at not extending the proper courtesy?

She raised her eyebrows and held his gaze for a moment.

Molly put filled bowls of stew in front of the men and gave Alexina a small plate of buttered potatoes.

Peyton glanced at Molly. "No stew? Is she not well?"

"Our new Miss ain't developed a taste for game, Sir."

Boyce huffed. "Well, you'd better develop a taste because we eat what's available. No one gets to choose."

"What is it you'll eat?" Peyton asked Alexina.

"I'm partial to beef, but I enjoy pork, fowl, fish, and young lamb."

"Seat," Peyton said, "Kill a bullock."

Boyce turned red. "A bullock! Those are for sale."

Peyton's voice was low but authoritative. "We have twice as many as last year. We can eat one or two. In fact, hold back four. I like beef, too."

"Thank you," Alexina said softly.

Peyton nodded.

Molly smiled.

Boyce scowled.

Chapter Thirteen

The removers arrived the next day. Many of the residents of Applewood rushed to see the massive van and the six huge draft horses. As Alexina greeted Mr. Anderson, Peyton stepped up.

"Mr. Woodleigh," Alexina said, "please meet Mr. Anderson, a friend of my grandfather. Mr. Anderson, my fiancé, Peyton Woodleigh."

Anderson thrust his hand toward Peyton, who paused and regarded the man. He pursed his lips, then shook the man's hand.

"Mr. Woodleigh," Anderson said. "Kindly tell Tom, the supervisor, where to put Miss Poole's belongings."

"She can tell you." He turned toward the barn.

Anderson shrugged as Peyton strode away.

There was no excuse, and she did not wish to begin their relationship by defending his discourtesy. She smiled at Mr. Anderson. "Do you normally accompany your client's property?"

"No, Miss Poole, but this shipment is special, and I had to make certain all went well. As it happened, we were accosted by bandits. Rest assured, nothing was taken."

"No one was hurt?"

"I didn't say that, Miss. No one in my employ was injured. Try not to think about it."

Don't think about it? How can I not? Mr. Anderson's expression advised her of the subject's conclusion.

She focused on directing the men where she wanted her belongings. First out of the van were the items she planned for the study. She stood at the door giving exact locations for the writing desk, the mahogany bookcase, a leather wing chair, and two side tables. She flitted back and forth between the pairs of movers giving orders where she wanted her bedroom furniture placed in the large bedchamber, sending other movers into the guest room with tables, chairs, and chests. The men left the remainder of the furnishings pushed against the walls on both sides of the empty space as far from the roof hole as possible.

As the van pulled away, she shelved the columns of books into the case and transferred papers to the slots in the elegant writing desk. A few hours later, standing at the door, she smiled wide. The room looked exactly as she imagined a gentleman's study to look.

At supper, Boyce came in last and took his place at the table. He glared at Alexina. "What business did you have rummaging through the papers in the study? How will we find our work?"

Alexina leveled her glare back at him. "I didn't change anything. I took the papers from the boxes and put them into slots." She turned to Peyton. "It's a good desk, with a proper inkwell and writing surface. It should serve you better than the table."

"I've been in the study," Peyton said.

"Everything is there," she said in a firm voice.

He turned his head to her. "It will do."

Under the table, Molly brushed her ankle against Alexina's leg, grabbing her attention. Molly bobbed her head to Boyce and winked. Alexina understood it to mean approval for standing up to Boyce and acknowledgement for Peyton's support.

Alexina buttered her bread. "I noticed some wonderful drawings in one of the boxes. No doubt, one represents the track for your shower-bath. I also saw designs for a fruit press and a distiller. Quite impressive."

Molly pointed at Peyton. "Our Young Lad, an engineer, he is. I told you he was brilliant."

"Molly," Peyton grumbled.

"Oh, he's too humble. I don't mind bragging about his genius."

"Molly," Peyton said louder.

Alexina patted Molly's hand. "No need to embarrass Mr. Woodleigh. I saw the work." She cast her glance across the table at Peyton. She hoped he saw the admiration she felt. "Will you build the machines?"

"We already have," he said.

"Hie! Hie! See there?" Molly said.

"I do see," Alexina said, with true esteem warming her eyes.

Chapter Fourteen

Alexina woke early to dress and take breakfast with Peyton. She chose a pale green cotton frock with a dark green band under the bustline, with matching bands at the sleeves and hem. The dress still had wrinkles even though she had laid it out the night before. Her bosom size had increased since she had worn it before leaving to work at the Greenfield School. The fabric strained, and the only way she could fit into it was to push her breasts slightly upward. A tailor would have to let out a little of the seams because she felt uncomfortable sporting such a cleavage. She selected three small combs, the porcelain tops fashioned into pink roses surrounded with green leaves. Two combs swept her hair back over her ears, and the third stuck in the top of a thick braid tied at the end with a green ribbon. Green jade drop earrings completed her look, and she was pleased with the image in the large cheval mirror sitting next to the tall chest of drawers. She picked up her step as she heard Peyton's voice in the kitchen.

She reached the kitchen in time to see Peyton wash his hands under the pump spigot. Molly handed him a towel. As he dried, Alexina entered the room.

"Good morning, Mr. Woodleigh," she said with a smile.

He nodded.

"Lovely weather. What are your plans on this fine day?"

Peyton's forehead furled into grooves. He cocked his head and stared at her. Grabbing a leather pouch, a palm-sized, well-filled purse from the table, he stuck it in his pocket. "I'm going to Turnersfield to order barrels and to see the magistrate." The sound of hoofs on the gravel outside the kitchen door meant he would leave right away.

When he left, Alexina plopped down on a chair at the small table. "I've irritated him."

Molly sat across from her. "Nay, just confused him. He's not used to anyone asking what he's about. Don't pay it no mind. If he's going to be a husband, he needs to change just like the rest of us. Porridge?"

"Yes, please," she sighed.

A few hours after Peyton rode away to Turnersfield, the fancy white carriage and matched dapples owned by Rufus Smith stopped outside of Stone House. Sissy opened the door, and the young man who had met Alexina in Turnersfield stepped into the room that now contained her furniture. He removed his top hat, bowed, and gave Alexina a bouquet of roses. "I had to see if you were safe."

The comment took her by surprise. "I'm fine. Would you care for tea?" The regrettable invitation came from her training. The proper thing to do. *What is wrong with me?*

"I would." His head swiveled right and left as if he had not been in the house before. "I see your dowry has arrived."

"It has. But how did you know these things represent my dowry?"

"Oh!" He turned to Alexina with his face reddening as if he had been caught stealing something from the windowsill. "I conjectured."

Molly, Dutch, and Sissy stood like statues, glaring at the man.

Alexina wanted the visit to be over as soon as possible. She turned to the three ladies. "Shall I help getting the tea?"

"Nay, Miss," Dutch said. "We'll bring tea." They left.

When Dutch moved out of earshot, Rufus grabbed Alexina's hand.

"Mr.—"

"Rufus. Won't you please call me Rufus? I am your neighbor, and I hope to be your friend…or more."

"It would not be appropriate for me to call you by your first name. We hardly know each other."

"Then I beg of you, call me Neighbor Rufus, and I shall call you—"

"Miss Poole for now, and then I shall be Mrs. Woodleigh."

"Oh, Miss Poole! I worry for your safety."

"I assure you, Mr. Smith, you need not have concerns on that account."

"Dear Miss Poole. This is no place for a woman of your culture and education. You will surely languish in this valley. And as soon as you come to your senses, send someone to me, and I shall rescue you from that barbarian."

"Mr. Smith!"

"Neighbor Rufus."

"Neighbor Rufus, you must not insult my fiancé. Nor should you invite me to flee from what is to be my home. You should go now." She accompanied him to the front door.

He opened the thick portal, turned, and hung his head. "My apologies, dear lady, but please know my behavior stems from my genuine concern for your well-being." Letting out a barely audible whine, he put on his hat. Neighbor Rufus had reached his rig when hoofbeats pounded nearby. Rufus turned ashen and froze with one boot on the ground and one on the carriage step.

The pounding horse gait did not stop at the barn but sped toward the house. Peyton slid off Dragon and dashed to the carriage. "Get," he growled.

Rufus clambered inside, pulled the door shut behind him, and rapped the velvet ceiling with his walking stick. The driver shook the reins, and the carriage took off.

Peyton watched the rig, then turned and stared at Alexina.

Alexina clasped her hands behind her and searched her mind for something to say. She chose, "Your business went well in Turnersfield?"

"It did, and, it seems, none too soon." He snatched up the horse's reins and stomped to the barn as if he put out a tiny fire with each step.

Alexina tread heavy steps to the oak door, still open, and would have slammed it if the iron hinges cooperated. If there had been a lock bar on it, she could have banged it into place, but she found nothing to abuse. "Impossible man."

Clinging to her deportment training, she calmed and began to inspect a box along the wall. The box stuffed with hay held two sets of dishes and glassware. All had survived the trip. Mr. Anderson's record remained unblemished. Later she would decide what to do with them. She then went into the master bedchamber to look through one of the trunks with her personal items. Her bed against the wall with its intricately carved headboard had four high posts. The feather mattress, enclosed in satin, was on it. Having slept on the handmade mattress topped with the sheepskin, she elected to keep Peyton's soft cloud-like one and send the one from London into the guest room to replace the floor mat.

The dresser, bed, chest of drawers, cheval mirror, and wardrobe gave the spacious master bedchamber a more proportioned appearance. Coupled with the fireplace and shower-bath, the room took on a cozy, more elegant look. It still greatly needed draperies and carpets, but the room pleased Alexina, and she felt her woman's touch had begun to show. Unpacking her things for this, soon to be her shared quarters, happily occupied several days.

Chapter Fifteen

"Oh, Miss, come quick!" Sissy announced. "The magistrate is here."

Alexina closed the drawer of the chest. "Why is *he* here?" She checked her hair in the cheval mirror and smoothed her ivory linen dress.

"I don't know, Mistress."

A portly man dressed in a dark suit waited outside the front door, accompanied by a young man so similar in face he had to be his son.

"Miss Poole, I presume? Where's the bridegroom?" The man cradled a leather-bound book under his arm, and the young man held a valise.

Alexina crossed her arms in front of her. "Yes, I am Miss Poole. May I inquire as to why you require *the bridegroom?* I assume you're referring to Mr. Woodleigh."

"I'm here to perform the wedding service."

"You don't mean today?"

"This minute, as soon as the gentleman appears."

Putting her hands on her hips, she stood rigid. "No. I'll not do it."

"Have you changed your mind?" Peyton's voice sounded behind her, with a hint of anxiety.

"No, Mr. Woodleigh, I've not changed my mind. I will marry you, but not this way. What I want—*demand*—is a proper ceremony. My trousseau includes a wedding gown. I will wear it in a church when I speak my vows."

"What's today's date?" Peyton asked. He had until Monday, his birthday, to marry and fulfill the requirements of the deed.

"The twenty-seventh," the magistrate answered.

"Reserve the church in Turnersfield for Saturday," Peyton said. "At noon. If that meets with your approval, Miss Poole."

"I need to speak with you first. Please, excuse us." She grabbed Peyton's sleeve and pulled him from the room into the hall. Alexina stepped closer to him. "Are you in a hurry, Mr. Woodleigh?"

He furrowed his brow. "I must wed by Monday, my twenty-fifth birthday, to keep my land."

Her heart double-beat. *This is the reason he upheld the marriage contract? Not to have a wife and family?* She clenched her teeth. Her first thought was to return to London. It was clear, though, he loved his land. She could not allow him to suffer such tragedy. Forcing herself to relax her jaw, she did not contest the date.

They returned to the magistrate, who gave a nod. "Saturday, as you say, Sir, Miss. Let us now go to a place where we can sign the documents."

In the study, Alexina pulled out the slanted lid of the desk, where the magistrate plopped down the heavy leather book showing the gold leaf title, *Register*. After flipping through the pages, he selected a pen from a groove on the side of the desk, dipped it into the inkwell, and wrote in the book.

He handed the pen to Peyton. He signed.

The magistrate gave the pen to the look-alike younger man. "Here, Wills, you're old enough to witness an official document."

After Wills added his name, he passed the pen to Alexina, who wrote on the line below Peyton's.

"We need another witness," the magistrate said.

Molly, who had been standing in the study doorway, said, "I'll fetch Daisy."

"Not Daisy." Alexina held out the pen toward Molly. "I'd prefer you to be my witness."

Molly put her hand to her cheek. "Oh, Miss, such an honor. But I've not writ my name for so long now, I can't remember how Rene taught me to spell my married French name."

"I'll help you. Say your last name." After hearing the surname, Alexina wrote two versions, Jeaneau and Janots, on a scrap of foolscap on the desk. "Is it one of these?"

Molly clapped her hands and pointed to Janots. "That's it,

ending with a squiggle."

Alexina put the Janots sample next to the witness signature line. Molly carefully copied it on the appropriate space.

Alexina glanced up. Peyton watched Molly as she bit her tongue and copied her signature, slowly and carefully, into the register. His eyes softened, and a tiny smile lifted one corner of his mouth.

"Do you need me further?" Peyton asked. "Will there be anything else required of Miss Poole and I?"

The magistrate dug in his valise for a wad of papers. "I've some documents to complete, but the signing is done."

Peyton left the study.

After writing a few words, the magistrate stopped. "Get him back. I need to be paid."

"I can pay you," Alexina said. "How much?"

"Two pounds for coming out and doing the—"

"I'll get it," she said.

When she returned, the magistrate made a few more scrawls on a certificate, rolled the curved blotter upon it, and held it out. "Congratulations, Mrs. and Mrs. Woodleigh."

Alexina read the paper that said on top, *Certificate of Marriage.* "What? Our wedding ceremony is not until Saturday."

"That's the religious portion of the marriage. This," he thumped the register then the papers, "is the legal portion. In the eyes of the law, you and Mr. Woodleigh are wed." He took the two pounds from her hand.

"Oh," Alexina said and sat down hard on the desk chair.

Molly patted her back. "Take no mind of it, Miss. In your heart, you ain't married. And our lad don't know about the legal portion, so he won't feel wed, neither. On Saturday, when you say your vows, you'll be true married. Right now, though," Molly said with a curious urgency, "you best go to where you keep your money." She gestured her head out the door.

Alexina dashed to the guest room, where she found Daisy with one hand in the keepsake box and another clutching the purse with the remainder of her yearly stipend.

"What are you doing?"

Daisy, never displaying quick wits, floundered. "Uhm, I'm... uhm...searching for something I lost."

"When you came to me, you brought nothing. How is it, then, you could have lost something?"

"I'm sorry, Miss. I won't do it again." She scurried out of the room, making the all-too-familiar whining sound.

Molly came in. "Trouble, that girl. It'll turn worse if you don't get rid of her."

Alexina closed her eyes hard. "I can't just send her out. She's alone, with nothing."

Molly sighed. "I know you can't. You're a good heart, you are. But let me put my mind to it."

"No trickery. Daisy must wish to leave on her own."

"I understand. I know our good lad has chose well. You're a lovely girl, good heart, and kind soul."

Alexina picked up the keepsake box. "I'd better move this into the big bedchamber." She entered the large room and put the enameled box on the elegant dresser. "It's my room now."

"Aye," Molly said, following her. "Let me help you unpack some of your clothes."

The two women removed the finery from one of the trunks. Molly opened the two doors of the intricately carved, mahogany wardrobe inlayed with colorful woods. The tall piece dwarfed Peyton's small, roughly constructed wardrobe situated next to it. Inside each door, enclosed shelves awaited small items—hair ornaments, jewelry boxes, assorted containers, and bottles. As the trunk emptied, the wardrobe filled.

At the bottom of the chest lay the wedding dress. Alexina gently spread it on the bed, smoothing out the bell skirt and puffed shoulders. It was creamy silk, with pearls sewn along the curved neckline.

Molly stood over the dress, marveling. "That's the most beautiful dress I've ever seen." She fingered the ivory lace covering the satin top. "You should try it on."

Alexina agreed. The dress had belonged to her mother. If it required alterations, they only had a few days to complete them.

Clad in her slip, Alexina allowed Molly to help with the dress. The top buttoned in the back down to the high-waist skirt. Puffy sleeves contracted into lace tubes to her wrists, where silk cuffs boasted scalloped pearl edging. Looking into the mirror, Alexina positioned the headpiece, a matched silk circlet twisted with rows of pearls. Attached to the circlet, lace, matching the dress, cascaded onto her shoulders.

Molly stepped back a few paces. "Now I know for sure. You're an angel sent from Heaven. You just need wings."

They both laughed, and Molly helped her remove the wedding

garments. They folded the dress and headpiece and lay them on the shelves of the wardrobe.

Alexina opened the door to Peyton's wardrobe, which contained two shirts, one pair of tweed plaid trousers, and another pair of worn serge pants. On one of the shelves, several pairs of socks and men's woven undergarments lay neatly folded.

"No suit?"

Molly shook her head. "Men don't have much need for suits here."

Alexina searched the shelves. "I don't see a tie."

Molly shook her head again. "No need."

Alexina took a dark blue silk sash from her wardrobe door. "I'll cut it lengthwise and sew the pieces. This should make a good necktie." She draped the sash around the pointed collar of the white shirt and tied a soft bow, satisfied with the idea. Pulling out the men's undergarments, she draped them over her arm. "It appears Mr. Woodleigh has more unders than outerwear."

"Why do you say that?"

"Well, not counting the leather breeches he works in, he has two pair of trousers and three pair of unders."

"Three? I only see two on your arm."

"Two here, one pair he wears."

"Ha! You think the men wear unders with their leathers? I'm afraid it's skin against skin. Do you think men in the city wear their unders all the time?"

Alexina knew they did. She and Hester had expended a lot of effort checking out the tight trousers of the men. The side buttons stretched the fabric across the front, showing lumps and bumps, assuring the young ladies of the fleshy equipment underneath. But to their unrelenting aggravation, the woven underwear had smoothed the shapes to such a degree that they couldn't even imagine what lay beneath those tight trousers.

"Mistress?" Molly said.

"Oh, uhm, yes. In the city, when men wear cloth trousers, they wear their unders."

"We both have much to learn." Molly grinned. "Just wait until your wedding night."

Alexina, with her limited knowledge of the nuptial night, was thinking just that.

Chapter Sixteen

The smell of roasting beef in the evening brought Alexina away from her unpacking. Molly set the table as Dutch sliced meat from a huge dripping joint.

"Can I help?"

"Nay," Dutch said. "The Mistress of Applewood Estate does no housework."

"Peyton works with the men," Alexina argued.

"He doesn't so much work as he occupies hisself with interests, you see," Molly explained.

Swiveling her head again, Alexina said, "I'm sure I can find an interest to occupy my time. Have you seen Daisy?"

Molly put a cup down on the table just a bit harder than before. "She's gone."

"How?"

"Left by her own understanding, Mistress, just like you wished."

Alexina tapped her foot, waiting for more information.

"She's with the Wagon Girls."

"How can that be?"

"See here, now, Mistress. There came a vacancy in one of the wagons when Emerald left. It happens once in a while. Gone off with a Garry man. That's the town near the north pass, where them wagons are. They're getting married."

Alexina remembered why her predecessor at Greenfield School left. "Was she going to have a child?"

Molly pulled at her ear. "Granny won't let that happen. She has a tonic for that."

"I see." Alexina didn't see but couldn't bring herself to ask for further detail. "I think I know what the Wagon Girls do, but Daisy?"

"You're a sweet thing, and being pure, you assumed the same of that girl."

"I don't understand."

"Of course, you don't. The way Daisy soaked up Granny's Sick Tonic said the truth. She enjoys her drink, and when a poor gal enjoys drink, there's only a few ways to get men to provide it. While you were going through your trunk, I took Daisy out to the Wagon Girls' camp and told her she could have good food, all the drink she wanted, and earn gold while doing it. Even dim-witted, that girl jumped at the opportunity, recognizing her good fortune."

"She did?"

"Sure as sunrise. With that yellow hair and white skin, she'll be popular. Men love those pales ones. Them pink nibbies on that gal will earn her double." Molly put her hand to her mouth. Oh, excuse me, Miss. I shouldn't have said that."

Alexina pictured the watercolors from the book, *The Naughty Menu at Corrinne's Table.* Pulling together the pieces of her limited knowledge, she said, "The Wagon Girls please men for money."

Molly stood on her tiptoes to match Alexina's eye level. "You know about women who do that sort of thing, right?"

I do now. Although exactly what they do…. Alexina nodded slowly.

"Aye. You have some questions, don't you? But you can't bring yourself to ask. Don't you worry. Soon you shall know all you need."

Alexina pictured the watercolors again. This time she became Corrinne, and Peyton's face replaced the gentleman. *Pink nibbies? I wonder if my new husband will appreciate my pink nibbies.* She bit her lip, not knowing whether she should be happy or frightened, uncertain about her abilities. *It won't be long until my wedding night. I hope my questions will be answered. Please let Molly be right. I so want to do just fine.*

Chapter Seventeen

Before dawn on the following day, Peyton came into the kitchen and waited for Dutch to make the porridge. Little Jim flitted into the warm room and sat quietly at the table. After Little Jim finished eating, Peyton jerked his head toward the outside, and Jim flew out of the chair.

They walked to the lake as the sun crept over the ring of hills. Standing on the top of the grotto, Peyton threw a canvas bag down into one of the small boats tethered to the posts driven into the rocky ground between craggy, moss-covered boulders. Jim hopped downward like a sure-footed goat and, without words, untied the boat, waiting while Peyton selected an oar. Peyton dug the oar into the soft mud to launch the boat. They drifted away from the shore on the ripples of the lake water.

"Fish?" Little Jim asked.

"Maybe," Peyton said, sending them toward the other side of the lake with a swift stroke of the oar.

When they reached the far shore, Peyton pulled the boat into a groove between the sand and the high bank. Little Jim followed, climbing over the lake rocks into the swampy area close to the base of the ridge. Removing his notebook from the bag, Peyton made a quick drawing of the marsh birds that pushed their beaks into the mud. Little Jim watched intently as the sure strokes of the charcoal stick rendered the images of the marsh inhabitants. Finished with the sketch, Peyton sat under a large tree and pulled his knees up. The boy sat down next to him and pulled his knees up too. Peyton had come out to this place, the swamp between the lake and the ridge, to think. With only the winds and the soft flutter of bird wings, he could clear his mind of troubles and reason out solutions. Little Jim, a perfect companion, went quiet as always, sensing better than any adult when silence was needed.

In the tranquility of the wilderness, Peyton focused on the present situation. Although totally different from him, there was something familiar about her. Her beauty and grace appealed to him in a way no other woman had. The effect troubled him, and the best way to control trouble was to stay away from her. He could do that until Saturday when she would become his wife. After that, he couldn't avoid her. More troublesome than that was, he didn't want to avoid her. She would be his, a diversion, a sharp right turn in his life's path. A beautiful departure from the comfortable normal he had established in the valley.

Alexina had already changed the daily life in Applewood, especially when she wore that green dress with the emerald ribbon dancing at the end of that lovely flaxen braid. His eye had been caught by the sparkling gold chain she wore, which disappeared into the vertical shadow, that sultry indication of her rounded breasts waiting underneath the soft fabric. A stirring near his inseam made him pull at his leather breeches. Her eyes, which had been so blue when he'd first seen her, had turned turquoise because of the green frock. He visualized a brooch his mother wore, a large turquoise brooch with a pink cameo in the shape of…his *mother's* brooch, the woman he never let into his thoughts. He swore and picked up a rock, heaving it so far it made a plop almost to the far shore of the lake.

"Alexina." He said her name aloud. "Enough." No more thoughts about women, even if she did look so lovely in green. "Come on, Jim." He extended his hand to the boy. "Let's see if we can get a few jumpers."

They raced to the boat, Jim winning. Peyton tossed the bag into the boat and shoved off. With a few hard strokes, he pulled the oar from the water and banged the side, making hollow wooden booms. Three fish jumped nearby. Again he banged, and more fish jumped. Taking a net from the bag, he inserted a long reed handle.

"Ready, Jimbo?"

Grinning, the boy stood.

Peyton banged the side of the boat as hard as he could and shouted, "Hoo-Hoo-Hoo!"

Five fish jumped around the boat, and Little Jim stretched outward, holding the net. He caught one of the fish in midair. Peyton quickly grabbed the handle and landed the fish. "Good eating tonight."

The sides of the ghoulish silver-pink flesh moved as the gills pulsed. Large black, unblinking eyes shifted within the oversized sockets.

The boy's normal smile widened, then he imitated the sucking lips and, with his fingers flittering on his neck, mimicked the creature's heaving gills. Keeping his smile, Little Jim made a face at the creature beside his feet. Then, Jim rubbed his stomach and swept his hand over the water.

"Right, then. Get ready for some more." *Alexina likes fish.* He swore softly to himself for having the thought and banged the boat with more strength than necessary.

Chapter Eighteen

Arising early, Alexina pinned her hair back into a full bun with tortoiseshell combs and selected one of her favorite dresses, a white cotton organdy with embroidered pink and yellow flowers on the bodice. The kitchen hummed with activity as she took her place at the table.

Even though she came for breakfast early to share breakfast with Peyton, the plates in the sink indicated he had been there and gone. "Where has Mr. Woodleigh gone this morning?"

Molly wiped her hands on her apron. "Visiting his thinking place across the lake. Our Young Lad needs quiet sometimes to think. He takes a boat over to a spot—a few acres of swamp, I think."

"What is it like?"

"Ain't none of us been there. We leave it be, you know, just for him. Granny would love to take a look at it. She thinks there might be some lilies growing there that would make good medicine."

"Granny should ask him," Alexina said, and reached for the honey pot.

"Oh, no. By invitation only. We honor his ways. So far, he's only invited Little Jim. Granny will wait."

Her betrothed had made himself scarce since the magistrate had visited. Was he avoiding her even more because she was now his wife? Or did he want to absent himself from the wedding planning?

After breakfast, she unpacked the last of the trunks. Rufus called once again, uninvited and unannounced. She met him in the arched doorway, blocking his entrance inside.

"Good morning, Neighbor Rufus."

"Good morning, dearest neighbor Alexina. I understand your wedding is scheduled for tomorrow. I beg you…reconsider."

"I will be married soon, Neighbor Rufus. I wish to be married, sir, and although you claim your behavior takes in my best interest, I request you cease your cause."

"He doesn't love you. He's only marrying you because—"

"Stop."

He spread his arms in supplication. "I do love you. And I'll accept you under any condition."

"Mr. Smith, leave instantly."

He took a few steps backwards. "I'm going. But remember, I'll take you under any circumstances, including joined in the state of wedlock."

Thrusting her hand out to grab the ring in the middle of the door, she stepped back, bringing the door with her, and closed it with a solid thunk. A wave of sadness flowed through her. She knew the reason her new husband honored the contract but thought she had seen a look in his eyes when they first met that reflected her own feelings.

A lump in her throat swelled, and her eyes watered. She dashed a hand across her eyes, straightened her spine, and lifted her chin, refusing to weep. The Greenfield School had provided enough examples of weepy, spoiled wives, the sodding mothers who had used tears to excuse their husbands' lack of interest. No weeping for Alexina, even if her legal husband was hiding from her.

That night when Sissy called dinner, Peyton's absence angered Alexina.

Molly brought the pan to the table. "Our Bright Boy brought these fish for you, Miss."

"How joyful," she said with a hard edge to her voice. "How can he be so rude? Now I don't see him at all."

Molly stroked Alexina's hand. "Try to overlook his bad manners. Our Good Lad keeps control of himself. You weren't what he expected, and he doesn't know what to do. He'll figure it out. I promise he will not disappoint you. Give him time. Here." She put a piece of fried fish on Alexina's plate. "This will make you feel better."

Savoring the first bite of the tender, sweet, moist fish with crispy skin improved her mood. Having more and enjoying the tang of the sauce served with the white meat produced a positive effect on her outlook. It was not proper that she should burden these kind people with her worries. She said, "The lemon sauce is the best I ever tasted."

"Lemon?" Sissy looked puzzled. "When's the last time you laid eye on a lemon, Molly?"

Molly laughed. "Not since Rene nicked one from that vendor in Cardiff. Um, borrowed," she amended. "But I think our young miss means the shore thyme." She pointed to a few small red-rooted bushes drying upside down in the window. "We call it that because of the leaf shape. We don't know what it is, just one of the mysterious weeds growing in the valley. And this one is the most odd. It grows in the shallows of the lake. The dried leaves make a tea what calms the stomach, rids headaches, helps bring on sleep. The stems, boiled down to a jelly, have a lemon flavor, and that's what you're tasting. But we have to be careful not to eat the roots."

"Poisonous?"

"Nay. The juice from the roots can make a stain hard to wash away. No taste. Pretty color, though. Granny uses it in her medicines."

"Like a colorant?"

"Powerful dye. Remember the tonic Daisy hankered for? Just Jack and honey and shore thyme root."

"Such a lovely red," Alexina said. "Aren't those ugly fish pink? Do they eat the roots?"

"I don't know. Perhaps Master Peyton does," Molly said.

Alexina sniffed. "The next time I see the elusive Mr. Woodleigh, I'll ask. I expect we will see him Saturday at the church."

"Indeed, we will," Molly said.

Chapter Nineteen

When Alexina awoke Saturday morning, Stone House seemed more quiet than usual. The absence of footsteps, chatter and clanking of the pots and pans made the place feel hollow. In the kitchen, Molly greeted her with a cup of tea and a bowl of steamed grain.

Before taking her seat, Alexina went to the half door and stuck her head out. "Where is everyone?"

"They've started their journey to Turnersfield."

"At eight-thirty?"

"It's a long walk, Miss."

"They're walking to Turnersfield?"

"We only have so many horses, the one carriage, and a few carts. Granny, and some others like you and me, get to ride, but the rest have to get there afoot."

"Molly, I didn't consider the inconvenience I caused insisting on a church ceremony." Alexina pushed her cup away.

"Don't fret on it, Miss. Long walk or not, we love a good party."

"There's to be a party?"

"Indeed so! The Jack'll be a-flowing tonight. Eat, Mistress. We should be getting you dressed."

In the master bedroom, the ivory silk dress covered with lace and studded with seed pearls lay on the bed with the headpiece next to it. Although it had been made for her mother, it fit Alexina when Molly relaxed the ties in the back at the bustline.

Molly stepped back, looked to the ceiling, saying, "How lovely. Just like a dream."

Alexina checked her image in the mirror, pulled the pearl

necklace and earrings from the box in the wardrobe, and put them on as a final touch.

At eleven, Seat pulled a carriage up to the front of Stone House with Sissy and Dutch in the rear-facing seat. Alexina and Molly got in and sat opposite them. Seat took his place on the driver's perch. The carriage, a contraption appearing to have been repaired with various parts of other coaches, had its top folded down. In its day, many years before, it had most likely been a fine vehicle. Even in the current dilapidated state, the ferns, feathers, bunting, and blossoms transformed the old hack into a royal conveyance. The splendid accouterments of the large gray horse, his mane braided with ribbons, the harness wrapped with silk sashes, suggested a serious celebration as its destination.

"Pretty horse," Alexina remarked. "Shouldn't this size coach have a pair?" She had seen four-seat coaches in London but always pulled by two matched horses.

Molly nodded. "We only have Silverton, but not to worry, he's stronger than two. I don't remember where Master Peyton bought that horse, but the animal was pitiful. He could barely walk on them bleeding cracked hooves, and he looked like a skeleton. A few weeks of Granny's salve cured his feet, and a few months grazing on the wild grains fattened him. Our Good Lad went to the meadow every day with apples and carrots."

"He's the best carriage horse I've ever seen," Seat said. "Right, boy? Yep. You and Dragon, fine fellows, both!" With a shake of the reins, Silverton set off in a smooth motion.

At eleven fifty-five, Seat hopped from the driver's perch to open the door for the ladies.

Alexina made her way to an alcove on the side of the old Norman church. Sissy held a bouquet of white flowers bunched together with a string and tied with white ribbons. She took a sniff of the sweet blossoms and handed the spray to the bride.

Alexina peeked into the sanctuary. To her surprise, the seats were filled. In the back row sat six women decked out in bright colors and less than tasteful accessories. Five had dark hair, making the one light-headed woman more prominent. Daisy! Bedecked with beads and golden hoop earrings, sporting red lips, pink cheeks, and eyebrows darkened with charcoal. Her hair, fashioned into stiff long curls, fell onto a bright pink dress and gave the woman a peculiar attractiveness. Alexina gaped at the woman, with a jaunty white plume upright among the curls—her former maid, who looked nothing like the pasty-faced, woe-begotten waif who cried and moaned every hour.

Molly came next to her. "See, even the Wagon Girls are here. This is quite the event, Miss—or should I say Missus?"

"Mrs. Woodleigh," Alexina whispered to herself. She listened in the alcove to a few of the Gypsy women who sang tunes, beautiful and enchanting but unknown to Alexina. At the songs' conclusion, Molly gave the bride a gentle nudge into the aisle.

Alexina's gaze fastened on Peyton as she walked to where he stood at the altar. He wore a white shirt, his tweed trousers, and the blue bow tie she had made from her sash. Clean-shaven, his hair tied back with a ribbon, the look on his face, although somber, bore a bit of a smile.

Alexina reached Peyton's side. The warmth from his body and the clean man-smell mingled with his appealing face overwhelmed her, and she barely heard the vicar speak until the church became silent.

Peyton looked at the vicar, then turned his face to her.

"The ring?" the vicar asked.

His jaw twitched, and he shook his head.

"Oh," Alexina said. "I already have it." She quickly pulled the chain from her bosom and removed the wedding band, which had been with her since her mother died.

Peyton mouthed the words, "Thank you."

The vicar took the band, passing it to Peyton. "Place the ring on her finger and repeat after me."

Peyton repeated the wedding vows, never taking his thankful and warm regard from her. Alexina repeated the promises, and the vicar instructed the groom to kiss his bride.

Peyton put his hands on Alexina's shoulders, leaned in, and kissed her. This kiss, no ordinary one, represented a species of hearty, sturdy kisses, full of promise. The kiss from his supple lips grew from light pressure into moderate force and lasted much longer than it should have. With her eyes closed, she drank in the taste of his lips and the sweet smell of his breath, a kiss that stole her breath away. Her speeding heart made her lightheaded, but she would not lose a second of this moment and willed herself upright and fully conscious of the proceedings. Without thinking, her lips parted for more, and her body experienced a wave of heat followed by an all-consuming tingling. When he ceased contact, she opened her eyes.

The vicar's mouth dropped open, then stumbled on the words,

"Man and wife."

A Gypsy cheer, sounding more like a battle cry, echoed off the thick stone walls of the ancient church. In spite of her shallow breathing, Alexina focused on the man who stood next to her. Peyton winked at her, lay his hand on her back, and escorted her to the entry. Little Jim ran past them out the door and led Dragon to the steps. After Peyton helped his wife into the festooned carriage, he bowed to the occupants and mounted Dragon.

Seat took his place on the driver's platform and shook the reins.

Alexina would have liked Peyton to ride next to her, but it would have displaced one of the ladies, and she had already inconvenienced many of the valley folk as it was. Dragon eased into a trot and kept abreast of the carriage all the way to the pass. Seat slowed on the narrow gravel, the crunching sounds echoing a thundering announcement that the celebrants had returned to the valley. Peyton forged ahead through the pass and into the valley.

Chapter Twenty

Peyton slapped the stirrups against the horse's flank. Dragon took off with a leap, and Peyton leaned toward the animal's neck, decreasing wind resistance, and let the horse fly. The horse and rider becoming one had been Peyton's reaction to stress. He couldn't identify the stress he felt today, the odd elation. Drawing energy from the horse's speed, he let out a yell, much like the hurrah in the church when the vicar pronounced them wed. As he entered the valley, the thin hills were a blur, and soon he saw the thatch of Stone House. He relaxed his hold on the reins, and Dragon dropped into a cantor. Upon reaching the barn, he stabled the horse and headed toward Stone House. Most of the folk were on their way home from the church and would be coming back for the party.

The carriage made the grating sound announcing the arrival. Peyton jogged the last few yards with the carriage and helped the ladies out. Alexina was last. He put his hands on her waist and lifted her from the carriage, bypassing the worn step.

She whispered, "Thank you, Mr. Woodleigh."

He answered, with a slight smile, "You are welcome, Mrs. Woodleigh."

She was his wife, Mrs. Woodleigh. It felt good to say it. As he started to say the title again, the idea that the same title belonged to his mother quelled his good mood. He turned his face away from the lovely woman, his wife, so she could not see the hate that would surely show on his face. He walked with her into Stone House, where Molly and the other women circled the bride. He went into his bedroom and stood frozen until his hateful sentiment decreased. Never had he seen a woman so beautiful as she had been today. Still feeling some of the hate that had raised its vile head, he removed the tie she, his wife, had made him. Carefully folded, he wasn't sure where to put it. He laid it on the bed. Would they be in that bed tonight?

Chapter Twenty-One

More people filed through the pass and into the valley. Spirits were high, and the folks laughed and sang.

Alexina excused herself to change out of the elegant dress. Turning to enter the bedroom, she came face to face with her husband. His face betrayed a mental battle waging. Whatever caused him distress, she wanted to help, to share his unease.

"Peyton." She touched his cheek. "What is wrong?"

He gently removed her hand from his face and kissed it. Then he shook his head, and wearing his day clothes and leather boots, he strode hard on the flagging.

What did that mean? How could she understand the anger and the kiss? The joy she experienced from the ceremony and the exuberance of the Wanderers faded. Perhaps that night, they could share their feelings. She picked up the tie she had made him and took it to one of the carved cabinets. Pulling out a small empty drawer, she kissed the tie and put it away.

She chose a blue cotton dress sprigged with tiny blue roses and green stems. After donning it, she held her shoulder length hair back with a wide blue silk ribbon. After she checked her image in the mirror, she hurried outside and down to the barn area, where a fire pit snapped and filled the air with fragrant smoke.

Peyton stood with a group of men around the pit, over which an entire gutted bullock had been raised on chains. A rotisserie held the meat, and one of the men had already assumed his turn at the handle.

Alexina wanted to join her new husband who had kissed her so wonderfully, but she was delayed by a trickle of women to wish her well and who had brought small presents. She took the gifts back to Stone House, which was now full of ladies working on a feast. Molly, Sissy, and Dutch provided a wooden bucket of punch surrounded by a plethora of unmatched cups. Alexina pictured her massive cut glass punch bowl and more than fifty elaborate glass cups still packed with the dishes. Having no experience, she had not thought about punch bowls or even considered supervising the party. She leaned against the stone wall of the kitchen, thinking she had a lot to learn. And, after the wedding kiss, she wanted to learn everything she could to live up to her duties and please her new husband.

Molly rushed to her and pulled her to the table. "Mistress Woodleigh!" Dipping a cup into the bucket, she offered Alexina a drink. "Here's to our new lady!"

The crowd in the kitchen shouted various hails and drank.

Alexina tasted the pink fruity drink. "Thank you. All of you. I can't tell you how much I appreciate your help in these last days."

The group cheered and swarmed around the bucket for seconds. Alexina, having never tasted so rich a punch, wanted more and made her way toward the container.

"Here," scolded Molly. She swished her hand for the group to make room. "Mistress first."

Molly filled the cup to the top. The cool drink had a slight tingle to it, reminding Alexina of the minuscule bubbles in expensive French champagne.

"Delicious," she proclaimed.

"It's for us, the women," Molly explained. "We made a few gallons yesterday. Them crocks' been cooling in the spring behind the house."

Alexina remembered seeing the *cooler,* as Molly called it, a large wire basket sitting in a depression of the spring that gushed from a colonnade of smooth rocks. Milk, butter, and other items must have been displaced for the crocks of the wedding punch.

She pictured the spring. Under the cooler, more rocks formed a white-water cascade, with water rushing around successive wire baskets. That, Molly had described, comprised the intricacies of Peyton's washing apparatus for their clothes to be cleaned by nature.

Cup in hand, Alexina followed Molly and Sissy and the bucket of ladies' punch out of Stone House and into the yard. She made her way through the growing crowds, outwardly acting at ease but desperate to find her husband.

Chapter Twenty-Two

Peyton saw her and stepped behind a tree to watch as she greeted many of the valley folk. Even at a distance, she looked lovely in the soft blue dress. Her eyes matched the bluest sky, the one they enjoyed that day.

Earlier, when she had come out of the small room at the church and walked toward him, he could not speak or think; he could only behold. Now she, with her velvety skin and warm lips, belonged to him. Would she have him intimately? He couldn't shake the thought. She definitely had not backed away from his kiss. He wished he had thanked her more for saving him from embarrassment by offering the ring on her chain. Maybe he could trust again. Except what did a woman like that want with *him*?

From all his reckonings, he considered himself an outcast, landed but without wealth. He had done well since he left school, but it would be years until he could be considered wealthy and gain respect. He took great pride in Applewood. His *Product* was becoming known in the area, and he sold all they could make, but that wasn't enough to attract a high-born lady. His eyes followed her path among the folk, smiling and gracious. Although it made no sense why she had agreed to marry, he could not will his thoughts away from her, this attractive, refined woman, now his wife. Could he place his arms around her, give her a tender caress? And tonight…. To help divert from those notions, he rejoined the group of men whose conversation had not changed in his absence.

Chapter Twenty-Three

Alexina thanked the last of her well-wishers. The yard bustled with folk, and the smell of the roasting beef had taken on a powerful appeal. An appeal of greater proportion, however, leaned against the wall of the barn, glass in hand, talking with a large crowd of men. She didn't have the nerve to interrupt his conversation, but she walked here and there talking to the children, trying her best to capture his eye.

She moved closer to the barn, which threw a long shadow in the afternoon sun. Men appeared with tables and lined them up one against the other in the barn's umbra. Chairs likewise appeared, and bedsheets served as tablecloths. Dishes, steaming and chilled, materialized, and before long, the crowd eased over toward the laden table.

Just as Alexina fixed her gaze on Peyton, she saw him look away. Following his line of sight, she noticed the crowd part, allowing a small, slightly bent, gray-haired old woman to walk through. The parting folk moved aside as if this person were royalty. It didn't take much to figure this old lady was the famous Granny Doctor. Behind her, like ladies-in-waiting, walked five of the most unattractive women Alexina had ever seen.

Molly broke through the crowd and grabbed Alexina by the hand. "Come. Granny wants to meet you."

By the time Alexina got close to the old lady, Granny was seated. With a simple point from the old lady, a man brought a chair.

Molly's grip on Alexina's hand kept her upright. "Mistress Woodleigh, this is Granny."

"Pleased to meet you," Alexina said, and had the urge to curtsey. Perhaps this occasion replaced her missed opportunity to be presented at court in London.

"Sit," the old lady said in a thin but commanding voice. Granny took Alexina's hand and turned it palm up. With her gnarled finger, she traced the lines. The old woman with gray eyes full of spirit and authority flashed as she spoke. "Yes, I see. It's right. Foretold. A long life. Many children. Wealth and happiness."

"Thank you."

"It won't be easy," Granny added. "But anything worth having ain't. You should know that. The harder, the sweeter."

Molly stood behind Granny and rolled her eyes. After taking a long swig from her cup, her lips turned up into a naughty grin. "Ain't truer words ever been spoke!"

Alexina didn't quite know what Molly meant, but when the other ladies laughed, she did as well. "Thank you, uhm, Granny."

Someone handed Granny a mug, and the conversation came to an end.

Molly whisked Alexina away.

"Granny tells fortunes by reading palms?"

Molly shook her head. "Granny tells fortunes because she knows. She looks at palms because that's what people expect." Molly peered into her cup. "Where's that girl with the punch? I'm going to need more. We'll be eating soon, and then we'll have music. You ain't seen a party until you been with the Wanderers." Molly held her cup aloft, and a young woman refilled it with ladies' punch. "What do you think of the party so far?"

"Fine." *It's my wedding day, and I'm not sitting even close to my husband.* Molly had enough punch that she slowed her speech as if searching for words. *How much better can it get?*

The five unattractive women who had followed Granny took seats at the long table surrounding the old lady.

"Who are those women with Granny?"

"Ah, those are Granny's students, except two—Anabel," Molly pointed to a young woman with a badly drooped eye and a severely turned club foot, "and Sofia." The second girl had a face resembling a pig, her nose flat with nostrils rounded in the middle.

"Oh."

"It's our custom." Molly took another swig. "Just as our most beautiful girls become the Wagon Girls, the females most desired by men, so do our unattractive girls, the ones unwanted by men, become our doctors."

"I don't understand."

Molly made a face. "It should be clear. What husband wishes to have a beautiful woman who would be desired by other men? He's better off with a pretty girl or a plain one. So, according to tradition, when we know a girl will become a beauty, she must accept her role as a Wagon Girl. She uses her gift for the good of the tribe. She shares her gold with us, and we provide her with a wagon, clothes, food, and protection. On the other side, when we know a bright girl won't outgrow her ugliness, she's dedicated to healing. She'll stick with her training and not be tempted to leave her trade to become a wife and mother."

A shot of anger pulsed through Alexina. "That's not fair!"

"Of course, it is. It's more fair than the accident of being born a queen or a pauper. The destinies of the beautiful and the ugly are known at an early age, and both fates provide well for the girls. When Granny trains a girl, other tribes pay us well for their services. They pay us with gold earned by their own beauties."

"You said all but two were students. I see five."

"Two replacements. Granny won't live forever. The one with the bad eye and club foot, Anabel, will replace Granny. Sofia, the other, will go to another tribe, free of charge, with the understanding she can be called back if something happens to Anabel. The first thing Sofia will do is train her own replacement in case she's recalled."

This was not the kind of conversation Alexina expected on her wedding day. Nor did she appreciate the barking dogs, or chickens running around the yard, or the hawk that swooped down to snatch a newly hatched duckling.

"It's life," Molly said. "Better get used to it." She lifted her mug and took a long drink, then held up her cup close to her breast, a place of honor. "Want more punch? Don't you like it?"

"I like it fine." *I can see how much you enjoy it.* "What's in it?"

"Special recipe." Molly was slurring her words and had trouble with the word *special.* "Wine we cap until it makes little bubbles, sweet grape juice, and *Product.*"

"What is Product?"

"What we make here. Jack, you know, hard cider, and Clear Jack."

"I have never heard of Clear Jack."

"You'd call it apple brandy. Our special product, the one everyone wants. Hail! Clear Jack!" She swung her arm over her head.

"Apples!" Molly lost her balance and wound up in a chair. She patted the seat next to her. "Here, sit. Let's eat."

Alexina looked down the length of the table. At the head, with no vacant seats around him, sat Peyton, accepting a full plate offered by Sissy. At that moment, the crowd noise abated as a cart filled with women came rumbling in. The Wagon Girls, clad in their colorful dresses, with hair flying, hooted and hollered to the top of their voices until the cart skidded to a halt. Men rushed to help them down, and each girl was swung around by men taking their turns.

Five Wagon Girls, the dark-haired ones, ran to Peyton, kissed him, and wished him well.

It was the first time Alexina had seen him smile, and she didn't like it one bit. Then they marched across the yard to her, introducing themselves, giving their best wishes.

She didn't wish to extend the audience with the Girls but tolerated their introductions. Each one had a gem name—Ruby, Sapphire, Citrine, Amethyst, and Garnet.

Daisy, now the sixth Wagon Girl, did not come by, nor did she kiss Peyton. As she passed Alexina on her strut toward the vacant end of the table, she put her nose in the air. Men smiled and whistled as she sauntered past, and with each call, she moved her hips in greater arcs.

Sissy brought a plate for Alexina, who tasted a spoonful of the grain pudding and a bit of the seasoned pork.

Molly joked and laughed during the meal. "Having fun, Mistress?"

Fun is not the word I'd use. My husband, far away at the end of the table, has just been kissed by…those…Girls.

Molly ogled each man as he passed by. "Hmm, I wonder how generous some of these wives will be tonight." Her words had become slower in order to get them out with a semblance of clarity. "I mean, us widows, see…well, some wives look away, you know, just like they do if the men want to, uhm, visit the Wagon Girls." She took a sip. "Of course, the Girls don't charge the tribe fellows, just the townsmen. Hey, Seat!"

Seat got up from his chair and came to them. "Yeah? What?"

Molly smacked his bottom. "Nice seat, Seat."

Seat smiled wide. "You know what they say." He pulled Molly up and kissed her, then grabbed her butt cheek through the skirts. "There ain't an ass so crooked, there's no Seat to fit it."

Alexina's face burned. *What am I doing here?*

She looked at the half-eaten plate in front of her. The roasted vegetables and creamed potatoes had been the best she ever tasted, but their superior flavor had been wasted. By the time Alexina finished her plate, she'd had enough celebrating. She got up and walked away.

Molly, stumbling, ran after her. "Hey, you ain't leaving? The music and dancing's not started. And when it's dark, they bring out the good Product. No one should miss a tribe party."

"A tribe party? It's my wedding reception." Alexina thrust her chin forward and glared at the other women. "This is supposed to be a solemn, blessed day. And what do I have? A barnyard full of drunks, and a cartful of whores! No thank you."

Alexina stepped around Molly, not looking back, confident that if Molly had heard the insults, she wouldn't remember or care.

Chapter Twenty-Four

But someone else heard her. After gaining the courage to approach his new wife, Peyton had arrived behind her just in time to witness her complaint and Alexina's sidestep, which preceded Molly's fall. He caught Molly before she reached the ground. Holding the woman up, he watched Alexina stomp back to Stone House.

Seat strode up and looped Molly's arm, jerking her away. "Hey! She's my girl for tonight! Go get your own."

Peyton had gotten his answer regarding how close he would get to his wife. *She thinks they're drunks and whores. The valley people. My people.* He cursed himself as a fool.

A young lady with a pitcher offered Peyton some men's punch. He nodded, let it fill to the top, and drank it without a breath. He rejoined the men, who still leaned against the barn wall.

Chapter Twenty-Five

The heat of anger pounded on Alexina's face. In addition, she felt alone. Everyone in the valley reveled outside the walls of Stone House, laughing and enjoying a hearty time. She rested at the kitchen table and hung her head. Too embarrassed to go back, she sat for a few minutes thinking of what to do.

"Not enjoying your party?" asked a masculine voice.

She turned and left the chair.

Boyce, showing his teeth in a threatening grin, advanced. "Noisy, aren't they? Why, no one could hear a thing with all that going on. Imagine."

Alexina backed toward the half door, her heart in her throat.

Boyce downed the last of his drink and sat the ceramic stein on the counter, then wiped his mouth with his sleeve. "There, nice and neat. No foam on my mustache, see?" He twirled the hairs on the top of his lip and made a pucker.

"Don't come any closer," she warned.

He didn't answer but pressed forward.

The half door swung open, almost hitting Alexina. A fair-haired boy skipped into the kitchen. He wrapped his arms around Alexina's waist. "Con-grads-lay-son," he managed.

Boyce's upper lip curled back as if he had just tasted bitterness. "Little Jim. Little simpleton. Imbecile peasant. You worthless little shit, always underfoot!"

The boy puffed out his chest and held his hand up, fingers spread wide to ward off Boyce.

"Ahhh," Boyce growled and loomed toward the child.

Alexina drew the boy closer, enclosing her arm over him. She moved aside with the child still in her grasp. "Leave us."

Boyce stomped, opening the half-door with his boot. "I wasn't going to hurt you. Just my way of saying con-grads-lay-son, too." The door creaked out on its hinges and returned with a slam.

"Bad man," whispered the boy.

"How brave you are."

"Like Master Peyton? You tell him?"

She sighed. "If I get the chance."

The sound of hoofbeats brought Alexina to the half door. Sneering as he rode by, Boyce drove his heels into the horse's side.

"Don't you want to be at the party?" Alexina asked the boy.

He nodded his head, gave her another hug, and skipped out as if nothing had happened, and he hadn't been called those horrible things.

Alexina couldn't return to the celebration. She walked slowly to the bedchamber where she lit the mantel candles, the stout wax pillars enclosed in the cut glass globes, part of the dowry. It would soon be dark. No one had started the fire or prepared the bed. Finding the French soap that smelled of lemons, she used the water still warm in the ewers for a shower-bath. She put on the lace gown, her wedding-night dress that, with one pull of the ribbon, would fall away. Lying on the big bed, she hoped Peyton would leave the revelry to pull the ribbon.

As the festivities wound down, a nightingale called for its mate. She wished she had a call to summon the man she loved. She fell asleep, still wishing.

Chapter Twenty-Six

Alexina entered the kitchen the next morning. Molly, Sissy, and Dutch busied with their tasks. Seat, Phillip, and Tad had finished their breakfasts. Everyone was amiable, working happily.

"Good morning, Mistress," Sissy said. She filled a bowl with porridge and placed it on the table. "Cream and honey?"

"Yes, thank you," Alexina took her seat.

Molly brought her own bowl and sat across from Alexina. "Great time we had last night." She made a puzzled face. "Did you leave early? Most of the evening's become a blur. I hope you had a good time."

Alexina used her spoonful of porridge as an excuse not to address the reference to her early exit. She waited for a minute. "You and Seat seemed to have something in common, as I last recall."

Seat took his last bite, nodded heartily, and excused himself from the kitchen.

Molly laughed. "Aye, Seat and I had some exciting… conversation, 'tis true."

Alexina gazed around the room. "Are you all quite well?"

The occupants of the room looked one to another as if the question had been absurd.

"No ill after effects from the Product?" Alexina looked to Molly. "I believe you took more than a few cups of the ladies punch, and—"

Molly slapped the table and laughed. "You mean was I pickled? I was, indeed. So far, in fact, I couldn't stand. Good thing Seat is so strong! That, I remember clearly."

"No headache? No sick stomach?" Before the long illness, her mother had taken Alexina on frequent visits to country manors, where, after the lavish dinners, many of the men, and a few women, imbibed until they couldn't talk or stand. Those people weren't heard from until late the next afternoon or sometimes that night. Servants made constant trips upstairs to attend the afflicted, offering medications of every sort to help cure the after-effects from the drinking. Even Grandfather Geoffrey drew the line with his nightly port and would only drink as much as he thought he could handle without having a headache the next morning.

"Nay," Molly said. "Our Product has no after-effects, no matter how much you drink. It's why we can sell all we make."

"How do you account for that property? A special recipe?"

Molly looked to the others and shook her head with the rest of them. "Nay, no special recipe. We make it like we've made all of our brews. It must be in the apples. This valley has many secrets and delights. Can you see why our Product sells so easy?"

"I can, indeed." *We could make a fortune in London. If the Clear Jack tastes as good as the ladies' punch, everyone who has ever been stricken with the day afters would pay dearly.*

Molly leaned in toward Alexina. "Mistress? Mistress Woodleigh?"

Alexina came out of her deliberation. "Oh, sorry." She pushed the bowl away. "Would you show me the orchard?"

Molly picked up both bowls. "Of course. It's a lovely walk."

The two women left via the back half door and took the path toward the barn. All the trappings from the party had disappeared, and the festive site had become a farmyard once again. Molly called the names of the vegetables in gardens as they strolled by—corn, beans, potatoes, and other crops, each patch in neat rows, well-tended and weed-free. Although Alexina had been to country manors, the closest thing to gardens she had seen had been hedges formed into mazes. She hadn't given thought to where the vegetables on her plate had started life. It pleased her to walk among those vital articles.

Alexina stopped walking and looked at the ground. "Molly, last night I said some things that I shouldn't, and—"

"Everyone does that. One of the beauties of the punch. We don't care! I can't remember anyway. Don't worry."

"Thank you," Alexina said.

By the time they reached the orchard, the size amazed her. From her reckonings, the orchard covered at least a half-mile and grew along a quarter of the lake's edge. It hadn't looked so large when she had seen it from the hills at the pass. Some of the trees had blooms, and sweet smells wafted in the air like perfume. Other trees had small fruits and buds, while a few tall, willowy trees had yellow and red mottled fruits appearing to be ripe.

Alexina stood on tiptoe to pull an apple. She bit into the fruit. The juice ran from the perforated skin into her mouth and down her chin. Her hand became sticky with goo.

"Oh, my! That's the sweetest thing I've ever tasted. As sweet as honey. Sweeter than sugar."

Molly reached for an apple. "Aye, these be the sweet ones. Nothing like them I ever had, and I been plenty-traveled, for sure."

"What pies, what juice, what marvelous foods you must make with these."

"We don't usually eat them. All the apples become the Product, you see." She swept her hand toward the crops. "We have plenty of vegetables, berries, pears, and other fruits, so we don't bother using the apples."

Alexina took another bite in spite of the running juice. "Oh, no. These apples can't be sacrificed for liquor." She counted the willowy trees. "Ten."

Just then, the little boy who had rescued her from the unpleasant encounter in the kitchen the night before came running to them. The boy stopped and grinned at Alexina.

"Hello. You're the boy who follows Peyton, aren't you? Little Jim. Thank you for wishing me well last night."

The boy did a cartwheel. He pointed to the apple.

"Delicious. Would you like to taste?" She offered him the unbitten side of the fruit.

He shot away from them and ran to the tree. Grabbing a branch, he hoisted upward onto a higher limb.

She hastened to the tree. "No! Little Jim. Come back. You might get hurt. Come down this minute. Slowly, carefully." She used her teacher's voice to make certain he would obey. The boy frowned but climbed down and returned to her. Alexina squatted at his eye level. "Listen, Little Jim. You could have fallen and gotten hurt." She brushed a lock of blond hair from his forehead. "You will be careful, yes?"

He nodded.

"Very good boy," she said, and tussled the hair she had just smoothed.

Molly put her hand on Alexina's elbow to help her stand. "You care about that boy?"

"Of course."

"You know he's simple, hare-brained?"

Alexina cocked her head. "That doesn't matter. He's a wonderful child. I'd be blessed to have one that sweet."

Molly said unintelligible words, licked her thumb, and pressed it on Alexina's forehead. "Now you will."

"What?"

"You've heard of a Gypsy's Curse? You just got the Gypsy's Blessing. Never fails." She added, "Either one."

Little Jim rammed into Alexina, ending with a tight hug. "Con-grad...."

She kissed the top of his head. "Congratulations. Well, done, Little Jim, and thank you. I see why Peyton likes you so much."

Little Jim beamed and ran off.

She turned to Molly. "I hope he's careful."

"Why?"

"Because simple or not, he's some mother's little darling, a precious child."

Molly stepped close, bringing her face a few inches from Alexina's. Her brown curls blew in the light wind. "You couldn't be more right. He's *my* little darling, the last of Rene that I have." She mumbled more unintelligible words and crossed her heart. She touched Alexina's breast. "Now you have my pledge. I owe you my complete loyalty in every way. And when a Gypsy makes that pledge, it's for life."

Alexina didn't know what to say. She stood, dumbly staring at Molly.

"We don't make those pledges often. Not even to Master Peyton. I'll always be loyal to him, but for you, Mistress, it's something special."

"Thank you." Uncomfortable and unsure of what to do, she changed the subject. "Shall we gather some of these apples? I have a few ideas."

Molly spread her apron like a tarpaulin, and Alexina filled the cloth with as many apples as they could pick. She gathered her own armload, and they returned to Stone House.

Later that afternoon, they took a bushel basket to the orchard and filled it with the sweet fruit, each holding the handle to share the weight. On the slope upward to Stone House, they rested for a minute on a log bench near the barn, where a day before, they'd enjoyed the celebration.

Alexina leaned forward. "The Wagon Girls?"

"Aye, I thought you might want to know a bit more on them."

"How long did they stay at the party?"

"That, I don't know for certain." Molly tapped her forehead and made a face, a symbol of her unclear memory. "But not long, I'd think. They have their work, and they work special on…uhm…events, you understand."

"Oh, of course." *Understand? No, I don't.*

"What are you about here, Mistress? You already know what they do. Aye…you want to know who they do it with. No husband left with a Girl last night."

How does she know what I'm thinking? "So, no angry wives this morning."

"If you mean do the wives dislike the Girls, then I can tell you that wives respect and admire them. Everyone has a job in the valley, and Girls perform services, often helping a wife. Say a woman is feeling poorly and ain't able to take care of her man. She sends him to see the Girls, and a few hours later, he comes home satisfied and appreciative to his woman. Plus, the real service the Girls offer to the tribe is taking pressure off the young unmarried gals."

Alexina had to think on that. The expression she felt forming on her face prompted Molly to continue.

"A mother must keep her daughter pure until her wedding night. When a fellow gets itchy, he lets one of the Girls scratch it."

Alexina shook her head. "It's not right for one unmarried girl to lay with a man, but acceptable if she's an unmarried Wagon Girl?"

"Aye! I see you appreciate the wonderful arrangement. Simple and effective."

Molly makes it sound so logical and moral. "What happens to a girl when she gets old and no longer beautiful?"

"She becomes a teacher and maid for the new girl who replaces her."

Alexina stood and slid her hand into the loop of the basket, having had enough information for the moment, especially the part where no husband had gone back with the beautiful women to the wagons parked at the northern pass.

By the time they returned with the apples, dinner was about

to be served. Alexina was grateful that no one had mentioned Peyton, and as much as she wanted to know his whereabouts, she couldn't bring herself to ask. At supper, she and the three ladies quietly dined on the remnants of the food from the previous day's party, and no one commented on the absence of the Master of Applewood.

At bedtime, Alexina bathed and put on her wedding nightdress with its ribbon woven through the loops, waiting for the loving pull. She listened for the lonely nightingale to call for its mate but heard no call. Had the nightingale found its love? Would she find hers?

Chapter Twenty-Seven

For the second day, Alexina did not see Peyton. Allowing the disappointment to pass, when the activities of breakfast had finished, Alexina implemented the first stage of her experiment, learning to pare apple skins.

"You mustn't do this," Molly advised. "It's our job."

"Don't think of it as work. I'm indulging in an avocation, interesting research."

After a short dialogue, Molly acquiesced, fetched a small, sharp knife, and demonstrated the art of skinning fruit. Molly pared ten to each one that Alexina peeled, but by the end of the afternoon, they had all of the apple pieces floating in a large copper kettle. With help from Sissy and Dutch, the four women hefted the cauldron to hang over the flames of the fireplace, where after two hours, the water sizzled and drops hissed over the top onto the embers.

"How long will it take to make syrup?" Alexina asked.

Dutch dipped a wooden dipper into the liquid and examined it. "Long time." She spilled a little into a cup of water. "Can't let it get dark. Needs to stay together in the cup, not mix with the water, and be careful it doesn't turn into a ball."

The three ladies peered into the cup to see the unfinished sample. While cooking the chickens Seat brought to them for supper, they checked the status of the syrup every few minutes. Seat and Little Jim joined them for the evening meal, and no one mentioned Peyton.

For a third night, Alexina prepared herself in hopes that her new husband would appear. She unwrapped the fancy soaps she had brought from London and replaced the hunks of lye soap that sat in a dish by the shower-bath. She pressed each bar to her nose and inhaled the rich aroma. One, molded into the shape of a flower, smelled of orange blossoms. Another, a diamond shape, had the soothing fragrance of sandalwood, and a third, leaf shaped and tinted purple, gave her the tangy scent of lavender. The aroma perfumed the room as she stroked the purple bar against her skin under the warm shower. As she bathed, she wished her husband had been there to assist her with the chore. A hollow feeling emerged deep within her, and she didn't know how to deal with it. The gaps in her knowledge frustrated her, but the frustration increased, for she craved his touch and knew from the little red book and her own need just exactly where that touch should be employed.

In the morning, she came into the busy kitchen, where she saw no sign of her husband. The copper cauldron had been removed from the embers. Hastening to the kettle, she dipped the iron spoon hanging from a ring on the edge and watched the light amber liquid coat the spoon and move like thick honey in its path around the bowl. When the steam abated, Alexina tasted it. With the intense flavor of apples, the sweet syrup exceeded her expectations.

Sissy took the spoon. "Can I taste? We waited for you."

Dutch and Molly gathered around, and each took their turn with the syrup. The women declared never having tasted anything so delicious.

"T'will be fine over bread," Molly said.

"A sauce for cobblers and pies," Sissy added.

"Hard candy," Dutch said.

"All of that," Alexina agreed, "but I'm thinking of something that will sell—for gold. Can we get some Product?"

"Aye," Molly said. "We haven't opened the batch still aging, but we always keep some of last year's around—you see, for events. I'll get Tad to give me a small cask."

Later that morning, the ladies experimented with combinations of Clear Jack and syrup. Alexina kept track of the amounts for each. In a few hours of mixing, they came up with the perfect blend. Using the recipe, they successfully made the same beverage three separate times. Alexina dug through her chests and found three cut glass decanters. The women poured the mixture into the glass bottles, sat them in the middle of the kitchen table, and stared at the pale liquid shining in the sun. Alexina swore everyone to secrecy until she had figured out the next step to her plan.

Molly passed around cups with the blends that had not made the grade. At first, Alexina protested, claiming ladies shouldn't imbibe in alcoholic drinks. When Sissy countered that it was truly experimental work done as an interesting avocation by a genteel lady and good enough not to be wasted, Alexina couldn't refute the logic.

They drank the cast offs. While the ladies dispensed with the unwanted examples, the smallest remarks became amusing, and within the hour, the four laughed until they could laugh no more.

"See," Molly said, "I think our Product makes people happy. Come to think on it, I've not encountered anyone becoming mean. And I've for sure seen that before settling in the valley."

"Happy drunks," Alexina said and giggled. "We need a name for our new blend."

"And," Molly said, moving to be near the window, "a lovely color." She reached for the small plants that hung upside down to dry. "Shore thyme." She snapped off the roots from the plants and threw them into a pan. "Granny's colorant."

"Brilliant!" Alexina exclaimed, and although the idea had merits of genius, it caused the four women to burst into laughter.

The laughter stopped. Boyce came in through the back door and wiped his feet on the brush mat. In a flash, Molly threw her apron over the cut glass bottles. Sissy gathered the empty cups and put them in the sink. Boyce cast a sour look at Alexina as he passed them and entered the study.

The ladies looked one to another, saying nothing. The half door creaked open, and Little Jim bounced in, breaking the silence in the kitchen.

Boyce and now Little Jim. Alexina hoped Peyton would follow.

Molly crooked her finger to the boy. "Do you know where Master Peyton is?"

Little Jim shrugged.

"How about Dragon?" Molly asked. "Is he around?"

Jim shook his head.

Chapter Twenty-Eight

Peyton had set up his bed in the barn since Alexina arrived and slept there the night of the wedding party. He felt at home there, at ease with horses and the fragrance of fresh hay. Although he couldn't remember his life as a young boy, he knew his family, being of the gentry, had owned horses, but the animals had been served by grooms and stable boys

On the day he fled Harrow, he had crept into a stall in an unknown barn and spent his first night in the company of a horse. At daybreak, the old mare awakened him by gently snuffing at his shoulder. The sweet hay smell on her breath and the soft, warm touch of her muzzle was something he would never forget. From that experience, he vowed to have horses about him, well-kept and loved. People had failed him; animals would not. And they never had.

The morning after the marriage, he stood in the doorway of the barn and gazed at Stone House, longing to see his new wife. She didn't approve of him or the Wanderers. How could she? The two of them were different. Was the only thing they had in common a paper their parents had signed years ago? *Another way my mother betrayed me.* He spat and shut the mental door on what little he remembered of his past.

He had not slept well, not just because he left the bedchamber, but howling on the south ridge disturbed him. Determined to find out what made the commotion, he saddled Dragon and set off to check his property. He did this on occasion, not as much to establish the state of the valley as to be alone, to withdraw. But the howling needed evaluation.

First, Peyton rode south and took the trail that led to the top of the ridge. The view included the entire valley, and he never tired of seeing the estate from this vantage. The west lands and meadows on rolling green hills fed the sheep, goats, and cattle. Deer and game flourished in the northern boundaries that had been left heavily wooded. The eastern pass slivered between the hills at this distance, narrowing and pointing the way out of the valley. A clear blue lake edged along the southern ridge where sparkling waters and swampy areas dotted the space between the shore and the beginning of the ridge. The bounty of nature's beauty lay resplendent before him.

In the valley's center sat Stone House and the great barn that had been built since he arrived. The barn provided a large measure of pride, as he had helped gather the stones and worked alongside the men to erect the building to his specifications. From the barn to the lake, rich fields prospered, some planted from the seeds of the wild grains growing in the valley, and others from seeds he had traded for product and animals. This plan of conservation regarding the wild game, fish, and fowl had served them well. Life in the valley thrived for him and his people.

His people. Not Alexina's.

He recalled the day he arrived at the valley with nothing but his deed in hand. Wagons peppered the clearings, and animals grazed untethered. When he approached the first wagon, he met Tad, a young man about his age. Tad called his father, and before long other men gathered around Peyton as he proclaimed himself the owner. Soon the crowd parted, and a grizzled old woman approached. Peyton showed his deed to Granny, but she brushed it aside.

She put her hand on his chest. "I see the truth in it." Then she touched his forehead. "I feel your intelligence."

That was all. Granny turned and left, but Peyton understood her unspoken request that the people stay in the valley and help him farm it.

Another howl from the direction of the western ridge took his attention away from his memories. Dismounting, he wrapped the reins loosely on the stirrup and let the horse graze. He removed his spyglass from the canvas bag, slung over Dragon's saddle and followed the hill rim until he detected movement. Wild dogs. They could be as bad as wolves, long gone in this region. His decision to check the property had been providential. He would need a few days to see if the beasts had wreaked havoc on his land or livestock. Tracing the hilltops, he searched for evidence of predation. To the north, bright blue painted wagons caught his eye. The Wagon Girls. In his glass, he saw several of the women taking clothes off a line. A fair-haired woman stood out among the dark girls. That vacuous blonde who had come with.... Without conscious thought, he moved the glass toward Stone House. He could make out two moving figures heading toward the orchard. He instantly recognized Molly and *her.*

Somehow, he could tell they enjoyed each other's company. Judging by her body language, Molly seemed content, even happy, with no malice from Alexina's words from the night of the party. Animated, the two women walked with faces toward each other, gesturing and sharing confidences. If Molly had forgiven his wife, why couldn't he? He lowered the spyglass. "Drunks and whores," he said to himself, recalling Alexina's statement on the night of their wedding celebration. What else could the Wagon Girls be called? And Molly had been so deep in her cups, no other description but drunk would fit. When he first came to the valley, the men drank every night until he put a stop to it. On the occasions when they celebrated, the Valley Folk imbibed to the degree that some could hardly walk.

Another howl brought him from his deliberations. His holdings, over a thousand acres, needed him.

Chapter Twenty-Nine

Four days since the wedding and Alexina had not seen Peyton. *Will he ever return to the house? Why did he leave?*

She washed and cleaned her teeth, then slipped into a morning dress. Smells emanating from the kitchen tempted her appetite, and she longed for a strong cup of tea.

"Good morning," she greeted Molly when she entered the room.

Molly jerked her head toward the closed study door.

"Thank you," Alexina said and hurried out of the kitchen, heading toward the study. She knocked, then pushed the door open and entered.

Peyton sat at the writing desk with his notebook propped at an angle. "The household knows not to disturb me when I'm here."

"I'm not the household." She drew herself up and tilted her head. "I waited…on the night of our wedding. And I've waited three days since. This is the first time I've had the chance to speak with you."

"Well, what is it you want?"

What does he think I want?

His eyebrows rose in response to her hurt and surprised expression. Her hands grasped together at her waist, white-knuckled. He looked to the desktop and bit his lip. "What can I do for you?" These words were soft, gentle, regretful.

She advanced, close enough to feel the warmth of his body. "I want a home, a caring husband, and children. I want to please you."

His startled gaze searched hers. The ancient clock above his desk struck loudly in the silence.

"Anything else?" His gaze shifted from her face, pink and wide-eyed, to the floor, obviously regretting his tone.

"No." She whirled, her linen skirts making wispy sounds on the stone floor. Pausing in the doorway, she gripped the frame. "I'll expect you this evening. After supper. In our bedchamber." She closed the door sharply.

Chapter Thirty

Peyton put the notebook and pen in the drawer and leaned back in the sturdy chair. He hadn't wanted a wife. Not even a beautiful one. How long *had* it been since he had lain with a woman? Months ago, with one of the Wagon Girls. The Wagon Girls required nothing, forgotten the next day. This woman, though.... Well, if she wanted him, he would give her what she wished. Tonight.

His concentration shattered, he left the study. A boom of thunder stopped him in the empty expanse between the bedrooms and the kitchen. A light rain fell through the hole in the roof. Furniture and trunks hugged the walls on both sides, the goods belonging to her, his legal wife, who in a few short weeks had brought a bit of refinement and order to his household

He left the house and jogged to the barn. "Carl, when the rain ceases, get some of the men to help you gather lake reeds to repair the thatch on Stone House. Our lady's things might get wet."

Chapter Thirty-One

That night Alexina bathed and donned her special nightdress, as she had since her wedding night. The bright moon cast a light through the thin burlap curtains. She lay back against the puffy pillows, the lace of her gown touching her back. The illumination cast dancing shadows on the intricate carving of the bedposts. She loved this bed, where most likely she had been conceived, created from a consuming love between her parents, a cherished union of devotion and commitment. Her mother had mourned daily for the loss, years after her father's death. *Will I be fortunate enough to experience even a small portion of that sentiment?*

The door creaked, and a ray of buttery lantern light from the hall spilled onto the floor. In the soft radiance, Peyton entered and walked to the shower-bath. After dropping his clothes, he cranked the shower's mechanism. Alexina bit her lip. She had married a bold and beautiful man. His muscles rippled as he bent and reached. Alexina's curiosity fixed on his body as he stepped onto the raised platform. He pulled the handle releasing the water, and turned, facing her. She had never seen a naked man before. His tanned upper torso showed patches of dark chest hair, contrasting against the pale skin of his abdomen and below. As he bathed, his manhood changed. Grew. Stiffened. She caught her breath at the sight of him, this man, her husband. He lathered, and the air of the room caught the orange scent of the French milled soap. Then he pulled the lever, rinsing the foam away.

Stepping from the shower, he toweled, all the time maintaining eye contact with her. As he dried, Alexina left the bed. Her heart fluttered like a tiny bird as she pulled the ribbon on her nightdress and let it fall. Peyton dropped his towel in the same movement and walked slowly toward her.

"The beams from the window have formed a halo around you and turned your hair to silver." He brushed a long curl from her shoulder. "Lovely." His dark eyes roved her form from head to toe. "Your clothes concealed the curves of your waist and hips." His hand moved from her hair, across her collarbone, down her arms and to her breasts. Her nipples drew into tight buds, fairly begging for his touch. He did not disappoint, and rolled them with his thumb and forefinger as he cupped the fullness. Her back arched into him.

"Perfect in the moonlight." He pulled her to him, nuzzling her neck and ears. She mewled, and he, in turn, breathed faster. Alexina backed to the bed until she reached the feather mattress. Her knees buckled. Peyton caught her in his arms and laid her on the bed. He knelt beside her and guided her hand to his groin. She released her hold, but he restored her grasp.

"Touch me."

Chapter Thirty-Two

"Oh," she said and coiled her fingers around him. She grasped the flesh now like a branch, exhaled a staccato breath, and closed her eyes. His touches felt wonderful, and she wished to please him. Peyton turned on his side and ran his hands down her belly, stroking until he reached the soft floss, where he probed and caressed. She parted her legs, inviting him.

Suddenly she knew. Feeling his size and hardness, it became clear how men and women achieved their union. The new knowledge thrilled her, but as she visualized what was to happen, a wave of fear made her shudder. Her eyes flew open, and she bit her lip. She turned her head against the pillow, waiting for the fear to pass. She desperately wanted him. The hollow within her demanded to be filled. But she didn't know enough. The uncertainty frightened her more. She squeezed her eyes shut and became rigid.

"Alexina!"

She opened her eyes wide and stared at him.

He stopped his touch and sat up. "I thought you wanted me, but I've seen that look before. Like a wounded deer. A trapped hare."

She turned her head away from him. Then she spread her legs wider.

"I'll not take you like this."

She didn't know what to say and kept her face toward the wall.

"What do you think I will do, take you like an animal? Is that what you think of me, a brute impaling an innocent victim? Look at me."

She couldn't look at him. His rudeness and constant

disappearances confused her. But she wanted him as her husband. *The fear will pass.*

The bed moved, then the door creaked. When she looked back, she was alone. *What happened*? She was willing to submit. The sight of him had taken her by surprise, even frightened her, but only for a moment. *Why didn't he consummate our marriage? What did I do to fail him?*

In the morning, as she dressed, she reviewed her brief encounter with Peyton. He must be disappointed in her. She had been bold enough to demand he perform his husbandly duties, then behaved like a coward. He was not the only one disappointed. How she longed for more of his touch and his kisses.

She went to the kitchen, and the quiet increased her sadness. The members of the household were engrossed in their breakfast. Alexina didn't know for sure if the workers in Stone House who sat at the table knew about her unproductive encounter with Peyton but based upon the looks on their faces and the previous *no secrets in the valley* comments, she assumed they had the knowledge of what had transpired.

"Good morning, Mistress," Sissy said, handing her a cup of tea.

Seat finished his plate of ham with eggs and wiped the last bit of yellow with his slice of bread. He stood. "I'm picking the rest of them sweet apples for you today, Mistress. I'll store them in a bin in the cask barn if that's good?"

"Thank you. They will be all right in a bin?"

"Sure. They'll last for months. As soon as the other trees start dropping, we'll pick them and start the brewing. I'll keep the sweet ones separate. They won't be juiced with the others."

"Will that affect the taste of the cider you make this year?"

He shook his head. "We already have half of the sweet crop, enough for taste."

Alexina pointed to the chair Seat had just occupied, indicating she wished him to stay. "Please, will you tell me what you do to make the Product?"

Seat got a strange look on his face as if he thought everyone knew about the Product. He pulled at his chin. "Well, you see, we pick the apples, and when there's enough for a batch, we put them in the press and squeeze out the juice. Then the juice goes into barrels to ferment."

"You don't do anything else to the juice?"

"No, Mistress. Nature does the work. After a few weeks, the bubbles have most popped the tops off them barrels. That's what we call Jack, but some people call it hard cider. We sell our Jack to the towns around the valley."

"Cider comes only from apples?"

"Hard cider. Telling the truth, Mistress, our folk can make hard drink from anything. Before we came to the valley, we made it from potatoes, cherries, grains, and once even from cactus. But them apples," he pointed in the direction of the orchard. "They's something special. That Jack is better than anything I ever tasted."

Alexina paused, hoping her interested expression would bring more information.

"Since Master Peyton and the blacksmith made the distiller, we have Clear Jack. You'd probably call it apple brandy. And fine it is, too. Why, the taverns around the valley beg for it. I believe Master Peyton will try to sell it in Kerrstead."

"Would selling it in Kerrstead make a larger profit?"

Seat pushed back his unruly curl, thinking. "Don't know much about the money. Boyce takes care of the selling and collecting. We just make the Jack."

"I see," Alexina said. "Thank you."

Seat left, and Molly sat down across from her.

"Does Mr. Woodleigh share his profits from the sale of the brandy?"

"Don't think it ever came up. We don't need any money, other than what the Wagon Girls share. We get half of the Clear Jack."

"Half?"

"Never measured, but we get what we need. The Girls get a barrel for entertaining, you see, and the rest we use at our events."

"The Wagon Girls—they entertain with the brandy?"

"What's on your mind, Mistress?"

"The Girls. Daisy. I can't imagine her...."

"You mean Pearl Pink?"

Alexina laughed. "That's her new name?"

Molly sniffed. "Ain't that a pip? Hmph. Pearl indeed. Rotten oyster would have been a better name. Although she's doing well. Got her own following already, and it's barely been a week or so. She's put on at least a stone. Wears a curly wig. You'd not recognize her."

"You've seen her?"

"Nay. But there ain't no secrets in the valley, Mistress."

She didn't have to say it. Alexina could read it on Molly's face. The Valley Folk already knew her first night with Peyton had been a failure.

Alexina did not wish to think about it right then. "What do the wagons look like? Are they fancy?"

"Aye, they are. All silk and satin curtains, and carpets on the floor."

Alexina pictured her bedchamber and all the other rooms of Stone House. Bare floors, cold and moist in the middle, with no carpets or draperies.

Molly smiled. "If you want to know more about the interior of them wagons, you could ask your friend, Neighbor Rufus. They take pity on the poor fool and only charge him double!"

Alexina laughed along with Molly. She sympathized for the pathetic little man who found love-for-gold at an inflated price.

Chapter Thirty-Three

After breakfast clean up, Alexina called the women to the table. "I believe we have a good recipe for our brandy. What about the color?"

Molly placed a small jug on the table and poured a bit of the content into a ladle. The spoon held liquid of the deepest ruby. "Boiled roots of the shore thyme. No taste, just color."

Alexina had donated three crystal decanters that came in her dowery. From her pocket, she produced a thin hollow reed and sucked the reed until the weight suggested fullness. Placing her finger over the top, she moved it to the open neck of the decanter. One drop, two drops, three. Molly put the glass stopper on and shook. The red swirled like tendrils in a whirlwind, and they watched as the pale amber changed into an ash-rose tint. Dutch repeated this several times until the liquid achieved a dark, clear ruby color.

While the tint spread in the bottles, Alexina regarded the walls of the great room and then the hole in the thatching. The longer her furniture and possessions stayed stacked, clinging to the sides, the more likely mildew could appear. She cleared her throat to get the others' attention. "So, Phillip is the best carpenter in the tribe? I should ask him about the windows and shelves."

Molly bobbed her head. "Aye. He's a quick mind and skilled hands. He is head carpenter."

"All of you have specific jobs? How did you decide to work in Stone House?"

"Granny told us, the widows, to take care of the Young Master. He needed care, and we needed a job and guaranteed meals."

"And now you have to work harder because I'm here."

Molly smiled. "Aye, that's true." She held her grin until her eyes twinkled, and she let out a laugh. "We love taking care of you." Then she went to the half door and called for Phillip.

By the time all the decanters received the exact ration of colorant, Phillip appeared.

"Yes, Mistress. What can I do for you?

The carpenter listened as Alexina told him what she wanted—shelves, wooden valences for the windows, and storage boxes that matched the color of her display cabinet. Phillip drew a picture in the ashes of the fireplace, and it suited her. *I hope he's as good as Molly claims.*

It had been an hour since the women used the shore thyme. The particles had settled to the bottom, and the liquid had achieved a perfect clear color. Alexina fetched paper and pencil from the study and made notes on the drops. They poured the decanter contents into a large jug and tried it again on the second round, and having matched the color, did it again with the third.

Three cut glass decanters sat on the table. A beam from the morning sun flashed through the window, causing the crimson contents to sparkle and glisten. The four women made a simultaneous cheer in praise of its beauty.

Dutch removed the decanters, and Molly pushed the big jug into the pantry away from sight when they heard footsteps growing louder as someone approached the back door.

Boyce, in his usual coarse manner, entered and sneered at the group seated at the table. "Did I interrupt your game of Whist? Need something to do?" He opened the door to the bread oven next to the fireplace and pretended to be disappointed. He glared at Dutch.

Dutch left her seat and opened the pantry door, bringing out a bag of flour.

Boyce walked over to the table and put his hands on his hips. He cocked his head at Molly and Sissy.

Alexina didn't wait for further intimidation. She crossed her arms in front of her. "Can I help you with something, Mr. Boyce? I don't appreciate you interrupting my staff meeting."

He blanched at her scolding. "Staff meeting?"

"Of course. In well-run institutions, competent superiors hold them regularly."

His eyes reflected the insult she had made on his supervisory abilities. Dutch left the flour on the counter and returned to the table.

"What do you want, Mr. Boyce?" Alexina demanded.

"We are going to Kerrstead."

"Oh, to order casks and barrels?"

He fluttered his eyelids as a way of dismissing her question. "Do you have a list of purchases?"

"I do," Alexina said and ran to the bedchamber where she kept her list.

When she returned, Peyton was standing in the kitchen with Boyce. She added the carpentry needs and handed him the list.

"Give it to Boyce," he said.

She took a step closer, locked eyes with him, and said, "I'd rather give it to *you*."

He took the paper and examined her requests. "What's this for? Sanding papers? Brushes, stain, and shellac?"

"To build shelves in the dining room." She pointed to the empty area in the center of the house. "Also, would you mail these for me?" She placed a stack of letters in his hand. "And don't forget the coffee and sugar."

"Hmmm," he said, folded the paper, and shoved the letters into his belt. "I won't forget."

Boyce came from the study with a ledger. Peyton engaged in a momentary look with Alexina, then nodded to the women.

"Good day," he said, then left, joining Boyce and Phillip, who waited outside.

Alexina watched out the half door as Boyce climbed into the torn seat of the carriage. Peyton stroked Silverton's snout, and heading toward the driver's seat, patted the horse's rump. Lithe and muscular, he climbed up into the seat, and with a snap of the reins, the carriage took off.

Chapter Thirty-Four

The sun slipped behind the hilltop, leaving a rosy glow in the blue and mauve sky. Alexina heard what she now knew was the sound alerting the residents that someone had come through the pass. Stepping out the front door, she recognized Applewood's dilapidated carriage, which passed by her, stopping at the barn. Peyton and Phillip disengaged Silverton from his harness.

She hoped Peyton would join them for dinner, but he and Phillip strolled to the first small stone building where the Wanderers lived. Disappointed, she returned to the house and entered the kitchen, at the same time Boyce appeared at the back door with a box. He put it on the floor and left. The box contained the sanding papers, the stain, the brushes, and the shellac. Next to that sat a smaller box with coffee and sugar.

The purchases made her smile. What had Ignace Smith said about the house needing a woman's touch? Her presence had already made a difference.

Between the secret brandy and supervising the new dining room, I have a lot to keep me busy. She recalled the sign in the meeting room at the Greenfield School. *We are sculptors of the human condition. Sculpt with Patience.* She looked down at her hands. *Patience.*

At bedtime, she closed the bedchamber door. She required privacy, and the nagging fear of Boyce being near made her wish the door could be locked. She didn't like being alone in the house after Dutch, Sissy, and Molly left for the night. Sliding under the blanket, the lonely nightingale returned with her melodious but despondent song. Alexina had stopped feeling sorry for the bird and took comfort in the fact she wasn't the only one devoid of a mate.

In the morning, Seat joined Alexina and the Stone House staff for breakfast. She welcomed the company. For all the elite individuals she had known in the country manors, she couldn't remember one who could match Seat's wit, and for most of the time in his presence, they enjoyed continuous laughter.

When Alexina saw Molly heading out to the spring where the women washed clothes, she followed. Molly gave her a questioning look.

"For supervisory purposes," Alexina explained.

Molly felt for the dryness of the sheets and pulled them from the line. Alexina shadowed Molly to the rocks, where dry clothing and towels had been spread by the washwomen.

"What are you about, Mistress?"

"Uhm, I don't want to intrude in your privacy, but...."

Molly folded a few towels before she spoke. "You can ask me whatever you wish. If I think your nose has gotten too far into me business, I'll let you know."

"Are you and Seat involved?"

"Involved? Aye, I know what you're asking. Let's just say when I'm needing comfort, I find a dependable Seat."

Alexina couldn't help but laugh. "I see." Armed with her recent information on the amorous activities between men and women, she did see. "Might you get married?"

"Married?" Molly looked like she'd just bitten into a worm. "Nay, nay! We're friends who give comfort and lend a hand—or whatever body part what's in need of service. You understand."

Service? Friends? Alexina pulled a towel from the flat stones and folded it.

Molly took the towel from Alexina and placed it in the laundry basket. "I'd get married again, to the right fellow. As much as I like Seat, he ain't the right seat for this bottom's lifetime. Anything else, Mistress?"

Alexina shook her head and accompanied Molly to the house. As they neared the back door, Phillip, and two men unknown to Alexina, had their arms full of boards.

Alexina approached Phillip. "The shelves?"

"Just so. Let's see if I got it right."

Phillip and his helpers walked past the kitchen and on to the great empty space with the two large windows centered in the back wall of Stone House. The assistants held a board between the two windows.

"Perfect." Alexina admired the curved edges and the deep grooves in the shelf boards just as she had drawn them.

For the next few hours, she and Phillip directed the men where to place each shelf. They marked lines between the windows. On the other side of the window casement, Alexina drew a space with the thick pencil to show where she had planned to suspend draperies. By the time they finished, long lines on the stones showed where the new shelves would hang.

"We'll work on them here in Stone House if you don't mind," Phillip said. "That way, if you don't like what we're doing, or you want to change your mind, you can tell us straight away. We can start now if you wish."

"Please," she said.

Phillip's eagerness to satisfy her gave Alexina the feeling she had been accepted as an authority, the Mistress of Applewood.

The men set up their work and began to sand the shelves. The sound of the rhythmic scratching and the smell of the sawdust fascinated her. She barely noticed the aromas from the kitchen, which usually alerted the household that supper was done. Phillip and his men left, and when Alexina came into the kitchen, she found the table set, the food ready, and those who would dine there that evening standing in wait.

"Oh, excuse me. I didn't mean to delay supper."

The workers assured her the delay created no inconvenience, but it was full dark by the time the kitchen could be considered done for the night. Dutch left, and, after putting the last pots away, Sissy followed.

"Molly," Alexina said. "We need a name for our secret brandy. Do you have any suggestions?"

Molly pulled out a chair at the table, pushing her mouth sideways. "Let me think.... The drink comes from apples, the fruit that tempted Eve. Our valley is a paradise, like Eden, and our brew is the color of the finest apples." She drummed her fingers on the table. "Paradise Temptation, Eve's Apple, Eden's Lure?"

Alexina competed with, "Eve's Gift, Eden's Blessing, Paradise Tribute."

They played with the titles, using combinations of words, but to no avail. Nothing captured their fascination.

They ran out of possibilities. In the quiet of the kitchen, boot scrapings at the back door sounded louder. Peyton came in.

Peyton stood next to Molly's chair. "Why are you here so late?" He crossed his arms over his chest.

"The Mistress and me were just talking."

"Little Jim has already gone back to the wagon. It's going to rain. Let me get an oilskin, and I'll walk you."

"No need, Young Master. I can go."

"It's not safe. Your wagon is a long walk, and I believe there are wild dogs in the hills. You must not go about alone at night, Molly." He shot an accusing look at Alexina. "Leave before nightfall." He directed his gaze to Alexina again. "No matter what the mistress wants."

Peyton left for the barn to get the oilskin.

Alexina dropped her head. "I'm sorry I kept you. Where is your wagon?"

"Me, Sissy, and Dutch live in the last wagon, past the grain fields."

"All of you and Little Jim? So crowded?"

"We spent our whole lives in them wagons until we found this valley, and our Good Lad let some of us build houses. Rene and I had the fourth house. Here comes Master Peyton now. I'll say goodnight to you, then. See you in the morning."

Peyton waited at the back door with the oilskin held high. Large drops started to hit the windows. She hadn't thought about Molly or where the woman slept. Since coming to Applewood, Alexina had become aware of the inequities of class. *How much we have taken for granted.*

Molly knocked at the bedroom door the next morning. She peeked into the room. "I thought I heard you moving about. Here!" She rushed to the bed. "You're the mistress. You'll not make the bed."

"I can help, can't I?"

"See here, Mistress. You'll put me out of a job. And don't I love touching these fine linens, too."

Alexina went to the other side of the bed and helped pull the sheet. "Out of a job. Would you consider being my personal maid?"

"I'd for certain consider it. I don't know if I would make a good one."

"You'd be a far sight better than Daisy."

Molly nodded. "What would I have to do?"

"What you do now, take care of me. But you'd have to live here in Stone House."

Molly smoothed the sheet quietly. "Hmm," she said after a minute. "I'd be in the guest room? Could Jim-boy stay, too?"

"Of course."

"What about Master Peyton?"

"Do you think he'll object?"

Molly shook her head. "Nay. He doesn't give much thought to the house and what we do here. And I know he'd want the best for you."

Alexina felt a little wave of warmth at that comment but dismissed it as foolish.

"Listen to me, Mistress. Don't you doubt for a minute about him caring. He don't show what he should. He needs some time, *that* man."

Alexina pulled her shoulders up in a way that said, *I wish it were true.*

"It's true," Molly stated in her usual way of reading Alexina's thoughts. "I would love to be your personal maid."

"I don't like being alone here at night."

Molly didn't comment as she fluffed the pillows. "Right, then. Dutch has made them grain cakes for breakfast, the ones the Good Lad likes so much."

"Dutch knows a lot about breads and pastries. How do you account for that?"

"I don't account for it because I don't know." Molly finished with the bed, picked up the soiled towels for washing. She held the door for Alexina, and they headed for the kitchen.

"What are Sissy and Dutch's last names?"

"Sissy's last name is Crowley. I don't know Dutch's. She joined us in Wales right before we came to this area."

"You've never asked her last name?"

Molly stopped and turned to Alexina. "Mistress, when Dutch joined us, Granny gave the go-ahead, and the rest of us trust Granny. Dutch never said, and we never asked. We don't need to know where Dutch came from or why she wanted to join us. Does that bother you?"

Oh, how I wish it didn't. "I won't let it bother me; how's that?"

"Just fine, Mistress. Our lad has done good wanting you."

But does he really want me?

Molly began walking again toward the kitchen. "He wants you."

Chapter Thirty-Five

Peyton normally took his breakfast at sunrise. Alexina had tried to get up in time to eat with him, but it took her so long to get ready she usually missed him. Sometimes, like this morning, he came back to Stone House.

He passed the kitchen on his way to the study.

On his return, Alexina hurried to him. "Mr. Woodleigh, I have asked Molly to be my lady's maid. Have you any objections? She'll need to move her things into the guest room."

"Suit yourself," he said. "You're in charge of Stone House."

"Thank you." Her brain raced for something else to say to keep him there. "I will need some things for the house."

"Boyce and I are going to Kerrstead tomorrow. Make a list."

"May I go? Some of the things I'll need to personally select."

Peyton paused for a minute. "Very well. Be ready early. It's a long ride."

"Early."

After breakfast, Alexina asked Molly to come to the bedchamber. "You'll go with me tomorrow as your first lesson in being a lady's maid. Let's see what you can wear."

Molly pulled the sides of her skirt and looked in the mirror. "You're saying I ain't right-dressed?"

"We can fix that." Alexina drew out a yellow calico skirt and pale-yellow blouse from her carved chest. "See if this fits you."

The blouse strained against Molly's bosom. "I'll have to move the buttons."

"Good," Alexina said. "And Daisy left the duster I bought her in London. You'll need that."

Molly took the thin beige coat and draped it over her arm.

"Will it cause you any problems with Sissy or Dutch to move here?"

"They'll be glad for the room in the wagon. They know Master Peyton told me to look after you. And this will make it easier for me with Jim. You'll have to tell me what a good lady's maid should be doing."

"You'll catch on quickly."

The following morning, Alexina and Molly were ready at sunrise and waited at the kitchen table. Boyce and Peyton came into the kitchen for their meal.

"Why are you so dressed up?" Boyce asked Molly.

"I'm going into town with my Mistress."

"She doesn't need you to go to town."

Alexina put on her best authoritarian facial expression. "Molly is my lady's maid and should accompany me into town, Mr. Boyce."

Molly bobbed her head. "That way, she ain't alone, see? Makes it proper."

Boyce rolled his eyes and sneered.

Peyton didn't say anything but reached for the butter and spread it on a piece of bread. Alexina took that as a sign he agreed with her. She didn't know much of Peyton's background, but it was obvious he had been brought up in high society. *Didn't Mother select him?* Alexina and her mother had enjoyed the company of London's finest families, and up until her illness, they had lived a society life. She recognized the training in Peyton, even if he had adopted the unrestricted life of the valley folk.

After breakfast, Peyton called for the coach. Molly put on her duster and helped her mistress with hers, as Alexina had instructed her earlier.

The top was down on the coach, as it promised to be a sunny day. Molly and Alexina, assisted by Peyton, took the front-facing seat, and Boyce sat alone in the back-facing cushion. Peyton climbed to the driver's bench. One cluck to Silverton, and the carriage smoothly rolled forward. Outside the valley beyond the pass, the early spring weather felt cooler, the sky overcast and gray.

Alexina bent close to Molly's ear. "I noticed the valley is sunny most of the time."

Molly responded close in. "It's like Eden, Mistress. When we left Garry and came through the northern pass, Granny said this would be our home, and the sun would shine on us for a long time. I thought she meant it as a blessing, but sure enough, the sun shines in our valley like no place else I've ever seen."

Alexina put her hood over her head to shield from the cold they encountered once the carriage left the valley. She had informed Molly on the merits of wearing a duster when traveling. Molly pulled the string at her neck to close the hood, opened it, and did it again with obvious satisfaction.

After two hours, Peyton pulled the coach off the road and into an area alongside a stream. He disengaged Silverton and led the horse to the running water. Boyce hopped down from his seat. He frowned at the ladies but extended his hand in a gesture for assistance.

"No, thank you, Mr. Boyce," Alexina said.

"You?" he asked Molly.

Molly shook her head. Boyce left, headed to a different direction from the stream, and disappeared into a copse of trees.

"I don't want that man touching me, either," Molly said. "Bad apple, that fellow."

"What does Granny say about him?"

"She doesn't trust him."

"Has she told that to Mr. Woodleigh?"

"I'm not sure what she said. But the master thinks he needs the man. Boyce knows business and such sort. Our Lad don't want to bother with trade or dealing with people."

"I see," Alexina said. She recalled Boyce's sinister behavior when she had come into the house during the wedding reception.

Peyton left Silverton at the water and returned to the coach.

Alexina cleared her throat. "Would you help us down, Mr. Woodleigh?"

He pulled out the metal step from the bottom of the coach. Alexina's foot found the step, and she extended her hand to Peyton. "That step is wobbly. I thought it might give way." With his hands around her waist, he lifted her to the ground but kept his hands on her longer than needed. She stood behind him while he squatted and looked up underneath the coach's chassis.

Shaking the mechanism, he moved it about. "I'll try to fix it. Be careful when you use it." He stood and extended his hand to Molly, who cautiously put her foot down on the step.

After a half hour, when Boyce returned, and Silverton's harness had been fastened, Peyton helped the ladies mount the coach, and they continued their journey. By the fourth hour, they reached the outskirts of Kerrstead. In front of the public stable, a groom took hold of the horse's reins. Boyce pulled the step and stood waiting, but neither woman would allow him to catch their gaze. He stepped aside, allowing Peyton to take his place.

Boyce sneered at their disregard. "Well, I'm going to the bank."

Alexina sat up and extended her hand to Peyton. "Excellent! We should all go to the bank."

"What?" Boyce made a face.

Alexina touched Peyton's shoulder, experiencing a tingle from the feel of the hard muscles under his shirt. "Mr. Woodleigh, you should present me to the banker. That way, I can establish an account with merchants, and your banker will know who I am."

The slight movement of Peyton's head showed his assent. Boyce left before Molly had disembarked. Alexina and Peyton walked side by side while Molly remained a few strides behind as she had been instructed.

"Mr. Woodleigh," Alexina said, "kindly slow your pace so I may keep up with you."

Peyton slowed but said nothing as Alexina inched a bit closer to him. When they reached the bank. Boyce had already taken a seat in the lobby.

A clerk came from a closed door and approached Peyton. "Mr. MacAdams will see you now, Mr. Woodleigh."

Boyce rose to join Peyton, but Alexina inserted herself between them, with Molly close behind. Boyce was forced to enter the office after them.

Mr. MacAdams bowed his head in a greeting. "Mr. Woodleigh, good to see you. You will be making a deposit soon, I trust. This is the time each year when you sell your brandy, is it not?"

Peyton nodded. "Soon." Then he cleared his throat. "MacAdams, this is my wife, Mrs. Woodleigh."

MacAdams bowed politely. Alexina put out her hand, and the banker took it. "Lovely to meet you, Mrs. Woodleigh." He cast a quick glance at Peyton. His expression was clear, with an unspoken *Well done, Woodleigh.*

Peyton's face brightened, and he cast a quick look of pride to his new wife.

She eased her hand from MacAdams's grasp. "My pleasure, sir.

Pray, tell me what you require to start a new merchant account."

MacAdams took a card from his desk and wrote on the back. "This is all you should need, madame."

"Thank you, sir. I shall take my leave. Good morning, Mr. MacAdams." She deliberately did not send adieu to Boyce, hoping he would understand his position as an employee and an underling to her.

Alexina smiled at Peyton and gestured with her eyes for Molly to leave. By the time they got close to the bank's exit, Peyton caught up and held the door. "Three o'clock at the stables. Please."

"Of course, Mr. Woodleigh." She smiled. "Do have a good day."

"Hmmm," he answered. "Thank you."

"Molly and I have shopping to do. You will be purchasing casks?"

"Yes, and other things. Three o'clock. It's important we get back to Applewood before dark."

"I understand. We will be there on time."

Along with the nod, Peyton had the ghost of a smile. That tiny gesture warmed her heart, and she had to will herself not to skip down the boardwalk.

Chapter Thirty-Six

Peyton's mood lifted a notch higher after Alexina's lilting wish for him to have a good day. He should wish her the same, but unable to converse with this woman, his wife, his answer was, "Hmmm." He couldn't deny the feeling of pride he felt when she waltzed into MacAdams's office. The banker recognized her class immediately and offered the appropriate respect. Peyton advanced a few notches up the rung of the banker's esteem for uniting with a woman who acted like an aristocrat. The honor increased when MacAdams gave him the *well-done, Woodleigh* eye message. How long had it been since Peyton had been surrounded with society etiquette? Hadn't he left that behind at Harrow? Did he want it again? *She's a woman and can't be trusted.* He watched her leave and took in the wave of her hips and the grace of her walk. He needed to remove the thoughts forming in his mind, remembering her scent, the feel of her body, the sweet breath on his face, and the night they almost....

Casks! Yes, he must go to the cask maker and pay the exorbitant fees for the small barrels they needed for their Clear Jack.

Chapter Thirty-Seven

As her first order of business, Alexina needed to visit the drapers. It didn't take long to find the shop with the white columns and the gorgeous fabrics in the window. She and Molly entered, checked the displays, and walked around. The walls were sectioned with shelves, each with its own vibrant color of cloth. Alexina spotted exactly what she wanted—heavy burgundy brocade with an intricate gold design. She met the proprietor and showed him MacAdams's card. Using hand to shoulder as a measure, the owner pulled thirty portions, calling them yards. She ordered the yardage to be delivered to the stable before three.

Next, they stopped at the tailor's shop and conducted business with him. After the tailor, they called at the grocers, started an account, and gave him the list of things, including vanilla flavoring, chocolate powder, and spices. The grocer promised to deliver the goods promptly. After the grocers, they found the dry goods store. There, Alexina ordered needles, pins, thread, thimble, several sizes of shears and scissors, a long measuring tape, and other items on the list. She felt elated at completing her purchases and looked forward to making the drapes.

"Hungry?" Alexina asked.

"Aye. Dutch gave me a small basket for our lunch."

Alexina tapped her purse. "We will be dining like fine ladies today." She indicated a restaurant down the street. The windows, decorated with gold leaf, allowed the many gas lights of the dining room to glow as an invitation to rest and consume.

"When we enter," Alexina said, "someone, perhaps the

maitre'd, will show us to a table, and someone, probably a waiter, will bring us a menu."

"What's a menu?"

"A list of foods and prices."

Molly cast her gaze down as she walked. "That's where Daisy had it all over me, Mistress. That menu might as well be blank."

"I'll read it to you. Daisy didn't have that much over you, however. I bought her a book when we traveled, a child's book, and she couldn't find her way through it."

"I'd sure enjoy being able to find my way through a book."

"And you shall. I'll teach you."

"If only we could do that for the children of the valley."

Molly was right. *Why shouldn't I bring education to these people? At least the children.*

"You are a good influence for us, Mistress. Look at what you're doing—decorating, teaching me society ways."

"Can Granny read and write?"

"Nay. She calls writing the devil's scratches."

"How does she keep her medicines labeled?"

"I don't know. I wouldn't go asking her. She keeps her secrets close to the bone."

Molly's eyes widened as they entered the restaurant. They were seated, and Alexina ordered for both of them. They sat quietly for a long time.

"You've not much to say, Molly?"

"I've got plenty to say, but you told me a good lady's maid don't talk unless talked to, so I'm waiting."

"So, I did. Oh, Molly, you will work out just fine." Alexina refused the wine menu the sommelier offered. "Have you given more thought to our secret drink's name?"

"I have. How about Eden's Joy?"

"Perfect! Molly, you are someone special."

"As you are to me, Mistress…to everyone in the valley."

After they dined and the bill was presented, Alexina took money from her purse and paid. She told Molly about tips.

They strolled about Kerrstead, and Alexina asked questions. "The banker expected a deposit from the brandy sales. What do you know about that, Molly?"

"It's almost Tasting Day. Then we sell the Product, the one ready from last year."

"Explain that, please."

"Like Seat said, after the harvest, we make Jack in big barrels. From the Jack, we make the brandy, Clear Jack, and that goes into the aging barrels for six months or so. Master Peyton won't let the men drink around the campfire at night like they used to. Now the men go home to their families. Our Young Lad has changed us for the better, especially the drinking. But we drink on special occasions, like weddings."

Alexina rolled the memory around regarding the drinking at the wedding. Peyton was wise to limit their access to alcohol.

"So," Molly continued, "we all look forward to our *events,* especially Tasting Day, the best party of all year, the night we taste the Product from the aging. And what a time we have, singing and laughing! Some of us get so pickled we pass out around the fire."

"And that will be soon?"

"Aye."

"What if the Product isn't good?"

"It's always good. Besides, the tavern owners don't care. They will buy all we provide. Master Peyton lets us keep part of our stuff. We save it for special, and Tasting Day is the most special, I can tell you. It's always a rip-snorter."

"And no after effect next morning?"

"Nay, not a headache or bellyache. That's why it's so popular even if it didn't taste good, which it always does."

"Peyton drinks on Tasting Day?"

"Becomes a bit pickled. We might get him to dance, like last year."

"Really?"

"Aye. We got a good laugh at him a-twizzlin' around."

Alexina needed to think about that for a while, and neither woman spoke as they walked toward the end of town. At three, the big clock in the town's center rang the hour just as they turned into the stable where they were met by Peyton, a glowering Boyce, and a pile of purchases. Boyce had his leg up, his foot resting on a large mass wrapped in brown paper.

"If you please, Mr. Boyce," Alexina said. "That is my drapery fabric upon which your dirty boot rests. Kindly put the purchase in the storage of the coach."

Without words, Boyce loaded the purchases. Peyton helped the ladies into the old coach, after which Boyce sat alone in the rear-facing seat. For the hours-long trip back to the valley, Boyce alternated between sneering and staring at the countryside.

On one occasion, Alexina shot him a high-born lady sneer. She couldn't read his facial expression in response. Unease? Yes, and it gave her a rush of triumph. *Oh, how I wish he'd say Yes, Mistress.*

Chapter Thirty-Eight

Shortly after sunrise the next day, Molly rapped at the bedchamber door, first softly, then louder, and peeked in. "Good morning, Mistress."

Alexina sat up. "What?" The frail light of morning splintered through the burlap curtains. A rooster crowed from the yard.

Molly entered and went straight to the large wardrobe. "I thought you might want to rise early. Master Peyton sent word to Dutch he's taking breakfast late and would like to have them honey grain cakes he likes."

Alexina stretched.

Molly pulled a dress from the peg. "Meaning, the master will be here in a quarter hour, just enough time for you to get dressed and let me do up your hair."

Alexina yawned. "Oh!" She jumped out of bed and headed for the washstand.

Molly hurried to the fireplace and poured warm water into the pitcher. Then she placed muslin undergarments on the bed. "I saw a lady in Kerrstead yesterday with her hair all done up, just so. I think I can do it for you."

Alexina washed while Molly rooted through the wardrobe for hairpins and adornments to match the pattern of the dress. With everything she needed on the counterpane, Molly then buttoned the back of the peach and aqua striped cotton frock. Next, Alexina sat in the brocade seat of the mahogany chair. Molly held the hairbrush while she studied for a moment, then went to work.

"Aye," Molly said and started a wide braid at the top, adding an inch of hair at a time. At intervals, she added silk orange blossoms with the hairpins. At the end of the braid, she curled the remainder into a bun and secured the bottom with the rest of the silk flowers.

Molly stepped back. "Hie, hie. Ain't you a spectacle of beauty."

Alexina picked up the hand mirror and used it to see the back of her head in the oval chaval glass. "As long as I'm not a spectacle."

The two women rushed into the kitchen and took their places at the table. The warmth of the room was suffused with the aroma of the honey grain cakes. Sissy served the coffee.

Boots scraped outside the back door. Peyton entered and breathed in the aroma. "Smells good, but different."

Dutch brought him a plate. "It's that vaniller, good sir. What the mistress brought from the city."

He lifted his gaze from the plate and met Alexina's. His lips parted in an *O*, and his eyes sparkled as he stared for a moment. "You look pretty, Mrs. Woodleigh." Holding up clean hands, he said, "I have been mucking out the stalls. But I washed up in the barn basin." He bit his lip and looked away. "I would have used the shower, but the door was closed."

Did he just apologize for his appearance? "I beg your pardon, Mr. Woodleigh. You can use the bedchamber at any time."

He nodded as his response.

Sissy gave him his tea, and he studied the cup. The three house women had unpacked the boxes with the dinnerware. That morning they took breakfast on the china Alexina had brought as her dowry.

Alexina held up a plate. "It's our everyday china, Mr. Woodleigh. I hope you don't mind."

His raised eyebrows and the far-away look suggested he thought about the past. He lifted the cup to his lips but didn't drink. Once again, he regarded the cream background and the pink roses, surrounded by thin green stems and tiny blue forget-me-nots.

"You don't care for the pattern?" Alexina asked.

"It's familiar," he said and drank the tea. His face tightened as if the pattern brought back a bad memory, things of his youth he wished to forget.

"I can put it back in storage if it displeases you."

"It's fine," he said in an *I don't want to talk about* it way.

The diners halted their activities at the sound of heavy stomping on the boot scrape at the back. Boyce came in and glowered, offering neither nod nor greeting. A chair skidded across the stone floor as he pulled it, then thudded forward as he took his place at the table. He accepted a cup of tea from Sissy and slurped it.

"I enjoyed our trip into town, Mr. Woodleigh," Alexina said, turning her head away from Boyce's stare.

"Hmmm," Peyton responded.

Alexina swiveled in her seat gracefully and pointed to the vacant part of the wall in the puddles. "Phillip has made the most wonderful shelves for the area between the windows, which will be the dining room. I plan to make draperies from the brocade we bought yesterday and will put a pair there," she pointed, "and in the dining area."

"More tea," Boyce commanded.

Peyton put his knife on the plate with a hard click and fixed his stare on Boyce.

"Please," Boyce said grudgingly.

Alexina looked down at the cakes on her plate. No one said anything.

Peyton cut a piece of the grain cake and ate it. Then he pointed the fork at Boyce. "We need to be more considerate of the servants." He cleared his throat. "Not servants. Volunteers, since I haven't paid them. And be polite to my wife." He looked at her.

She couldn't stop the smile that seized her lips.

No one else spoke. Breakfast continued in silence.

After the meal, Peyton left for the study and Boyce followed, shutting the door with a serious thud. Molly excused herself to check on Little Jim.

In the bedchamber, Alexina and Dutch unwrapped the brown paper from the drapery material and unrolled it on the bed. Alexina measured several times and marked the cuts with pins. As she inserted the last pin, Molly came in.

"Mistress, word is tomorrow will be Tasting Day."

The pincushion dropped on the fabric. "And?"

"Tomorrow afternoon, you might want to take a stroll and end up at the barn, maybe show some interest in what the men do around here."

Tasting Day, according to Molly, was the biggest party of the year. Word traveled fast, and Applewood became a beehive of activity. The movements of the valley residents reminded Alexina of a clock's hand when the winding key is forced forward. She tried to concentrate on the draperies, but the excitement became contagious, and she couldn't trust herself to cut correctly.

With everyone working to make extra food for the party, the residents of Stone House were consigned to nibble on leftovers, bread, and butter for supper. Dutch and Sissy departed early for their wagon, and Molly said goodnight after sunset. Stone House fell quiet and feeling the loneliness, Alexina retired early, too.

Remembering Boyce had been in and out of the study all day, Alexina assumed he had come back to work late when she heard the sound of a squeaking drawer in the study. She closed her door and considered putting the mahogany chair under the handle. Step sounds accompanied by lantern rays shining in the door cracks distressed her. Lying in bed, she tried to decide what to do. Should she race to the door, throw it open, and order Boyce out of the house? Insist he not come there at night? No, she didn't have to open the door.

"Leave me alone," she said harshly. She tensed her muscles, gathering her nerve to face him, but the light faded, and the footsteps retreated.

Chapter Thirty-Nine

Peyton had never seen Stone House so quiet. Although he knew the house had occupants, the place had an empty feeling. He went into the study to consult his notebook one more time. He had been keeping comprehensive records of the orchard since he started working with the Wanderers who made the cider and now the brandy. He knew details of his trees, when they bloomed, the yields and the proper time to start the press. The tall willowy trees with the sweet apples showed a lower production than the past years. He would have to speak with Seat about that.

Traditionally, by Tasting Day, they had gathered enough apples to start the press, and by the time they had pressed their stock, other trees yielded more fruit. They would be busy for weeks from morning to night, processing the juice. When the juice reached hard cider stage, they would take half of the supply and distill it into Clear Jack. For two years, the Clear Jack had proven to be popular, and they could sell all they had.

Peyton had been saving his profits. He wanted to start paying his workers. Not that anyone ever asked for money—the Wagon Girls provided what they needed—but he wanted to share the profits for their hard work. Letting them live in Applewood no longer represented proper compensation.

Tasting Day had become the celebration for a bountiful harvest, but it also heralded weeks of intense labor ahead. Soon they would sell last year's Product, and when the profits had been collected, he would pay his bills and, for the first time, distribute most of what was left to the workers. According to the ledger Boyce left in the slot of the writing desk, the bank balance was close to two thousand pounds. A wave of pleasure flowed through him from his success, for he had done this himself, working alongside the Wanderers. No one had given him an advance or provided support for his business. The only help he had had, other than his workers, was Boyce, who kept the accounts. Ironic that now he was near to his goal, he had a wife, something he had not wanted.

She was something he very much wanted. But what he needed was a long hot shower. He stowed the ledgers and notebooks and picked up the lamp. His boots made soft echoes on the flagging of the quiet house. He stopped at the bedchamber door and wondered if he should intrude. She said he could come in any time, but he had been so dirty and disheveled at breakfast, how could he present himself in the bedchamber? He regarded the portal in the lamplight for a moment.

"Leave me alone," she said from the other side of the door.

The words came through the wooden door loud and clear. He backed away and headed for the stream behind Stone House, where the women did their wash. He put the lamp on a flat rock and removed his clothing. Two towels that hung that day in the sun would serve as a washcloth and dryer. He didn't like washing at the chilly cascade. After all, hadn't he built a shower-bath? *Why did Alexina change her mind about letting me use it?* He dipped the first towel in the water at dabbed at his face. *A fine bath for the master of Applewood.*

Dropping the wet towel, he thought about a truly fine bath nearby, at the Wagon Girls' camp. He pictured the ring of wagons and inside the area the lovely circular tent. Gossamer curtains fell from the top of what the Girls called their "Sultan's Bath Tent." Inside the fascinating gazebo, a wooden dais held a large copper bathtub.

Peyton had enjoyed quite a few washes there, baths like no other. This bathing required the skills of all the Girls. Ruby and Garnet kept the tub full of hot water, while Opal rubbed unguents and foaming agents into his hair and skin. Citrine wielded her razor with dexterity, resulting in a shave that left his skin like satin, and never a nick. He smiled at the thought of allowing someone to hold a blade so close to his neck, especially when he was so vulnerable. Amethyst kept his hair trimmed with her precisely honed scissors. Then he submitted to a detailed rinsing. Sapphire, the wittiest Wagon Girl, would command him to stand while she examined him closely. "Ah ha!" she'd say and put her lovely dark eyes near his navel. "A speck of dirt remains. Girls! More soap!" Then she would rub his belly and pull the sea sponge downward, where she would once again exclaim, "Another speck of dirt. We need to pay better attention to our favorite guest." They would laugh and tease, their thin batiste bathing gowns growing wet, showing their charms while they rubbed his tender parts. Based on her vast experience on just how far to go, Ruby would step in and say, "Enough stroking! We must preserve his energy. After all, he has the six of us to please tonight."

And he had always done his best not to disappoint them. When Peyton came for a bath, the camp shut down to all other business. They never charged him for their bathing services, claiming the activities to be sport rather than work.

Putting an icy towel to his face, Peyton pictured the Sultan's Bath Tent and the copper bathtub, remembering the wet gowns clinging to perfect bodies. But he didn't want the Wagon Girls to bathe him this night. In place of the six lovelies who would lavish their cleansing attention, he thought about the fine woman who slept in his bed behind the closed door in Stone House. Perhaps someday that woman would inspect his navel, giggle, and say, "Dirty, dirty, dirty!" He thought about Alexina plying him with warm water and soap...*Enough of that!* He plunged the towel into the cold spring and wrung it out over his head.

Chapter Forty

Even though she rose early the next morning, Alexina was disappointed at Peyton's absence and dined with the three ladies at breakfast. She couldn't focus on the draperies with the fuss and anticipation of the biggest party of the year happening all around her.

Molly took her aside and suggested it might be a good time to enjoy the fresh air outside in the yard and pointed out that Peyton was most likely working in the barn.

Alexina entered the barn and stood for a moment taking in the large wooden building. Above her head, large beams displayed the saw marks that had fashioned single, huge oaks into roof supports. Thick thatch let no light in from above—only the cracks between the upright wallboards allowed rays of sunshine to penetrate the atmosphere. The men's conversation became hushed. Peyton looked up from his work. She stood where two beams of light glowed from cracks in the upper walls. Walking out of the golden shafts toward him, her rose-sprigged muslin dress moved softly, and her dainty black leather shoes made muted taps on the hard-packed floor.

"Today is Tasting Day?"

Peyton nodded.

Boyce entered. "What do you want?"

Peyton cleared his throat.

"What can we do for you?" Boyce asked in a milder tone.

She threw Peyton a quick *thank you* glance. "I thought I'd see the barn. Where are the casks?"

"In the cask barn," Boyce said bluntly.

"I hoped to try a bit of the Product." She directed her request to Peyton.

"Of course. You want the first taste," Boyce said with a narrowed-eyed look. "I'm sure you'd love it. Let me get the cup we pass around for the first sample. Maybe someday we'll get it washed."

She caught her breath. Peyton stepped close to her. "Everyone uses the same cup. Tradition," he said quietly.

"Still interested?" Boyce asked.

"Perhaps later." She turned to leave.

"Wait," Peyton called to her. "I always take the first taste. But tonight could be different. And we will use a clean cup."

Boyce muttered as he left, "I'll be in the study."

Alexina didn't know what to say. She had brought so many changes, and perhaps the differences added to the conflict between her and Peyton. "I don't need to taste it. Thank you." She picked up her skirt and hurried from the barn.

Chapter Forty-One

After a few minutes of silence, a voice from the back of the barn laughed. "Our Young Master has himself a fine pie for dessert."

"Cherry," another voice said.

"Yep," said a third, "still warm on the window sill, untasted."

Peyton's eyes darted around the barn. They knew he hadn't slept with her. After the years here, he understood there were no secrets with these people.

"Best he takes a slice before it goes cold, or some thief steals that sweetness from the sill."

They meant Rufus Smith, who had visited Alexina twice. Peyton remembered the look in the man's eyes the day she came to Applewood. She belonged to Peyton, but perhaps the workers were right. Would the pie cool?

"Get back to work," Peyton directed.

He stomped to the stall and threw a measure of oats into Dragon's feeder. The image of Smith practically foaming at the mouth slipped into his mind's eye. The vision of Alexina with the barn's soft light surrounding her like an angel's aura, the untouched, undoubtedly, sweet pie, blinded him from all other objects.

Chapter Forty-Two

Alexina returned to Stone House. Everyone worked at a dizzying pace. Sissy pounded the dasher in the cream crock. Dutch sifted large bowls of freshly-milled flour. Molly and Little Jim peeled mounds of potatoes and carrots. To keep out of the way, she returned to the bedchamber. It wouldn't hurt to read the instructions regarding how to sew large hems into the draperies. Again.

In the late afternoon, Molly stuck her head in the door. Aye, Mistress. Sorry I've ignored you. Can I do anything for you?"

"You can tell me what to expect tonight. I am invited, correct?"

Molly's curls bounced with her laughter. "Of course! We can't wait to see how you enjoy our Tasting celebration. Don't eat supper—come hungry. And thirsty!"

"What shall I wear?"

"Something you don't mind getting rust, soot, and cider on." Molly picked up the hairbrush and waggled it toward the chair. "Let's get you beautiful, and I'll tell you about the Tasting." Molly stroked the bristles through Alexina's hair. "First, we'll eat. I doubt there's any better food in the finest London restaurant. Then we'll send the children to bed in one of the houses. We drew straws to see who minds the young ones. Poor Sally." Molly chuckled. "Then we'll start with ladies' punch."

"Would you like to use my punch bowl and cups?"

"Nay. Once we get going, there's no protecting fine glasses. We'll use our mugs. That is if you don't mind drinking out of the old ware."

"I don't mind. Then what?"

"Our musicians will play, we'll sing, and after a few passes of the Clear Jack, we'll dance. You'll love that!"

"What kind of dancing? Jigs? Waltzes? Flings?"

"I heard of Jigs and Flings. But we do Gypsy dances."

"I don't know those dances."

"No need to think about it, just listen to the music. Around midnight, the ladies will go home and wait for the men."

"You'll be here tonight, then?"

Molly slowly and emphatically shook her head in the negative.

Alexina read the silent message. "Where does Seat live?"

"He has a room in the loft of the cask barn."

"Oh, I've not seen that room," Alexina said.

Molly smiled wide. "I have!" She put the brush away and tied the hair ribbon. "I need to help set up the outside table. It will be dark soon, and they will light the fire. Come when you see it get real bright. We're going to have a wonderful time tonight. You'll see."

The sun set beneath the ring of hills in the western part of the valley, causing a rosy glow with streaks of purple and blue. Not long after that, flames flickered from upright logs burning in the barnyard. She checked her image in the long mirror. Her blue chintz dress with white lace at the rounded neckline and medium length sleeves matched the ribbon Molly had tied behind her ears. Alexina ran her fingers through the cylinders of golden curls. Pulling out a small drawer from the wardrobe, she found a pot of red colorant and rubbed a bit on her lips before she gave a light swab on the apple of her cheeks.

On her way to the back door, she ran into Boyce entering the study.

"Mr. Boyce. I don't want you working in the study at night."

He sneered with a fake grin. "I rarely work at night, but I thank you for considering my hours. You must know I only take orders from Mr. Woodleigh."

She controlled her face even though as soon as she turned away, she would feel the flush of anger. "Very well. I shall speak to my husband."

"You do that, Mrs. Woodleigh. Have at it."

Chapter Forty-Three

When Alexina arrived in the barnyard, the same place as her wedding reception, she found the women, children, and Granny's disciples sitting around the fire pit.

"Welcome," Sissy said, "We waited for you. Let me get you a plate."

"Thank you, Sissy. I don't mind serving myself tonight. Please." She addressed the group seated around the fire. "Eat. Don't wait for me." Then she whispered to Sissy, "Are we supposed to wait for the men?"

She shook her head. "They're bringing the barrels and the casks. They'll eat when they get here."

The children sprang up and made a mad dash for the table. Moving only slightly slower were the rest of the women.

Later Granny appeared and walked around the fire pit, greeting the partiers and patting the children's heads. Tad brought the old woman a chair, and someone handed her a plate and mug. Alexina had filled her own plate, and by the time she returned to the fire, Tad held a chair for her.

Molly had been right about the food. Alexina had never tasted such rich, agreeable fare. Many of the foods at Applewood had been new to her, but tonight the gravy excelled all others she had ever tried. When a teenage girl brought around a jug of the ladies' punch, Alexina took a whole mug full.

The sound of male voices grew closer as the men carried several small barrels toward the fire. Peyton carried two casks, one on each shoulder. He lowered them to the table. As he sat the second one down, a cheer arose. Seat drove a spigot into the end of one of the casks and filled a cup.

Peyton put the container to his lips but paused. He searched the crowd in the firelight. His gaze lit upon Alexina, and he approached her. "Clean cup," he whispered.

She took it and let a few drops roll on her tongue, then down her throat. The strong brew infused her palate and nose with rich apple flavor, tasting wonderful until the alcohol found its head. Her eyes watered as she breathed out like she was a fire-breather.

Then Peyton took a long swig. He put his hands in the air and shouted, "Yes!"

The crowd cheered. Women jumped up and piled food onto plates for the men. Alexina rose from her chair to fill a plate for her husband, but Sissy handed Peyton a plate already loaded. The crowds separated them. The party started.

Peyton scanned the crowd. He stopped as soon as his gaze lit on her and held his cup in the air. She smiled with pleasure, although it was unlikely he would join her. The men kept separate from the women while they ate and drank, which everyone did in great quantities.

As the serving platters emptied, more Jack and punch circulated. Soon the laughter became loud and raucous. Sally, the unlucky straw-puller, gathered the children, who made the rounds with goodnight kisses. The gaggle of little ones followed the woman to the house where they would spend the night.

When the music started, a few couples began to dance. As the music picked up speed, more dancers joined, and their movements became wilder and more frenetic.

Someone in the crowd shouted for the music to cease and called out, "Master Peyton! Time to dance!"

"Dance! Dance! Dance!" The chant grew louder.

Molly and Dutch pulled Alexina to her feet, and at the same time, some of the men pushed Peyton toward her. The music started again, slower in tempo, and the onlookers began to clap with the beat of the music.

Alexina swallowed hard. She didn't know the Gypsy dances.

Molly stood in front of her. "Like this." She swayed her hips. "Now, you, Young Master." She turned around, grabbed Peyton's hands, and placed them around Alexina's waist. "Closer. Now, both of you, move about."

Peyton stepped closer until his hard body pressed against

Alexina's softer curves. His warm breath tickled her neck as they swayed to the beat. She enjoyed this dancing. It seemed natural, not like the waltzes and mazurkas, where she had to mentally count the beats. She relaxed with Peyton's arms wrapped around her.

"Why have you not come to me?" she whispered, her lips close to his ear. Peyton did not respond but continued to hold her close until the music ended. Alexina tilted her head back and smiled at him. "I want to be with you,"

He searched her face. At last, he said, "I want to be with you, too. But you fear me."

"Only for a moment. I wish to be your wife.

He nodded. "Later."

She smiled and watched him walk back to where the men gathered around the cask.

In a few minutes, the music started again, a slower tune. Dancers entwined in sinuous motions. He came to her with open arms. She stepped into his embrace, and they moved as one. Her heart pounded with his touch. With his lips against her ear, he whispered, "Wait for me in our bed."

For hours the routine continued. Music and dancing, time for eating and drinking, then the dancers returned to their circles until the music next roused them near the fire pit. When the embers cast a pulsing orange, Granny dug around in her fabric bag. She called to Tad.

Molly leaned toward Alexina. "Granny is going, so it's time for us to quit. The men have some serious tasting ahead. Best we not be here."

The old woman whispered in Tad's ear, after which he held up his hand to quiet the crowd. "Granny will take her leave after she has a word with Master Peyton."

When the old woman stood, the other women stood as well. Alexina joined the retreating revelers returning to their homes and picked up a lantern to light her way to the front door. As she entered, Boyce emerged from Peyton's study. She paused, holding the light high to assure identity—both ways. She didn't recall seeing Boyce at the Tasting. He rolled his upper lip into a snarl and turned on his heel toward the dark kitchen, his boots clomping. The back door creaked open and slammed shut.

In her bed-chamber, she washed the smoke from her hair, using the shower-bath, and pulled a stool near the fire. Separating the tresses, she combed, stroking them smooth, allowing the warm air to dry them. She formed a braid and tied the end with a ribbon. Her nightdress lay on the bed. She donned it, climbed into bed, and waited for her husband.

Chapter Forty-Four

Peyton and the other men drew close to the fire pit, occupying the seats the women had surrendered. Granny approached Peyton and gestured for his audience. She handed him a small bag. "To make the way easier." Then she gestured to Tad, took his arm, and left.

Peyton didn't open the bag but put it in the side pocket of his leather breeches.

Seat brought out a second large cask and rammed a tap into the bunghole. The Clear Jack gurgled from the spigot. Carl held tin cups under the flow, timing the next cup's position as the present cup filled. Peyton got the first cup, and in accordance to the unofficial standing of the men, they waited for their portion. When all held their Product, they waited for Peyton's toast.

He lifted his mug. "To Prince Jack, all hail!"

The men, in unison, lifted their brew. "All hail Prince Jack." Everyone emptied their cups without taking a breath. They slammed the cups on the nearest flat surface and laughed heartily. They laughed and drank until the cask could not produce another drop.

Carl put down his empty mug. He wiped his mouth with the back of his hand. "Well, now, time for pie!"

Tad, who had returned from escorting Granny home, stood up and brushed off the back of his pants. "Aye! I could do with some pie. Sweet pie."

A voice from the group laughed and said, "Master Peyton, shouldn't you be having some sweet cherry?"

The men laughed, and Peyton stood, grabbing Tad's shoulder for support. He slurred his words. "Right. Pie." He pulled at his breeches and thought about the delicious treat waiting for him at Stone House. Peyton reached into his pocket and brought out the bag, revealing a small cork-stoppered bottle, Granny's Special Oil. On any other night, Peyton would not have reacted so genially, but this was Tasting Night, and right now, he wanted that cherry dessert.

Peyton held the vial up, letting it glisten in the dancing firelight. "Oh, yes," he said in garbled words. "One should always make the way easier. Especially with dessert."

Tad slapped Peyton on the back, nearly knocking him down. Peyton shoved the vial into his belt and staggered toward the row of lanterns. He seized a handle and headed for the house, clumsily swinging both parts of the kitchen door wide. The lantern lighted his way. He didn't knock but opened the door and leaned against the wooden jamb.

Alexina lay under the comforter, the rich glow of the lantern falling on her form. She raised up on her elbows. "You're here."

He paused for a moment before kicking the door shut. Soft light drifted about the walls and floor as he approached the bed. Lowering the lantern, it clanked on the floor. He bent over the bed and regarded her in the shadowy illumination. "Aye, I've come to you, wife."

Alexina crawled from underneath the cover and rose to her knees. With her small hands on his shoulders, she kissed him softly. He returned the kiss, coaxing her mouth open and dancing the tip of his tongue on hers. At the same time, he fumbled with her ribbon around the neckline of her nightdress. When it loosened, she shrugged, allowing the thin batiste to slip off her shoulders and pool on the bed. She sat back and slid her legs free of the gown. He placed the vial on the bedside table and stripped his own clothes off.

Crawling next to her, he kissed her neck and slid his hand down to caress her breast with a light touch. She responded by running her fingers through his chest hair and kissing his ears and face, making her way to his lips. The late moon cast silver upon their bodies. He breathed deeply of her sweet smell, which took second place to her sweet-tasting skin. His virgin bride displayed no hesitation to touch him intimately, and when he parted her legs and stroked her, she moaned, drawing him closer.

He spread her thighs wide and moved between them. Alexina's fingertips skimmed over his buttocks and around his thighs, grasping his manhood and squeezing. He closed his eyes and inhaled deeply to steady himself before he could enter her.

He pushed his arms straight, sat back, and reached for the vial. "Rub this on me. It will make it easier."

He pulled the cork and the fruity aroma of the oil mingled with the fragrance of Alexina's body on his fingers. A small pool of fluid puddled in her hand. She rubbed it on him.

"More," he whispered breathlessly.

She ran her hand up and down the shaft. His heart raced from the touch. The intensity of her touch brought low moans from his throat. She applied the oil more vigorously.

"Stop," he said in slurred words.

She increased the pressure.

Peyton grabbed her hand to stay the movement, but it was too late. He curled over and groaned as if in pain. He hit the bed with his fists.

"What's wrong? Peyton!"

He pushed her away and stood, glaring. He swore and grabbed his clothes from the floor. Stomping and staggering, he fled the room, leaving the door ajar.

"Peyton, come back!"

Chapter Forty-Five

She left the bed and ran after him. In the hall, she slowed her step when the kitchen door slammed shut. Confused, she washed her hands in the basin and returned to bed. She propped herself on the pillows and waited. He did not come back. She rose early, hoping to find Peyton at breakfast so she could demand an explanation for the night before

In the kitchen, Dutch pulled a loaf of bread from the brick oven next to the fireplace.

"Top of the morning," Molly said. "Porridge? Eggs and ham? Maybe some fried bread?"

Alexina looked around. "Where's Peyton?"

"Haven't seen him this morning," Molly said, and pushed a bowl of steaming porridge across the table. She put a spoon and a pitcher of cream next to the bowl.

Alexina sat and stared at the bowl.

"We have an excellent batch of Jack this year, Mistress," Molly said, sitting down with her own bowl. "Should bring a fine profit."

The backdoor slammed against the wall. Everyone turned as Boyce tramped into the room. "That's me and Mr. Woodleigh's business, you understand?"

Molly scooted the chair backward loudly. She rose and moved behind Boyce, sticking her tongue out at him.

Boyce glared at Alexina. "It's men's business. Not your concern."

Alexina stiffened, but she wasn't in the mood to address this beast properly. She pictured herself as the headmistress at the Greenfield school and spoke with as much dignified scorn as she could conjure. "Do you wish to have an audience with me?"

"What I wish," Boyce grumbled, "is to be served my breakfast and have silence from women."

Alexina plunged her spoon into the porridge. "Molly, Sissy, Dutch? I need you to come with me."

Molly threw her towel on the counter. Sissy rose from her chair. Dutch made a dubious curtsey to the man, and they followed Alexina out the back door.

Alexina picked up her skirt and headed for a clump of lavender. She plucked a few sprigs and sniffed them.

"What can we do for you, good Mistress?" Molly said.

"What you can do for me is, let *that man* get his own breakfast and eat it in silence."

"Right, then," Molly said, smiling.

Dutch looked back at the window where Boyce waited. "I fancy a walk. How about you?"

"I'm for it," Sissy said.

The four women strolled around the clusters of aromatic plants growing in the garden behind Stone House.

"Poor Boyce," Sissy said.

Alexina turned to the woman. "You have pity for him?"

"He's probably bristly 'cause he don't get no love...or nothing else. He ain't wed, and the Wagon Girls won't let him in their camp."

Alexina rolled her bottom lip. "They won't let him in?"

Sissy shook her head. "Not in any way! Citrine run him out with a razor."

"Why?" Alexina asked.

"He come into camp one time saying his status be the same as Master Peyton, so he should get their services for free. Citrine grabbed her razor and said if he didn't git out, she'd fix it, so he didn't need services, ever."

Great, I get an empty bed, and my husband gets free privileges in the camp.

Dutch put her hand on her hip. "The new Girl, though, Pearl Pink, she got low standards, that one. She might be tempted, with gold, to service *Boyce*."

As if on cue, the three staff women simultaneously made a face and a collective *euew*. They waited until Boyce exited the Stone House before returning to the kitchen.

Later that afternoon, Alexina cleaned an area on the floor of what would be the new dining room. She laid out the items she needed, including the measuring ribbon, shears, her new needle cushion, and a package of assorted needles to work with the bolt of fabric for the draperies. As she measured, activity on the roof interrupted her. Bits of reed rained down, barely missing the fabric now spread out on the floor.

She left her needlework, stood under the hole, and looked up. "Hello?"

Carl popped his head through the opening. "We're fixing the roof, Mistress."

Alexina put her hand on her forehead to shield the glare. "Oh, do be careful."

"Not to worry." He showed her a portion of the rope he had tied to his waist.

Returning to the draperies, she worked while hammers pounded and the wind shuffled through the new reeds. Peyton must have reassigned men needed to work the presses, just for her. Now the refined furniture of her dowry would be protected from the elements. Ready with the shears, she held her breath and boldly cut the fabric.

Days passed, and she hadn't seen Peyton. Every morning at breakfast, she inquired about him, but the women who ran the kitchen had not seen him.

One morning Molly held Alexina's elbow. "Do ya wish to talk about anything, Mistress?"

Alexina did, but she could not. She swallowed the lump in her throat and shook her head.

"He's got his ways, see? Be patient. Give him time. It'll turn out fine."

Each day Alexina sat at her sewing until dark, working on the seams and hems. After a week, Phillip hammered iron brackets into the window frame and later that day produced what had been a sapling, now smoothed and cut to the perfect length to become the curtain rod.

The next day, Alexina had the curtains sewn, pressed, and ready to install. She pushed the sapling through the wide channel at the top of the fabric. Moving a chair close to the window, she climbed onto the seat and lifted one end of the heavy draperies. With effort, she struggled to lower the rod onto the bracket. Once the end was in place, she repositioned the chair to the other side.

As she bent to grab the free end, Peyton's voice said, "What are you doing?"

Distracted, she lost her balance, and the chair tipped. She made a grab for the window frame. Before she toppled to the floor, Peyton scooped her into his arms, and they both fell, slowly, protected, and covered by a wealth of soft fabric.

"Are you hurt?" Peyton asked.

She shook her head.

"Are you sure?" He ran his hand down her arms and flanks.

Alexina put her arm around him and pressed her lips against his ear. "Only in my heart is there an ache," she whispered.

Peyton froze.

"I so wish to be your wife. Please tell me what I did wrong."

He responded with an inarticulate noise and held her tightly. "Nothing. You did nothing wrong. I'm the one who is sorry." He nuzzled his nose against her neck. "You smell like orange blossoms."

Alexina brushed her lips against his face. They were bound together so close in the heavy panels of fabric that she could not tell if she felt his heartbeat or hers. She held her breath lest the movement cause their embrace to cease.

"I want you as my wife too."

"Will you—?"

"Whoa-ho! What happened?" Tad and Carl pulled the fabric away from them.

Peyton jumped to his feet and extended his hand to Alexina.

Smiling, she said, "Thank you for saving me."

Peyton nodded and gestured for Tad to grab the middle of the rod and Carl to lift the other end. The three men hung the heavy rod and curtain over the window.

Molly and Dutch arrived and viewed Alexina's decorative masterpiece. Now the smooth, shining, stained shelves were flanked by the large windows draped with rich burgundy brocade.

Alexina watched Peyton. Without him saying it, she knew he approved. He studied the wall with his hands on his hips and nodded. Alexina's warm feeling of accomplishment vanished when Boyce clomped into the room.

"We should take some product samples tomorrow," Boyce said.

Alexina touched Peyton's arm. "You are going to town?"

"Kerrstead."

"May I go with you? I have to pick up mail and some other items."

"Make a list," Boyce growled.

Peyton turned to her. "Can you be ready early?"

"Yes." *Especially if you come to our bed chamber tonight.*

He cleared his throat. "I'll be working on the samples most of the night."

His explanation gave her a thin branch of hope to hold on to for the future. "Thank you for your help."

Boyce shot her a glare as he turned away. Peyton stole a quick parting glance and strode through the kitchen, Molly and Dutch following in his wake.

Alexina surveyed what had once been an empty space between the kitchen and bedchambers. All the debris was removed, curtains and shelves lined the wall, and the roof had been repaired. She eyed her furnishings still piled against the wall.

"Tad and Carl? Would you move my dining room furniture into our new room?"

As Alexina tied the draperies back with sashes, the men brought in the furniture. She directed where each item should be. After dusting and rubbing the wood with oil, she invited Molly to come and admire the space.

"It's so grand," Molly said. "I feel like I'm in a castle."

"I dub thee Stone House, of Castle Applewood, the Woodleigh Estate," Alexina said.

Her spirits lifted. Only one more thing could make her life perfect. She had sensed Peyton's attraction to her on the first day, again the night of the Tasting Party, and it had been there today under the brocade avalanche. She needed to be patient a little longer.

Chapter Forty-Six

Alexina awoke before daybreak. She dressed quietly, allowing Molly to sleep in the guest room because Little Jim had run a fever all night. A light rain drizzled, casting a gloom in the bedchamber that the lamp couldn't ease.

She did her hair in a simple bun and selected an ivory linen dress with lace at the sleeves and neckline. The mirror revealed flashes of white and red lights shining from the small diamond and ruby pendant around her neck, the piece of jewelry she had worn for many years.

Alexina selected a carrying basket for shopping. Rummaging through her wardrobe, she unearthed her purse containing what was leftover from the annual stipend Ignace Smith had given her and slipped the bills and coins into the basket, along with a few small books.

Sissy and Dutch had just arrived. In lieu of eating breakfast in the kitchen, Alexina wrapped buttered, sugared bread in a napkin and added it to the basket. The carriage sounded in front of Stone House, and holding a towel over her head, she hurried into the vehicle.

Because of the rain, Alexina had brought scraps of the brocade to stuff in the holes of the carriage roof. At the start of the trip, the patches held the rain at bay. How much moisture could they hold before they dripped on the worn upholstery and the occupants? Perhaps with the money the Product brought in, they could have the seats and the roof repaired.

Boyce took a seat across from her.

"It's raining. Why aren't driving?" she asked.

He scowled. "My employer has more control over the horse. He drives."

A chill stiffened her. "Your employer doesn't beat his horses. Perhaps that's why he can control them."

Alexina fished through her large basket and brought out the book. Each time she looked up from her page, she felt Boyce's cold stare.

"Would you care for something to read?"

"I don't read women's literature," he huffed

She fingered the reading material, none of which could be considered light reading.

Every so often, she peered out the flap that served as a window. Peyton's oilskin cape dripped from the mist, and fine rivulets streamed from Silverton's flank. Because of the danger from wet roads, their pace slowed, and after four hours, they arrived in Kerrstead, the streets still damp from the rain. The sun peeked out from gray clouds.

When they pulled into the stables, Boyce hopped down and strode into the street. Peyton lifted Alexina down to prevent her from putting weight on the unreliable metal step. His hands rested on her waist. She caught his gaze and smiled. There, ever so slightly, on the corners of his lips, was a quiver, a gesture, a signal of his interest.

Peyton removed the oilskin he wore and shook the rain away. Alexina brought a towel from the basket and touched it to his face. When he didn't protest, she rubbed vigorously, toweling the moisture from his hair and neck. For a moment, she imagined them together in the shower-bath, she with soap in hand massaging suds into his skin, he enjoying her touch and insisting he had not yet achieved an acceptable level of clean. She fought the smile forming on her lips.

Alexina draped the wet towel over a rail. "Will you come with me to the tailor?"

Peyton scratched his nose. "Why?"

"I have a present for you."

The corners of his mouth twitched. She looped her arm into his, and they left the stable.

Boyce waited at the boardwalk in front of a pub. "I'll be at the Toad and Crown," he said and strode heavily away like he had to extinguish little embers along the board sidewalk.

When they entered the tailor shop, Alexina asked Peyton to wait in front of the mirror while the shopkeeper retrieved her order.

"What's this?" Peyton asked as the tailor returned and displayed two shirts and a dark woolen suit.

"When you brought Molly and me to town last time, I gave Mr. Bittle one of your shirts to copy. I measured your tweed pants, and the tailor has made this for you." She held out the dark suit pants and jacket. "Here, try them on. If they don't fit, the tailor can alter them, and we can take them back with us today." She eyed Mr. Bittle, letting him know it was an order rather than a request.

In moments, Peyton came from the back room wearing no boots but looking marvelous in the clothes, which fit perfectly. Alexina turned him around to face the mirror.

"How handsome you are!" she said.

Peyton turned from side to side and stretched his neck to see the back, moving his broad shoulders to check the fit. Alexina retrieved a black ribbon from her arm basket and finger-combed his damp curls, which she tied into a tight cue. "Every man should have a good suit." She didn't remember how she came by this bit of wisdom, but she was certain of its logic.

"Thank you," Peyton said quietly. "It's been a long time since I received a gift."

"Then you're overdue." Alexina brushed a bit of thread from the lapel. "Well, what do you think?"

"It's fine and fits very well." Peyton went to the back room to change. The tailor carefully wrapped his new clothes in brown paper for the trip home.-

Alexina touched Peyton's arm. "I must go to the post office, the grocers, the dry goods store, and then the drapers. Would you like to accompany me?"

He hesitated. "I need to take samples of the Product to the taverns."

"Of course," she said.

"Meet us in front of the stable at three o'clock. We must be on the road by then. The rain makes the road treacherous in the pass, and there's no moon."

"I'll be there," she promised.

Walking away, she turned and caught him watching her. She waved and crossed the street to the post office, where she found her packages and letters.

When she removed the brown wrappers from the packages, she could barely believe what she read. The items exceeded her expectations, but she didn't have time to examine the contents—books from the Royal Academy of Science. Shoving the postal items into her shopping basket, she hurried to the stable to store them in the old phaeton. Her next stop was the dry goods store. She chose the items from the shelves and stood at the cashier's counter.

The proprietor folded his arms on his rotund gut. "I must speak with Mr. Woodleigh, please, before I dispense any merchandise."

"Why do you need to speak with Mr. Woodleigh? I set up the account with you."

"Because the previous bill has not been paid."

"I will speak to my husband and will return later with the payment."

She crossed the street to the grocers, selected a few things, and asked for a package of cinnamon.

"Nothing until the bill has been paid," the lady owner said.

One bill unpaid may be an oversight, but two?

Alexina walked briskly to the drapers. She inspected many bolts of fabric, and based upon the progress of the dining room, she decided on more fabric. After her pleasant start that morning with Peyton, she was keen to achieve a positive outcome. She would make the bedchamber inviting to her husband.

She found a lovely dark blue damask with a gold design. "I'm Mrs. Woodleigh. I would like thirty yards of this."

"I remember you, madame," the draper said. "I'm sorry, Mrs. Woodleigh, I cannot extend further credit."

"Credit? Have you submitted your bill to the bank?"

"Most certainly, madame, but your husband hasn't released the funds."

"I'm sure this will be taken care of today."

"Perhaps, but I won't dispense further goods until the current bill is satisfied."

"Of course," Alexina said, controlling her emotion. She pulled a twenty-pound note from her reticule. "Will this do?"

"Yes, it leaves but a small balance."

"I will go to the bank and get the rest of the money."

"Thank you, Madame."

Alexina headed down the street to the bank and demanded to speak with the manager. Mr. MacAdams came out into the lobby. "How may I help you, Mrs. Woodleigh?"

"I would like to know why the merchants have not been paid."

"I'm afraid I'm not at liberty to discuss these matters with you."

"Why not?"

"I only discuss the fiscal details with Mr. Woodleigh or Mr. Boyce. And," his voice took a condescending tone, "most ladies don't bother themselves with their husband's finances."

"I am not most ladies, sir."

"But accounts are difficult to understand, and I don't have the time to explain debits and credits."

"I assure you, sir, I will understand."

"Mrs. Woodleigh, Mr. Boyce—"

Alexina pulled her spine up straight and locked eyes with the man. "Mr. Boyce is in my husband's employ, a worker, whereas I am Mr. Woodleigh's wife, legally allowed to view his account."

"But, Mrs. Woodleigh—"

"Mr. MacAdams, I wish to see his account now, or must I seek legal force?" She didn't know whether she was legally allowed to see the account, but Hester had told her the headmistress used that ploy many times with parents who become irate or threatening.

"Please be seated in that office." He pointed to a door. "I will bring you the ledger."

The tactic worked. Alexina sat at the table in the small office and waited. When the ledger had been placed on the table, she started at the last page and worked backward, so she could see what had taken place while she had been at Applewood. Large sums of money had been deposited last year, as expected. After all, the cattle had been sold, and Molly said last year's Product had been profitable. But Alexina couldn't understand the large expenditures, one paid to Henry and Sons Carriage Builders, or the Carter Feed Company. Other payments, such as one to H. Green, Silversmiths, puzzled her.

"Mr. MacAdams, bring me the invoices for these payments."

"Mrs. Woodleigh! I must say this is highly irregular."

Alexina fixed him with the stare she had seen the headmistress apply with instant effect. MacAdams backed from the room and returned with two large boxes.

She sorted the invoices by bills she thought were sound and those in question. The second pile dwarfed the first. She could not believe what she saw. A new barouche, custom-built in white enamel, crimson velvet upholstery, red spokes, and a design rendered in mother-of-pearl for the door? And horse fodder? The animals of Applewood browsed on the rich grasses and wild grains in the valley, and even Dragon and Silverton, Peyton's favorites and hardest working horses, ate the same oats and cereals the residents consumed. She had to look twice at the invoice from Mr. Green, the silversmith, who had billed the account for a twelve-piece silver tea service.

Mr. MacAdams stuck his head into the doorway. As he did, she heard the bong of the large clock in the lobby. "Mrs. Woodleigh, please. The bank closed at three, and now it is five. I really must lock up."

"Oh, I didn't realize I'd been here so long. Please store these carefully. I may need to return." He gathered the invoices and stuffed them into the boxes, walked her to the door, and locked it.

She rushed to the stables. Peyton leaned against a thick wooden support.

"I'm so sorry," she said.

Peyton glared.

"I must talk to you—."

Boyce stepped around the column stopping her mid-sentence. "You're late!"

Peyton gestured to the building across the street. "The inn."

"We're not going back to Applewood?"

"It's too late to go through the pass."

"Forgive me for holding us up. Let me explain."

"Silence," Peyton said. His teeth compressed so tightly the muscles made knots in his cheeks.

"But I must speak with you!"

He held his hand up. "Go."

"They have a room for us?"

He glared and did not speak a word.

"Peyton, listen to me. I have a good reason for not being here on time."

Peyton grabbed her hand and marched her across the road into the inn.

The timbers of the Tudor style building bowed, making the inn look like it would fall over. The plaster between the dark planks had not been whitewashed for so long, patches of green mildew grew in the pits and gouges.

"Be ready at sunrise." Peyton turned toward the door.

"Peyton!" She stomped her foot, but he continued away. When she turned, she faced the corpulent proprietor, whose reddened face must have matched her own. He jerked his head toward a dark stairwell and held a candle high. She followed him up two flights to a tiny, musty room that had a cot barely big enough for one small person.

"I'll bring you a bowl of soup," the proprietor said.

She used the cold water in the pitcher to wash her face and hands. After finishing the watery chicken soup, she slept in her slip under a thin, smelly blanket.

Chapter Forty-Seven

In the morning, the innkeeper rapped a harsh summons on the door. Alexina readied herself and headed down to the dining room, where a woman served tea with bread and butter. This could not compare with the richness of the same simple meal from Applewood. She had taken a few bites when Peyton appeared. He greeted her with a grim expression, neither a curve to his lips nor a twinkle in his eyes.

Boyce walked in behind him, glaring. "We slept in the stable because you got the only room."

Alexina imagined the pleasure she would have throwing her steaming tea at the man. Instead, she wiped her face of expression. She needed to talk to Peyton without having Boyce suspect she knew about their finances.

The somber trip back to Applewood made her wish she had not come, but now she knew what had happened to Peyton's money. Boyce sat facing her, sneering and scorning with his gaze. Most of her discomfort came from the question of whether this horrible man suspected she knew about the bank situation.

When they reached Stone House, Peyton stopped at the front door and said nothing as he helped her down the unreliable step. Boyce watched her every move. She pushed the heavy oak door and winced at the carriage sounds as it continued on with both men. In the kitchen, she breathed a sigh of relief to find Molly there enjoying tea with Sissy and Dutch.

Stepping slowly toward the table, Alexina caught Molly's attention. Immediately she rose and took her mistress by the arm. "Come with me, please." Molly guided her to the guest room and closed the door. "We were worried about you."

"How is Little Jim?"

"Oh, fine. Granny gave him a bit of her Fever Brew, and now he's right as rain. But you? Are you all right?"

"No! I need to speak with Peyton. Without Boyce."

Molly gave a quick shudder. "That man." She closed her eyes and mumbled a few unintelligible words. "Today, the men are turning the manure piles with hay. Master Peyton will most likely help, and he's sure to take a shower afterwards. You can speak with him then. Boyce won't go into the bedchamber, but you can. Make sure you leave the door open for the master."

"Good idea," Alexina said.

"Is there anything I can do to help?"

"No, but I'm grateful you're here."

Molly's brown curls bobbed as she nodded. "I'm here, Mistress. Rest sure on that."

Toward evening Alexina checked the stock of the sweet apples Seat had stored in the cask room. She took a walk to the ten trees providing the fruit for the women's brew. The trees were picked clean. Seat had done a good job. This thing with Boyce interrupted her plans with Eden's Joy now. She would have to reconsider her actions.

As she left the orchard, she noticed far off lightning and the distant rumble of thunder. Beyond the pass, a storm raged.

She had not seen Peyton. On her way back to Stone House, she wondered when he would come inside to bathe. As she approached the back door, Molly and Little Jim walked rapidly toward her.

"The master's in the bedchamber," Molly said.

"Thank you." Alexina hurried into the house and to the room. She closed the door behind her as Peyton toweled dry. "I must speak with you."

He held his hand out. "Silence. There's nothing to say." He wrapped the towel around his waist and tied the ends.

She needed his attention. Recalling the headmistress at the Greenfield School, Alexina adopted the woman's tone of command. "Oh, but there is. And *you* must listen."

Peyton jerked his head back at her harsh words.

She drew close. "I returned late to the stable because I spent the entire afternoon going over your account at the bank."

He took a breath, obviously ready to hurl a reprimand.

She put her hand to his face. "Silence!" she said, returning his directive. "Your account is down to two hundred pounds."

A furrow formed between his eyebrows as the information sank in.

"And I know you haven't ordered a custom-fitted carriage, or a team of matched horses to pull it, or a twelve-piece silver tea service. None of the accounts that I started have been paid, and I saw bills for things you don't use, like grain for your horses. I doubt you've been withdrawing twenty pounds at a time *in gold*."

He shook his head.

"Boyce has not allowed the banker to pay the legitimate bills, like the casks you ordered on your last trip to Kerrstead."

"I don't understand."

"Think about it," she demanded.

He turned his head and pointed at the closed door. There, golden light from a lantern revealed the shadow of someone leaning against the crack. Peyton leaped toward the door and pulled it open. Pounding boot steps retreated on the flagging, followed by yells from the women in the kitchen.

Peyton returned, holding his towel to his waist. "It was Boyce. Help me dress. I've got to catch him."

Alexina shook her head. "It's storming outside the valley. The pass is dangerous."

Peyton gathered his clothes and boots. Thudding horse hooves sounded in the packed dirt outside of the house.

"I can't let him get to Kerrstead before me."

"You don't have to go after him."

"First thing in the morning, he'll get the rest of the money!"

Alexina relaxed and smiled. "No, he won't."

"What?" Peyton said in a confused voice.

"Let him go. He won't get anything. In this weather, it will take him all night to get there, and you can stay here warm and dry."

"What are you talking about?"

"He won't get the rest of your money because as I left the bank, I told Mr. MacAdams not to pay out or allow a withdrawal unless you authorized it personally."

Peyton put his hands on her shoulders and turned her to face him. Then she saw what she had waited for a long time. Peyton laughed.

"My beautiful, wonderful, clever girl."

"Yours?"

He pulled her close. "Yes, mine." He kissed her and let the

towel slide from his waist.

Alexina melted into his embrace, responding with her lips against his. She clasped her fingers around his neck.

Peyton swung her into his arms and carried her to the bed. She pulled at her buttons with a swift dexterity she didn't know she possessed. He helped removed her blouse, then her skirt, and her undergarments. He kissed her neck and moved the kisses down to her breasts.

Alexina felt like she would crawl out of her skin. She had imagined this so many times and had the other two near-misses to build on.

Peyton caressed her, rubbing and massaging as he worked his way down. Then he pressed his body against hers. She moaned softly and ran her hand down his belly toward his groin. Finding what she searched for, she moved into place.

"Please," she said.

"Don't be in such a hurry," he whispered in her ear. "Enjoy."

"I *am* in a hurry. I don't want anything to get in the way of becoming your wife."

He chuckled softly and pressed his lips against her cheek. "Relax, my precious Alexina."

She closed her eyes hard as he spoke her name.

"My dear, beautiful wife," he added.

"Now!" she demanded.

"Very well, if you insist!" He laughed again.

Her hollow insides demanded to be filled. She opened her legs, inviting him. He pressed against her and slid his hands under her buttocks. Then he stopped and sat up.

"Peyton!" she cried, nearly hysterical from her need.

"Did you hear that?"

"No," she said in three syllables. "Don't stop."

"There! Listen."

Alexina sat up and heard the unmistakable cry, "Fire! Fire in the barn!"

Chapter Forty-Eight

Peyton jumped from the bed and seized his clothes. He pulled on his breeches. Alexina ran to where he left his boots. While he buttoned his shirt, she helped him with them.

He stood for a moment and regarded her. "I'll be back." He took a few steps away and returned to kiss her long and hard. "Don't go out there. Promise me you'll stay here where it's safe."

"Peyton...."

"Promise me."

She nodded. "I'll stay. Please. Be careful."

"I will," he said, and ran from the room.

She stood still and thought about the last few minutes with him, her husband, almost. Cries from the other side of the house brought her out of her contemplation. She grabbed her dressing gown from the wardrobe and rushed from the bedchamber. In the kitchen, Sissy, Dutch, Molly, and Little Jim pressed together, straining to see out the half door. Alexina went to the front door and, against the dark of night, saw flames shooting upward from the barn thatch. Men shouted and ran, bringing out the animals. Women and children were silhouetted against the flashes of fire as they gathered to watch the conflagration. Some of the women made their way to Stone House, and soon the house filled with the watchers and those that feared their safety from the wooden wagons.

During the night hours, the fire raged. Women made beds for the children, who succumbed to sleep. As the young ones lay about, Molly called, "Little Jim? Where are you?"

Soon the mothers joined her search.

Molly, usually calm and cool-headed in a crisis, grabbed Alexina's arm. "I can't find Jim! I think he's gone to help Master Peyton. I heard someone say Dragon is missing."

Another hour passed, but they still hadn't found Jim. A loud crack was heard as the flaming roof of the barn gave way. Parts of it fell into the middle, and a mass of the blazing reeds were hurled like torches into the surrounding areas. The shouts and bellows of the workers increased, building into frantic cries.

In the midst of the frenzied firefight, Dragon, *sans* rider, his reins hanging and his coat dripping with water ambled down the path from the pass. Hearing the whinny, Alexina ran to the arched doorway at the front of the house. She retied the belt of her dressing gown and held the skirt up to hurry to Dragon, who huffed and stomped, pitching his head back and forth. The whites of his eyes rolled as he swayed, frightened by the fire and the noise. She approached the horse, spoke softly, and stroked his neck.

Boyce had stolen Dragon, so Peyton couldn't catch him. To slow Peyton down further, the thief had set the barn on fire. But where was Boyce? Dragon couldn't have been all the way to Kerrstead and back in the hours since Boyce took him, especially since the storm still thundered outside the pass. Storm! Why couldn't it rain here? She cursed the good weather they enjoyed in their magical valley.

The men's shouts increased, grabbing Alexina's attention. The flame light had died down with the collapse of the roof. Although the sun made dark purple hints above the hills, it was not yet sunrise in the valley. She could just make out two groups of men carrying something toward Stone House.

Blackened with ash from fighting the fire, they brought in two casualties. Alexina dropped Dragon's reins. The men put Peyton, red and oozing from his burns, on the bed. Two more men carried Little Jim, singed and coughing, and placed him on his cot in the guest room. Granny soon followed, worn and frayed from her work during the night treating burns and cuts.

She barked orders. A pair of her helpers rushed into the guest room to administer aid to Little Jim. Granny carefully pulled off pieces of clothing stuck to the burned flesh on Peyton's body. With little discussion, the old woman used gestures and looks to command her disciples, who understood her arcane sign language.

Peyton moaned. Granny snapped her fingers, and one of her attendants handed her a bottle and spoon.

"Open," Granny whispered.

Peyton parted his lips, and the medicine flowed into his mouth. A moment later, he inhaled a deep breath and fell asleep.

After a few minutes of his regular breathing, Granny cleaned his body, removing bits of wood and cloth. One of the helpers handed her a wet cloth. Alexina recognized the smell immediately. The cloth had been doused with the Product, their apple brandy. The old woman dabbed at the clotted ooze running down a long gash diagonally from his navel to his groin.

Alexina stood next to the bed and observed Granny's sure touch and gentle application. Peyton's red, raw wounds alarmed her, and she bit her bottom lip as more damage appeared from Granny's cleansing.

Another helper brought in large thick leaves from a succulent plant that grew in the herb garden. With a long stroke from a flat knife, the top skin of one leaf parted, and the woman separated a long piece of green gel. She put it into a mortar and began to work it with the pestle until it became softened goo. Granny, who pulled the long gash closed with needle and thread, pointed to Peyton's burned forehead. The next helper smoothed the goo onto the area while the first woman prepared another leaf. Each time Granny pointed to a burned spot on Peyton, an assistant gently introduced the preparation. In an hour, Peyton's skin looked almost green with the many patches of gel. Neat black stitches held the white skin of his belly together in a long seam.

When Granny turned and nodded, another helper brought her white cloth strips, which she placed around Peyton's head, arms, and legs, and put wide pieces of cloth over his abdomen.

Granny pulled back Peyton's eyelids and nodded to her students.

She turned to Alexina. "We'll come to change his dressings twice a day."

"Granny, I…I—"

"Hush, girl. Listen to me. He's burned, but we can take care of it."

"Please don't let him die."

"We've done what we can. You'll be here with him?"

"Yes. What can I do to help?"

Granny put a bottle of white opaque fluid into Alexina's hands. The small bottle, flat on two sides, had been etched with a flower shaped like a poppy, and next to that, two closed eyes.

Granny cleared her throat in her way of saying, "Are you

listening?"

She snapped to attention. "Oh, yes, Granny."

"Only give him a teaspoon if he asks. This can't be given freely because it can invade his mind and make him a slave to it."

Alexina understood. During the last year of illness, her mother had fallen prey to the comforts of laudanum. Based on Granny's warning, she suspected this medicine far exceeded the strength of common laudanum.

Alexina looked at the bottle she held. "He gets a teaspoon only when he asks for it."

Granny nodded.

She cast a look in the direction of the guest room. "What about Little Jim?"

Chapter Forty-Nine

"Little Jim," Granny said with a sigh, "got too much smoke. He'll be sick for a while but will come through. He's not to get any medicine. Even if he says he has pain." She pointed to the bottle. "This can affect breathing, and fresh air is what the boy needs most now. I'm telling you so you can keep an eye on Molly."

"Yes, Granny. Thank you."

Alexina climbed onto the mattress, leaving enough room not to disturb Peyton. The softness of the sheepskin soothed her. It didn't take long to fall asleep.

Peyton's moans woke her. She sat up, heartsick because of the bandages covering most of his body. The irony of the first time sharing her husband's bed did not escape her.

He's alive. That offered a good substitute for what she had hoped to be her first night with him.

He moaned again.

"Peyton, are you awake?"

He barely whispered, "Did Granny leave something for me?"

"Yes. But she told me to wait until you asked for it."

"I'm asking," he rasped.

Alexina put the spoon to his lips.

He choked. "That's awful."

She held a glass of water and bid him to sip. The next sip went down easier. He took another. She dabbed his mouth with a napkin.

"Dragon—?"

"Boyce took him. Something happened because Dragon came back alone with the saddle at a slant and blood around his mouth."

Peyton took an easier breath. "The pass. Dangerous at night. Rain. Boyce wasn't a good horseman." He let the last word falter and began to breathe with the slow regularity of a sleeper.

Molly stuck her head in the bedchamber. "Mistress, come and eat the midday meal. I'll stay with our hero."

Alexina gazed upon the man, covered with dressings. "Hero?"

Molly came to the bedside and winced at the sight of Peyton, still and bandaged. "He got all of the animals out of the barn. Then he heard that Little Jim went in to look for Dragon. The roof had just fallen, and the men tried to hold Master Peyton back, but he ducked through the burning wood to get Jim." Her words stumbled over tears. "My boy is alive because of that man."

The stress, the lack of food during the fire, the hours of fitful sleep, and now hearing the report of his actions overwhelmed Alexina. The room swayed like a whirlwind had taken over. She barely had time to find a chair.

Molly bent Alexina over, guiding her head over her knees. After a minute, Molly squatted next to the chair. "Let me help you to the kitchen. Dutch can sit with the master for a while."

Alexina agreed and allowed Molly to escort her to the table.

Seat ate with bandaged hands. "How's Master Peyton?"

"Resting."

Sissy brought a plate. At the first bite, Alexina realized her hunger. She ate and thought about the fire and the damage. "Did anyone else get hurt? What about the barn? The cask barn?"

"Minor injuries," Molly said. "All tended by Granny and her students. I don't think we lost more than a few chickens."

Seat added, "The barn has no roof, but we'll start gathering reeds. We watered the area around the cask barn. Master Peyton had us build it away from the barn and the house, so the wind couldn't carry sparks. Everything, including your stash of apples, is fine."

The mention of the apples triggered a thought. After finishing her plate, she gathered the mail she had picked up in Kerrstead. The ride home opposite Boyce had been so dismal that she hadn't given her postal items much thought. She thanked Dutch for watching Peyton and pulled her chair to the window to examine her mail.

I can't believe it. The first of what turned out to be outstanding responses to her inquiries came from the Royal Academy of Sciences in London.

Dear Mrs. Woodleigh. I am pleased to answer your many questions regarding the propagation of trees, namely apple trees. Your surname brings pleasure to me and my fellows, for there was no one who possessed more knowledge on the subject than Clive Woodleigh. Surely there must be a relationship? I am sending you copies of his work in the subject of propagation. I am also including his book regarding grasses, grains, and herbs. Based on your questions, I believe you will find this information valuable. I am at your service for future queries. Respectfully, John August, Botanist.

Clive Woodleigh, the name on her marriage contract, Peyton's father!

She could barely put the book aside to look at the other mail. Catalogues, instructions, books, and information were gathered and sent by her friend Hester. *Bless that woman. How much effort did it take for Hester to research and collect the items? Oh, Hester, my dear ally. I expected no less. How can I repay your efforts? I'll think of something.*

The afternoon passed quickly as she read the catalogues and pamphlets, plus the many letters answering the numerous questions she had mailed weeks before. Every so often, Peyton would awaken and ask for water. Alexina said a mental thank you to Dutch, who had brought a thin hollow reed that Peyton used to draw the water from the glass. He slept on and off and only asked for the medicine once more before Granny came that evening and changed the dressings, then applied the gel from a large bowl. She nodded as she checked each raw wound.

"Strong," she mumbled. Placing a few pillows behind his shoulders, Granny insisted he rest in that position to help his breathing and circulation.

Alexina didn't ask any questions, clinging to the assurance that Granny, with little conversation, gave the air of competency Peyton required to live. Alexina understood why the Wanderers esteemed the old woman, her value exceeding gold.

The next morning Dutch came with broth in a porcelain container looking like Aladdin's lamp. Peyton sipped from the small pot easily.

While all remained quiet, Alexina spread her reading on the vacant spaces of the bed. The hours flew by as she assimilated the vast amount of information. She made notes and read some things two and three times to understand better.

On the third day, Peyton asked to sit up. Granny had Phillip bring in a wooden wedge that enabled Peyton to elevate. Although he didn't engage in long conversations, Peyton kept awake for longer and took nourishment more eagerly. Granny was pleased with his progress.

A few days later, Granny removed his bandages. The wounds, some still red and oozing, had begun to scab. Granny brought in additional medicines, some that smelled unpleasant and some that looked like pond slime. Alexina asked no questions, for she trusted the old lady completely and wished that some of the doctors in London would be willing to train under this medical genius. Granny checked the pain medicine bottle each day.

When the bottle's level reached less than a quarter, Granny held it up to Alexina but directed her words to Peyton. "This is the only bottle he can have. When it's gone, there will be no more."

Peyton stopped asking for it. When the level of medicine didn't change after two days, Granny smiled. "He has not disappointed me." From then on, Granny left the treatment to Alexina and told her to call if needed.

Peyton began eating whole meals. Alexina shared the meals in the bedchamber and rarely left his side, all the while studying and making plans.

A few weeks after the fire, although still red and healing, Peyton sat up and crossed his arms over his chest. "I'm bored. What is it that has you so rapt?"

"Wondrous things, my husband. Wondrous. And when you are ready, I will share what I have learned."

"Don't make me wait for wondrous things, wife. Share them now."

It had been what Alexina waited for. She now understood most of what she read and put a few of the items on the bed in front of him.

"I wrote to the Royal Academy with questions about apples and growing trees. This is part of what they sent me." She handed him the letter and book his father had written.

Peyton read the letter and leafed through the book. "My father? Was a Fellow of the Royal Academy?"

"You didn't know?"

"I don't remember my father. I only knew he left me a deed to a large piece of land called Applewood." Peyton returned to reading.

Alexina waited for him to pause, but he didn't stop. She cleared her throat. "Excuse me, but I have something very special to show you. But I must leave for a few minutes to get it."

Not looking up from the pages, he nodded.

She returned, bringing a tray with a small bottle plus two glasses and an elaborate decanter full of the beautiful crimson brandy. She cleared her throat again to get his notice. "Taste." She poured him a small glass.

He took a sip, then another. "That's incredible. I know it's apple brandy, but…? She poured from the small bottle and handed him the glass. "Try this."

He sampled the next one. "Absolutely delicious? Honey from apples? And why didn't you give me this while I took that nasty pain medicine?"

"Oh, no. I needed your tasting ability to be perfect."

He smiled. "Pray tell me. What's in this bottle? I've never tasted anything like it."

"You know the sweet apples on the tall, graceful trees? The ones with the mottled red and yellow fruit?"

"Yes."

"Have you ever considered making Jack from them alone?"

"Not enough fruit for us to waste the effort. All the apples go into the Jack together."

"This," she held the small bottle of pale amber fluid, "is syrup from those apples. I'm afraid I confiscated half of the apples from those trees."

"On whose authority?" He winced with the smile that accompanied his tease.

"Mine. I am the Mistress of Applewood. My commands are almost as royal as yours."

He smiled. "I wondered why those trees didn't produce as much this year. Now I know what happened to them, but I must hear how you came by this. Do continue."

She tapped the decanter. "This is our secret recipe. Your Clear Jack is mixed with the syrup and a little colorant from the shore thyme root." She could see he didn't know about the plant. "The little shrub that grows in the shallows of the lake."

"Hmm," he said and shook the empty glass for another sample. "It's incredible. *You* did this?"

"Don't be insulting. Of course, I did—well, with help from a few others. Actually, I couldn't have done it without Molly, Sissy, Dutch, and Seat."

He sighed. "I understand. I couldn't do without the folk." He traced his finger over the book. "When did you do all of this?"

She bit her lip and looked down at her hands. "All those days after our wedding, when I didn't see you. I needed something to do. After we made the syrup, I needed more information, so I've been writing letters and having anyone going into town post them."

He looked away. When he turned back, he bore the same serious look as he had before his accident. "I see."

The room stayed quiet for a few minutes.

For the first time, she noticed the sound of a branch scraping against the window. She didn't understand his solemn countenance. Perhaps he didn't wish to be reminded he had made himself scarce, but she had told him the truth. He had ignored her, and she found a way to occupy her time. And it took the form of something close to his interests. In fact, it was something wonderful that he had not thought about.

Did I say something wrong? Have I annoyed him? "Are you angry?"

He nodded.

"Forgive me."

"Nothing to forgive. I'm angry with myself, Alexina."

I love it when he speaks my name! I shouldn't be so excited, but I am. It sounds so good.

He picked up the book and started to read. She sat quietly on the edge of the bed for a quarter hour as he continued to pore over the pages. Finally, he laid the book down on the bed and shut his eyes.

"You need some rest now."

She got up and went to the kitchen, gathering her thoughts. Taking a cup of tea from Sissy, she sipped it. *Once he started reading, he hardly knew I was there. I have so much to discuss with him. So many questions I need to ask, personal things. Perhaps I made a mistake giving him the correspondence or telling him about Eden's Joy. Shall I hold off giving him some of the other literature? If I don't hold off, I may never get to talk with him. He's confined, the perfect time to get to know each other.* Peyton had been pleased, but by what, the items she had in her possession? She so wanted him to be pleased with her. Would she be satisfied to have him pleased by what she had accomplished?

When the time came for a renewed application of the healing gel, Peyton refused, anxious to read the work he had before him.

"I don't want that stuff on me. It will get on the documents. I'm healing," he protested.

Alexina sent for Granny, who came and checked his wounds.

She didn't insist he allow the treatments.

"Doesn't surprise me," Granny said in her thin, reedy voice.

"He wants to get up," Alexina complained.

"Let him get up." Granny left the room.

Peyton demanded more of the correspondence and asked if she had any more examples of written experiments or monographs. She gave him a few more.

Although his wounds looked angry and red, Peyton sat at the table for his meals and at the lovely desk when he worked in the study. He still required a lot of rest. While he rested, Alexina talked to him, asking questions about what he had studied in school, hoping he would tell her what he remembered of his past. He said little about his school days. What he remembered of his early youth, he was reluctant to share. She didn't press. *All in good time.*

"Please listen to me," she said one morning as he carefully put on his shirt.

"All right." He sat down on the bed.

"I have a plan. I believe we can sell the new brandy in London. You have done well in this area, but there exists a huge potential with the wealthy. The absence of the after-effects coupled with the wonderful taste would make anyone want to consume it. We will charge a hefty price, and people will pay. We can recoup the money Boyce stole."

Chapter Fifty

Peyton's head fell back into the pillow. "Regain my loss? Tell me how."

He listened with growing interest as Alexina gave him an overview of her plans to sell Eden's Joy in London.

"Of course, I want to get back the money Boyce stole, but I don't want to deal with the kind of people in London I escaped from years ago. Let me think about it."

She shifted on the bed next to him. "What is it you must think about?"

He rolled his lip, then shrugged, letting out a sharp groan from the movement. "Very well, make your plans. I believe I'll rest."

Days later, Alexina heard voices echoing from the other rooms that sounded different from the usual. She left the bedchamber to see who had come.

Molly stood in the open arched doorway. Most valley folk entered by the back and usually didn't wait for an invitation to enter. Alexina knew this visit must be important, carried on in an uncommon formality.

"Mistress, we have visitors," Molly said with singular solemnity.

Granny came in, and she was not alone. Behind her were five of the beautiful Wagon Girls. Trailing them was Sophia, Granny's droopy-eyed, club-footed assistant, whose abject homeliness was even starker in comparison to the Girls. Sophia wore plain tan muslin. The Girls wore colorful dresses, each with a vibrantly hued band setting off their curvaceous waistlines.

Obviously, the visitors waited for a proper invitation. Alexina didn't know what to do. *Should I let those women in my house? Yes, I should. I am Mistress of Applewood. I want to have a place as one of the Valley Folk.*

"Do come in." She stepped aside and bade the women to enter. Sophia made eye contact but didn't speak.

Alexina recognized the Wagon Girls but didn't know them by name.

"Hello, I'm Sapphire," said a tall woman, whose hair hung in full dark curls, large dangling earrings poking through. Her white silk blouse had been pulled together with satin cords held in a channel along the neckline. Her wide blue waistband separated the blouse from the green paisley skirt. Her lacy petticoat peeked out in a saucy fashion.

"I'm Ruby," the next Girl said.

The introductions went around to Citrine, then Garnet.

After Amethyst presented herself, she lifted up a bag, like each of the Wagon Girls held. "We've come to see Master Peyton." She turned to the other girls for a second. "If that suits you."

Alexina felt the weight of Granny's eyes upon her. "Yes, of course. I'll show you to the bedchamber." As she led the way, she wondered if perhaps these women already knew the path. Alexina held the door open. "Mr. Woodleigh? You have visitors."

Peyton opened his eyes and struggled to sit up. Citrine rushed to the bedside and helped him.

Granny put her hand on Alexina's arm.

I must go. I don't want to witness this. "Granny," Alexina said. "Would you care for tea?"

They headed for the kitchen as the door to the bedchamber closed firmly behind them.

Alexina suspected Dutch, Sissy, and Molly had known ahead of time about the visitors. Dutch rarely baked tea cakes, but as they sat down, she pulled a tray of thin cakes from the oven. The rough table sported a lace cloth and had been set for tea.

Alexina worried her lip and stared down the hallway leading to the master bedroom, desperate to know what was taking place in the bedchamber. After all, these girls had been with her husband in a way she had not. But surely they wouldn't be—

"Tea?" Sissy said. "Mistress?"

"What?"

Molly laughed and rolled her eyes towards the other end of the house. "I can't imagine where your mind is right about now."

Alexina's cheeks grew hot. "Sugar?" As she reached for the bowl, she caught Granny's stare, which could speak louder and clearer than her voice, and said, *Well done, Mistress.* Alexina licked her lips and stirred the sugar into her cup.

Dutch put the cakes on the three-tiered plate matching Alexina's dishes. The cakes tasted nutty and delicious, truly melting in her mouth. She recognized three flavors, chocolate, vanilla, and cinnamon, the flavors she had brought from her shopping in Kerrstead. "Dutch, I've never had such wonderful tea cakes."

"Thank you, Mistress."

The ladies engaged in a lengthy conversation about making tea cakes. Grateful for the diversion, Alexina did not think about the activities taking place on the other side of the house.

When the last of the tea and cakes had been consumed, Alexina heard a commotion and left the table.

Sophia came into the kitchen. She motioned to Alexina. "Come with me."

Chapter Fifty-One

Alexina followed Granny's student, Sophia, into the bedchamber. Peyton looked almost as robust as he had when she first laid eyes on him. The Girls had cut his hair and given him a shave. He wore a new nightshirt, white linen trimmed with a row of pleats at the collar and sleeves. The sheets had been pulled up to his waist.

"Look." He moved the sheet aside and hiked his nightshirt to his navel. "No more stitches."

His wounds were still red but dry and healing.

Alexina cast her gaze around the room. "Thank you, all."

One by one, the visitors departed, leaving the couple alone.

"You look so much better. I couldn't have done what they did." She swept her hand across his forehead and cupped his chin. "We are lucky."

Peyton pulled her hand to his lips and closed his eyes. "Thank you." He let out a deep breath and relaxed.

When his sonorous breathing began, she sat at the writing desk that Tad and Carl had moved into the bedchamber. While Peyton slept, she continued her correspondence. Her pen scratched furiously as she wrote letters needed to market Eden's Joy. Since Sophia had ordered Peyton to rest the whole day, he stayed in bed and let Sissy and Dutch fuss over him with food and wine from Applewood's fine vineyard.

Several hours after the evening meal, Alexina showered and readied for bed. She crawled in next to Peyton and felt the same desires he had complained about since he began to heal. Sophia had given instructions for him not to have any activity, especially *that* kind until Granny gave the go ahead. She added that if he couldn't control himself,

Alexina would have to sleep elsewhere, and one of the students would sleep in a cot near him to monitor his recovery.

The whippoorwill's plaintive call took on a new meaning as she lay next to her husband in the dark.

In the morning, the gravel crunched under the wheels of the drayage cart belonging to John Sutton of Turnersfield. He stopped the cart at the front door. Alexina held up her hand as a signal to wait for her to run to the bedchamber to get money for the bundle of mail he waved at her.

Giving him what he needed for the postal charges, she took the mail then returned to where Peyton lay sleeping. At the desk, she slid the dagger-like letter opener to unseal the brown wrapper of a small package. She unfolded the paper cover, which revealed the book entitled *Propagation of Fruit Trees*. She quickly opened it and started to read. The contents included drawings and instructions on how to graft trees.

"Good morning, wife," Peyton said in a low volume. "What has your interest?"

She rushed to his side. "Look! You have ten Eden's Joy trees, but this book says you can transplant branches onto other trees, and they can produce the apples."

"Let me see that."

She gave him the small book. He scooted up in the bed, impatient while she fluffed pillows behind him. The pages flew at a fast pace as he leafed through, looking at the drawings and reading the explanation of each illustration. Looking up from his reading, he put the book aside and kicked off the covers. He struggled to get up.

"What are you doing?"

He winced as he made his way to the rough wardrobe that held his clothes. Opening the cabinet, he pulled out his breeches and shirt.

"Peyton?"

"You saw the book. We can increase our Eden's Joy production. No time to waste if we are going to have a crop for next year. I must get started now."

"But you aren't healed. You can't go out into the orchard."

"Yes, I can," he said as he pulled on his breeches. In a few minutes, he was dressed and headed for the back door, passing the ladies who kept the house. Alexina followed him as far as the door.

"Mistress?" Molly said.

"He's going to the orchard!"

Molly, Sissy, and Dutch sat quietly, not reacting to this news like Alexina thought they should.

Hands on hips, Alexina said, "I need to speak to Granny!"

Molly dispatched Little Jim to the circle of wagons belonging to the Healers. Before long, the gray-haired old woman came through the back door.

"Granny! Peyton has gone to the orchard to work."

"And?"

"He mustn't do that. He hasn't healed."

Granny smiled. "He'll do what he can and come back to rest."

"But, Granny—"

She pushed two cambric bags tied with twine into Alexina's hand. "Herbal tea and a sleeping powder. Give him a draught of this when he comes back from being outside."

"But, Granny...."

Granny continued to hold the bags in Alexina's fingers. "Mistress, why don't you have some herbal tea now?"

Alexina regarded each occupant of the room, waiting for support regarding her complaint. The silence told her she had none. Alexina dropped her head. Granny let go of the tea sachets.

In two hours, a group of men brought Peyton, weakened and dirty, back to Stone House. Alexina led the men into the bedchamber, where they deposited him on the big bed. She cleaned his face with a rag and took off his boots. Tucking him in, she held the tea draught up to his lips while he took a few sips.

"I did it, Alexina. I grafted a branch. I'll do more tomorrow." His head fell back onto the pillow, and he fell asleep.

He had looked so good after the Girls and Sophia had worked on him. She ran her gaze over him. He lay there in deep slumber, still sweaty and dirty. The Wagon Girls were no longer her competitors, but perhaps she had a new one—fruit trees.

Chapter Fifty-Two

Each day Peyton dragged himself out to the orchard for a few hours until he could do no more. He used the techniques he had read in the book the Royal Academy had sent. When he could toil no longer and was near passing out, a few of the valley men hauled him back to Stone House, where he allowed Alexina to apply a wet cloth and give him tea before he fell asleep. When evening came, Alexina crawled into bed with Peyton, snuggled as close as she could without disturbing him, and slept.

Every day he worked a little longer outside, sometimes staying until the time of midday meal. Alexina watched the clock on the mahogany credenza in the parlor to monitor the time when the men brought him back in a canvas bed held by two poles.

"I'm getting better," he said every day.

She countered with, "Perhaps that would be true if the exertion didn't hinder your recuperation."

Alexina continued to write her letters and frequently had one of the men ride into Turnersfield to post them and collect her incoming mail. She received multiple catalogues and numerous letters from Hester.

One afternoon while writing at the desk, the sound of horses outside the house disturbed her. Opening the front door revealed Rufus descending from his fancy rig.

"Good day, dear Neighbor—"

She shot him a warning glance before he could say her name. "Good afternoon, Mr. Smith."

Smith stepped closer to the door, expecting to be invited inside.

Alexina didn't move.

He pulled at his chin, appearing to be confused at her inhospitality. "I heard in Turnersfield you had a fire."

I don't like our business being the subject of gossip.

"Neighbor Alexina?"

"Oh, yes. We lost the roof to our barn. It's being rebuilt."

"I also heard Woodleigh had been badly burned, but no one sent for a doctor. Is Woodleigh dead?"

"Mr. Smith!"

"If so, I am here at your service, dear lady."

"We didn't call for a physician because Granny Doctor treated him. He is recovering nicely, thank you."

"Granny Doctor? Oh, yes, that witch healer. You must not value Woodleigh if you left his treatment up to her." He chuckled. "So tell me true, he lives?"

"Mr—" Beyond him, two men with an empty stretcher headed for the orchard. It meant Peyton had reached the end of his energy and would be coming back. She wiped emotion from her face. "He lives. Granny is an extraordinary medical practitioner. By the way, have you seen our cask barn and press?"

"No. That beast Woodleigh runs me off as soon as I get here. Are you offering to show me?"

She smiled. "I am. Follow me. Oh, and instruct your man to park your rig in the back, please."

Rufus gave word to the driver, who immediately moved the fancy white vehicle.

She took off at a brisk pace, and Rufus hurried to catch up with her. As they passed the barn, a bundle of reeds fell down from the roof and hit him on his head. He stumbled, then looked up at the men who worked above them.

Alexina put her hand over her mouth to conceal her grin. She waited while he stood and rubbed his sparsely fuzzed forehead. He brushed debris off his fine trousers. "I reckon we should be more careful and not get too close to the construction." She cast a quick glance over her shoulder, and sure enough, the men were coming up the path with Peyton in the canvas bed.

"Walk this way." She beckoned with her hand. The door to the cask barn was open, and the fragrance of juices coming from the press enveloped them. Tiers of casks lined the walls.

"My, oh, my," Rufus said. "What a press. Of course, I wouldn't have any knowledge of such things, this common work, but I must admit this press is remarkable."

She extended her hand toward the next room of the cask barn, the distilling chamber. Upon entering, the fermenting smells battered their senses.

"What does this thing do? It smells like…I don't know what."

"Fermentation, I believe. That," she pointed to the vat with its curled tubing, "is the distilling machine designed by Mr. Woodleigh himself."

"I don't believe it. He probably just told you that."

Alexina figured sufficient time had elapsed, allowing Peyton to be returned to the bedchamber. "Thank you for coming. The tour is concluded."

"You wish me to leave?"

His words matched the hurt in his face. The tiny bit of sympathy that stung her departed in a moment. "Yes. I have things to do. Unannounced visitors cannot expect an extended call."

"True," he said. "But if I announce my visit, Woodleigh will decline, and then I can't see you at all." He paused as they walked toward the back of Stone House. "Too bad about Mr. Boyce."

"What do you know about Boyce?"

"The drayage man from Turnersfield found a dead body in a ravine just beyond the pass to this place. It was Mr. Boyce."

"Thank you for informing me. He left the night of the barn fire, and we had not heard from him since."

"I see, hmmm."

Standing in the shade of Stone House, he waved his hand at the driver, who shook the horses' leathers. When the chaise arrived, he bowed and put Alexina's hand to his lips. "Farewell, lovely lady. My offer still stands, don't forget."

Alexina pulled her hand away. "Good day. I'll not encourage you to return."

He climbed into the rig. "I need no encouragement. All I need is the memory of your sweet face." He held up his walking stick and rapped the roof of the vehicle with the brass head. The driver took off.

When the clamor of the horses echoed in the pass, she rushed into the house. Peyton lay still on the bed, sleeping. She dipped a towel in the warm water of the ewer and cleaned his face.

He opened his eyes. "Thank you. I rest better after you care for me."

She cleaned his neck, carefully avoiding the red and angry wounds. After the tea, he slipped into slow, regular breathing, and she wished they could have a long conversation. Peyton had devoted his waking time to reading and his limited energies to working in the orchard. Alexina told herself that for the time being, she best served him by working on their plan to sell Eden's Joy and recouping their financial losses.

Chapter Fifty-Three

The next morning when Alexina brought Peyton his breakfast on a tray, he sat up and smiled.

"Look," he said.

"What?"

He pointed to the sheet over his hips where the linen peaked. He flung back the cover, showing what she had only seen at night. In the light of day, that which she had desired stood straight and tall.

"Oh!"

"Granny was afraid the gash to my groin might have damaged me for life."

Her hand went to her throat. "Peyton!"

"But, as you can see, I'm mending in the right manner. I haven't achieved such loftiness since the fire." He returned the sheet to cover his torso. "When Sophia removed the stitches, she cautioned me not to be *active* because even though the skin has mended, the muscle underneath has not, meaning I can't...."

Alexina, still holding the tray, sat next to him on the bed. "We'll wait until you heal completely. That's all there is to it."

He pulled her arm toward him, mindful of the tray until their faces almost touched. "It will be worth the wait. You'll see."

A shot of heat ran through her body, starting deep within her. It would be worth the wait.

After putting the tray on the bed, she placed a napkin under his chin. "Why don't you stay in today? I have much to tell you about the plans. I'm excited regarding our preparations. Things are coming together. I know we will be able to sell Eden's Joy."

"Whatever you want, my dear."

She smiled at his words, sweet words, the same ones Rufus had said yesterday at his unexpected visit. The endearment coming from Peyton sent ripples of pleasure through her. *First, his words give me physical excitement by his wanting to bed me, and now I joy to his words of sweetness. If I can partake of all of these emotions from his mere words, what can I expect when we finally come together? How can I possibly wait?*

Peyton folded her small hand in his. "My dear?"

"Sorry, I couldn't help but envision what lies ahead…when you heal."

"Uhm, perhaps we should change the subject." He pointed to the tent forming under the sheet again. "I'm weak, not only physically, but in spirit. I don't know how much temptation I can handle."

She coquettishly smiled and batted her eyelashes. "I must resist temptation as well, Mr. Woodleigh."

He chuckled and then made a sharp moan. "Don't make me laugh. It hurts."

"See here, Dutch has made your favorite sweet grain cakes." She smoothed the butter over the cake, then drizzled honey on top.

He let her feed him. She held the dripping cakes to his lips, then brushed them lightly with the linen napkin if he didn't first lick the excess sweet with his tongue. His tongue moved along his mouth, the act causing her to review the promise of their future union. She very much wanted him to heal and thought he should rest.

"So, can I talk you into staying in bed today if I promise not to tempt you?"

"No. I need to work as much as possible. The grafting takes a long time, and the more I accomplish, the more sweet apples we'll have for next year."

"You do it yourself? Have you shown the others how to graft?"

"Not yet. The more I do, the more I learn. Then I can teach the others."

"I would really like to go over the plans to sell the brandy. I've almost completed them, and I need your endorsement. You should know and understand how I've allotted time and our limited resources—"

He held up his hand, indicating he had taken enough nourishment. He kept his hand up to stay the conversation. "I don't need to know. I'll do what I can in the orchard and leave the rest to you. When the time comes, just direct me."

She sighed. "Very well. I'll continue with my strategy. But sometime in the near future, you must give me an audience regarding my ideas."

He struggled to get off the bed. Alexina selected his breeches and helped him with his shirt and boots.

Chapter Fifty-Four

In a few days, Alexina's plans were finalized. She spent hours arranging the timeline and made several copies. Soon she had thick envelopes stuffed with instructions. Everything—businesses, addresses, cities, and inns—became part of her itinerary for success.

One afternoon Peyton announced he had completed the grafting process. He took off his shirt to show his healing wounds. "Granny says in a few days, I can resume my activities. When can we leave?"

"Tomorrow," she said. "Let me write a few more letters to tell those who expect us when we will arrive. Oh, Peyton! Go rest now for our journey!"

Chapter Fifty-Five

Alexina had the plans for their trip to London worked out, written down, and committed to memory. She'd figured each action and cost to the last pence. None of those plans excited her, however, more than the knowledge that Peyton would be free of his work and could pay suitable attention to her alone. Remembering his promise that the wait would be worth it gave her a thrill that started in one place, reverberated through her body, and circled round back to the same spot. Sometimes it excited her so much she couldn't concentrate on the moment. They would be leaving the next day. She needed to focus and oversee the entire process so nothing could be overlooked.

Most of the following morning was spent loading the carriage with their luggage and the casks containing Eden's Joy. Sissy packed a basket with sandwiches and other foods to last them until they reached the outskirts of London. The blankets would be left in the old chaise while it was stored at a carriage rental agency.

Just as Peyton and Alexina were ready to leave, Carl brought Granny to Stone House in a cart and lifted the old woman out of her seat as if she were a bundle of wheat straw. While Peyton had a few last words of instruction for Carl, Granny took Alexina aside. The old woman turned Alexina's palm over and peered at it. "A long journey."

I know that.

Granny gave a look that said Alexina should not be thinking but listening carefully. "It won't be an easy trip." Then Granny put her hand on Alexina's breast. "Think with your heart, Mistress. Time comes when your heart knows the truth, and you must give your trust when you least think it earned. Allow love to accept help from an unexpected source."

"Granny, that doesn't sound like a good prediction."

"No prediction, Mistress. Advice. Now the prediction. Success in many quarters."

Granny rolled Alexina's hand into a soft fist and then kissed her cheek, an action providing much surprise for Alexina.

Alexina and Peyton bid adieu to Applewood, with both of them sitting on the driver's perch. Peyton held the reins with one hand and grasped his wife's shoulder with the other. Silverton held his head high. The even clip-clop of the large horse's hooves resonated against the high ridges and onto the narrow gravel causeway leading from the bountiful valley.

They stopped near a river to rest Silverton and take lunch. Alexina spread the blanket and opened the food basket. During the meal, Alexina brought out two large envelopes. "While you labored in the orchard, I spent my time planning our strategy for selling Eden's Joy. I wished to tell you about this beforehand, but you have been so worn out—"

He leaned over and kissed her cheek. "So exhausted I haven't been able to make love to my wife." He kissed her again. "But tonight, my darling, we will make up for all the time we lost."

That hollow feeling formed inside her, the demand for attention.

"These are the plans."

Peyton gathered the papers and stuck them back in the envelopes. "I can't concentrate with you so warm and close." He patted the blanket that served as their table. Pulling her near, he nibbled her ear. "You know, we don't have to wait for tonight if you can tolerate the chilly wind."

She looked around the field, her heart speeding and thumping in her temples. "Could someone see us? Where is the nearest village?"

He sighed. "Pretty close. We may not enjoy total privacy right here."

"Oh, Peyton."

He nuzzled her neck. "Tonight, then, at the inn." He jumped up and extended his hand. "I want to get there as soon as possible! So get moving, woman."

Peyton returned Silverton to the traces, and they headed eastward, reaching the desired inn just at nightfall. Dinner was included in the price, and they were led to a table. They admitted to each other they could skip dinner and go right to the room. Mindful of the budget and strict plan, Alexina pointed out they must stick to both. As the last plate was cleared, Alexina brought out the two envelopes again. "Try to concentrate. These," she said, opening one, "are your instructions. I have everything mapped out to the finest detail."

He spread the papers on the table and looked them over, every few minutes catching her gaze and sending a subtle message that made her blush.

She selected a sheet and turned it so he could see. "The itinerary. The day after we get to London, we will go to Grandfather's and pick up the money."

"What money?"

"I wish we had talked about this before, but now will have to do."

He scratched at the back of his head. "I'd rather have something different in my thoughts, my darling."

"Yes, yes. I completely agree, but please, indulge me for just a few minutes."

"Hurry," he said, smiling.

"I have Grandfather's gift money for our traveling expenses. Luckily, I didn't give it to you earlier for deposit. We'll stop in northern London, where I've reserved a buggy and driver. The next day we'll visit Grandfather. I wrote and told him to sell enough of my inherited jewelry to obtain five hundred pounds."

"Your jewelry? Oh, my sweetheart. I don't want you to sell—"

"Silence," she said, in mock anger. "We need the start-up money." She traced her finger on the paper. "Next, you will go to this place and order fifteen glass decanters—"

"I can't concentrate on directions. I'll read them when we get to London. Right now—"

"One more minute. We'll be staying at your house, and—"

The smile vanished from Peyton's face. "What do you mean, *my house*?"

"The Woodleigh House, on Cross Street. With your mother."

Peyton's face turned ashen. "What are you talking about?"

"Grandfather has little furniture and no guest room. I wrote your mother, and—"

"My mother!" He slammed the table with his palm, making the papers shake. Other diners became quiet. "What in the *hell* do you think you are doing?"

Chapter Fifty-Six

"Peyton, I don't understand."

"This exceeds idiocy. Who told you to write my…that woman… she doesn't want—"

"I wrote her and said we were coming to London and I'd like to meet her. I asked if she had room for us to stay there for a week. I hadn't met her and thought—"

"You thought? Obviously, you didn't think very clearly."

"Don't insult me. I have planned this to the finest detail."

"You don't know that woman. She doesn't want us there."

Alexina fumbled through her envelope and pulled out a letter. "But she does. Look."

He turned his head away, not willing to view the letter as if it offended his eyes.

"I'll read it to you. *Dear Mrs. Woodleigh, I will be leaving London on the day you wish to visit. However, I will stay long enough to make your acquaintance, for I am very interested to meet the woman who wed my son. I will assign a room, and you may stay in my absence. Also, as I have a double stable, you may store your horse and conveyance. Be sure to accommodate your vehicle and animals properly. Mrs. Bertha Woodleigh.* You see, she wants us to visit."

"You're a complete fool," he snarled. "She mocks you. Yes, she's interested in meeting you…to abuse you."

"But she invited us to stay."

"Because you asked. That…harpy. She's a slave to propriety. She'd prefer death to having anyone know she refused a request to stay."

"Well, we have no alternative. That is where we will be staying."

Peyton shot from his seat like it burned him. "Never! I'd rather sleep on the street."

Alexina stood. "I won't sleep on the street, Peyton. I'll be staying at Woodleigh House with or without you."

His nostrils flared, and his breathing became shallow. "Good night, Alexina."

"Good night?"

"I'll bed down with Silverton. I've spent quite a lot of time sharing hay with horses since you've come into my life." He stomped away.

"Peyton, come back." She hastily gathered the papers and followed him. He ignored her pleas as he made his way to the back of the inn. She grabbed his arm as he entered the stable. "Peyton, please. Can't we talk about this?"

"You mean what you should have done before you wrote to... *her?"*

"I tried to talk with you."

"Let me be."

She let go of his arm. He moved stiffly through the stable and seized a hayfork. Stabbing at a mound of hay, he pitched a load into Silverton's manger. Keeping his back to her, he pulled the padded bench from the carriage and threw it into the corner of the stall.

She sighed, returned to the inn, and climbed the stairs to the room, where the fire cast a dancing radiance on the walls.

Chapter Fifty-Seven

Alexina ate breakfast alone and wrapped Peyton's portion in a table linen. She waited with her carpetbag on a bench outside the inn.

Peyton pulled the carriage up to the bench. In a grim voice, he asked, "East or back to Applewood?"

"East, then south to London. I've invested time and effort in this plan. I wish to see it through."

He hopped from the driver's seat and held the door open, indicating she would not be sitting beside him. When they stopped to rest, he pulled the rig near a river but took the horse downstream and stayed there, in view but not in speaking distance. At the end of the day, he let her out at the front of the inn, and she didn't see him again until the next morning.

On the third day, they neared the outskirts of London and stopped when they reached the agency where she had reserved a buggy and driver. Peyton leaned against his old carriage. Alexina went into the office with the letter of confirmation.

The clerk behind the desk read the letter and made a face. "I'm sorry, Mrs. Woodleigh, but the buggy you reserved for today is not available."

"Yes, it is," she countered. Taking a small catalogue from her basket, she pointed to a drawing. "I ordered a Rockaway. I can see it from here parked in the drive. I know that is the one I ordered because I requested a large basket boot for our luggage."

The clerk pulled at his collar. "Yes, madame, that is the coach you requested. Unfortunately, it has been promised to another customer."

"Although sad for the other customer," she said, "it has no

effect on my plans." She waved the confirmation letter in his face. Her volume increased. "You will summon the driver forthwith. I have a schedule."

Peyton came into the office with a look of curiosity. He folded his arms over his chest, waiting to hear the conversation.

"See here, madame," the clerk stammered.

Peyton strode forward, placing his hands palm down on the counter. "What is the problem?"

Alexina answered without turning to face him. "There will be no problem." She focused her stare at the clerk and allowed the anguish of the past few days to color her words. "Fetch your manager. Or better still, the owner."

The clerk hurried from his post, pale-faced.

A man, sporting great mutton-chop whiskers and wearing a business suit that should have been cut a little more generously, came out of his office. His mouth was set with determination. "I'm Ezra Schaeffer, the owner." He addressed Peyton. "You wished to speak with me, sir?"

"Mrs. Woodleigh," Alexina said, grabbing the man's attention.

Peyton stepped back and shoved his hands into his pockets.

"Mrs. Woodleigh?" Mr. Schaeffer cleared his throat and shifted his considerable weight from foot to foot. His discomfort of having to deal with a woman instead of a man showed as his eyes darted toward Peyton and then back to Alexina. After a pause, he directed his words at her. "I'm afraid you won't be able to hire a coach today. We have but one, and that is promised."

Alexina held her confirmation letter in front of Ezra Schaeffer's face. "See the date on this letter? Show me a request that predates my reservation."

"Excuse me?"

"You said it is promised. I believe it is promised to me, but if someone has hired it before me, then I shall go elsewhere."

"I don't understand," Mr. Schaeffer said.

"Clearly, you must have the proper paperwork for the rental. Show it to me."

"Madame—"

"Mrs. Woodleigh," she said, allowing the irony of the situation to increase her temper.

"I can't. I—"

"Then I am first. I will take the coach. Summon the driver."

The fellow cast his glance to Peyton, who silently leaned against the doorjamb. Peyton's head movement and shrug gave the undeniable message that the matter had been concluded.

Alexina pictured the headmistress at the Greenfield School. She willed herself to assume the role, and her voice became sharp and threatening. "Mr. Schaeffer, this letter of confirmation represents a legal contract, meaning you are obliged to stand by your word. I am lawfully entitled to hire that rig and the driver. Do I need to summon legal force?"

"Legal force?"

Alexina didn't know for certain her claim would be upheld or whether she could find a person with the authority to enforce the contract, but she bet Mr. Schaeffer didn't know it either. The tactic had worked with Mr. MacAdams.

After a pause, Mr. Schaeffer nodded. "Do you wish to hire a horse as well?"

"We have our own horse, and according to your letter, the storage of our vehicle is included in your price." She reached in her purse. "Here is half, as agreed. The other half to be paid upon return."

Mr. Schaeffer peered around Alexina and saw the pitiful old thing they had come in.

Her gaze followed his view, and she guessed his thoughts. "Our formal carriage is in for repairs, and we had to utilize an old one we keep for emergencies," she explained, lest he wonder if they could pay the remainder of the rental.

"I see."

"The driver?" Alexina asked.

The man sighed. "Joseph Pemberton. He should be here soon."

"I have contracted for noon. Every half hour he is late will be deducted from the fee."

Alexina figured she would go all the way with the attitude. She concluded it couldn't hurt for Peyton, her almost-husband, to see how things could be handled when necessary.

"Yes, madame," Mr. Schaeffer said. "Curtiss?"

The clerk obediently appeared.

"Run to Pemberton's house and get him here, quick."

Curtiss nodded, glancing at Alexina, who held her jaw firmly and didn't flinch. Alexina waited in the hiring office while Peyton and a helper stored the old carriage.

Within the hour, a man in a gray livery uniform entered and

took off his cap. "Mrs. Woodleigh? Joe Pemberton, your driver." He bowed his head. "At your service."

Alexina stood. "The Rockaway is ready?"

"Yes, madame."

Pemberton sped ahead and held the door of the smart new buggy. Peyton stood aside for her to enter and then sat next to her. The vehicle dipped as Pemberton took his place on the top. A slight jolt meant they were on their way.

Alexina put the travel basket between them and removed the envelopes. "This is yours," she said curtly and placed the envelope on his lap.

Peyton pulled the cord on the window blind, sending it upward and looked out the glass.

"Open it," Alexina said, exasperated.

Peyton did not respond but crossed his arms over his chest. He continued to stare out the window.

"Mr. Woodleigh, do you wish to sell Eden's Joy and replace the money stolen from you? Stolen, I might add, because you did not take enough interest in your own business and allowed a scoundrel to fleece you?"

That got his attention. He turned his head swiftly and breathed sharply out his nose.

"Regardless of how you feel about me, if you wish to accomplish this mission, you must do what I have written on your list. Read it. Now."

Peyton removed the first paper and gave it a cursory examination. He took out the rest of the material and compared it to the list on the outside of the envelope.

When he had read the last page, she cleared her throat for his attention. "To sum up the information, the first day you pick up the money from my grandfather, Geoffrey Downing. Then go to Assim's. See the address? As directed, order fifteen glass decanters and leave them in the buggy. After that, note the places you must visit and what you should order. Pay attention to those catalogue pages. That way you will know the appropriate prices. It wouldn't hurt to negotiate for a lower price."

He nodded.

"You must leave word at Grandfather's where you can be contacted. When I have filled the decanters, I will take the samples to sell. I will need the carriage every other day for my part of the mission."

He nodded again.

"We must complete all business by Sunday morning because this carriage is due back in the afternoon, and the budget does not allow for overages. Understand?"

He nodded, narrow-eyed and nostrils flared.

Chapter Fifty-Eight

Peyton understood but didn't like the tone she used to impart the information. A tone from his past, one of the few things he remembered from his youth. *Like her....*

He shook his head, quashing the unpleasant memory.

"Mr. Woodleigh," she said coldly.

His eyes dwindled to slits. *She says my name like a curse word.*

"Peyton," she said, changing the sound of her voice.

He didn't hear her now, having learned to ignore unkind words like the ones he had endured at school when the other boys taunted him. Peyton had been smarter than most of the boys and retreated into his studies for solace and comfort. He had desperately wanted a tender word or gesture from his mother when he came home on holiday. There had been none for him, even when he stood in front of her quietly waiting for anything, the slightest indication she had feelings for him. How he wished he could have thrown his arms around her and buried his head in her warmth. Eventually, he learned there would be no affection from that source. It had become necessary to turn his emotions inward to a place where he could learn to control his own feelings. He discovered the ability to withdraw from any sensation, reaction, or manner, making him immune to anguish. Summoning this ability, he became a granite statue sitting next to this woman who had invaded his sanctuary at Applewood.

Alexina gently tapped his hand. "Peyton, we've had a miscommunication. Pray tell me what caused you to avoid an encounter with your mother. Perhaps—"

His stony face became enraged. "A miscommunication! You

must be a simpleton of the highest magnitude."

"Simpleton?" Her face became flint. After a pause, she softened. "I wish to resolve this...situation. I am your wife, I—"

"Wife! You've been causing trouble since you came to Applewood. Why did you have to change everything? Why couldn't you have kept things as they were, left me alone? Things were fine until you came."

"If you feel like that, why did you want to take a wife?"

"I didn't want a wife. As an addendum to my deed, I had to be married before my twenty-fifth birthday in order to keep my land. Believe me, that was the only reason I signed that contract."

Her sweet pink face turned white. Those rosy lips thinned and became gray.

Why did I say that to her? It was true in the beginning when I read the addendum to the deed, but when I saw her in the carriage, I wanted her. Since she had come into his life, so many things had improved. She brought class and elegance into Stone House, making it more comfortable and warm. *The valley people love her, including Granny. She uncovered Boyce's treachery and rescued what little we have left our savings. Ours. And what about Eden's Joy?* He believed her plan could recoup their losses by selling the brandy to establishments catering to society people.

Peyton looked at the heavy envelope he held in his lap. *I'll apologize, but I'm not sure what should I say. I need a few minutes to think.* He opened the flap, removed several sets of papers, and reviewed the contents, seeing detailed directions on what to buy and where to go. *All this work and planning. I couldn't have done this. I would have just borne the loss and plodded on. Not Alexina. She's willing to fight and gain success. For me. Now I've hurt her with my words.*

Chapter Fifty-Nine

Alexina choked back the tears. She would not cry. Not in front of him. *How could I have been so wrong? Did I see the care in his eyes because I wanted it so? Did I mistake the tenderness I felt when he kissed me and touched me? The sparks I felt…were they just mine? I must stop loving him. There's no purpose for it.*

Peyton leafed through the pages she'd given him.

I know this plan will work. At least he can regain what he's lost financially. What have I lost? Something I never had?

She stifled her emotions. Rummaging around her mind, she summoned the words of Ovid about how to fall out of love. *How did that go? Find a physical flaw on the one you love and focus on its unpleasantness?*

She stared at Peyton as he looked through the papers. Searching his face, she tried to find a flaw. *I see nothing but perfection on that sculpted face, fashioned with such elegant proportions Michelangelo himself couldn't have done better.*

As she contemplated Peyton's physical appearance, anger slowly replaced the wretchedness. She could cope with anger. Allowing the fury to well up inside her, she clenched her teeth in rage. *How could he treat me like this?* As long as she had been at Applewood, she'd tried her best to serve him, offering him her heart and attention. *How did he repay me? When he wasn't ignoring me, he barely spoke to me. I'll not have this conduct any longer. I will see this plan through, and then I'll not return to Applewood. Perhaps I can get another position in London. I have a week to make my arrangements. With his money restored, he won't miss my presence.*

As she continued to stare at him and perform her mental deliberations, he turned to look at her. She hurled a piercing look.

He shook his head and put the envelope down between them.

Alexina's eyes followed his movement. She found her words. "You don't approve of my plan? I have everything written down. If you follow it to the letter, this mission will be successful, and you should be able to sell your brandy. You can return to Applewood with enough money to start a large production, after which you can pay your workers, hire an honest supervisor, and not have to worry."

His words had an icy crackle. "I have no difficulty with your instructions. What I have difficulty with is your behavior."

"*My* behavior?" She crossed her arms in front of her chest. "What colossal nerve you have."

"I don't know what you will say or do. You have perplexed me since you came to Applewood."

She glowered. "I have perplexed you? Does a word exist meaning bigger than colossal?"

He set his jaw. "Not only have you confounded me at every turn, I can't trust you."

The unmitigated gall! She held her hand palm forward to him. "I'll not dignify those comments with a redress. However, I must understand and incorporate the changes you have forced upon this strategy." She thumped her own envelope. "If you will not take advantage of the prearranged accommodations, then I warn you there is no room in the allotted budget for you to hire a room."

"I'll find my own accommodations."

"Then I shan't trouble myself over your lodging. Pick up the money from my grandfather's house mid-morning tomorrow. Leave word with him where you can be contacted. If all goes as planned, you need not meet with me, but a few times, then you can go back to Applewood and start production."

Peyton acknowledged her words with a barely audible throat rumble. For a moment, his facial muscles went slack as if he'd heard bad news. A slight elevation of his head and a nod purveyed the idea he didn't care. Knowing him for the past months, she could read his *do what you wish.*

They rode in silence until Mr. Pemberton slowed the pace, and Silverton made a comforting clop-clop on the cobblestones. In a few minutes, the vehicle stopped, and the buggy's springs moved as Pemberton descended from his perch and swung the door out.

"This is the address, Woodleigh House, Cross Street and Randolph Road."

Peyton refused to look at the corner house they had reached, staring at an unfocused spot across the street.

Alexina took the driver's hand as she found the step with her foot. "Thank you. Please check the stables in the rear." She pointed around the corner. "Just there." The edge of a building behind the house had two large doors, each crossed with boards forming an *X* for support. "You may keep the horse and buggy in that stable overnight. Here," she gave him a note and some change. "You must buy feed for the horse. And I require a receipt for the feed purchase."

Pemberton tipped his hat in an obsequious manner. "Yes, madame."

"You will pick up the cab at eight in the morning and stall the horse at eight each evening. I'm sure my husband…." The word stuck in her throat. "Will give you instructions on the care of his horse. I may check on your performance."

"Yes, madame."

Then she pointed at him, using her headmistress voice. "Mr. Pemberton, I bid you, remember *we* hired your services. When you have discharged us to our destinations, this cab remains empty until you once again fetch us." She paused. "This horse is ours. My husband…." She shot an ugly look at the buggy's interior, having had to use his title again. "Will know if the horse has been run. Do you understand my meaning?"

"Yes, madame. I understand. I'll remember."

"Good," she said and moved her gaze to the boot. "My cases?"

"Oh, yes, madame." Pemberton released the lock on the boot and removed her two pieces, one a carpetbag, the other a large-handled slender basket. He sat the baggage on the front doorstep. "Very good, madame," Pemberton said. He backed away, facing her as if he had been dismissed by Queen Victoria herself.

Alexina waited until the cab turned the corner toward the stable and had time for Pemberton to check the site. When he pulled the horse about and set on the cobblestone road, she rang the doorbell.

Chapter Sixty

Peyton lowered the cab window and stuck his head out to see Alexina watching the Rockaway until it turned the corner. He then gave directions to an inn called the Toad and Pond.

Peyton's recollections of his boyhood started when he was ten, his first year of boarding school. At eleven, he had been allowed to come home during the summer break. At that time, he found his mother had left for Italy and would remain for the entire season, relinquishing his care to the housemaids. Perhaps his association with those kind and gentle women gave him his affinity for the wandering people who had settled in his valley. That summer represented the best time in his life, for, in that brief period, he'd experienced a close connection to another boy, one he could call a friend.

Raymond Bates, a man of color, had been hired to repair the stables and a few other things at the house. A hard worker, he arrived early and stayed late, with an attention to detail that impressed young Peyton. Best of all, Raymond brought his son, Ike, with him as an assistant. Ike, the same age as Peyton, was a bright boy and took a liking to the lonely lad who lived in the fancy house. With time on his hands, Peyton often helped Raymond and Ike. Although unschooled, Raymond knew things and shared the information with the boys, often tracing designs in the sand to show how things worked.

One day, as Raymond described gearing, Peyton ran into the house and brought out pen and paper. Raymond drew designs with exceptional clarity and line. The drawing showed cogs and wheels and how turning one could make the other turn and, combined to shafts and gears, could be used in unlimited applications. It was that day

Peyton decided to discover as much as he could about engineering.

During those days with Raymond and Ike, Peyton learned about their desire to become innkeepers, to buy a business of their own. At that time, Raymond had an eye on an inn for sale, the Toad and Pond. Peyton hoped that by now, Raymond had bought that inn.

The buggy came to a halt in front of the Toad and Pond.

As Pemberton held the cab door, he had a sympathetic look on his face. "I couldn't help but overhear the ruckus, Mr. Woodleigh."

Peyton glared at the man.

Pemberton clucked his tongue. "From what I heard, the missus threw you out of the house. Forgive me, but you're young. I know what you're about, poor fellow. You got it bad for the lady."

"What?" Peyton sputtered.

"Yes, sir. You got it written all over your face. I understand. I'm married to a looker, too. Them beauties, they get under your skin, and you can't help yourself. Let me give you a piece of advice if you don't mind." Pemberton continued without allowing Peyton to deny the situation or stop the man's self-acclaimed wisdom. "It's worth it. Just put up with her ways because when you love that kind of woman, life is Heaven when she's happy. And don't forget, that woman is with you, and she could have been chosen by a hundred others, see? You'll be back in your house before you know it."

"Thank you," Peyton said gruffly. "Wait here. I'll be a few minutes."

Pemberton tipped his hat and climbed up on his perch.

Peyton entered the tavern and, as soon as his eyes adjusted to the dark and smoky atmosphere, he recognized the young man behind the bar.

"Ike, do you remember me, Peyton Woodleigh?" He extended his hand.

Ike rushed around the bar and shook hands vigorously. "Peyton! Yes, of course. It's so good to see you. It's been years. Heard you moved north. Back for good?"

"I'm in London for a week." He scratched the back of his head and shifted his weight from one side to the other. He wasn't accustomed to asking favors. "Would you be willing to let me work in your stable in exchange for lodging?"

Ike made a face showing his discomfort. "I would, but we only have three rooms, and they are taken."

Peyton felt grateful Ike had not said anything about not having enough money to rent a room. "I could sleep in the stable."

"Very well," Ike said, the confusion starting to show from the juxtaposition of their former roles. "Sure. Would you like a drink? On me?"

"Thank you. I would. Allow me a short time." Peyton returned to the buggy, which was still waiting at the curb. He eyed the small stable behind the inn and realized the size prevented storing a vehicle. He would have to allow Pemberton to park the rig at Woodleigh House. Mentally reviewing the itemized errands on the list, he knew he had no other tasks for the day. Removing his bag and a small cask from the boot, he dismissed Pemberton. Should he remind the man of the strong warning Alexina had delivered earlier regarding using the rig as a city cab? Pemberton already knew how to deal with *this kind of woman,* as he said, so the man needed no extra reminders from him. Then Peyton thought of the advice the driver had offered about being in love with a beauty. He shook his head at the ridiculous notion that *he had it bad for the lady.* He reminded the cabbie to be at the Toad and Pond at eight-thirty the next morning, then dismissed him.

Peyton returned to the bar and found his drink waiting. He took a sip. *This brandy is awful.*

"You don't like it?" Ike asked.

Peyton regretted that his facial expression revealed a dislike of the drink meant to honor a childhood friendship. "Thank you, Ike. It's fine." He dug into his bag and brought out a bottle. "Here, let me treat you to a drink."

Ike reached under the bar and brought out two clean glasses. Peyton poured the sparkling ruby fluid. He held his up in salute to Ike, who responded in kind.

Ike took a small sip. His face brightened, and he took a longer sip. "My God, man, what is this? I've never tasted its like before. Tell me."

"Brandy made from the apples in my orchard."

"I must have it," Ike said and moved closer to Peyton.

Peyton reflected for a moment. Alexina had predicted this exact reaction. Tomorrow, according to the notes she had given him, he would procure flasks, which she would then fill and take to potential buyers. Now, without even trying, Ike wished to have Eden's Joy.

"Peyton?" Ike said.

"Oh, uhm, I only have this small bottle with me."

"I'll tell you what," Ike said in a bargaining tone. "Give me that bottle, and I will make sure you have a room for the entire week. I can evict one of my tenants. He needs to go anyway."

Alexina had mapped out the entire plan, and Peyton didn't know if the bottle she had packed in his bag had been for his own use. Perhaps he shouldn't meddle with her plan.

"Peyton?" Ike tapped his fingers on the bar. "Look, I'll add your meals. As much as you want. What do you say?"

Meals! Bloody Hell. He hadn't thought about how he'd eat when he told her not to worry about his arrangements. But then, he hadn't been the one to make those contemptible arrangements either. Peyton thumped the cork stopper. "Meals and a private room for the week in exchange for the rest of this brandy?"

"Yes," Ike said, clearly pleased. "And let's talk about future purchases."

"Perhaps later, Ike. I hadn't planned on selling my brandy." It was true. He was not supposed to be selling it. That area of expertise belonged to the lovely, intelligent Alexina Woodleigh. He whispered a low grunt, stifling his thoughts about her.

Chapter Sixty-One

After the buggy turned the corner, Alexina approached the door of Woodleigh House, turned the key on the doorbell, and cast her gaze down Cross Street, feeling an instant of abandonment. She bit her lip. Had she been too stringent? *What difference does it make?* She was Mrs. Woodleigh in name only and couldn't make things worse by preserving at least some of her dignity. She would not permit him to speak to her like that again.

Her thoughts were interrupted when the door cracked open. A woman, who was older than Molly but resembled her, smiled.

"Can I help you?"

"I'm Mrs. Peyton Woodleigh," Alexina said, banishing her annoyance to the married name.

"Oh!" the woman exclaimed. "Come right in." She grabbed Alexina's hand and pulled her into the foyer. "I'm ever so glad to meet you." The woman stepped back a few paces and took a long look. "I'm Bridget, the head housekeeper. We've so been wanting to see you. Oh, let me look at you. Of course, our dear little Peyton would choose someone like you." She turned her head toward the parlor. "Sam, come get the luggage." She stepped closer to Alexina. "Where's Peyton?"

Alexina stiffened her spine. *I'll not make excuses for his rudeness.* "Mr. Woodleigh has declined to come."

Bridget nodded. "Doesn't surprise me. What did surprise me was the letter with the news he had married and would be coming here. Tsk, tsk," she said, sucking her teeth. "Bad blood between them. I guess you know about that."

Too late, but I do. Alexina nodded.

A tall uniformed man approached them.

"Sam, get Mrs. Woodleigh's luggage on the front step and put it in her...uh, room." Bridget took Alexina's hand again. "The last we heard, Peyton had bolted from Harrow. A few years later, the accountant told Mrs. Bertha the taxes were paid on Applewood, so we knew he was there. Oh, yes! I can see it now—you, the Mistress of Applewood. Such a house! I'll bet you have many servants. You'd need them."

"Yes, a few," she said.

"Where is your personal maid?"

"My maid? Oh, uhm, she couldn't come. I'm afraid I'm by myself on this trip."

"Too bad. We, the entire household, will be leaving this afternoon."

A younger woman in maid's garb came into the room.

"Sara, prepare the tea cart for our guest." Bridget smiled at Alexina. "You must be famished from your trip."

"Thank you. I would love tea."

Although she still smiled, Bridget's tone changed. "Mrs. Bertha is in the study. I'll announce you. Be back straightaway."

Alexina waited in the foyer, but the bright smile had vanished from Bridget's face when she returned. "Mrs. Bertha will see you now. Follow me, please."

Alexina trailed the woman through the main hall.

Bridget stopped abruptly and turned. "A word, if you don't mind, Mrs. Woodleigh."

A chill passed through Alexina at Bridget's words.

"Mrs. Bertha.... Well, I remember when sweetness and goodness ruled this house. In her heart, she's a good woman, although it might not seem so to someone who doesn't know her. Keep that in mind, young Mrs. Woodleigh."

Bridget recommenced her task as escort. She stepped back and allowed Alexina to enter a large paneled room decorated with rich furnishings. A lady sat by the fire reading, her feet on a cushion. The woman was still attractive. Her dark hair, streaked with gray, was pulled back into an intricate bun. She kept her head down toward the open book, her eyes not rising above the wire spectacles she wore.

Bridget crossed the threshold and continued until she stood in front of the woman.

"Mrs. Bertha Woodleigh, please make the acquaintance of Mrs.

Peyton Woodleigh."

Alexina approached the seated woman until she stood next to Bridget.

"Mrs. Bertha!" Bridget mildly scolded.

The woman removed her glasses and looked up but maintained her position. She took her time closing the book and placed it on the table next to the chair.

Alexina flinched at this breach of etiquette and obvious snub. The woman did not seem infirm, so why did she not stand or offer her hand in welcome?

Bertha Woodleigh regarded Alexina with a cold, hard stare.

Alexina moved closer and extended her hand. "I'm so pleased to meet you, Mrs. Woodleigh. I've looked forward to this since...I wrote you my introduction."

"I received no introduction letter, young woman, only a letter announcing you would be coming to London and wished to stay here. Did you write that yourself?"

"What?"

"Can you read and write?"

"Of course, I can."

"Parlez vous Francaise?"

Alexina's face grew hot. *"Oui, Madame. Hablo Espanol und Ich spreche Duetche ebenso."*

Bridget shot Alexina a pleased expression.

"I see," Bertha Woodleigh said.

"Have a seat, young Mrs. Woodleigh," Bridget said, throwing a glare at the older Mrs. Woodleigh.

"Thank you." Alexina sat in the chair facing Bertha and waited for the woman to respond with the proper point of manners. After an uncomfortable silence with Bertha staring, the scrutiny became akin to a hole being burned into the wood with a red-hot rod.

Finally, Bridget broke the silence. "Look at her, Mrs. Bertha. Isn't she lovely? So fair."

"She's fair," Bertha said grudgingly.

"Thank you," Alexina said, glad to have the conversation started again. "And thank you for your invitation to visit."

Bertha sniffed. "Invitation!"

"You must have been as curious to meet me as I am to meet you," Alexina said sweetly.

"Oh, I was curious, to be sure. I wanted to see what kind of woman would marry my...*son*." She let the word "son" slip from her tongue as if she had tasted a bitter herb.

"I regret you didn't get my letter of introduction," Alexina said, allowing the insult to slide away, "wherein I detailed my family history. I left the letter with my solicitor, who promised to address and mail it. He obviously made a mistake."

"A mistake, indeed."

The new silence weighed heavily in the room, eventually broken by the sound of Sara pushing a wooden cart. The wood wheels thumped over the thick silk carpet, making the teapot and cups rattle.

Bertha stood and pointed to Sara. "I did *not* order tea!"

Bridget put her hand on her hip and faced Bertha. "You should have. But I told Sara to bring that cart."

Bertha's eyes narrowed. "So, you think I'm running a hotel and a restaurant?"

Bridget made a disgusted face and shook her head. "Young Mrs. Woodleigh, may I pour you tea and offer cakes?"

"No thank you," Alexina said. "Perhaps I should go. I apologize for the inconvenience. I will find another place to stay." She, in fact, had no other place, nor did she have room in her budget for accommodations. Grandfather's house? The dusty, closed-off rooms with only a small settee, but worse, his unpredictable behavior?

"Oh, no!" Bertha said, the disdain dripping from the words. "I'll not have anyone say I did not offer hospitality to my *daughter-in-law*." Once again, she spit the words as if they inflamed her tongue. "Besides, as I said in my *invitation*, I won't be here, so it makes no difference to me where you stay. We leave immediately." She called to Sara. "Have Sam bring the carriage round. Now." She turned to Bridget. "Show Mrs. Woodleigh to her room." Bertha Woodleigh walked away but stopped. Stepping close to Alexina, she said, "I suppose when I die, my *son* will claim this property, but for now, you will get nothing from me."

"I don't want or need anything from you." *That isn't true. I require a place to stay.* "I came with the sincere intention of meeting you."

"Well, you've achieved your goal, then, haven't you?" Bertha said. "Do not go to the upper floors. Be aware, the door to my bedroom and office are securely locked. Understand?"

Alexina would not allow the insult to land. "Of course, I understand," she said sweetly. "And if the table turned and you were visiting at my house, I'd do exactly the same thing. After all, trust needs to be earned, regardless of the family relation."

Bertha's eyes expanded as the insult took root in her mind's garden. She sniffed and pivoted, stepping briskly away.

Alexina felt good for a moment. The feeling faded quickly. *Perhaps Peyton is justified with his wrath.* He didn't want to come here. Did he try to protect her, but she didn't see it?

Bridget patted Alexina's arm. "Well done, young Mrs. Woodleigh! You are just what she needs. Perhaps some fences will be mended now."

Alexina didn't want to know what Bridget meant. She had to fight to keep her composure.

"Come," Bridget said with a loud sigh. "I'll show you to your room."

Alexina followed.

"As I said," Bridget explained, "she really is a good woman. I've been here a long time, worked my way up from chambermaid to housekeeper. This place had been such a happy home. Before I came, she had been married to a horrible man, a peer, who had two dreadful boys from his first marriage. Lord Dunforth beat his horse once too often, and the thing stomped him to death. I came here to Mr. Clive's household when she married him, and not a nicer man existed on this earth. Mrs. Bertha loved him so, and he returned that love. When she had little Peyton, and those two awful boys went off to school, this place seemed like Heaven. Then Mr. Clive had that house in Applewood Estate built for Mrs. Bertha, but she didn't care for it up there. The winters were harsh, and her social life was in London."

"Harsh winters?" Alexina asked. The winters in the valley were mild.

"Mr. Clive had his work, and she had her social life. He divided his time between his work up north and his family here in London."

Alexina listened to the history, putting aside the anger that had formed from the acid dialogue she'd just experienced. It mildly registered that they headed to the rear of the house.

"I never saw a couple so devoted to each other." Bridget made a questioning face. "Well, seems I did. They had friends who were as much in love. And that couple had the cutest little girl. Peyton adored that child. But then…well, that's something else. Where was I? Oh, yes. Mrs. Bertha wanted more children, Peyton being such a pleasure, such a loving little boy. Like a doll, he was. One winter's night, Mr. Clive returned to London during a frightful sleet storm. Poor little Peyton had been running a fever, and it became worse. Mr. Clive panicked and went out to find a doctor. Another carriage slipped on the icy roads and swept both of them buggies right into the Thames."

Alexina stopped and grabbed Bridget's hand. "Oh, how terrible."

"To be sure. Mrs. Bertha was beside herself with grief, and the next day she lost the baby she carried. Poor little Peyton, burning with fever and didn't have his mummy to comfort him. In fact, in her misery, she blamed him for the death of his father and unborn sister. Me and the other servants took care of him, and as soon as she could, she sent that boy off to school."

"Poor Peyton," Alexina whispered.

"Poor both of them," Bridget amended. "And that's not all.

Alexina barely noticed they traveled down the service steps.

Bridget continued her description. "The fever hurt him. When he regained his health, he had no memory of his mother or father. That was more than Mrs. Bertha could bear, a little stranger in her home whose young face reflected the face of his father, her beloved husband. After Peyton went off to school, she had a change of heart and wrote him to come home if he wished, but he wouldn't answer her. She wrote several letters, and he refused to correspond. After that, she would have no more to do with him and avoided the times he came home for the holidays. That boy had changed, no longer the happy, loving child he had been. He was sullen and reclusive."

Alexina knew precisely what Bridget meant.

"Well, young Mrs. Woodleigh," Bridget said with apology. "Your quarters." She pushed open the door of a small room.

"Oh," Alexina said, not knowing what other response would suffice. "Maid's quarters?"

Bridget scratched her nose and nodded. "So sorry. She's being extra mean. I guess the thought Peyton might come here affected her. But the room is clean and cozy."

Alexina's carpetbags sat in front of a huge wardrobe.

"This is Mr. Clive's old closet. She wouldn't part with anything of his. His items are stored in the empty quarters here in the basement." Bridget opened the door of the wardrobe. "Here's some room for your things." She moved to the fireplace. "There's extra coal." She pointed to a full scuttle. Then she gnashed her teeth for a second. "I wouldn't advise you to eat any of the food in the pantry.

"Have no worry on that," Alexina said. "I wouldn't eat a thing of hers if it meant the difference between life or death."

Bridget put her head back and laughed heartily. "Good on you, Mistress. She's met her match. And I'm glad you didn't let her heartlessness run you out. You've a right to stay here. After all, it really belongs to Peyton, being the only son. He could well turn her out, you know."

"The only son? You said he had two step-brothers."

"Bad eggs, them. One died as a result of cheating at gambling, the other killed by an outraged father...if you get my meaning."

Sara appeared in the doorway. "Mrs. Bertha says to come right now, or you'll not have a job tomorrow."

Bridget clucked. "So she always says. But I'm coming." She kissed Alexina's cheek. "Forgive my impertinence, but I'm so happy you have come. Here is a key to the back door. By now, you must understand you can't use the front entrance." She made the clucking sound again. "I hope to see you again, young missus, and I so hope to see Peyton. Tell him how much I miss him. I know you must make him proud and happy. He did good choosing you." She hurried out of the room.

Alexina sat on the small bed and let out a huge breath. *He didn't choose me. Our marriage meant he could keep his property, which was odd if he owns this house.* She shook her head with the confoundedness of this information and looked out a small window. Obviously, this room occupied the most rear of the basement. She could see the stables and a bit of yard, the grass wet with the light rainstorm in progress.

She reviewed her plan. This afternoon she must speak with Grandfather Geoffrey. Hearing a noise, she looked out the window again. The smart new rig with Pemberton atop pulled in front of the stables.

Chapter Sixty-Two

Alexina hurried to find her way out to the stables. She had to use the service steps, enter a narrow hall, and exit a back door. On the top of the rear iron steps, she steadied herself by grabbing the handrail.

"Mr. Pemberton." She waved to him for attention rather than stepping from the overhang and getting wet. After a second hail, he hopped down from his perch and came to the steps.

"Yes, madame?"

"I'll need to travel to 103 Academy Street. Do you know where that is?"

"I know my way around London. When do you wish to travel?"

"In a quarter-hour."

"Very good, Mrs. Woodleigh. It gives me time to unload your things. I'll bring them in."

"I have what I need." Pride caused her to not want him to know she occupied the maid's residence. "Leave the canvas bags in the boot of the rig."

"As you direct, madame. I'll be in front in fifteen minutes."

"No…pick me up here. I wish to leave unobserved." It was the only reason she could think of to use the back door, chafing at the idea of justifying her movements to Pemberton, a man of service. *What has happened to me? A strict budget, putting up with a harpy to acquire a room and worrying about when I'll eat. Peyton Woodleigh, that's what!* The anger she felt with him earlier resurfaced. No matter how pitiful his problems he had as a boy, *she* was paying the price.

Returning to her small quarters, she unpacked a few things. Now on her own and fending for herself, she looked around the room.

The bowl and pitcher on the washstand would be her only source of cleaning. She hadn't asked about where she could get warm water. And the facilities? Surely the small cabinet beside the bed held a pot.

The cabinet did hold a small pot. *But where should I empty it?* She hadn't emptied a pot before. The cesspit had to be somewhere in the basement or outside. And no one to ask. *I'm glad I didn't have that tea.*

She had become aware of the privileges of high birth at Applewood, but the point would be made even clearer here, where she had no maid service at all. And she had to use the back staircase, the one built for the servants and workmen.

Holding her basket ready with the folded lists, she waited under the portico at the back door. Pemberton pulled the rig as close as he could. She darted down the steps and into the open door of the buggy.

The rain made the trip longer than it should have been. Alexina estimated it would take forty minutes on foot but should have been only fifteen by hack. Stalled traffic, people darting in and out of the carriages, and black umbrellas looking like a garden of dark morning glories added to her gloom. Sitting alone in the cab, she could not avoid the thoughts creeping into her mind. Peyton had told her he didn't remember his father. Now she knew why. That poor little boy came out of a serious illness, not knowing who he was or what had happened. Then he had been denied his mother's care and devotion. Her own childhood differed from other girls her age. During the years Alexina should have been involved with parties and balls, she stayed at her mother's bedside. By the time the illness had taken Edwina, Alexina had missed her window of eligibility. Alexina didn't remember her father because she was very young, but the memory lived on through her mother's constant tributes. After his death, she had been her mother's only focus. When her mother could not bear living in the family house, the two of them had moved in with Grandfather. Edwina frequently claimed the reason they accepted so many invitations to country manor homes had been to get a break from Geoffrey.

From their numerous visits away, Alexina had met many possible suitors, and her path had lain before her like that of any other Regency girl, which meant exposure to young men of good families, coming out in society, being presented at court, and all of the trappings of entitlement.

All of that had ceased when Edwina took ill. In his own grief, Grandfather Geoffrey had offered Alexina no solace, no support.

The only person available had been Ignace Smith. After her mother's death, Ignace suggested she leave Geoffrey's household, who, in his opinion, had spells of madness. She would be better off in the position of governess or teacher.

Returning to her current situation, she swallowed her ire and sat up, stiffly vowing to review her status and come up with a design for her own life. That is when she completed the plan she had slaved over for weeks so Peyton Woodleigh, her husband, the man who had not wanted to be a husband, could regain his lost fortune.

The cab stopped in front of Geoffrey Downing's house, the home she had known during her mother's illness.

Pemberton jumped down from the driver's seat and held the door. "Orders, madame?"

"Mr. Woodleigh has the cab tomorrow all day." She wanted to ask where Peyton had gone, but pride kept her from inquiring.

"Shall I put up the cab and horse at your house, then?"

My house? "Yes, the Woodleigh House. Unless Mr. Woodleigh needs you."

"Mr. Woodleigh has dismissed me for the rest of the day, madame."

She took the envelope off the seat and started to put it in her basket when she saw the brown edge of another envelope already there. Reading the front, she slapped it down on the seat. *Peyton didn't take his envelope!*

"Mrs. Woodleigh?" Pemberton said, holding the door of the rig.

"Yes," she answered vacantly and moved toward him. She extended the envelope. "Please see that Mr. Woodleigh gets this right away. He will need it for tomorrow."

"Right, madame." He helped her from the rig and tipped his hat as she climbed the steps to the front door.

"I won't be needing you for the rest of the day."

But where was Peyton?

Chapter Sixty-Three

Peyton took his luggage up the narrow wooden stairs to the room Ike had given him. He breathed relief, for this room represented the first good accommodation of his travel after sleeping in the stable or on the seat of the chaise. A low fire made the room warm. The cozy fire, the wood paneling, and spotless wooden floor, coupled with the light coming from the diamond shaped panes of the window, made this room inviting. He could rest. The bed pleased him with its clean linens and soft mattress.

Alexina's image crept into his mind. This large bed could accommodate two with room to spare, but he remained alone.

He shouldn't have allowed Alexina to face that woman, who by name and biology was his mother. Peyton reclined on the bed and let out a long breath. But Alexina insisted on it. In fact, she had become very much like his mother, with a look that could render him to ashes if he but uttered one syllable when she upheld her plan of action.

He closed his eyes. *That's not fair to Alexina.* He reviewed the past months and how things had changed at Applewood, most of them good changes. If she hadn't been there, Boyce would have taken all the money, and perhaps he would have lost his valley to taxes. And Eden's Joy....

His reflections stopped when he heard the knock.

"Mr. Woodleigh?"

Peyton recognized Pemberton's voice. "Enter."

Pemberton held his hat and the envelope. "Mrs. Woodleigh bid me take this to you."

Peyton flinched when he saw he hadn't brought the instructions.

"Thank you. How did she know I left it?"

"She found it when I took her to Academy Street. Not too pleased about you leaving it, I might add."

Peyton scratched the back of his head. "I don't suppose she would be. Did she ask to be fetched from the house at Academy Street?"

"No, sir."

"I will see you tomorrow."

Peyton stood in the hall as the driver left. Smells from the kitchen wafted up the stairwell, reminding Peyton he hadn't eaten anything but the hard-boiled egg Alexina had given him in the morning.

He went into the tavern and ordered his evening meal. The fare didn't disappoint him, being hearty and tasty, but it didn't compare to the rich, delicious food from the valley.

Pemberton's information about Alexina going to her grandfather's and not asking for a ride back to Woodleigh House made him wonder if her interview with the Beast of Woodleigh didn't go well. He didn't think it would have. He pushed the bowl away, no longer interested in his meal. He wished he had asked Pemberton if Alexina had brought her luggage to the house on Academy Street.

Returning to the room, he reread the orders for the next day, orders carefully and clearly written by someone who had put a lot of time and effort into this strategy. They had not had an opportunity to go over the instructions. *My fault for throwing such a fit.*

Chapter Sixty-Four

Alexina waited on the top step. No one answered the bell. She tried the handle and let herself in. *Why isn't the door locked?*

She came into the parlor and found him napping in his favorite chair. "Grandfather?"

He sputtered, looked up, and cried, "Oh!" Jumping to his feet in a surprisingly spry move, he grabbed the poker sitting by the fire. Brandishing it toward her, he said, *"Arrêtez-vous! Voleur! Défendez-vous."*

Alexina's shoulders slumped. She threw her traveling basket on the chair near the fireplace. "Grandfather! Put down that poker." All of the events that had so vexed her replayed in her mind. She sagged and moved her things on the floor to make space for her to sit. "Grandfather, it's me, Alexina."

He laughed. "So it is. Welcome, my darling granddaughter."

"You know me then?"

"Of course. I merely had a farce with you for humor."

She shook her head at him. "I'm not amused. I didn't need that." Might as well get straight to business. "Oh, Grandfather, please tell me you sold the necklace."

"The necklace?"

She left the chair in a blur and sprinted to the parlor desk where he kept his mail. "I sent you a letter." She rooted amid the stack of correspondence. "Grandfather. You did open it, right? You sold the jewelry? I need the money for tomorrow to keep on schedule."

"Why do you wish to sell your jewelry? It belonged to your dear mother."

Her legs went limp. She grabbed the edge of the chair and sat down hard. "I need the money, five hundred pounds, to start a business venture. I wrote you and asked you to sell as much of the jewelry as needed to get that sum."

"Hmph," he said. "One of the least necklaces would fetch that price. But put the worry of money to rest. Tell me about your venture." He peered at her. "You don't look well. Have you eaten?"

Embarrassed, she shook her head.

"Here, here. We shall go straight away to have a meal. Let me get my coat and hat. We'll talk over luncheon. How does that sound."

"Thank you, Grandfather, it sounds lovely." As a matter of fact, it sounded wonderful. She hadn't eaten since early that morning, and her stomach ached after refusing the tea that her ersatz mother-in-law had begrudged. Grandfather, when in his right mind, cared about her well-being.

Geoffrey Downing took her to a restaurant that overlooked the Thames. He ordered, and the food soothed her emptiness, at least in her stomach.

"Now," he said, looking up from his meal. "Tell me of your business venture."

Without reference to Boyce stealing the funds, she focused on the brandy. "We—that is, the people who work on the farm—press apples into cider and make apple brandy. We blend the brandy with a syrup to make a flavorful drink we call Eden's Joy."

"An aperitif?"

"Yes. An apple flavored-sipping liquor."

"And you think you can market this beverage?"

"Yes, Grandfather. I do."

"I would like to try this creation you believe is worth selling your valuable possessions to produce."

"I have brought some with me. You can taste it later."

"Very well, Granddaughter. We shall see to that. But now tell me about your life in the north."

"Haven't you been reading my letters?"

Geoffrey looked at the plate. "Sometimes, I don't read all of my mail."

She let out a puff. "I purely wish you would."

"You know," he said as he put the napkin to his mouth, "I have my rational times. I'm not always mad."

She bit her lip. "I know."

"Years ago, when your father died, your mother could not bear to stay in their home. I had to promise not to meddle in her or your business. Because of that, and that only, do I not ask questions of you. It does not mean that I don't wonder or worry. I so want you to volunteer the information I crave. That is that you've found love and harmony. Granddaughter?"

At that moment, Alexina fought the words forming on her tongue. "Perhaps some other time," she managed to say.

"Dear girl! Will you release me from my pledge this very minute? You are one who has not disappointed me, and I so wish to serve you."

"I release you from your pledge," she said with a sigh. "However, I won't agree to answer questions I find too personal. Please understand."

"I understand. But at least I can be of help to you now without worrying about breaking my word to your mother. Now, the first thing I wish to discuss is your business relationship with that reprehensible miscreant, Ignace Smith."

"Sometimes, Grandfather, I feel that man has not served me well."

"Oh, my dear! How sweetly you describe the work of a crook."

The luncheon check came, ending Geoffrey's discourse. He paid and escorted Alexina to the front, where they caught a cab back. The rain had increased, and the road was jammed with traffic.

In her grandfather's house, they sat in front of the fire, allowing the radiant heat to warm them from the chill of the wet. After a while, Geoffrey opened the cabinet holding his collection of wines and ports.

"This would be a good time to try Eden's Joy," Alexina said. She opened her basket and removed the bottle of ruby fluid. She offered Geoffrey a glass.

He took a small taste, held the glass to his nose, examined the color, and took another, longer drink. "Unbelievable! This is what you intend to sell?"

"Yes. You do…like it?"

He took a careful sip. "Marvelous. Simply splendid. I'm afraid if I had a large supply, I would surely be tempted to imbibe beyond reason. I would have a terrible time the next day."

Alexina moved close to him. "Ah, but you would not. Not only does it taste good, but it does not leave the partaker with troublesome suffering afterwards."

"How can that be?"

"I can't explain it, Grandfather, but I have seen this myself. Those who overdrink and enjoy the intoxicating properties have no ill effects later on."

"If this is true, and I can scarce believe it, you can name your price. Everyone will clamor for it. I ask that you allow me to help you in your venture."

Alexina shook her head slightly, not wanting to take the conversation further.

"Granddaughter! I am a businessman. Yes, yes, albeit a little dodgy at times, but that is because I've had no purpose. My club affiliation can only give me so much distraction. This!" He waggled the glass, "This is what I need. Have I not proved myself years before with my business prowess?"

Alexina didn't know about his business prowess. She had never considered where her grandfather had gotten his fortune if he indeed had a fortune.

Geoffrey clinked his glass against the bottle, asking for a refill. "See here, girl. You have no experience in marketing. I do, and what I might lack, there are others at the club who can fill the need. Let me think on this overnight. Do nothing further until you hear from me."

"Grandfather, I need that money. My husband will be here in the morning to pick it up."

"Money? What does he need money for?"

"To purchase what he needs to increase his press and distiller. He will need many things." A wave of sorrow came over her.-

"Yes, of course. He will need to enlarge his processing. He will have the money tomorrow sharp. Five hundred pounds, you say? No problem."

"Then you sold my necklace?"

"Let this be up to me, girl. It will be wonderful!"

Alexina recognized the happy intoxication produced by the drink. She recalled sitting in the kitchen with Molly, Dutch, and Sissy disposing of the unwanted samples of Eden's Joy, feeling silly and happy, and the world had become so amusing. Perhaps a glass would suit her right now. But she didn't want a false elation, for when the effect wore away, she would still be unwanted by the man she loved.

"It's late, Grandfather. My accommodations are across town, and I must be on my way."

"I'll get a cab for you."

She thought about her limited funds. "I can walk."

"Absolutely not." He went outside to flag a cab. When one stopped, Geoffrey took out his wallet and removed a bill. He handed it to the driver. "Take her to—"

"Cross and Randolph," Alexina said and stepped carefully into the small rig.

Arriving at the Woodleigh House, gas street lights cast a soft glow, but not enough to dispel the gloom from the darkened structure. Alexina climbed the slippery back stairs.

After entering, Alexina made her way to the small chamber by way of the service stairs and the back hall. She didn't know where the lights were, so she ran her hand down the wall as she tried to remember how to access the room. Finding the brass knob on the door, she walked carefully and felt the carpetbag near the bed. Feeling around the hard surface of the bedside table, she recognized the touch of metal and matches close by. The light of the match made it easy to turn the key and touch the fire to the gas lamp. The room illuminated in the yellow light. She was alone, and every creak and rattle frightened her. Adding coal to the fireplace, she briefly thought of Peyton and wondered if he shared a barn and what he had eaten. She got into bed, pulled the blanket up to her chin, and took four cleansing breaths, the way the headmistress had instructed the teachers when they encountered bad-tempered or edgy children. *Unfortunately, we weren't taught how to handle fractious husbands.* She turned over and went to sleep.

Chapter Sixty-Five

In the morning, Peyton consulted his list and found Pemberton had taken him to the proper address, the home of Geoffrey Downing. He rang the bell.

A woman answered. "May I help you, sir?"

He disliked confrontations of any sort but found his business voice. "Mr. Downing, please. Peyton Woodleigh calling."

He wondered if Alexina was in earshot. If so, he toyed with the notion of apologizing for his behavior. Perhaps he could explain his ire against staying at Woodleigh House.

The lady opened the door wide to admit him. "Yes, sir, Mr. Downing expects you. Please follow me." She led him into the parlor. "Wait here."

Within minutes Geoffrey Downing approached him, hand out to shake. "I'm Geoffrey Downing, Mr. Woodleigh. So very glad to make your acquaintance."

Peyton nodded, his way of returning the greeting. He did not enjoy meeting anyone of society, but this man seemed genial.

Geoffrey looked about. "Where is my beloved girl? Does she wait outside?" He pulled the draperies aside to see the shiny smart rig still parked in front.

"No, sir," Peyton thrust his hands into the pockets of his suit pants. "I thought she might be here."

Geoffrey shook his head. "I've not had the pleasure of her sweet company since dinner last evening. But you aren't here for idle chatter. Here." He pushed a leather wallet into Peyton's hand. "This is what our dear girl has ordered. I'm so looking forward to this new and glorious enterprise. So be off to your assigned tasks, as I am to mine. Best of day to you, young Mr. Woodleigh."

Perplexed by the commentary, Peyton stuffed the wallet into his back pocket and returned to the cab, still trying to sort out the meaning of the old man's words. He consulted his notes and found nothing regarding Mr. Downing being involved. The old gentleman had just given him a fortune in cash with barely a how-to-do, fulfilling the number one task on Alexina's carefully crafted list. He read the number two task, which stated he should go to the next address and purchase fifteen glass decanters. He gave the directions to Pemberton, who coaxed Silverton into a jaunty clip.

Chapter Sixty-Six

At Woodleigh House, Alexina washed with the water in the china pitcher she had set by the fireplace. She located the cesspit, and to her disdain, emptied her own pot and slop bowl. Peering out the small window gave her a view of the stables. Surprisingly, Pemberton was closing the door. She considered running to stop him, but with the hallway and service stairs, there was not enough time. Plus, remembering her list, she knew he would be on his way to pick Peyton up for the assigned tasks. Having to share the rig became nearly impossible since they were not together. She would have to decide whether to spend her allotted funds on breakfast or a cab to her grandfather's. She had planned on taking breakfast at the Woodleigh House. Her well-laid plans had met with major snags. *All because….* It did no good to pin blame. She needed to work around the obstruction.

Finished with the hairbrush and a quick check in the small mirror sitting on the dresser, she picked up her basket. She would choose a cab over breakfast. Twenty minutes later, she sat in her grandfather's parlor to wait. The sounds of stomping on the doormat heralded his arrival. She rushed to the front door.

"Hello, my dear. Best of the morning. Come, come. We've much to do."

"Good morning," she said, placing a kiss on his forehead. "Did you get the money, Grandfather?"

"I did, indeed, and gave it to that stalwart lad. I expected you to be with him, but here you are. Your man said he has taken lodging at an inn called the Toad and Pond." Geoffrey pulled at his chin, looked aside, and bit his lip. "I certainly hope that young man belonged to you!"

Alexina put her hand to her mouth. She hadn't had the chance to introduce Peyton. Things seemed to be spiraling down into a ruinous chasm.

"Forgive me, Grandfather, for the breach of etiquette."

He peered deep into her eyes. "Not to worry. I think I see. You and your young man have had a spat."

Alexina let out the breath she had been unconsciously holding. *A spat. If only that were the case.* "Yes, a spat."

"Well, then. I know well of those matters." Turning his head to the painting over the fireplace, he chuckled. "We had our spats, didn't we, my angel?" He returned his attention to Alexina. "Ah, scrapping with the one who has your heart. Not to worry. Great awards can be derived from the part that follows. I speak of the reconciliation. And, if you're not already familiar with the process, you will soon find the joys to be gained from its occupation. So, take cheer, the darker the conflict, the sweeter the resolution!" He turned. "Eh, sweet Abigail? Why, I regularly vexed you just so I could take you in my arms and plead my apologies…to which you would flee into the bedchamber. Once I had gained entrance, I would cuddle you, and…." He turned back to Alexina. "Right, then." Geoffrey Downing removed his coat and hat from the hall tree. "Time to see some folks." He escorted Alexina out the door and down the steps and waved for a cab.

Inside the cab, Alexina thought about Peyton. *The Toad and Pond?* Her jaw grew tight. *He can't afford an inn. And I didn't give him money for food. I expected to share the coach, too. And now I have to decide whether I will buy food or take a cab, and he takes a room at an inn!* That five hundred pounds had to cover the purchases on the list. Only a little of that was to be used for food. What a mess. *Now I'm here in a cab with my half-mad grandfather.* Perhaps she could sell more jewelry. "Grandfather! I have things to do this morning. I must be about to make appointments."

Geoffrey patted her hand. "You must leave this to me. But it's fair to tell you of my plans. As soon as I sent your man—"

"Peyton," Alexina said.

"Indeed, Peyton. After I dispatched him with the money, I ran to the club to reserve the meeting hall for next Saturday night."

"Why?"

"For our banquet, of course."

"Grandfather, we have no funds for that sort of thing. I have figured this plan down to the pence, and as it is, I might have to—"

"Tut, tut, girl. Hush, listen and learn the ways of commerce. I've reserved the hall and hired a caterer. Your young man...Peyton. Uhm, yes, that's it, Peyton. Or was it you who mentioned he'd be buying fifteen glass decanters for the presentation of your samples of Eden's Joy? Excellent move, by the way. Now, we must make haste to the printers for the invitations."

"Invitations?"

"Yes, girl. Keep up. Invitations to our banquet, where we will not only present you and, uh, what's his name...?"

Alexina shot her grandfather an annoyed glare.

"Peyton," he added. "To the proper people. But where was I? Oh, yes, we will introduce Eden's Joy."

"Grandfather."

"If I know anything in the world of business, it's who to pitch what to, you see. And most of these right people belong to my club, and those who don't won't be let into this investment opportunity. See?"

Alexina put her face in her hands.

Geoffrey took her hands away and held her face by her chin. His voice became soothing. "There, there. Not to worry. Your old Gran is hell-bent, you see, chafing at the bit. Just give me my head, girl. Let this stallion, albeit long in the tooth, fly. We'll finish first for the big win. Won't you trust me?" He thumped his chest. "Listen to your heart."

Granny's words surfaced in her memory. "Yes, dear Grandfather. I will trust you." She sat back in the seat of the cab and tried to relax. *How much worse can this get anyway?*

In ten minutes, they entered the print shop. Geoffrey gave the printer exact directions and insisted the invitations be ready by ten the next morning. Back in the cab, he told her the next stop was to be the silversmith. Upon arrival, Alexina recognized the name, Green Brothers, that she had seen on the embezzled invoices MacAdams had given her.

In the showroom, Geoffrey ordered bottle neck chains in sterling attached to an oval pendant. On the pendant, he ordered engraved block lettering saying "Applewood Estate," and below that in large script "Eden's Joy."

"For the decanters," he explained. He turned to the salesman. "These are to be ready by Thursday, at five. Understand?" After the salesman promised, Geoffrey took her by the hand. "To luncheon."

She agreed, for she had not eaten but a single crust of bread she found that morning left in the basket Sissy had given them. She didn't mind that it was hard and stale, and anything for lunch would be a feast.

Grandfather Geoffrey selected a restaurant near a small park—fortunately, the same park where Alexina had arranged to meet Hester later that afternoon. At the conclusion of the meal, she bid Geoffrey goodbye with the promise to return to the house later that day.

The park was a short walk away, and when she arrived, Hester waited on a bench near a large tree. She bounded up and greeted Alexina with a tight squeeze.

"Hester, how wonderfully good to see you."

"Lexy, superb friend. I can't tell you how I've looked forward to this day." Hester hugged Alexina and stood back. "What can be the matter? You aren't well. I can see it. Are you ill? Tell me this instant." She took Alexina's arm and led her to the bench. "Here. Sit. Let the sun shine on your sweet face."

Alexina sat and turned her head away from her friend.

"Lexy!"

"I'm not ill but have much on my mind. I wish to thank you for your efforts. Please know I couldn't have gotten this far without you." Since the dinner on the first day of the travel, where she felt her life had become so hostile, Alexina found solace and comfort in this warm and sympathetic woman.

"You can count on me. I don't like the strain I see on your face."

"Please," Alexina said. "Let us talk of other things." She felt vulnerable at that moment and feared if Hester pried even the smallest amount, the result would be disastrous.

"Right, then," Hester said. A wide grin spread on her face. "You have been wed these many months, and you have written me many letters. Do you not recall our pact regarding wedded ladies? Lexy! You have divulged nothing of the information we sought so earnestly. Enlighten me before I shake it out of you."

It was more than Alexina could bear. She put her hands up to her face.

"Lexy?"

"I know what happens. But I have not experienced the event."

"Not experienced? Your letters said—"

"That I liked living in the valley and the people there were kind to me. And that I cared for my husband. But.... Oh, Hester!" She began to sob. "He doesn't care for me. I thought he did, but I saw it because I wanted it to be so. I am not his wife in the eyes of God."

"Lexy," Hester said in a breathy tone. "What happened?"

"He only married me to keep his land."

"What does that mean?"

"His father left the property to him on the condition he marry by age twenty-five."

"I've never heard of such a thing. When a father dies, the oldest son inherits. Simple."

Alexina sat up and wiped her eyes with a linen hanky. She considered the comment. "That is how I've always heard a man inherits. I don't understand."

"There may be some circumstances when a person is gifted assets with conditions, but not an estate. We should consult my brother, a solicitor."

"But the contract?"

"A marriage contract has nothing to do with inheriting real estate. Or I don't think so."

Alexina bit her bottom lip. "Peyton doesn't pay attention to finances or writing letters or things involving legal matters. He focuses on his farm, the animals, and the produce."

Hester made a face. "Obviously, he doesn't focus on his wife."

Alexina wiped her eyes. "Imagine if he found out the marriage had nothing to do with keeping his property. It's almost amusing. He did not want a wife."

"But you aren't his wife if you haven't…."

Chapter Sixty-Seven

When the cab stopped, Peyton compared the name in the window with his list. The location of the Haversham Glass Company was exactly where it should be. Catalogue page in hand, he entered the store and showed what he wanted to the salesman. Luckily there were fifteen of the decanters in stock, and within a half hour, the items were being wrapped in brown paper. Peyton and the salesman stowed three boxes with his purchases in the roomy boot of the rig.

The next stop took him to a store which sold many things, including cork stoppers. He showed that clerk the picture on the catalogue page, displaying a cork affixed to a metal stopper with a cut glass faceted knob. Trying the stopper with his just-purchased decanter and finding a perfect seal, Peyton ordered fifteen. Within a short time, he stored that package next to the decanters.

His three chores—the money, the decanters, and the stoppers—had been accomplished in a short time. He dismissed Pemberton, admonishing him against using the rig for hire, and returned to the Toad and Pond for the midday meal.

He ate, barely noticing the food. Although tasty, he missed the food from Applewood. In his room, he paced, not relishing being cooped up in the confines of the four walls. Fresh air! That's what he needed. He hurried from his room and picked up a swift pace as he walked the streets of London.

He spread his arms over his head with a feeling of freedom. His injuries had been a long time healing from the fire, and now his vitality had returned. He breathed in a full measure of air and then coughed, remembering that London's atmosphere was not conducive to large inhales. As he marched, he reflected on the last months, all of the changes and events.

Things had been just the way he had wanted in his valley. Then, that addle-brained mouse of a man, Smith, had come bringing the contract—oddly, just in time to save his property from confiscation. Confiscation? He wished he had paid more attention to the study of legal aspects. In school, he had focused on engineering. He had long put out the notion of having brothers—he knew he had them, stepbrothers, anyway. Inheritance—he should know about those things. Every once in a while, a bubble of memory would surface from his early childhood, but only a shred, not enough for a full memory. He had hidden like a turtle pulled into a shell, happily devoid of any family encumbrance, there in Applewood. Then, *she* came. His life turned upside down. Stone House, the building, made of stone walls and reed roof, had been transformed into a home, complete with elegant furniture and fancy china.

The Wanderers had embraced her fully. Granny, the one who all looked up to, had endorsed Alexina. Did that mean Granny had been taken in?

The more Peyton thought about it, the more he questioned his conduct. He knew of all people in the world Granny would not be fooled. Had he been mistaken to accuse Alexina of wrong-doing? After all, had he actually spoken of his loathing for his mother and all people of high birth? He had barely conversed with her at all as soon as he started reading the materiel she had given him, especially after he read the book on grafting. His every waking minute had been devoted to the orchard. And hadn't she made the syrup which created Eden's Joy, that noble elixir of flavor certain to restore his lost fortune? He believed the special drink would bring his account back to the amount he had so hard won and accumulated to increase production and pay the Applewood workers. He laughed in a moment of revulsion, thinking he agreed to take money from the very people he despised, the high society of London, to restore that which he had lost by his own apathy.

But even so, didn't she turn on him after they rented the cab? He had seen looks like that and the tone of her voice. Yes, he had experienced both from the woman who bore him. The title caught in his throat. Her, his mother, who had cut him straight to his heart with her coldness and treated him as if he didn't exist. But Alexina wasn't like his mother. As he walked, he weighed her goodness against the things he had stacked against her. He pictured that lonely bed in the inn, the one big enough for two. Remembering her softness, the smell of her skin, the lovely face. And hadn't she taken such good care of him while he recovered from his injuries? Her shortcomings had far been exceeded by her virtues. He must find her and beg forgiveness. At that moment, he realized he had given his heart.

Striding onward, he reached a park. Across the minor expanse through the trees, his eye stopped on a bench occupied by two women. One sat tall, and the other was Alexina.

Here was his opportunity! He picked up speed approaching her. As he did, Alexina put her hands to her face and broke down in sobs. Impulse made him run to her aid, but as he got closer, the words between the sobs made him stop.

"I can't go back to Applewood, Hester. I just can't."

He ducked behind the nearby tree.

Hester put her arm around Alexina. "If you don't want to go back to that valley, then you shan't."

Peyton watched the woman slide her arm around Alexina.

"I can't bear to see you like this, my precious friend. We shall visit my brother. He can help you obtain an annulment."

"Annulment?"

"Surely you've thought of that if you don't wish to return to his estate."

Alexina wiped her eyes and struggled to speak. "I would have no way to pay your brother since I've given all my assets as dowry. I have nothing."

"We can work on that, too. I don't know that much about the law, but there must be something we can do to free you from your husband and retrieve your goods."

"I wonder if my stipend of one hundred pounds a year is considered his."

Peyton pulled back behind the tree. *I didn't know Alexina had a stipend. One hundred pounds a year? That's where she got the money to pay off the merchants in Kerrstead. But it is hers, as I wish for nothing, nothing but her.* He leaned forward to hear more of the conversation.

"All questions to ask my brother Bob. What about staying with your grandfather?"

"I don't know. It's not possible right now. He hasn't a place for me."

"Listen, you must not fret. I will ask regarding positions of governess or teacher."

"No one will hire me if I am wed."

"We must start on the annulment immediately."

"I don't know, Hester. Allow me to complete my tasks here in London. I can't think properly at the moment."

"I understand. Let me do whatever I can to help you."

Alexina sighed. "As always, Hester."

As Alexina sobbed, Peyton couldn't make out her words, but he had heard enough. She would not return with him and would annul their marriage. Could he blame her? He had been beastly. He turned over the words she had said to him, how he had been unkind to her. He walked back through the park stiff, feeling disemboweled, empty. He had given his heart. Would he be able to get it back?

Chapter Sixty-Eight

Alexina wiped her eyes and took a cleansing breath. "I must think about what to do, Hester. This is a decision which shouldn't be made in haste." *How can I leave the one I love?*

The conversation lapsed into descriptions of the Greenfield School by Hester, and accounts of the valley and the Wanderers by Alexina, until the sun hung low in the sky.

"I must return to the school, my friend. It was difficult to get the day off, and I had to promise the headmistress I'd be back before dark. We wouldn't want to set a precedent for the other teachers now, wanting time away and all that!"

They both laughed at the idea of setting bad examples for the other teachers. Alexina managed a tiny smile. "If the headmistress knew of our mischief!"

Hester rolled her eyes. "Then I'd be bereft of employment."

Alexina dabbed at her nose with her hanky. "Grandfather expects me to return. I am so glad to have seen you, Hester."

Hester hugged Alexina and brushed back a stray wisp of hair. "Let me know what you wish to do. Bob and I are at your service."

"Thank you. Hester, I can't stay here in London. I will return to Applewood."

"You love him, don't you?"

Alexina hung her head, then nodded. "No matter how I fight against it."

"You must listen to your heart."

That is what Granny said. If I listen, will my heart be broken further?

"Hester, will you visit me?"

"I will. I look forward to it. But if you have a change of mind, you know I will do all I can to assist you."

They parted. Alexina didn't mind the long walk back to Academy Street. It gave her time to think. She loved Peyton, and there was no way to stop it. She would return with him to Applewood, her home. She would still have Molly, Sissy, Dutch, and Little Jim. Perhaps Peyton would learn to tolerate her if she could stay out of his way. What a life! But better than a life without him at all.

By the time she reached the house, she had control of her feelings. Geoffrey, all smiles, welcomed her and whisked her away for supper.

After a grand meal, Alexina tapped her napkin to the corners of her mouth. "Grandfather, I don't wish to abuse your generosity. I mean, all these meals—"

"What? You don't enjoy my company?"

"Of course, I do. It's just that—"

"Please don't deny me this time with you, the one relative in the world who…." He groped for words.

She finished the sentence. "Who loves, admires, and respects you."

"Yes. That's it. Allow this old man to spoil you. After all, I only have this week with you, and to my advantage, you are having a spat with him…."

"Peyton," she added with a sigh.

"I haven't forgotten his name. Let's not talk about that, my dear. We'll talk about tomorrow morning. Get here early. We'll dine first and then be back to await the invitations. Ho, ho, pity them if they made any mistakes. They won't. I've used them before, but…. Where was I going with that? Oh, yes, then we'll see about what you will wear."

"Wear?"

"This is a formal affair. My granddaughter is being presented, and—"

"Grandfather. I'm wed." *Oh, the perfect irony of it all. Where were you when I needed to be presented?* She closed her eyes hard. *Where the eligible bachelors would have examined me like a prized horse and made their hollow advances to woo me? Would I have found someone to love then?* She thought back to the first time she'd seen Peyton. She knew his face from her dreams, the imaginings of a young woman who pictured the future with the ideal mate.

"I know," Geoffrey continued. "But I need a reason to host an elaborate affair, after which we will give decanters of your Eden's Joy as a gift. Then those who taste it will beat down your door to have it, to which you will seem surprised at their request and just not know anything about commerce. You will put hand to head, proclaim your aversion to crass money matters, and say they should consult your aged, dotty grandfather for information."

A smile formed, one so powerful that all of the unpleasantness of the past few days vanished. Then she laughed aloud. "You old rascal, you!"

Geoffrey pushed the seat back with his feet and hopped up from his seat at the table, where he did a formal bow. "Rascal Grandfather, at your service!"

The effects of his cleverness stayed with her in the cab Geoffrey hailed to take her to Woodleigh House, where the dark and somber building once again underscored her loneliness. She made her way up the steep back iron stairs to the back door and on to the dim rooms of the basement.

In the morning, she arose and looked out the small chamber window to see Pemberton opening the wide door on one side of the stable. He led Silverton to the carriage, and to Alexina's satisfaction, he carefully hitched the horse to the rig. *Peyton would approve.* A moment of anguish pulsed through her—almost her first thought of the day regarded Peyton. His face had been in her mind as she fell asleep the night before. *First in the morning, last at night.*

She thought about the tasks for the day. Peyton would need the cab. She could hire her own ride because Grandfather had invited her for breakfast. *Bless the old gentleman. He has been so helpful and attentive.* Was he different, or had she not appreciated him in the past? Making way from the back of Woodleigh House to the front curb, she hailed a cab.

During the rhythmic clip-clop ride, she wondered what her life would have been like had she stayed there after her mother's death. Ignace Smith had urged her to leave her grandfather, claiming his madness might escalate into something dangerous. What foolishness. She had done her grandfather a disservice in leaving him. *But isn't that part of Fate? Which road to travel? How can we know the right path until we look back on our footsteps*? At the Greenfield School, she'd met Hester, her marvelous friend. Then, her shoulders sagged into a sigh. *I might not have gone to Applewood and met those wonderful people and him.*

Being practical and not wishing to dwell on her recent troubles, she focused on the errands of the day. Hers had changed drastically, but Peyton's remained the same. Today he would be visiting a company that made brass valves and spigots the men at Applewood needed to use for fermentation and distillation. She had provided catalogue pages with drawings of various parts but left the selection up to him—that is, within a price range. Perhaps he would find the parts to suit him and have a few pounds left over. *Left over for what? Separate rooms on the trip back?* There she was again, whining about her situation. That just wouldn't do, and she upbraided herself for the folly.

This morning Geoffrey waited on the front porch for her arrival. His hat, coat, and walking stick in hand, he used the same cab she sat in and took her to dine. Alexina felt a bit guilty allowing him to lavish meals on her, but he continued to insist the favor had been his, that nothing could be better than a lonely man breaking bread with a lovely companion.

After the meal, they returned to find the messenger with the invitations waiting in the parlor. The engraved papers delighted her, as they exceeded her expectations. The elegantly designed invitations stated: *Mr. Geoffrey Downing requests the pleasure of your company this Saturday night at 8:00 p.m. at the Greek Club Dining Hall on Main Street, with the intent of introducing his granddaughter and her husband, Mr. and Mrs. Peyton Woodleigh, on their first visit to London since their marriage. Please R.S.V.P.*

Alexina could barely contain her sadness. A wedding reception in her honor. A sham reception, like the marriage she had entered. *Stop dwelling on unpleasantness.* She looked at Geoffrey with the question of "What next?"

"You have a good hand, my dear. Use my list of fifteen possible guests, and we will send them off post haste."

Alexina used Geoffrey's desk after tidying it for a space and addressed the envelopes. There had been a few extras, and she addressed one to Peyton at the Toad and Pond. In his envelope, she included a note.

As you can see, my grandfather has arranged for a reception in our honor. This dinner will provide the opportunity to present Eden's Joy. Please send the carriage for me at six-thirty.

Geoffrey gave the messenger the box containing the invitations and sent him on his way. Alexina put Peyton's envelope into her basket, wishing to see the Toad and Pond for herself.

"Now," Geoffrey said. "I'm not in any way an expert in ladies' fashion, but I know it's imperative if you want to make money, you must appear not to need it. Therefore, shall we check the trunks of clothes to find the most elegant gown?"

Alexina and Geoffrey entered the room that had once been hers, empty except for three large chests. Alexina remembered how full it had once been with the furniture that now graced Stone House. After going through the trunks, a coral-colored silk dress stood out among the rest.

Geoffrey pulled it from the others and held it up. "There! I remember your mother wearing this. I always liked how the color shimmered in the light. It will be perfect for you."

"I don't think I can fit into it, Grandfather. I've changed a bit, you see." She reflected silently on how her bosom had been pushed out from the tightness of her other dresses.

He pulled at his chin. "I'll ask Mrs. Pribble. She might know someone who can help."

Within minutes, Mrs. Pribble recommended two ladies who not only could alter the bodice but who were experienced with hair dressing and cosmetics. Geoffrey sent the housekeeper out to hire them immediately.

"Things are happening fast, Grandfather."

"Yes, yes, the way they should be. You can tell when a good plan is coming together by the speed in which things occur." He patted her hand. "Trust me, girl."

Alexina felt comforted with the words. She did trust him.

An hour later, Mrs. Pribble returned with two young women. They went to work immediately. Alexina tried on the lovely silk dress that shimmered various colors of orange and coral as the light caressed the fabric. They couldn't lace the back because, as Alexina suspected, the bosom of her mother's dress did not fit.

"Not to worry," the first young woman named Angel said. "What do you think, Chloe?"

"Plenty of seam room," Cloe said. "We can let it out in the bust. Hand me that chalk."

Cloe made marks along the seams that ran down from the scooped neckline to the point of the waist. There, now we can change the seams, and it will fit you perfectly. Let's talk about your hair."

"My hair?"

"You can't go to a formal event with your hair pulled back in a ribbon, now can you?"

Alexina hadn't thought about that. She hadn't attended formal affairs as an adult—that is, elevated to the status as available after being presented to society. During her mother's illness, Alexina stayed at home. Relegated to the rank of probable old maid and hidden behind the walls of the Greenfield School, she had had few social encounters requiring her to dress in the manner challenging her now.

Angel put her hand to her mouth, thinking. "Mr. Downing said to spare no expense. Silk orange blossoms right here?" Angel put her fingers above Alexina's ears.

"And long curls. We'll bring the hot iron and start early," Cloe added.

"Early?" Alexina looked from Cloe to Angel. "What do you mean?"

"Mr. Downing has hired us to dress you, which includes fixing your hair. We know the latest styles, and you are so pretty it will be a pleasure rather than work!"

Chapter Sixty-Nine

"Chloe, look!" Angel held a mass of coral silk. "I found this mantle in the trunk. It matches the dress, and if we removed the white lining, we have enough to change the skirt." She smiled. "Oh, Mrs. Woodleigh, we can make you a dress like no other. May we use this to remake your gown?"

Alexina had other things on her mind, and the fuss over the dress and hairstyles puzzled her. "Of course," she said. *Gowns? Silk flowers? Spare no expense? What is Grandfather getting me into?*

Angel and Chloe stood in rapt attention, obviously waiting for Alexina's excitement regarding the work they would perform for her. She wished she could muster the intense joy these two ladies shared in their ability to produce beauty.

Alexina nodded and managed a smile. "I can't wait to see the dress."

"You will be thrilled," Angel said.

If the man I love won't care, it means nothing. But she fake-smiled and said, "Exquisite."

"We will call early Saturday afternoon," Chloe said.

Alexina needed to dress at Woodleigh House, where she had unpacked her things. She gave them the address and asked them to knock on the back door of the house, where she would be. Hesitating, she did not explain why they couldn't knock on the front door.

The dressing experts departed, chattering about seams, threads, and hems, their hands and arms in full animation. Mrs. Pribble had been caught up in the cheeriness and sang in the kitchen as she did her work. With contagious excitement, Grandfather buzzed about the upcoming dinner and how important it would be to their success.

"Alexina, my dear." Geoffrey pulled a faded pink velvet box from his jacket pocket and opened it. "Here, you must wear this."

Sitting regally in its velvety channel, a diamond, ruby, and sapphire necklace sparkled in the muted lighting.

"Grandfather! That is the necklace I asked you to sell. Where did you get the five hundred pounds you gave Peyton?"

"Tosh, girl! You don't need to sell jewelry. Jewels are meant to be worn. You shall wear this and declare your wealth." He snapped the box shut and pushed it into her hands.

I am not wealthy. Alexina closed her eyes. *I have to choose between eating and taking a cab to travel across town.*

Geoffrey took her by the arm toward the front door. "Here now, let's dine early this evening. Afterwards, I have much to do at the club."

Alexina didn't protest. She needed the time to find The Toad and Pond to deliver the invitation. She hoped it wouldn't be too far away from Woodleigh House.

They dined at a small restaurant that served an excellent salmon. After the meal, Grandfather waved down a cab. He gave the driver money.

"You know," Geoffrey said as he held the door for Alexina, "With all this stimulation, I swear I feel twenty years younger. I'll walk to the club. It's only a mile or so. Here now, give your old granddad a kiss goodbye."

You've never asked for a farewell kiss before. She kissed his whiskery cheek.

"Ah, nothing like a kiss from a beautiful woman." He pulled at his chin. "Well, perhaps there are a few things better than a kiss."

"Grandfather!"

"Forgive an old fool, but I haven't felt so good since I can't remember. Now," he said, checking his watch, "tomorrow we have a busy schedule. Oh, and dress up." He waited for her to get into the rig, turned, and walked away with a brisk step, twirling his walking stick.

It made her laugh. *Even if he is half mad, at least he is enjoying himself. Each day is a mystery. Good or bad, we do not know what will happen next.*

"Where to, miss?" the cabbie asked.

"Do you know the Toad and Pond?"

"The inn? Indeed, I do. Is that where you wish to go?"

"Yes, please. And then, would you be able to take me to Cross and Randolph Street?"

"The gentleman paid me so well, miss. We can go across town twice!"

Alexina relaxed on the leather seat. Her thoughts came in a flood of visions. She pictured the Greenfield School, the trip to Eversham with Daisy, who constantly sniveled, and then meeting pathetic Rufus. She rankled at the memory of his warning about Peyton. What did he say? He thought she would languish in the valley, and he would rescue her from that barbarian. Alexina's throat closed as she choked on mental words. *He was right, but I love that barbarian.*

She banished those thoughts and concentrated on the vision of the lush valley and the wonderful people there. She wished Molly was sitting beside her. Molly would have something to say to make the situation better. And Granny…didn't she predict the trip? *Although not easy, I'd find success in many quarters? What else? Oh, yes. I should listen to my heart because the heart knows the truth.* She had already given her trust to Grandfather based on what Granny said.

Her thoughts came to a halt when the cab stopped. The driver jumped from his perch and opened the door. "Toad and Pond, miss."

Alexina stood for a moment, taking in the compact, three-story structure built in the Tudor fashion with white plaster between dark beams. "Please wait."

She entered through the massive oak door. Light filtered from the irregular paned windows. Food aromas blended with the smell of ales and smoke, combined with the low sounds of people enjoying their surroundings.

"Help you, miss?" a man said from behind the bar.

"Yes. Is Mr. Woodleigh here?"

"Yes, he has a room." The man looked at the ceiling, a reflex indicating rooms on the upper floors. "But he's not about right now, miss. He's just left."

"Oh." She reached into her basket and pushed aside the soft velvet box to grasp the envelope. "Would you see he gets this?"

He took the letter. "Of course."

After having another glance around the room, she returned to the cab.

That inn is nice. Where did Peyton get the money to stay there? He does have five hundred pounds. She shook her head, knowing his honor. He wouldn't take what wasn't his.

The London traffic had doubled since she left Grandfather, and rain threatened. Pulled between avoiding traffic and hours of loneliness in the dungeon of Woodleigh House, she gave the address of Cross and Randolph.

When the cab left her at Woodleigh House, she trod the iron steps of the back. Her mood and the weather made the place more solitary, somber than before. She inserted the key into the lock and felt the tumblers give. Should she return to Grandfather's? The notion of leaving didn't make sense. All of her things were here, and it would cause more bother than good. The whinny from the stable startled her. That meant the buggy and Silverton had been put up for the night. *But the barkeep said Peyton had gone out. On foot?* It was no matter. She had no control over his choices. She hoped he was sticking to the list.

Closing the back door, she remembered the shelf near the entry and found the matches to light the small whale oil lamp that would take her down the dark hallway and stairs to her room.

In the morning, she dressed in her best as Grandfather had asked and tread the outside iron steps. Pemberton led Silverton from the stable.

He tipped his hat. "Good morning, Mrs. Woodleigh. I hope you are well."

"I am, thank you. I return the wish. Would you be able to take me to Academy Street right now without discommoding Mr. Woodleigh?"

"Of course. Mr. Woodleigh does not specify a time for me. I wait for him in the back of the inn until he summons me."

Today Peyton is supposed to select and order the copper vats. "Mr. Pemberton, do you recall where you went yesterday?"

"Certainly. I drove Mr. Woodleigh to the All Parts Emporium near St. Katherine's docks. We had quite the time locating the place because it turned out to be more of a warehouse than an actual store."

Good. The Parts Emporium for valves and fittings is precisely where he was to go. He is sticking to the schedule.

Pemberton shook his head. "Abominable parking facility. The wagons and delivery carts flew by within inches of the carriage."

"Without incident, I hope."

"No damage was done." Pemberton patted Silverton's neck. "Good horse, this." He stroked down the horse's flank. "Other horses would have become unruly having to wait so close to the road for such a long time, but this one kept calm. I wonder if Mr. Woodleigh would consider selling."

"Mr. Woodleigh stayed for a long time in the establishment?"

"He did, madame. About the horse—"

"You'd have to ask Mr. Woodleigh, but…." She thought about Peyton's attachment to Dragon and Silverton. Then a moment of sadness took over. *If only he could develop such an attachment to me.* "I doubt he'd sell this animal. It means too much to him."

"Yes, madame. I believe Mr. Woodleigh knows what quality he possesses." Pemberton winked at her and nodded. He turned to the horse and backed Silverton into the traces.

When Alexina reached Grandfather's, the smells of breakfast promised ham and fresh baked bread. She eagerly gave her basket and cloak to Mrs. Pribble in the foyer.

At the dining room table, Grandfather Geoffrey folded his newspaper. "Ah, my dear. I waited to take breakfast with you. I hope you haven't eaten."

"Thank you, Grandfather. I'd love to share breakfast."

After their meal, Geoffrey hired an open carriage for the day and, passing through the Queen's Gate, they took a leisurely ride through Hyde Park, slowing to admire the boating on the Serpentine. They followed the lake until they reached Kensington Gardens.

Geoffrey leaned back on the horsehair upholstery. "Ah, I remember taking my lovely Abby to Rotten Row at every opportunity. How she came to love me has ever been a mystery to me, but I wanted the world to see my good fortune." His eyes watered then cleared. "You can't appreciate what your visit means to me. You have brought back many pleasant memories. A man shouldn't wallow in his miseries, and I had allowed myself to fall into that abyss."

Alexina took a long look at the man next to her. He seemed younger than she remembered. He couldn't have been more than sixty, yet she had always thought of him as doddering and aged. She believed his claim that she had energized and diverted him from his otherwise solitary and dim existence.

"I'm pleased to bring some happiness to you, Grandfather." *Even if you remain somewhat dotty.*

They toured for the rest of the morning. A light tinkling emanating from the gold pocket watch in his vest pocket elicited new directions from Geoffrey to the driver.

The carriage stopped in front of a huge palace-like house, where various buggies and rigs lined the drive and surrounding road. A footman decked out in dark blue and gold let them out.

At the entrance, a crimson-coated doorman took their hats

and coverings and led them to another servant, dressed in sage green velvet. Grandfather presented his calling card, and the man led them through high-ceiling chambers, where sweet strains of violins echoed from the hall.

Alexina halted to stop the clacks from her wooden heels. "Ah. Vivaldi! One of my favorites. Oh, Grandfather," she whispered, smiling. "You've brought me to a concert. Thank you."

Geoffrey pulled at his chin. "Uhm, yes...brought you. I'll just be there," he pointed to another doorway, "in the billiards room."

"Grandfather?"

"Enjoy," he said, picking up his step toward the other part of the mansion.

"I will," she answered softly. The servant opened the carved white doors to admit her to the conservatory, where a group of musicians with various stringed instruments played beautifully.

All seats were occupied with the exception of two, on either side of an old man who held a brass horn to his ear. She slipped into the seat left of the gentleman. The reason for the empty seats revealed itself after a few minutes. If she closed her eyes, the smell conjured the feeling of being next to wet sheep. In addition, the crumpled handkerchief dangling from his sleeve frequently came from its lodging to receive a huge amount of congestion from the codger's nose. Every so often, the neighbor would look at her and smile, displaying a set of ill-fitting ivory teeth. As he spread his lips, an extraordinary musty funk emanated. She pulled a handkerchief from her reticule and covered her own nose as delicately as she could, trying hard not to be insulting to the unfortunate man. As soon as the musicians took an intermission, she nodded to the old fellow and fled.

Looking around the room, she saw a group of people vacating their seats, no doubt proceeding to the buffet in the adjacent room. She hurried to fill one of the empty seats, thinking she would eat during the next intermission.

As soon as she sat, a young man rushed to the plush chair next to her. He wore a fine suit with lace bristling from the lapel and sleeves. His hair slicked back with Makassar oil, reflected the gas lighting glowing from the heavy crystal chandeliers and matching wall sconces. He smelled of spice and lilacs.

"As I live and breathe!" The young man raised his eyebrows and smiled. "If it isn't the lovely and enchanting Alexina Poole."

"I'm afraid I'm at a disadvantage, sir."

"The disadvantage belongs to me. You purely broke my heart, you know."

"I? Broke your heart?"

"You don't remember me?" He put his hand to his chest as if in pain. "But I can't have changed that much since we met at the Culver's Estate and then again at the May House in Leeds."

"I have been at both of those homes, but—"

"You must recall *me*," he said, annoyed. "For I certainly remember you. I told Mother the first time I laid eyes upon you that you were the one for me. Of course, your age at the time prevented me from proclaiming my heartfelt declarations, but I told Mother I'd wait and be the first beau to vie for your attention." He stood and bowed. "I present myself, once again. Harold Tennet." He pronounced his last name as French, sounding like *Tenay*.

She remembered him but mentally heard the name ending in the English mode, *Tenn-et*. "Yes, I do recall meeting you, Mr. uhm, Ten...."

"Tenay," he prompted, "From my ancestors in Normandy. But they are of no matter. Miss Poole! I waited for your coming out. But instead, you disappeared."

"My mother became ill."

"Such a shame, your absence. Absolutely devastating. A genuine blow to me." He dropped his head dramatically. Then he sneered. "Look at her." He pointed across the room to a rounded, red-cheeked young woman, strikingly unattractive. "Your disappearance doomed me to wed Hildegarde Stump." He sat down hard, and his shoulders sagged. "As much wealth as you, maybe more, but certainly not your equal in beauty and grace."

Alexina did not know how to respond.

"And you?" he asked, his dark eyes staring into hers.

"I have wed, as well." She looked around, searching for a polite means of escape.

A blue-velvet clad servant brought a tray of champagne. Harold seized two and handed one to Alexina. She took it, considering the glass as less a beverage and more of an anchor, mooring her to the seat.

"That doesn't matter." He took a sip.

"What doesn't matter?"

"Indeed, the fact we have attachments simplifies things."

"What things?"

"Come, come now. I do not wish to boast, but I can't help but know my own appearance. And I have certain skills of which I could boast but won't."

Alexina took a long sip and looked away from the annoying braggart. He cleared his throat for her attention. When she turned back to him, he held an unusual walking stick. The tan wood tapered to the floor ending in a silver tip. Letting go of the handle exposed a bizarre carving. As she examined the stick, he slowly tipped it to make the handle appear to arise from his trouser closure.

"I have pleased many of the women in this very audience. I would be delighted to please you." He laughed.

It took a few seconds for her to recognize the carving. She took in a quick breath.

He grinned at her reaction. "This handle is an exact replica of my endowment. The sculptor, a talented lady, enjoyed her work. Shocking, no? I love the look on the faces of my proposed lovers when they realize what I am offering."

Alexina stood and dashed the remains of her champagne in his face. "Shocked? Oh my, yes. I am shocked that you would think that toothpick would please any woman, even, as you claim, many of the ladies in this very audience. Why would I want a twig when I have my own tree trunk?"

Harold Tennet twitched, sending droplets of wine from his face into the air. Mouth agape, he let go of the stick, which fell clattering on the stone tiles. Hildegarde waddled hastily to her husband. Many people had heard Alexina's comment and held their hands to their mouths. The room echoed with laughter and twittering commentaries.

Alexina bolted from the conservatory and into the billiards room. Geoffrey saw her immediately and dropped the cue on the green felt. He rushed to her.

"You feel unwell?"

"Remarkably unwell. We need to go, Grandfather." Alexina cast her eyes to the floor and bit her lip. "I have shamed you. I'm so sorry."

"I'm sure you haven't done any such thing."

By the time they reached the front, the doorman already held their garments, and as they descended the steps, the carriage clopped down the road toward them.

In the seat, Alexina held her hands to her face. "I have said something terrible."

Geoffrey laughed. "I'd love to hear it, my dear."

She related the scenario, and when she got to the toothpick remark, Geoffrey threw his head back and laughed until he grabbed his sides.

"You find this amusing?"

"Amusing does not describe it. First, you must know that gold-digging popinjay surely needed to be put in his place. My pride that you achieved it goes beyond measure. Here now, listen to me. The unfortunate fact that you weren't presented may have saved you from that weasel. French, indeed. I knew his grandfather. Welsh, he was, and not a bad sort, but couldn't keep money in his pocket. The poor fool. Anyone who wished to could rob him with a few words. The family had almost nothing by the time that young idiot came around. Since he was whelped, his mother has been trying to find him a rich wife. He would have pursued you for your wealth."

"My wealth? You mean the hundred pounds yearly stipend you have allotted me?"

"I've not allotted you anything."

"You are my closest male relative. You have control over what my father left."

"I'm not your closest relative. Part of your money comes from your Uncle Simon. And I'll wager it's more like one hundred pounds a day."

"Uncle Simon? A hundred pounds a day? Oh, Grandfather, I thought you felt better. I mean…well, today seems to be a day for truths. I thought you weren't having delusions."

"I may have a delusion or two, but not about Simon Poole. However, seeing how your mother hated him, it comes as no surprise she wouldn't have told you about him."

Alexina shook her head and looked away.

"My dear granddaughter! Your disbelief crushes me. You have granted surcease of the promise I made to your mother, remember?"

Alexina sniffed. "I remember.

"Then, allow me to inform you of Simon Poole."

Chapter Seventy

Peyton had spent most of the day at the copper factory. Wagons filled with sheet copper brought in from Wales and Cornwall made deep grooves in the graveled drive as Silverton labored toward the loading platform. Even though he had come to choose multiple vats for distilling the apple juice, the formation and construction of the copper equipment fascinated his engineering interests. After choosing five vats, all with tight-fitting lids and brass accessories to ship to Applewood, he spent hours watching the workmen ply their trade hammering, bending, and welding the soft metal. The heat from the welding forge warmed the entire factory.

When he had satisfied his curiosity with the copper fabrication and concluded his business, Peyton had the rest of the late afternoon free. Even in the cool weather, the stink from the human sewage floating on the Thames persuaded him to ask Pemberton to take the long way back to the inn.

After making a stop at a bookseller, he dismissed Pemberton and settled in his room to read. His thoughts wandered to the image of Woodleigh House. Pemberton had told him Alexina had been there that morning, but the house seemed uninhabited, meaning each evening when Pemberton brought the carriage to the stable, the only light came from one basement window, and no smoke chugged out of the chimneys when he arrived to get the horse and carriage in the morning.

Peyton closed the book and put on his boots. Since he had arrived in London, the only exertion he tendered involved climbing in and out of a carriage and the fateful walk in the park. *I should be doing something worthwhile.* Standing at the leaded pane window, he watched a woodman below split logs for the inn's fireplace and stove. As the woodsman loaded split firewood into the bin, Peyton wished he could have a few axe swings at some tree trunks. He would be glad when he returned to Applewood. Except she would not be returning with him. *What can I do about that?* He paced the room, feeling confined. He needed to walk outside. And think.

His steps came hard and fast as he advanced on the sidewalks. The memory of Alexina in the park troubled him. The word *annulment* continued to ring in his ears. He crossed the busy afternoon street, dodging buggies and cabs, heading in the direction of Academy Street. When he arrived at Geoffrey Downing's house, Peyton banged the lion's head knocker a number of times, but no one answered. He stomped his foot on the doorstep and walked the few miles back to the Toad and Pond. He stopped at the bar to order an ale.

Ike pulled the long ceramic handle dispensing the golden brew. "How about some baked pheasant? A hunter brought them in this afternoon."

Peyton nodded. Although he didn't feel the hunger, he recognized the complaints from his growling stomach demanding supper. He hadn't eaten since early afternoon when Pemberton stopped at a street vendor to buy meat pies.

Along with the steaming dish, Ike laid an envelope next to the glass. "Here's a message for you, Peyton. A really pretty lady came looking for you. I didn't see you until now to deliver it."

Peyton read the invitation and reread it. *Why would she wish me to attend a reception given in our honor if she plans to seek an annulment?* He folded the envelope and pushed it into his vest pocket.

Chapter Seventy-One

"Your father had a twin named Simon. And more different two men could not possibly be. I admired Alexander for his kind disposition, keen mind, and clean lifestyle. Simon, although not an unpleasant sort, lived life on the edge. He was handsome and dashing, but the man needed constant excitement. He found it in gambling, horseracing, swordplay, and pursuing ladies. Some men didn't take lightly to losing, whether it be in cards or love. One sorry specimen, after losing his money, found out his fiancée had fallen for Simon. That man called for a duel, which he lost, as well. The family claimed Simon murdered the fellow."

"Murder? Dueling is not murder."

"Oh, it is when a peer claims it to be. Simon had to flee. He came to your father in the middle of the night, asking for money to leave the country. Alexander hid his brother and gathered all he could, then came to me. We had to be careful because agents watched the most logical places Simon Poole would be. After a few days, we got him passage to Australia. Your father extracted a promise from his brother. Should he die and Simon inherit, he would make sure your mother and you had access to the entire estate, all funds. Ignace attended the legal papers, and as far as I know, he administers it still."

"Grandfather, I don't understand."

"The only thing you need to understand is that bandit has full control over Simon's estate, truly yours by legal arrangement. I made the promise to your mother not to ask questions and interfere, meaning I had no right to know any information. When your father died, your mother, by way of Ignace, had access to what she needed. Instead of informing you, she entrusted that blackguard with the management. When she died, you didn't know what Simon provided you or information about your father's estate. Simon wrote me after moving from Australia to the United States, where he went into the commerce of river steamboats. His letter to me said he had made a fortune, and since he had no children, he made it all available to you. Although I don't know for sure what your father left, I would wager the amount was immense. Therefore, you have two fortunes."

Oh, Grandfather. I wish all you are saying could be true, but Mother would have told me something of this. Alexina had never heard the name Simon Poole or anything about wealth or fortune. *I never know when the irrational side of you will take over. Fortunes, indeed.*

"So, my dear, how about an early dinner?"

"Thank you, Grandfather. I'm afraid I didn't get to eat at the concert."

Geoffrey laughed. "You may not have ingested anything, but I imagine Monsieur Tennet," he chuckled at the mixture of French and English, "is getting a real mouthful of trouble from that German Frau of his!"

"Please, I don't wish to think about that horrid event."

"You'll laugh about it in years to come. Mark my words, girl. You have my blood in your veins. Now let's get the juiciest joint of beef we can find, with roasted parsnips and Yorkshire pudding." He patted her hand. "There's two things in life sure to pull someone out of a funk. The second one is good food."

Alexina could not help the smile that formed. One could never describe Grandfather as predictable. That word conjured thoughts of Peyton, another unpredictable man. *The two men in my life whom I love. Is that the reason I love them so?* A nagging notion pricked at her. *I definitely should pay Ignace a visit as soon as possible.*

Chapter Seventy-Two

Peyton sat on the chair facing the window of his room. He checked the list Alexina had given him, making sure he was on schedule. Tomorrow he would buy tubing, glass beakers, and measuring equipment. He had time this afternoon to accomplish tomorrow's tasks, but he didn't want to stray from the directive, and the list said to wait until tomorrow.

Although comfortable, the room confined him, and he still had a few hours of light left. A long walk appealed to him. He acknowledged Ike as he left the inn.

Once again, the thick, fetid air of London assaulted his nose. Out on the street, he pulled his collar up against a fine misty rain. His long strides helped to clear his mind. He didn't pay attention to where he walked until he realized he was on Randolph Street, within a few blocks of Woodleigh house. He paused, not wanting to go near the place.

It is just a house. He put his hands in his pockets and picked up his gait. When he reached the back of the house, he stopped and stared at it. Pemberton was correct. It looked unattended. No smoke belched from the chimneys, no clothes hung behind the stables, and all the windows were dark except for one in the basement. Alexina had said the household would be leaving. One of the servants must have stayed.

He would have walked on, but Silverton snorted from inside the stable. Peyton lifted the oak bar on the side entrance. The horse whinnied a greeting, inviting Peyton to stroke the sleek neck. As he spoke low words and patted down the animal's flank, he nodded with satisfaction at Pemberton's care. As an additional bit of affection, he poured an extra ration of oats into the manger. Resting on a bale of hay, Peyton took out the invitation given him and read the words again. Ike said a pretty lady had come looking for him, which surely meant Alexina had brought the invitation. She could have given it to Pemberton, but she brought it personally. And that reception? He didn't understand any of it. What he did understand was that he had treated her so wretchedly she wished to obtain an annulment.

He folded the paper and slid it into his pocket. However, distracted about the reception, the paper did not reach its destination but fell against the back wheel of the carriage. After giving Silverton another neck stroke, he returned to the inn. The rain changed from a mist to light drops, making him speed his step.

Chapter Seventy-Three

In the basement room, Alexina sat near the small window attempting to write. Having no proper surface, she used a wooden box from the large wardrobe that sat against the back wall. Balancing the box on her knees, she held the ink bottle with one hand and wrote with the other. Something made a noise near the stable, but her precarious position with the ink bottle prevented her from looking out the window until she finished the note. As the ink dried, she returned the box to the wardrobe, underneath a pile of men's clothing. The clothes fell as she moved them. She carefully refolded the man's suit and arranged the interior as she'd found it.

Alexina put the note in her pocket and made her way to the back door. She was glad she brought her umbrella because the narrow overhang of the back step barely kept the light rain away. She grasped the handrail and, holding up her skirt, cautiously climbed down the iron steps.

Lifting the bar of the stable's side door, she entered. Silverton chewed with noisy snorts. *Odd. Pemberton had put the horse away and fed him before I arrived.*

Alexina moved to the rear of the carriage and lifted the boot lid. Two casks lay under the canvas. She checked the note in her pocket, ensuring the words had not smeared from the rain. *Mr. Pemberton, please bring the box with decanters and the stoppers to the house on Academy Street at your earliest convenience. Also, please take the two casks into the house. Thank you, A. Woodleigh.* She placed the message on the driver's perch.

As she moved away from the carriage, she noticed something

near the back wheel, a folded paper. Picking it up, she recognized the invitation she had sent to Peyton. A lump formed in her throat. *Thrown on the floor?* Her shoulders sagged as she put the paper in her pocket.

The dreary rain on the iron stairs and dark house made the world gray. Back in the sparse room, she dressed in her nightgown and added coal to the fireplace.

Sounds by the stable woke her in the morning. The muted light from the window indicated the rain had not abated. She was glad she had left the note the night before. As she selected her clothes, she thought about what she and Grandfather would be doing that day. Because of the rain, she had to wait a long time before an empty cab passed the road. Her small umbrella barely covered her, and she feared the contents of her fan-shaped basket would get wet.

When she arrived at the house on Academy Street, Pemberton had already delivered the box of decanters and casks. In addition, the silversmith had delivered the engraved medallions.

After breakfast, she, Geoffrey, and Mrs. Pribble set up an assembly line. Mrs. Pribble used a funnel to pour the ruby liquid into the decanters, Grandfather Geoffrey topped them securely with the stoppers, and Alexina attached the chains with the medallions engraved with *Applewood Estate, Eden's Joy*.

After the bottles were completed, all three enjoyed a glass. Mrs. Pribble proclaimed the drink as the finest spirits she had ever tasted.

"You see, my dear granddaughter. Everyone will demand the brandy. Ah! The fame!"

Alexina suggested Geoffrey fill his own decanter with some of the leftover Eden's Joy. He happily promised to empty one of his port bottles that very afternoon and said he'd keep the casks there until Pemberton could retrieve them.

She left him to hail a cab to the headquarters of Ignace Smith. The front clerk tried to dismiss her, saying the full appointment schedule prevented an audience, but with unusual bravado, she walked past the clerk and into his office.

Ignace, with a tiny white ring of hair surrounding a large shiny bald patch, looked up from his work and frowned. Quickly the frown turned into a smile. "Alexina! I had no idea you were here in town."

"Peyton and I have business in London."

"I see. How remarkably well you look. Have a seat, dear girl. What can I do for you?"

She placed her slender basket next to the desk, sat in the chair, put her hands on her lap, and said, "Simon Poole."

Ignace's eyes widened, but only for a moment. "What about Simon Poole?"

She didn't respond but let the silence oblige him to explain.

"Ahem." He pulled at his necktie, then smiled again. "I imagine that fool Downing has spoken out of turn. That man! Poor little Alexina, having to deal with a lunatic."

Alexina remained quiet, her hands unmoving.

"What have you heard?" Ignace drummed his fingers on the desktop.

"Simon Poole is my uncle."

"That is true. But you would be far better off not knowing about him. Your sainted mother kept this knowledge from you for a good reason. But I will tell you. The man is a criminal. If he sets foot in England, he will most certainly be hanged. He fled to Australia, leaving debt and unhappiness with your family."

"He is my closest living relative, I believe."

"I wouldn't be too proud of that, my dear. In fact, you would be serving yourself a kindness to forget you ever heard of the villain."

"You have no contact with him?"

"Of course not. Why should I? And if I did, I would surely inform the authorities of his whereabouts."

"My yearly stipend?"

"Comes from a small trust left by your father." He rose from his seat and bent over to make eye contact. "Alexina, you must rely upon me to see to your interests."

He pulled her hand to urge her from the seat, a not so subtle way of closing the conversation. As he stepped closer, he brushed her basket, overturning it.

"Pardon me," he said and squatted to pick up the items. He reached for the pink velvet box.

Alexina did not miss the recognition in his face. His fingers closed around the case. He didn't touch another item but rose to a standing position and allowed her to restore the rest of the fallen items into the basket. She put out her hand to receive that which he held, but his fingers remained tight around the velvet box. "My box, if you please."

The hesitation in his manner bordered on rudeness.

"Ignace."

He let out a breath, and with a longing look at the piece, handed it to her. He looked away. "You are in London for an extended stay?"

"We leave Saturday morning."

"I see."

Chapter Seventy-Four

Alexina rose early enough on Friday morning to ask Pemberton to drive her to Geoffrey's house.

The driver tipped his hat. "Best of the morning, Mrs. Woodleigh. Can I be of service?"

"Yes. If it doesn't affect Mr. Woodleigh's schedule, I need to go to Mr. Downing's house."

"No worries, madame." He held the door."

She took her place on the seat. "Tomorrow evening—" she began.

"Mr. Woodleigh informed me I'm to arrive at 7:30 to pick you up here, at the Randolph Street House. Has there been a change?"

"No. That will be fine. Thank you." She couldn't ask him, a coachman, if her husband would be attending.

At Academy Street, Mrs. Pribble showed her to the parlor, where Geoffrey waited.

"Ah, things are coming together nicely, Alexina, dear. All invitees have responded, and only one will not attend. That means fourteen influential men with their ladies will sup at our table. Quite a crowd. Let's see, that makes twenty-eight, plus you, me, and…uhm—"

"Peyton," she said.

He laughed. "Got you! I know his name. I love to tease you." He cast a look across the room to the fireplace. "Remember how I teased *you*, my sweet Abby?"

Alexina silently praised Mrs. Pribble's timing as she brought in a tray of coffee and rolls, preventing a further conversation between her grandfather and his wife's painting.

"Today," he took a sip from his cup, "I'll confer with the caterer for last minute arrangements. I'm meeting him at the club." He nibbled at the sweet roll. "Then we shall do a little shopping. Would you like to accompany me?"

"Shopping? Doesn't Mrs. Pribble see to your needs?"

"Not for me! As you are in the big city, wouldn't you like to visit a fabric store, select a new bonnet, or browse a place that sells do-dads for fine ladies? I pretended not to enjoy shopping with Abby, but in fact, I did relish watching her intensely study hair ribbons or shoe buckles and such. Now I have this opportunity to do it again with you. We can go to Covent Gardens and order flowers for the banquet! Yes, of course. I forgot to do that." He pulled his chin. "Although perhaps the caterer takes care of that. Hmmm."

"We can ask the caterer when we see him this morning, Grandfather. And as for the shopping, I don't need anything. You know I live on a—" She didn't know how to describe Applewood. A valley? A farm? An orchard? Estate? According to the bottle medallions, it was a luxurious estate. "We don't entertain much, Grandfather. I don't need to buy anything, truly."

"Tut, tut, there. I insist, young lady. First, our dealings with the caterer, and then down to business with the shopkeepers—as many as we can work into an afternoon. Now eat well." He tapped the plate Mrs. Downing put in front of him and pointed to hers. "You'll need the energy to keep up with me. Geoffrey Downing prepares for the hunt! Ah, something amuses you, my dear."

"You, dear old man," she said, smiling. "Will you visit me in Applewood?"

"I will, indeed."

When they arrived at the club, a doorman ushered Alexina into the ladies' area, a paneled room with soft leather chairs and palm trees in large pots. Being a men's club, ladies stayed sequestered for the rare times one would chance a visit. In a few minutes, an attendant knocked and led Alexina down a long hall, which opened into a banquet area. The room smelled of cigars and the rich scent of the many meals consumed within the walls. An intense-looking man dressed in a silk business suit talked with Geoffrey as she approached.

"Alexina, meet Randolph Rawls, the caterer." Geoffrey turned. "This is my granddaughter, Alexina Woodleigh. The reception is in her honor."

Mr. Rawls bowed stiffly. "Woodleigh, a fine name to be sure, madame. I have the pleasure to make your acquaintance. Allow me to present you the menu." He handed her a paper showing the courses and selections.

Alexina paled at the list. "Excuse us for a moment, Mr. Rawls." She pulled Geoffrey aside. "Grandfather, these dishes are so expensive. I'll—"

"Worry not, sweet thing. I have already paid. We want this venture to—"

"I do not want to build a huge debt to you. We must tell Mr. Rawls—"

"Not another word, my pet. Trust me?"

They returned to Mr. Rawls, who had examined the table in their absence. "You approve, Mrs. Woodleigh? Can you think of something I need to add?"

"It looks marvelous."

"Rawls, what about flowers for the table?" Geoffrey said.

"We will decorate completely. Leave everything to us. We cater royal events, Mr. Downing. Rest assured, all will be seen to."

"Splendid. I will send fourteen decanters of special liquor tomorrow afternoon. Take utmost care with them, Rawls."

"We give utmost care to the smallest detail, sir."

Alexina believed he did.

"Very good. Come now, my dear one. The hunt is afoot!"

Alexina struggled to prevent Geoffrey from buying everything he saw. During their afternoon of shopping, she allowed him to buy her a bonnet, a new umbrella, a few embroidered handkerchiefs, and a pair of silver buckles for her black leather shoes. On their way back to Academy Street, her thoughts strayed to Peyton. Had he found all of the parts listed on the schedule? What was he doing at the moment?

Chapter Seventy-Five

At the store that sold the tubing, Peyton didn't find what he wanted. He looked at all of the offerings, but none suited the other items he'd ordered. The proprietor said he could obtain what Peyton wanted early on Sunday morning. He chose fittings and tools and other small items, things he could bring back to Applewood in the carriage. By early afternoon, except for the tubing, he had completed his tasks for the day.

Back in the carriage, Pemberton said he needed to pick up the casks at the Downing house. Peyton jumped at the chance to go. Perhaps Alexina would be there, and he could talk to her. He wasn't sure of what he would say, but he didn't want to return to Applewood alone. Would an apology be enough?

When they reached the house on Academy Street, Peyton sighed when Mrs. Pribble let them into an empty house. The decanters, resplendent in their cut glass-topped stoppers and the silver medallions proclaiming the Applewood pedigree, amazed him.

Peyton lifted the casks, one empty, another with a bit of the brandy. Ike had been so generous he would give some of this to him. Perhaps a glass of Eden's Joy would help his own mood, too. Happiness in a cup, Seat had called it. Peyton could use some happiness right now.

Back at the inn, Ike served baked fish. At the first bite, Peyton longed for the ugly pink jumping fish from his valley. He remembered how much Alexina enjoyed the dish and hoped he could do something to ensure she would be able to eat it regularly. In his room, a tall glass of the lovely colored drink brought him a bit of relief. He relaxed on the bed and thought about tomorrow evening's reception. He would get to see her. But then, what had she planned to tell him? He poured another glass of Eden's Joy and took comfort from it.

Chapter Seventy-Six

Alexina looked forward to her breakfast with Grandfather. The mornings with him had brought her enjoyment and a new understanding of the old man. The trip to London had not been what she had hoped for regarding her relationship with Peyton, but this new bond with Grandfather presented an unexpected gift.

"Tonight!" Geoffrey said. "Our big presentation. You will feel the pride of a successful venture, young lady. Exhilarating. Addictive!"

"I look forward to it, as well. I must be at Woodleigh House by two o'clock so the dressing ladies can work their magic on me."

"Magic? You need none. What a stunner you turned out to be, although you have always been comely, even as a small child. When you and your mother came to live here, I wished to have more of a hand in your upbringing, but Edwina wouldn't let me close to you. I blame that reprobate Smith for that. Alexander and I got on well. He didn't like Smith, either, but your mother, unfortunately, inherited my stubborn streak. And frankly, Alex couldn't say no to her any more than I could deny a single wish of Abigail's. When he died in that explosion—"

"You mean the mine collapse?"

"No collapse, Alexina." His voice became serious "Witness accounts clearly indicate an explosion. In fact, since the mine operated as an open pit, how could something that had no overhead collapse? The miners dug for gems in a river bed, richly endowed with precious stones. Alex described his work to me at length. Someone, a competitor perhaps, knew Alex would be there and blew up the mine. Foul play, my dear. But the Indian authorities, British miscreants, had been bought off to change the reports. Your mother refused my help in trying to find those responsible."

"Grandfather, I've heard nothing regarding this."

"Of course, you didn't. You know only what Edwina wished you to know. And I'm sure that bastard—er, excuse me, dear girl—that scoundrel Smith manipulated her every move."

Alexina had developed her own misgivings about Smith.

"Granddaughter," Geoffrey's voice once again became serious. "Would you allow me to investigate some matters on your behalf?"

At first, Alexina suspected the mad portion of the man's brain had spoken, but the clarity of his eyes and the set of his jaw convinced her he had his full faculties. "Do what you think might be helpful, Grandfather."

"Well done, my girl! Leave it to me. I'll have things on the straight path for you and your young man." He chuckled. "Peyton."

Geoffrey stood and brushed a few wayward crumbs from his vest. "I have work to do." He kissed Alexina's forehead. "I will see you tonight, my sweet girl. We will conquer London with my savvy and Applewood's recipe."

Geoffrey Downing left with a deliberate stride and a stature that seemed to Alexina to be a few inches higher.

She returned to Woodleigh House. At precisely two o'clock, according to the small mantle clock, she heard the clatter of a vehicle outside. She rushed to the top of the iron staircase and hailed Chloe and Angel, who struggled with multiple bags and a large box.

Alexina led the two workers of magic down the inside service steps and into the room.

Chloe swiveled her head, examining the room. "Rather small. Isn't this a maid's quarters?"

Alexina had dreaded explaining her accommodations and gathered her words. "I'm here alone, you see."

"You don't have a personal maid?" Chloe asked.

"No, my maid—"

Angel tapped Chloe's shoulder. "Of course. If she had a maid, she wouldn't need us. Don't you see? Being alone in the house, she'd have to worry about all the rooms, keeping them warm, lighting the lights, and all the things a maid would do. Selecting the smallest room in the house makes perfect sense."

"Brilliant, Mrs. Woodleigh," Chloe agreed.

Alexina breathed relief. *Why hadn't I thought of that?* Actually, it did make sense. What would she have done if she had the responsibility for the whole house without help? The maid's room had been comfortable and cozy. Good for one person. She hoped they wouldn't inquire why they had used the back entrance.

Chloe and Angel sorted their devices and instruments as if major surgery were to commence. A metal tray went into the fireplace to hold the curling rods. Angel opened a case of pots containing colored cosmetics and placed it on the dresser by the door. She removed an assortment of brushes and puffs from the case. Alexina waited on the bed as the women unfolded, arranged, and prepared their tools.

"Now," Chloe said. "Ready to see your dress?" She opened the box and removed the shimmering peachy satin creation.

Alexina took a breath. It was the most beautiful gown she'd ever seen. Its full skirt glistened in the light from the window. They had redesigned the bodice with puffy sleeves and a dropped neckline. She couldn't imagine them making such a change in the few days they'd had, especially the middle panel of the bodice, now radiating the soft sheen of pearls sewn in a swirl pattern. The matching lace formerly edging the cloak now edged the sleeves and shoulders.

Angel and Chloe grinned at Alexina's response.

"You truly are magicians! How can I thank you for your work?"

"Mr. Downing has thanked us generously, Mrs. Woodleigh. But more so does your delight."

Alexina allowed the two artists to fuss and groom. She didn't complain when they scrubbed her scalp and rinsed with a sweet-smelling tonic. Using a bellows-like apparatus, they partially dried her hair, then pulled locks and tightly wound them around the warm iron rods to finish the drying. With each long curl, they used an atomizer to fix the tress into a stiff cylinder. Pins secured silk flowers and tiny decorations.

As they worked, thunder heralded a rainstorm, and the room darkened.

"More light," Chloe demanded.

Angel turned up the whale oil lamp on the bedside table.

When her hairstyle satisfied the two ladies, they started on the make-up. In her youth, Alexina had experimented with a bit of her mother's cheek rouge, but that had been her only initiation to cosmetics. Chloe picked at Alexina's eyebrows with tweezers and then held up a mirror. For the slight difference, Alexina didn't think it was worth the amount of pain. But she sat quietly and let Chloe and Angel work.

They powdered, smudged, and brushed. When at last they proclaimed her face a success, Alexina looked in the mirror. For all of their labor, she didn't look painted and said so.

"Ah, you see," Chloe said. "That is precisely our skill. However, truth be told, you don't really need much at all. We are perfecting that which is almost perfect."

They all laughed and took a short break.

After a few minutes, Angel shook the crinolines to their fluffy best and helped Alexina step into them. Then Chloe carefully spread the gleaming silk skirt. They gently lifted it over Alexina's coiffed hair and fastened it. The pearl studded bodice came next, and as they pulled the laces in the back, Alexina wondered if she would be able to consume dinner safely.

Alexina unfastened the small pendant and gave the magicians the pink velvet box. Both Chloe and Angel gasped when they saw the gemstone necklace and matching earrings. Alexina had not paid much attention to the jewelry. She had been comfortable with what she usually wore, the small pendant, her mother's wedding ring, and unobtrusive earrings.

"Just like a princess," Chloe said. "You'd better hope Queen Victoria doesn't see you. You might be sent to the tower!"

The little mantel clock chimed six. Chloe and Angel busily collected their wares as Alexina plastered herself against the large wardrobe to stay out of their way. Within fifteen minutes, they had packed and were ready to depart. Both ladies gave Alexina a kiss on her cheek for good luck.

"Thank you so much for your good work," Alexina said, holding the bedroom door.

"Don't see us out, Mrs. Woodleigh," Angel demanded. "You don't want to catch your skirt on the steps. Oh, I do hope it stops raining. There are puddles everywhere. Mind the water. Have a wonderful evening."

Alexina looked at her new umbrella and thought it had been a good purchase, for the rain increased. Large drops pelted the window and the roof of the stable.

A few minutes after six-thirty, a carriage stopped on the side street. She picked up her reticule and the umbrella. At the rear vestibule, she opened the door and spied the carriage. Rain hammered down on Pemberton and Silverton. She turned to lock the back door, and when she finished, she spotted Peyton exiting the carriage dressed in the suit she'd bought him in Kerrstead. He stepped a few feet from the rig, his eyes riveted on her. As he stared, a Landau raced toward him, sending a tall sheet of mud and water cascading over Peyton and the carriage. When the water subsided, Peyton stood drenched with rivulets of dirty water streaming down his body.

"Peyton!" She grabbed the rail and put her foot on the first iron step.

"No! Stay there," he commanded.

She stepped back under the overhang. "Come up. We can dry your clothes."

He hesitated, then proceeded toward the stairway.

Chapter Seventy-Seven

Peyton took the drenched iron steps two at a time, reaching the landing before Alexina had unlocked the back door. Mud and rain dripped from him. As she held the door, he hesitated, looking at her skirt and then to his sodden clothing.

She pulled her skirt aside. "Come with me. We have to get you dry."

He followed her down the hall but stopped where the hall diverged, one way leading to the kitchen and the other to the service steps. Peyton gave her a quizzical look when she lit the small lamp at the stairwell. As she headed down the stairs, he followed. In the basement hallway, she held the lamp high for better illumination and walked to the last room.

"Why are we going in here?"

"It's the room your mother allowed me to use."

The light showed his face turning into a scowl. "The maid's quarters? That bitch."

"I don't mind." She reflected on Chloe's comments. "In fact, I prefer it here. Now you must get out of those clothes."

Alexina took a towel from the washstand. She moved closer, ready to touch the towel to his face and hair, remembering the day she had dried him in the stable. He had enjoyed it, but the look on his face now had no vestige of pleasure, and she wouldn't risk provoking him. Besides, if she touched him, she feared she would throw her arms around him and beg him to love her. Stiffening her spine, she handed him the towel.

Turning away, she bit her lip. She could tell by the moving

shadows he'd begun his own drying. She looked in the wardrobe for something, perhaps a larger cloth, to use when the small towel was saturated. In the wardrobe were bed linens and the man's clothing she had folded a few days before.

"I've found something." She took the garments from the shelf, turned, then pulled in a quick breath. He had stripped down to his unders. A bit of moisture glistened on the silky hair of his chest. Shadows from the lamp accentuated his muscles. She put the clothing on the bed and searched the dresser for the clothes brush.

"I'll brush these things while you finish drying."

Without making eye contact, she handed him the brushed trousers. With each item, she kept her gaze unfocused to maintain her dignity. Her resolve was worn very thin when it came to Peyton.

Alexina checked the wardrobe again and found shoes and silk socks. "Perhaps these will fit." First, she brushed the leather and worked the bristles into the silver buckles. She put them on the floor and went back to the wardrobe. A wooden box stored a top hat, gloves, and a fine cravat. These items far surpassed the simple suit ordered from Kerrstead.

She stepped from the small room to give him dressing space. When she peeked in, she could hardly believe her eyes. The clothes and shoes fit perfectly. He couldn't have been more attractive.

Her words came out in a bare whisper. "We must hurry. We are late already."

Peyton took the lamp from the dresser and held it high as they rushed through the hallway and up the service stairs.

What little daylight remained had been foiled by the rain. Alexina fumbled through her reticule to find the keys to the back door.

Peyton held out his hand, silently offering to attend to the lock. He opened the door and took the umbrella that leaned against the wall. He held it unfurled while she stepped under its protection.

After locking up, they moved onto the first metal step. Peyton wrapped his arm firmly about her waist and helped her navigate the treacherous iron treads. She held her breath with each step, not for the danger, but because he held her so close.

When they reached the bottom of the stairs, Peyton kept his hold on her, and Alexina did not pull away.

"So sorry, Pemberton," Peyton said as they hurried to the carriage.

The footman stood stoically in the rain under a wide umbrella.

"An inescapable aspect of my trade, sir. I am accustomed to inclement weather."

Pemberton held the door as Peyton grasped Alexina's waist and almost lifted her into the seat. He hurried in behind her.

Alexina stared at the oval window in front of her, forcing her attention to the rain and the streetlights that made soft shadows inside the cab. Although they sat apart, she could still feel Peyton's touch on her waist. His touch. She must keep control. All she had left in their relationship was her dignity. The silence in the cab magnified Silverton's even clip-clop on the stone pavement.

"You look…beautiful," Peyton said.

They made eye contact.

"Thank you. You look so handsome. Those clothes—"

The rig stopped.

Pemberton opened the door. He held the expansive umbrella drivers used for passengers. "We have arrived, Mr. and Mrs. Woodleigh."

Peyton got out first and lifted Alexina from the carriage to the pavement.

"Thank you, Pemberton," Peyton said and opened his own umbrella. "That will be all for tonight."

"Very good, sir. I shall see you in the morning. Do have a pleasant evening."

With a slight push against her back, Peyton escorted Alexina up the marble steps of the Men's Club.

Chapter Seventy-Eight

The marble entry gave way to the dark wooden panels inside the building. The low hum of conversations, the smell of expensive tobaccos, and the warmth of the many fireplaces provided a friendly atmosphere.

An attendant dressed in black took Alexina's capelet and Peyton's borrowed cloak. Another man in a green uniform took the invitation from Alexina and led them down a lengthy hall to the banquet room.

One elongated table draped in white had three huge vases of cream-colored flowers regularly spaced down its length. Dishes, glassware, and silver gleamed in the lights mingling from the wall sconces, chandeliers, and fireplaces that flickered warm orange and yellow. Men and women in formal wear stood in small groups sipping their before-dinner wine.

"Ah," Grandfather Geoffrey said in a louder than normal voice. He hurried toward them. "The happy couple has arrived. Attention, everyone!"

The room went quiet.

"Ladies and gentlemen," Geoffrey said, "I present Mr. and Mrs. Peyton Woodleigh, my granddaughter Alexina and her husband." He signaled to a waiter, who brought a tray of wine.

Geoffrey gave them each a glass. "A toast! To the Woodleighs. May they visit London often!"

The guests raised their glasses and said, not quite in unison. "To the Woodleighs."

Geoffrey whispered to a servant. The man gave a quick bow

and went to the far corner, where an orchestra waited. Soon the hall rang with sweet melodic strains.

Some of the guests started to dance. Alexina recalled the feel of Peyton's touch on her waist and imagined him whisking her around the dance floor. She felt him staring at her and quickly turned to him.

"Would you—?" he began.

"My dear!" Grandfather said and came from behind her. "If this fool man has not asked you to dance, I shall." He bowed and took her hand.

As she headed for the dance floor, she glanced back at Peyton, who had the same miserable look as when the sheet of water doused him on the street. Would she ever know what he had started to say?

Geoffrey spun her around to the three-beat rhythm of a waltz. At the next opportunity, Alexina looked for Peyton in the spot she had last seen him. He was gone.

"Your man doesn't dance?"

"He can dance, Grandfather." She mentally ran through several excuses. *No. I'll not make explanations for him.* The hostilities during their trip, her encounter with Bertha Woodleigh, and the other negative events in the last week flashed in her memory. He had told her she looked beautiful. But what did that mean? He had barely spoken to her that evening, not even regarding the unfortunate circumstance of his watery accident.

When the headwaiter called the group to dinner, the guests made their way to the tables, where each setting had names on small cards.

Geoffrey took Alexina by the hand and waited for Peyton. Then he put his arm around Peyton's shoulder and spoke in a low tone. "After the meal, do not engage in conversation. Be assured you will be pressed to do so. Refer all questions to me."

Peyton nodded.

"Grandfather?" Alexina said.

"Trust me, sweet girl." He sat at the head of the table and pointed to his left, where Alexina should sit. Peyton's card put him at the other end of the table, seated at the opposite head.

The first course consisted of spiced cold tongue, pickled relishes, and two soups, turtle and potato chowder. The next course, round of beef, loin of veal, stuffed fowl, and pigeon pie, was served with potatoes, rice, and a selection of vegetables.

Alexina picked at the food. Time dragged on until dessert

appeared, ginger cake with a thick brandied cream topping, chocolate pudding, and assorted fruit pies. The apple pie caught her attention, and she accepted a piece. *Oh, Dutch, how I miss you!* This pie could not compare with the delicious compotes and pastries she had eaten at Applewood. Tilting her head around the flower arrangements, she saw Peyton taking a bite of his dessert. The look on his face after swallowing suggested he, too, missed Dutch.

When the dessert dishes and wine glasses were removed, Geoffrey rose to speak. "Ladies and gentlemen, please accept this gift."

Fourteen servants brought the lovely decanters on silver trays with wine glasses and put them in front of each couple. As the guests examined the bottles, amid tinkling and low chatter, Geoffrey spoke again.

"The beautiful liqueur you have in front of you is brandy bottled at the Woodleigh Estate, Applewood. My granddaughter and her husband send their appreciation for welcoming them to London by way of their special recipe, Eden's Joy. Shall we toast? To health, happiness, and Eden's Joy!"

Like a well-trained army, the servants unstoppered the decanters and poured the rich red fluid. The guests stood and held their glasses high. "Eden's Joy," the guests said, then drank.

The silence in the banquet room made a huge contrast to the noise of the immediate past. Then, all at once, as if planned ahead, the guests took more of their brandy, all talking at once.

Geoffrey smiled wide and winked at Alexina.

"Thank you for coming," Geoffrey said. "May God Speed."

No one left the room.

Several men left their seats and bore down on Peyton, asking simultaneous questions. Alexina could not see him for the crowd. A few minutes later, the same men crowded around Geoffrey, firing statements and queries at him.

"Mr. Woodleigh cannot deny us this wondrous brandy," one guest said.

Another man stepped in front. "Please, Geoff, talk that man into an arrangement. Does he not know what he has here?"

Geoffrey casually dusted off a few specks from his vest and pulled out his pocket watch.

Another man pushed through the throng. "That brandy. I must have it. Woodleigh won't entertain my offers. Can you talk sense into the man?"

Geoffrey turned his head and winked at Alexina. "Tut, tut, gentlemen. I'll do what I can. See me on Monday. I will have had time to talk with Mr. Woodleigh. Perhaps he will let go of a few barrels."

By then, an audience surrounded Geoffrey. Alexina looked through the crowd and saw Peyton at his seat. She was unable to read the expression on his face.

Geoffrey turned his back on the people who demanded his attention. He extended his hand to Alexina. "My dear."

With her eyes still on Peyton, she accepted Geoffrey's offer of escort. Geoffrey beckoned to Peyton. As the three left the banquet hall, several guests tagged along, still pleading to acquire Eden's Joy.

Geoffrey waved his hands in the air. "Enough, please! I'll speak with you next week. Call on me at the Club." He hurried Alexina and Peyton down the hall to the great marble entry, where coaches waited on the street. The rain had ceased, and the night was crisp and clean.

Geoffrey hailed a cab. Before he could speak to the driver, one of the guests stepped in front of Peyton.

"My carriage is just there, Mr. Woodleigh. You will be going to the Woodleigh House on Randolph and Cross, I presume? I must pass that very house and would be honored if you'd share my carriage."

Peyton looked at Alexina, who looked at her grandfather. Geoffrey shrugged. "Go. I will find my own way home." He nodded and got into the cab he had hailed.

The exquisite carriage owned by Mr. Davies glided to the steps of the club. A footman held the door for Alexina and Mrs. Davies, who sat opposite from each other. The men took their places next to the women.

The soft springs of the coach created a floating sensation, and the sturdy, satin appointed interior subdued the clop-clop of the four horses on the brick street. Alexina had a flash of memory. *I was in something just like this a long time ago. My father held me in his lap. I remember! They talked about having another child.* The brief flash wasn't enough, and she wanted to remember more. She tried to ignore Mr. Davies as he extolled the extraordinary features of Eden's Joy and his persistence in wanting to buy it.

Peyton kept his face blank. When Davies paused, Peyton said, "Speak to Mr. Downing. He acts as my agent."

Davies leaned toward Peyton. "I understand your position—that is, being a gentleman farmer, commerce does not interest you. I will most certainly call on Downing, but I insist you agree to at least giving me first bid."

"Again, sir. See Mr. Downing."

"Ah, you drive a hard bargain, Mr. Woodleigh. I have been dealing in food commodities for twenty years. I see I've met my match at negotiations. Well done, sir."

Focusing on Peyton, Alexina tried to suppress her smile. Grandfather had been correct in instructing Peyton not to discuss selling Eden's Joy. The less Peyton said the more power Grandfather had for negotiations. The trip had provided her with a new and admirable opinion of the old man.

The coach slowed and soon stopped at Woodleigh House. Peyton thanked the Davies for the congenial ride. The footman opened the plush door and helped both Peyton and Alexina out in front of the dark house.

"Oh, dear, the butler forgot to turn the lights on in the front parlor," The lie came from Alexina, smooth as silk.

Mr. Davies leaned out toward them. "Shall we accompany you in?"

Alexina told Peyton with a look to back her up.

Peyton flipped his hand. "It happens all the time. The butler is old, but we can't do without him." Peyton tipped his tall hat. "Good night."

When the footman returned to his place, the coach left. At the sounds of the retreating coach, Alexina turned to walk to the back.

Peyton took a long step and grasp her arm. "What was that about, and why don't we go in the front door?"

"For the same reason we exited from the back. I have no key to the front."

"What?"

Alexina could make out his lip curling into a snarl in the light of the street lamp. "She,"—he said the word as if it were poison— "didn't give you a key to the front door?"

"It doesn't matter. The back door has served me well. It takes just as long to get to the servant's quarters whether one uses the front or the back."

They walked on a stone path in silence to the rear of the place. Once again, he put his hand on her waist as they descended the iron treads. Alexina said a silent thank you for the fifteen steps that allowed her to feel Peyton's touch. The front had only three.

Inside, Peyton lit the small whale oil lamp and preceded her down the narrow service stairs and through the hall to the last room.

Alexina slowed her pace. Peyton was here, with her, filling the small space with the warmth of his nearness. She tensed at the thought of the cavernous and dark house without his presence. As soon as he gave up the borrowed clothes, he would leave, and she would be lonely once more.

Chapter Seventy-Nine

In the room, Peyton dumped a few bits of coal into the fireplace. Alexina turned the key to the lamp to provide more light. Shadows flickered on the chair that held Peyton's still damp suit. He pulled a small stool from the corner, sat, and removed the elegant shoes.

The full skirt of Alexina's silk dress brushed against the bed and chair. "Would you please unfasten my necklace and untie my laces?"

His eyes glinted in the firelight. He stood, unhooked the jeweled necklace, and pulled at the ribbons crisscrossing the back of her dress.

Craving his touch, she blessed the dressers for drawing the strings so tight he had to spend time to loosen them, his fingertips and knuckles brushing against her back.

"Thank you."

She removed her nightdress from the dresser drawer and stepped out into the hall to have enough room to get out of her skirt and the crinolines. As she drew her arms from the puffy sleeves of the bodice, a mixture of emotions nearly overwhelmed her. The happiness she experienced from his presence became dread at the knowledge he would soon leave. The skirt and bodice lay on the floor. The scant light from the room fell in soft beams upon the coral silk, creating an undulating bed of warmth and pleasure. The evening had come to an end, and the crumpled outfit reminded her of the other portions of her life that lie in a heap. She shook her head to dispel the desolation that hung like a dark fog. As she removed her corset, it brushed against her breasts and reminded her of his touch. When the satin pantalettes slid across her belly and down her legs, she bit her lip to not beg for his attention. She leaned her hand against the wall and took a deep breath.

Finally, she donned her nightdress and buttoned the front.

Peeking into the room, she saw Peyton, clad only in his unders, carefully folding the loaned clothing.

The door creaked as she pushed it further open. "I'll put the things back into the wardrobe like I found them." He handed her the items, and she replaced them. "Peyton...." Her fingers worried at a silk flower dangling in her hair. A long curl fell over her cheek. "I need to talk to you."

"I know," he said.

"You do?"

"I know everything. I've been dreading it all week. I thought you might wait until this night." He sat hard on the stool and sighed, letting his shoulders down.

"Pray tell me what you think you know."

"I know you aren't returning to Applewood with me. I know you no longer wish to be my wife. I know you've started annulment proceedings. And I know—"

"You know all of this?"

"Yes, but—"

The emotions left her raw. Rage flashed through her. "You think you know so much. You aggravating, unbelievably arrogant man! You don't know anything!"

Alexina stomped her bare feet on the floor planks on her way to the door. She didn't know where she was going, but it was certainly out of that room.

"I'm wrong?" Peyton asked.

She punctuated her words with her exaggerated steps. "You. Are. So. Very. Wrong."

Alexina's feet lifted from the floor, and she sailed across the short distance to land on the bed. She couldn't say a word because his lips were on hers.

Her breath caught. His hand at her nightdress released the buttons with lightning speed. The nightdress parted. He trailed his kisses to her neck and down to her breasts. She tugged at the buttons on his unders.

"Make me your wife."

He nuzzled her neck and ran his hand down her belly. "Not now."

"Peyton!"

"You're not ready."

She pressed her cheek against his. "I have been ready since the day we married."

He sat up on his knees. "Alexina—"

"Now, Peyton, before the place catches on fire, or the wind blows the roof away, or—"

"Nothing can keep me from you."

"I'm not taking the chance. Now."

Peyton parted her legs with his knees.

She ran her hand down his groin and fondled him, guiding him to her. "Peyton!"

He pushed gently. She whimpered when she felt his hardness enter her. He pushed with more force. Her tissues separated and burned from his thrust. "Oh," she cried again as he pulled out and returned. With each thrust, the pain lessened. He gave a shout, then stopped moving and placed his face next to hers. She almost cried, not from pain, but for the sheer joy of being one with him.-

They lay quietly for a few minutes.

"I'm sorry I hurt you," he whispered.

"I welcomed it."

He pressed his lips on her cheek. "My brave, beautiful girl."

"Yours, Peyton, yours."

"Mine."

"Peyton, how I love you."

He rolled over and put his arm under her shoulders. "And I have loved you ever since…."

She sat up like a shot, leaned to the nightstand, and turned the key on the lamp to its brightest. "Since when? Since when have you loved me?"

He sat up next to her. "Ever since I saw you in the carriage that first day."

"You loved me then? But why…why didn't you…? I don't understand."

He ran his hand through his dark curls. "I didn't know you, couldn't trust my feelings. I didn't want to be…."

Alexina brought her hand back in an arc and slapped his face.

"Ow! What was that for?" Peyton said.

"What you put me through!"

Alexina's other hand swung toward him, but he grabbed her wrist, stopping the blow.

"All of this time. We could have—"

"Many things we could have. I know. But here we are together. The Woodleighs, man and wife."

Alexina stared at the wall, her teeth clenched. "I don't know what to say."

"Say you love me again. Tell me you will overlook my thoughtlessness and idiocy. Can we make this night one of forgiveness? Can this be the time we start anew?"

She rested her head on his shoulder. "We will start anew. Mr. and Mrs. Woodleigh. Together and loving."

He kissed her, running the kisses along her neck, down to her breasts, then sat up sharply. "Listen!"

"What?"

He hopped from the bed and pulled on his trousers. "Someone is in the house." Bending to pull the poker from the holder, he turned his head and put his finger to his lips. He grabbed a dish with a small candle and lit the wick from the flame of the lamp. "Stay here."

Chapter Eighty

Peyton crept down the hall.

Alexina reached for her nightdress until she saw the bloody stain on it. She hurriedly pulled her robe from the dresser drawer and tied the sash as she treaded softly down the hall after the dim light marking Peyton's location and caught up with him.

He blew out the candle, and they made the last few steps in the wan light of the streetlights shining through the windows. Peyton became a blur, and within a second, a bang against the wall preceded his low words. "How dare you sneak into this house, villain!"

The shuffling noises in the darkness were muted and confused. A struck match illuminated a small area, and soon the glow of a gaslight filled the room.

"Peyton!" Alexina ran to him as he pushed the large man against the wall holding a poker against the man's neck. "It's Sam, your mother's driver. Let him go."

Bridget, still holding the match to the wall lamp, blew out the petite flame. "Faith! It's our boy! Oh, dear one. Peyton, for sure."

He dropped the poker.

Bridget spread her arms. "It's your nurse. Don't ye know me?"

After a moment, he nodded. The door opened, and Sara, the chambermaid, holding a particularly shaggy Cairn terrier, walked into the foyer. Then another person, wrapped in a cloak, walked through the front door. The cloak slipped to the floor, identifying Bertha, who held a second terrier. She let it out of her grasp and hurried to Peyton. "Clive! my love! You've come back to me. Oh, Clive!" Bertha put her hand to her bosom and collapsed.

Catching her before she hit the floor, Peyton hefted her up in his arms.

Bertha opened her eyes and mumbled weakly, "Clive?"

Peyton's face blanched. "Not your Clive, Mother. I'm your son."

She fainted, her head resting on his shoulder.

"Mrs. Bertha!" Bridget ran to her. "Here, now. Take her upstairs to her room."

Alexina joined them. "Do you have the keys?"

"Which keys?"

"She keeps her bedroom locked," Alexina said.

"Oh," Bridget sucked in her breath. "Mrs. Bertha doesn't lock her room, young Mrs. Woodleigh. She told you that just to be mean." Bridget rushed toward the staircase. "This way, Peyton. Oh, but you know that. Sara, find some brandy for the mistress."

Alexina followed them to the bottom step. "I have some brandy. I'll get it."

Peyton nodded and took the steps with Bertha in his arms.

Alexina lit the candle and rushed down the hall to the service steps. In the small room, she rifled through her carpetbag to find her bottle of Eden's Joy. She hastened back to the main hall, where Bridget waited with a tray and glasses.

"Sam," Bridget said, "why don't ye put up the coach and horses? We've got a good hold on things here." She headed up the stairs. "Come, young Mrs. Woodleigh. I think my mistress will make good use of this pretty stuff."

Alexina entered the bedroom and knew she'd been there before. The memory flash of her parent's voices in the coach came back. She heard them clearly, laughing. There once had been joy in this room, and she had been part of it. She came to the bedside where Peyton stood.

Bertha's eyes fluttered open and studied him. "My boy? Peyton?"

"Yes, Mother." He stepped away from the bed.

Bertha's voice cracked. "Come back." She held her arms out. "Please."

He eyed her. "Mother…."

Bridget brought a glass of the scarlet brandy and gave it to Peyton as Bertha struggled to sit up. Bridget beckoned to Peyton for help. Reluctantly he assisted his mother to sit as Bridget stuffed pillows at her back. He put the glass to her lips, and she sipped. Then she grabbed his forearm, pleading with her eyes. "Peyton, please. Can you ever forgive me? I've been horrid to you. All of these years...." Tears streaked her cheeks.

He turned his head to Alexina.

Alexina put her arm around his waist. "Can't we make this night one of forgiveness? Can this be the time we start anew?"

Peyton's eyebrows came together, then he dropped his head. He sat down on the bed. "Yes, this is the night we start over."

Bridget took Alexina's hand. "I think we need to go downstairs and let some of these old fences be mended. Here," she said, lifting the tray with the bottle of Eden's Joy. "We should take this with us. I'd like to taste what magic melted old Ice-Heart."

Alexina left the bedside with Bridget. As she moved away, she noticed the unlit fireplace. A likeness of Peyton hung over the mantle. But how could it be? Of course, it was a likeness of Clive Woodleigh.

Jumbled scenes from her past raced into her mind. Voices and people. She recognized that portrait of Clive. She had seen it over and over. That face, looking so much like Peyton, had been the one she had seen in her dreams and imaginings long before she came to Applewood—the face of the man she would love.

"Are ye with me, young Mrs. Woodleigh?"

"Yes, yes, Bridget. I'm coming." She quietly shut the door. Alexina ran her hand along the carved banister as they took the carpeted steps. "I didn't think you were coming back for several weeks."

"We weren't supposed to return, but the country home we visited had typhoid fever, and when we went to another estate, they had a terrible ague. T'warnt safe, them homes. When we went to a third place, they were a-vomiting a-plenty. We knew we had to come back to dirty old London. So that's why we be so late coming in. Mrs. Bertha feared we would get sick."

Sara and Sam ate sandwiches in the kitchen. Bridget and Alexina joined them. They sat at a small table where they enjoyed healthy portions of Eden's Joy.

"To lost and found love," Bridget said and held the glass high. They clinked glasses and drank. "Oh, my," Bridget said and brought the glass closer to see.

"Delicious." Sara took another sip. "What is this?"

"Fine liquor," Sam said, "But I couldn't tell you just what."

"Apple brandy," Alexina explained. "Made from the fruit grown at Applewood Estate."

"Applewood Estate?" Bridget made a face. "I don't remember any apple trees, only acres and acres of lush lawn, and that beautiful house. Here, let me have some more."

Alexina sipped her brandy. "You have been there?"

"Aye, several times, until the mistress decided to stay in London and send poor Mr. Clive up there alone. I did so love that house. How she chose this place over that one defied me."

"You think the Applewood house is nicer than this one?"

"Of course. Elegant, sophisticated, and huge. They could have had so many visitors, but as far as I can remember, no one ever visited. And Mr. Clive designed that place just for her." She pointed to the ceiling. "After he died, no one went there at all."

The room grew quiet as they nibbled the food and sipped the ruby fluid.

"Well," Sam said. "I've had a busy night. I'm turning in."

Sara stood. "As soon as I clean up, I'm going to bed."

Bridget stretched. "Right. I'm as tuckered as I can remember. I'll check on the mistress, and then I'm turning in. You should go, too, Mrs. Woodleigh."

"It's been a long night for me, as well." *The best one of my life.* The drenching accident, the banquet's success, and Peyton's lips upon hers. She was his now. Forever. "I'm ready for bed, too."

Alexina ambled toward the service steps. *I wonder what's happening upstairs with Peyton and his mother. All those years apart.* In the basement room, she left the light burning low and crawled into the small bed. *If he intends to share this bed with me, he will have to get close.* She laughed softly. *Very close.*

Alexina awoke to kisses on her shoulder.

"Good morning, Mrs. Woodleigh."

"Good morning, husband. How did you manage to slip in next to me while I slept?"

Peyton brushed away stray curls from her cheek. "You don't know how good I am. You are about to discover many of my talents." He untied the robe she had used as a nightdress and ran kisses down her neck to her shoulder.

The muted light from the window suggested the time.

She stretched gently, carefully, not to dislodge his lips. "It's dawn. Why must you be up so early?"

"I have things to take care of." He traced his finger down to her breast and followed the path with kisses.

She gasped as the sensation sent a tingle deep within. "What things?" she managed to ask.

He slid her hand down his groin. "This, for one."

She wrapped her fingers around the hardness. "Peyton, did you just make a jest?"

"This thing is serious."

"You did jest. You have a sense of humor."

"That which was lost is now found," he said. "You have restored my humor."

"Hard truth?"

"Indeed, Mrs. Woodleigh." He ran his tongue over her breast and down to her navel. "I'm afraid I left you with a misconception last night."

"How is that?"

"Love doesn't hurt. Only the first time. Let me show you."

Chapter Eighty-One

Waves of indescribable pleasure coursed through Alexina's body, washing over and over, flowing to her fingers and toes. Her moan gained momentum until it bordered on a scream. Peyton gently put his hand over her mouth. When the sensations diminished, she caught her breath. Peyton began his own seizure of moaning. He eased and lay next to her, gasped, and let out a noisy breath.

"Peyton, what just happened to me?"

He pressed his lips against her ear. "Something wonderful."

"I've never.... I, uh—"

He moved her into his embrace. "Words fail you?"

She pushed her face into his chest and nodded against the dark silken hair. Inhaling, she relished the smell of his skin. "Peyton?"

"What, my darling?"

"Do you think you'd be able to do that again?"

He chuckled. "Over and over until I die of thirst or exhaustion."

She pushed away from him and stroked her hand over his chin, feeling the slight prickle of his whiskers. "Prepare for a life frequented by near-death events."

"I shall lay down my life for you at your will, my love." He rolled on top of her. "I'm prepared to offer my life now, in fact. However," he whispered, "we should strive to be less vocal. We don't want to alarm the servants."

"I'll keep my screaming to a minimum," she promised, and then a small moan escaped her lips, for her hero had begun to lay down his life.

An hour later, Peyton left the bed and sorted through the clothes on the chair.

"Where are you going?"

He made a face and uttered a low growl. "To see Mother."

"Do tell me about your conversation. You must have been with her for a long time because I fell asleep waiting for you."

He picked up the unders.

"Peyton?"

"Let's not talk about it."

"You have made amends?"

"Do you think I can just forget the last sixteen years?"

"You and I have put our differences aside."

"You and I had difficulties due to misunderstandings, outside influences. But she—"

"Peyton. Embrace your good fortune. This trip has gained us so much."

He nodded and resumed his attention to the clothing.

Alexina left the bed. "Granny Doctor predicted all of this, you know." She traced her finger along the large pink scar that made a path into his groin. No hair grew in the still-healing track.

"Granny? What did she say?"

"She told me the way would be difficult, but I'd find success in many quarters."

Peyton looked around the room. "Like servant's quarters. Since the first day I met Granny Doctor, I've listened to her." He hung his head. "Well, not everything."

Alexina cocked her head, waiting for further explanation. *Granny must have said something about me.* "What did Granny tell you about me?"

He took her hand. "It's what she didn't say, and I should have been paying attention. It would have saved us a whole lot of trouble. Granny can't be fooled by anyone. I didn't ask her opinion, and she didn't say anything about you. But she didn't warn me, either, and she would have. How could I have been such a fool not to trust you?"

"Do you think it's time to trust your mother?"

He sighed. "Perhaps." He pulled his shirt from the chair. "I promised to see her this morning before I finish the last of the business."

"What business?"

"The tubing for the distiller. The store manager promised it would be ready this morning. I'll need Pemberton to take me if we are to keep on schedule to head home."

"We need to do that. I have just enough money to pay for the rental carriage. I'll walk to Grandfather's. It's not raining."

He shook his head. "I have a little left from what you gave me." He lifted the jacket from the chair and dug into the pocket. "Here. Take a cab."

She hugged him. "It's so nice we are working together now. I have so many questions to ask regarding the equipment you bought, and—"

"We'll have plenty of time on the return to Applewood." He kissed her forehead and pulled on his trousers. "I can't tell you how happy I am that you are returning with me." He sat on the stool and reached for his boots. "I need to get going. The trip north has taken on a new attraction for me." He finished dressing.

She walked him to the door. "I'll see you at Grandfather's. Before noon, yes?"

"Yes," he said. He kissed her until she felt like butter left too long by the stove.

After his steps faded and the hall became silent, she dressed, carefully folding and packing her two carpetbags. After a thorough check of the room, she put the pink velvet box into her slim basket. She wanted it on top, so she could get to it easily when she reached Grandfather's house.

A soft knock on the door coincided with the snapping of the bags. "Come in," she said.

Bridget creaked the door open and peeked in. "Top o' the morning, young Mrs. Woodleigh."

"Hello. I'm almost packed and leaving soon."

"Mrs. Bertha has asked you to join her in her room. She takes her morning meal there, and she would like to dine with you."

"Very well." Alexina pulled the handle of one bag.

"Sam will take those for you."

"Thank you," Alexina said, truly grateful she wouldn't have to lug them upstairs herself.

Bridget held the door. "Some night we had, eh?"

Some night and an even better morning for me. "Yes, I say we all had an interesting time." She picked up the basket.

Bridget led Alexina to Bertha Woodleigh's bedroom. The light of day shining through the large windows gave it a bright and cheery atmosphere, at once evoking a flurry of memories.

Bertha looked up as Alexina entered. "Good morning, my dear, and let me say this right now. I am so very sorry for the way I treated you at our introduction. I will never forgive myself for what I have done."

Alexina searched for words but found none.

"Come, sit by me, please," Bertha patted a chair next to her bed.

The seat showed an indentation where Alexina imagined Peyton had been.

Bridget brought a rolling cart with sweet rolls, sausages, and scotch eggs. "Coffee, young Mrs. Woodleigh?"

"Thank you. Cream and sugar, please." *Well, this time I will take your food.* The memory of the tea cart made Alexina understand how Peyton couldn't forgive so easily.

Bertha took a sip. "I have been so awful to my boy, and he is my last living relative."

Alexina nodded and chastised herself silently for agreeing.

"When he was only nine, he became ill. My husband had a fatal accident trying to find a doctor."

Bridget had told Alexina the same story.

"I blamed my boy for that accident."

Alexina wondered if Bertha would mention she lost her pregnancy because of the grief.

"He was only a child. If that wasn't enough, the fever caused him damage. He had no memory of what happened before his recovery. When he recuperated from the fever, he didn't know me." Her eyes began to water. "He reminded me so much of Clive. I couldn't bear to look at him, so I sent him to a boarding school. When I realized how much I missed him, I wrote, but he wouldn't write or answer any of my letters. We have been estranged for all that time." Bertha dabbed at her eyes. "It is you, young woman, who has brought him back to me, and for that, I thank you."

"You are welcome." Alexina understood completely how Bertha felt. She had almost lost Peyton, too.

In dabbing her eyes again, Bertha's cup spilled. Alexina took her napkin and wiped the drops of coffee from the bedcover. When she returned to the chair, she knocked over the basket, and her things tumbled out. She picked up the pink velvet box and carefully brushed a bit of dust from it.

"That box belonged to Edwina Poole. How have you come by it?"

Alexina stiffened in the chair. "Edwina Poole was my mother."

Bertha put her hand to her chest as she had the night before and went pale. "My dearest friend." She broke out into a full sob.

Bridget, who had been out in the hall, came running. "What has happened?"

Alexina shook her head, surprised and confused.

"My own Winnie," she sniffed between words. "I never knew why she deserted me."

Bridget cast a glance at Alexina and bit her lip. "Here, now, Mrs. Bertha. Calm yourself."

Bertha took a breath and swallowed, using a few moments to get control. She looked at Alexina. "I loved your mother closer than any sister could. But one day, with no reason, I received a letter from her demanding I cut off all contact. It came by courier, an official document. I never understood why. And then," she dabbed at her eyes again, "when your father died in that explosion…."

Alexina handed the velvet box to Bertha, who snapped it open.

Explosion. Mrs. Woodleigh has called it that, too, like Grandfather.

Bertha touched her nose with the napkin. "I received another document saying I should stay away from all family members and not attend the funeral. My sweet Winnie didn't want me. It was right after that when Clive died. I thought perhaps Winnie would be by my side."

My mother wouldn't have been so cruel. I don't understand. "Did she call you Bertie?"

Bertha moved her head in a sudden movement to stare at Alexina. "Yes. Only Clive and your parents called me that. Why?"

Alexina leaned forward. "You were her last thought. She told me she knew she would be in Heaven soon, and she would wait for you just to ask why you no longer wanted *her* friendship."

Bertha's face showed confusion, and she shook her head. "I don't know what happened."

Alexina shut her eyes and tried to sort out Bertha's account of the past. It made no sense. She searched the room with her gaze and tried to summon memories. None came.

Bridget silently left, keeping the door open.

After a few minutes, Bertha took Alexina's hand. "How kind Fate can be to bring you two together. How is it you met Peyton? Did you move to the north?"

Alexina pulled her hand away. "I don't know why you are surprised. We married because of the contract you and my parents signed."

Bertha sat up away from her pillows. "A marriage contract?"

"Yes. When I was two, and he was five."

"There was no contract."

"But there was. I saw it and signed it not a year ago."

Bertha moved her eyes and bit her lip. "Wait a minute. Oh! Little Lexie. The darling little child who played so well with Peyton." Her eyes widened. "He adored you. But— That contract, it was a farce, a joke between us." Her nostrils spread, and a look of disgust swept her face. "That fool, Ignace, always tagging after Winnie. Everyone but Winnie could see how he yearned for her. He brought that little brat of his here, and the three of you played together. I forget his name, but he favored you and tried to keep Peyton away from you. Peyton wouldn't let that boy interfere with his time with you, and Winnie and I jested about having a marriage contract. Ignace surprised us with several copies. We signed as a lark. I don't know what happened to those contracts."

"I know what happened to two of them," Alexina said. "I signed one, and Peyton signed the other." Thoughts of the marriage contract made Alexina remember Peyton's caustic comments about marrying her to save his land. *All of that is passed. He loves me and I him.*

"I had forgotten," Bertha said. "In deference to Winnie, we used Smith as our legal representative, but I never liked him. When Clive found discrepancies in our account, we sent him packing. Clive, your father, Alex, and I tried to tell your mother how dangerous the man was, but she wouldn't believe anything bad of her cousin. Sometime after we sacked Smith, your mother sent that horrible document. I often wondered if trying to besmirch Smith had anything to do with that. It broke my heart to lose her." Bertha looked at the necklace again. "It's so beautiful. She loved this necklace. Your father did such a wonderful job creating it."

"My father created it?"

"You didn't know that?"

"I don't remember my mother wearing it."

"Your father was brilliant with gemstones. That's how he met Clive. They were members of the Royal Academy of Science, Clive a botanist and Alexander, a geologist. Alex worked for a company that produced fine oil paints, and he traveled the world looking for pigments. Somewhere in India, he found a beautiful red pigment that did not fade, but in the same place, he noticed the rocks had a variety of gems. When he returned from his trip, he encouraged us to invest in the land so he could form a mine. The mine paid off handsomely, and we who invested earned a great deal of money."

"I knew my father owned a mine, but I didn't think it was valuable."

"Indeed, it was. He quit working for the firm and became interested in cutting the gems. He became a wonderful jeweler." Bertha took the necklace from the box. "When he made this for Winnie, he made a small one for you and a stickpin for himself. "See?" She pointed to dual vacancies that appeared to be part of the design in the thick part of the necklace. "Your little pendant fit here and his stickpin here."

Alexina took off her pendant and placed it in one of the vacancies. It fit perfectly.

"You can appreciate how brilliant he was with jewelry. Let me show you something else." Bertha pointed across the room. "Would you bring that black lacquer box here?"

Alexina brought the box to the bed. Bertha opened the lid, lifting a top drawer that rode smoothly upward on hinged arms. "Look." She held an oval brooch. "He made this for me out of pink sapphires, black diamonds, and turquoise."

Alexina looked closely. Formed in faceted pink stones, she saw the ugly fish she had come to love from the lake in Applewood. The black diamonds formed the large eye. Rendered as a piece of jewelry, the fish looked gorgeous.

"Alex brought back a plant for Clive, the same plant he discovered that makes the pigment because the sap had the ability to grow roots on even the smallest part of a plant, even a leaf. But the plant lived in shallow water and only grew with the presence of this type of fish. So, Alex brought the fish and the plant to Clive for his research."

The jumping fish and the shore thyme. "Do you mean my father is responsible for the ugly pink fish and the plants that are so useful?"

"You know about them?"

"Yes, they both thrive at Applewood."

Bertha shut her eyes hard and sighed. "Applewood. Clive loved that place so much. I am truly sorry I did not share his love for the estate. I didn't like the cold or being away from the excitement of London."

Cold weather? The valley traps the heat for the winter.

"I have so much to tell you, Alexina. Oh, little Lexie. You were so beautiful. I loved you like my own daughter,"

The clock on the side table chimed ten bells. Alexina put the necklace in its place and stowed the box in the basket. "Mrs. Woodleigh, I must go. I will be late if I don't catch a cab right away. I'm due at my grandfather's."

Bertha nodded. "Geoffrey Downing. I remember him well. You don't have to hail a cab." Bertha rang the handbell on the bedside table. Bridget came in immediately. "Have Sam ready the carriage for Mrs. Woodleigh." She smiled at Alexina. "Now you have a few more minutes."

"Thank you, Mrs. Woodleigh."

"Oh, my dear Alexina. I am doubly sorry for our first meeting." Her eyes watered again. "Sweet young woman, could you bring yourself to call me Mother?"

"I will call you Mother Bertha."

Bertha wiped her eyes. "I wish it was that easy for Peyton."

"Give him some time. Why don't you come to visit? This spring? If you can get to Turnersfield—"

Bertha smiled. "I think I can remember the way."

"The drayage man, who also delivers mail, will bring you to us."

"Thank you. I'd love to come."

Alexina said her farewell and went downstairs. At the front door, she saw her carpetbags, and, in her newly-bestowed status as a welcomed guest, she used the front steps to exit Woodleigh House.

Chapter Eighty-Two

A few minutes after she arrived at her grandfather's, Mrs. Pribble admitted Peyton, who entered with a smile on his face. He approached Alexina and slipped his hand over hers.

"Good morning, young fellow," Geoffrey said.

"Yes, sir." He smiled at Alexina. "A good morning, indeed."

The hall clock struck rich tones, signaling the beginning of afternoon.

"We should be leaving, Grandfather," Alexina said. "I didn't plan to leave Woodleigh House so late. We need to return the rental to the agency, and our coachman is outside."

"He can wait a few more minutes." Geoffrey pulled at his chin. "I see the spat between you two has been concluded. Yes, that smile says it all, young man." He breathed in and blew out. "Nothing like a spat to make a union sweet, I say."

"Grandfather," Alexina said, casting a sidelong glance.

"Well, now, enough of that. Peyton, my boy, Eden's Joy exceeded all expectations. I should think you shall have more orders than brandy next year. I wouldn't mind putting in an order for myself. In fact, here is my down payment." He handed Peyton a leather wallet stitched at the open edges. "This represents my investment in your product. I'll come to Applewood to claim my barrel."

"Thank you, sir." Peyton stuffed the wallet in his jacket pocket.

"Do come, Grandfather. We welcome your visit."

"Don't be surprised when I show. I'll write first."

Once again, Alexina shot him her sidelong glance.

Geoffrey scratched his bald head. "I'll try to remember to write.

How is that?"

Alexina hugged him. "I love you."

Geoffrey allowed Alexina's long hug. He cleared his throat. "Mrs. Pribble, where's that basket?"

Mrs. Pribble came from the kitchen with a double-lidded basket. "He insisted I pack you a picnic lunch." She opened one side of the hinged top. "Bread, cheese, meat, lemonade, and apples."

"Apples?" Alexina picked an apple from the basket. "Just what we wanted." She winked at Peyton. "Thank you."

Peyton stepped forward and pumped Geoffrey's hand. "I don't know what to say, but I am grateful for all you've done."

"My pleasure, young sir. Make my granddaughter happy."

"I'm happy, Grandfather. Oh, and here." She pulled the pink box from her slim basket.

Geoffrey held his palm up. "This is yours, my dear. After your father died, your mother wouldn't wear it, but it looked ravishing on you."

"You were supposed to sell it so we could purchase materials. You supplied the money. It is yours."

"But, sweet one—"

"Besides, I have no use for it where we are. That is why I only brought a few pieces with me to begin with. It should stay here."

"Very well. I won't checker our last few minutes together with contention." Geoffrey walked them to the front steps. "Do be careful. Don't forget your get-away basket."

Alexina and Peyton thanked Geoffrey and left the house to step onto the stone carriage step at the curb. The carriage slid to a gentle stop. Peyton assisted Alexina in, and then he entered. He shut the finely appointed door with a reassuring thud.

Pemberton slapped the rein straps on Silverton's rump, and they were on their way.

"What is a get-away basket?" Peyton asked.

Alexina rolled her eyes. "Grandfather can be a bit dotty. I'm not quite sure what he meant." *But I remember the get-away present he gave me when I left for Applewood. That gift got us here to London.*

When they reached the rental agency. Alexina paid the balance on the rental and gave Pemberton a tip while Peyton and the groom switched their goods and Silverton to the old, ragged coach. Alexina sat on the driver's perch with Peyton. The old rig's seat, although worn and shredded in places, still offered soft seating, but being close to him trumped any type of comfort.

"What did Grandfather give you?"

Peyton reached into his shirt and pulled out the wallet. "Open it and see."

Alexina unlaced the leather cording and opened the top of the wallet. She fanned out multiple bills. "Two hundred pounds! Oh, Peyton. That's a lot of money."

He grinned with a sly look. "Two years stipend for you, isn't it?"

Her mouth formed an *O* before she raised her eyebrows. She had not told him about her money. "It is, but how do you know about it?"

"The same way I knew about the annulment. I saw you in the park with a woman. I wanted to…."

"To what?"

"To beg your forgiveness for my behavior. But then I heard you say you didn't want to return to Applewood. She suggested an annulment, and then you…."

Alexina looked away and took a breath. "Then I said I couldn't leave you."

"I guess I didn't stay long enough to hear that." He whistled. "Did you see how the clerk at the rental agency turned pale when he saw you?"

"Good. Now those who work there might think twice when they try to rent a reserved buggy that has been promised." Alexina kissed his cheek. "I'll not be that way again."

"Good," he said.

"And you must promise to never be angry with me in the future."

He pulled at his chin. "I can't make *that* promise, but I can promise never to speak to you harshly, and if a problem arises, we shall talk it over."

She moved closer to him. "If only we had communicated better before."

Peyton responded with the familiar "hmmm."

The weather remained fair and the roads clear. They made good time and neared the town Alexina had scheduled as their resting place for the night.

The road made a sharp turn, with clumps of trees on both sides preventing the view of the town. As Silverton slowed for the turn, a series of shrieks made the horse skitter and stop. Four men, their faces hidden by kerchiefs, ran from the forested area, two with guns and two brandishing knives.

"Get down," demanded a man with a white triangle tied around his face. He waved his pistol at them.

With lightning speed, Peyton pulled his pistol from under the seat and pointed the gun at the speaker. The gun cracked, and the man went down. Peyton reached for a second pistol, but the tallest of the villains jumped on the wheel rim and pulled Alexina off the perch. He held his knife against her throat.

The remaining gunman pointed his pistol at Peyton. "Down!"

Peyton hopped from his seat with his arms up.

The man on the ground emitted a long raspy breath. His white cloth turned red. The gunman turned to the tall fellow and pointed to the dying man. "You know him?"

"No," answered the man with the blue kerchief over his nose. "Our employer won't use those who know each other. Then we have no problem and can walk away."

The tall man turned the body with his foot until it tumbled down an embankment. While one brigand held his gun on Peyton and the other held the knife to Alexina, the third man tore through the carriage, paying extra attention to the carpetbags.

"Nothing here but a small purse, with thirty pounds. And a wallet, loaded!"

"There might be more. Search them," the gun holder commanded. "There's supposed to be a necklace."

The new speaker stood in front of Alexina. "Where's your jewelry? You have rubies and diamonds?"

"Just my necklace."

With a smile, the robber who held the knife against her cut the buttons one at a time down to her lacy bodice. The glint of the gold disappeared into her cleavage. He used his knife to lift the chain that held the glittering object. Leering, he grinned as he rubbed his fingers against her breasts, slowly fumbling with the pendant.

"So pretty," the ruffian said.

"Don't do that," Alexina pleaded. "I'll take it off."

Peyton growled. "Hurt her, and I'll kill you."

"You'd have to be raised from the dead to do that," the lone gunman said and elevated the pistol to Peyton's forehead. "We don't have time to mess with the woman, so get on with it."

Alexina, forcing her hand not to shake, handed the necklace with the small pendant to the man.

He looked it over. "For this little thing?"

"And the money," said the gunman, tapping the open wallet against his hip. He addressed Peyton. "You two, on the ground, face down."

They did. Peyton slid his hand over hers. "I love you," he whispered.

Choked on her closed throat and body-shaking sobs, she overcame the terror for a moment. "I love you, too," fearing it might be the last thing they said to each other. She moved closer, pressing against him, waiting for something, but she didn't know what. Muddled sounds gave her no indication of what transpired around them.

Chapter Eighty-Three

After a minute of silence, Peyton raised his head. "They're gone. Are you all right?"

"No." Words and sobs mixed, obscuring what she said.

He embraced her and whispered comfort. "We are alive and can have our time together." He scooted from under the carriage and pulled her out. Once again, holding her, he placed kisses on her moist face. "Better?"

She sniffed and calmed herself. "Yes." A large tear dripped off her cheek.

"It is all right, my darling."

Horses thundered on the other side of the thick patch of trees. Peyton kissed her cheek, then ran to Silverton and grabbed the leather straps connected to the traces.

The new alarm brought her out of her temporary breakdown. "No, Peyton! Don't go after them."

His nostrils flared, and he looked in the direction of the fading hoof falls. "You're right." He let out a breath. "I can't leave you here."

Alexina picked up the items strewn about. Peyton went down the embankment.

He returned and wiped his hands on a rag kept in the carriage boot. "He's dead." After reloading the pistol, he stowed it in the hiding place under the seat. "Let's get out of here." He helped Alexina to the driver's perch.

They stayed quiet until they reached the outskirts of the town.

A furrow developed between Peyton's eyebrows. "That money replaced what I thought we'd get in orders."

"At least it came from Grandfather. What would we do if we lost all of the businessmen's deposits?"

"I planned on using what we obtained to pay the workers at Applewood. And the taxes."

She rubbed her forehead. "And the thirty pounds were to have provided good accommodations and food. Now we have nothing but each other." She pulled his face around to hers. "That is worth a fortune."

Peyton smiled. "Love *is* a treasure, but we're going to get a little hungry."

She bent around and stretched to get the fat basket Geoffrey had provided. "We have Grandfather's get-away basket." Putting it in her lap, she flipped open one-half of the top. "Now I know what he meant by telling us not to forget this." Out came the apples, sandwiches, hard-boiled eggs, and the rest of the picnic supplies. She flipped over the linen napkin lining the bottom. Under the cloth was a ten-pound note.

"This is his get-away gift. That crazy, clever, wonderful old man."

Peyton took the note and stuck it in his shirt. "We'll not starve, nor will Silverton. Get-up, horse!" He slapped the leathers, and Silverton took off.

When the sun had set, and it was nearly dark, Peyton pointed to an area of trees away from the road. He tethered the horse, secured the rig, and they slept on a blanket underneath the timeworn phaeton. With a chorus of night birds as their company, Alexina and Peyton made love sweeter than the serenade.

In the morning, they dined on the remainder of the basket's contents. Silverton had grazed, and when they reached the next town, Peyton bought oats for the feedbag.

On the second night of the trip, they had enough money for a small inn they found, but the place looked so mean and shoddy, Alexina preferred her bed under the carriage, sleeping with her loved one rather than fleas, bedbugs, and mice.

Early the following morning, they made good time, but a hailstorm cut short their travel. Peyton struggled with the leather top as ice the size of filberts pelted them. Silverton shuddered and whinnied with each hit. Alexina huddled inside, but Peyton stood outside, soothing and calming the horse.

Heavy traffic caused by the storm made them break early for the evening. They stopped at an inn, but it was packed. Alexina bought food to go. Camped by a river that evening, they ate the cold meal.

"I'm sorry about these accommodations," Peyton said as he pulled the horse blanket over them.

"I've never been happier," Alexina whispered.

He pressed his nose against her cheek. "Nor I."

By noon the next day, they reached the gravel road that brought them into Applewood Valley. When the rig stopped at Stone House, most of the workers were there to greet them, including Granny Doctor.

Molly ran to the carriage. "Welcome home, Young Master and Mistress. Hungry?"

Seat ran to them and grabbed Silverton's collar. "I'll see to him."

Peyton hopped down from the seat. "I'll unload it later."

"Nay, sir. We'll take care of that," Tad said.

Molly grabbed Alexina's arm. "We've been expecting you. Heard you on the gravel."

Little Jim flew at Peyton. "Fish! They's fishing."

Peyton threw him up in the air and caught him. "Just like the fish in the lake, I caught you, Little Jim." He ruffled the boy's blond curls. "But we won't eat you."

"Not eat me?"

Alexina left Molly's side and bent low to Jim. "We'll have to throw you back. You're too small!"

Little Jim laughed. "Can I fish with Tom?"

Peyton looked around at the gathered folk. His lips thinned, and his brows came together. "Who's Tom?"

A large man broke through the crowd and stopped before Peyton. "I'm Thomas Lloyd."

Molly untied her apron and handed it to Sissy. She came to Peyton. "Tom…he's—"

"In my valley without permission," Peyton said.

"Sir." Tom gently moved Molly aside. "May I have a word with you?"

Molly returned to her stance, facing Peyton. "Young Master, you need to hear what Tom does—"

"Molly," Tom said with an authority that surprised Alexina. "Quiet. Let me speak with the master."

The crowd parted for Granny Doctor. Silently she took a place between Peyton and Tom, folding her arms over her chest. Alexina cocked her head at Peyton, reminding him to listen to Granny, either her words or manner.

Peyton nodded to Alexina. "I'll converse with you, Thomas Lloyd. Come into the house."

On their way into Stone House, Alexina turned to see Granny point at Molly, who halted and made no more attempt to follow. Dutch and Sissy busied in the kitchen while Peyton escorted Alexina and Tom into the study. Peyton faced Tom. Alexina sat in the desk chair

"Sir, while you were gone, I entered your valley uninvited. I will tell you no lies. I am a wanted man. I come from Wales, where I killed a man in a fair fight provoked by him. The man was the brother of the sheriff, and the sheriff did not want to hear my side. I've been widowed some twenty years now, and my children are grown, so I departed. I only wish to work and cause no trouble. I'm asking to stay in your valley. I know you are the owner of this fair place and a good man, according to them." His head tilted toward the outside. "Will you consider it?"

Peyton paced once around the room. "On trial. One offense, and you're through. Understand?"

"Thank you. I won't cause any problems."

"What do you do for a living?"

"I'm a cooper."

Alexina drew in a noisy breath.

Peyton relaxed his stance. "You didn't let Molly tell me that."

"I didn't want my occupation to affect your decision, sir."

"Do you know how much we need a cooper here in Applewood?"

The man drew his fingers through his thick hair. "I believe I do, sir. And I can make any size barrels you need. The best barrels, no leaks. I've made a few already for my keep."

Peyton put out his hand to Tom to shake. He turned to his wife. "We've got a cooper, Alexina!"

Chapter Eighty-Four

When Alexina and Peyton left the study, the aroma from the kitchen made Peyton pick up his step. Sissy put plates on the small table, and Dutch stood over a large black frying pan, focusing on its contents. She turned and smiled. "Fish and potatoes, the mistress's favorite."

Peyton made a face. "What about my favorite?"

Dutch flinched. "Your favorite?"

Peyton laughed and came to the stove. He bent over the pan. "Anything *you* cook."

"Oh," she said, her eyebrows up and her mouth open.

Alexina hugged Dutch. "He's developed a sense of humor."

Peyton slipped his arm around Alexina's waist.

"Oh!" Dutch said.

"Oh," Sissy repeated. "Welcome home, Master and Mistress." She pulled out the chair for Alexina.

Dutch brought the pan to the table. "Tonight, we have celebration. Big Party. When we heard you in the pass, we started to prepare a celebration for your great success."

Alexina savored a bite. "Our success? You didn't know how we fared in London."

"Granny predicted it. We knew."

"Success in many quarters," Alexina said, winking at Peyton and taking another bite.

At the end of the meal, Sissy cleared the plates, and Peyton leaned back in his chair. "We need a rest. Leave us be until dark." He stood, and with a small movement of his head, summoned Alexina.

They entered the bedroom, where Peyton had to put some muscle on the door's wooden bar to move it into its slot.

"I've never used that bar. Too heavy."

"Nor have I, but for this afternoon, I don't want us disturbed." He pulled her close. "Shower-bath?"

Peyton admired Alexina's body as the articles of clothing dropped to the floor. After kicking off his boots, he stripped, not taking his eyes from her. He cranked the handle of the mechanism that sent the large metal ewer on its track to the elevated tank. Taking her by the hand, they stepped over the low wall and into the shower-bath. Pulling the handle sent a gentle tumble of warm water over them.

Alexina handed him a fancy yellow soap. "For me, lemon. And for you...." She held a bar shaped like a clam. "Sandalwood."

"I'm very dirty, don't miss a spot," Peyton said.

She lathered the soap on his chest and down his arms.

"I am dirty in other places."

"I'm getting to that." She lathered his belly and down his groin. "I see." She ran her soapy hands to that which protruded. "All that travel...dirt from the road, dust in the air. I'll have to pay close attention here."

Peyton leaned against the back wall, enjoying his wife's touch. All the sultan baths he had taken at the hands of the Wagon Girls could not compare to this. "Please don't stop." For just a moment, he left his reverie to realize he had just pleaded with someone for something. It felt good. His body tightened, heralding the epitome of pleasure. He allowed himself a robust moan and slid down the wall to the floor.

He quieted and let the gentle touch of water rinse him.

Alexina extended her hand. "You have work to do, husband."

Peyton gathered his strength and examined her carefully. "Yes, I see I do." He rubbed the soap on her, energetically lathering until she was covered in white bubbles, then pulled the handle and rinsed her.

"You're done?"

"Not quite." He glided his hands on her breasts. "Soap is not enough." He pushed her against the wall and licked her nipples. "Spit bath," he whispered. "The best kind."

He attended her many soiled spots until she wrapped her hand around his erection and pulled him to her. He lifted her to the right height and, holding her aloft, slipped inside. He thrust until she cried out.

After restoring her upright to the stall floor, they dried each other. He swept her into his arms, placed her on the soft mattress of the four-poster bed, and lay next to her.

"Peyton," she said breathlessly. "You have no idea how many times I imagined us in the shower-bath together. It was better than I imagined."

He remembered the times he had wished for the same. What bright star had shone on him that he had her in his arms? His thoughts wavered between self-condemnation for his distrust and the elation of this closeness.

"Peyton?"

"I'm here." He kissed her. "I will always be here."

"Are you thirsty?"

"What?"

"Prepare to hover at death from thirst and exhaustion."

Peyton laughed for all the times he had not allowed himself humor and all of the missed opportunities. With Alexina, they had been returned to him.

"No laughing, husband. This is serious business."

"I love you," he said.

"I know," she whispered. "Show it."

At dusk, they were awakened by a sharp rap at the door. Peyton wrapped a towel around his waist and raised the bar. He peeked out and saw Molly.

"Sorry to disturb you, Young Master, but—"

"Not to worry," he said. "Is anything amiss?"

"Everything is wonderful, but the men have started the fire. You don't want to miss the celebration. Much merriment tonight."

He closed the door and returned to the bed, his shoulders sagging.

Alexina sat up, hugging the sheet to her chest. "What's wrong?"

"I wanted to pay the men. I have to tell them I can't."

"Don't you have Clear Jack? Can't you sell all you make?"

"Yes. But I give the workers a portion to make up for pay, and I haven't given the taxman his share. "

"The taxman?"

"Boyce." Peyton spat out the name like it was poison. "He arranged to lower the taxes by bribing the official. I don't know the man. I don't know what the sum will be. It doesn't matter. I don't have it."

"Don't think of it tonight, my love. Enjoy the homecoming.

Trust Granny's prediction."

"You are so good for me, Alexina. I regret—"

She put her finger to his lips. "Don't. Let's get dressed and join the party."

Chapter Eighty-Five

Peyton held Alexina's hand as they left Stone House for the party. The night air smelled of a rich aroma rising from the golden firelight. Logs glowed and sizzled from the dripping meats skewered over the pit. Kegs stacked against the barn wall foretold of the hearty drinking planned. The untapped kegs were a testament to the folk's respect for Peyton.

A wave of warmth passed through him. Nothing had changed here at Applewood except his perceptions. The folk had always admired him, but until Alexina came, he had been unaware of their true relationships, affection, and trust.

Someone shouted from the yard, "They're here!" The musicians played their lively gypsy tunes, and the reverie officially began. Peyton held up his hand to speak. The music stopped, and the crowd became hushed. He felt their eyes upon him.

"My friends…." The folks fell silent. Although he had lived among them and shared in the work and hardships, he had never called them friends. "Yes. You are more than workers. I give you my most appreciative gratitude. I went to London to sell Eden's Joy, and the brandy was a resounding success."

The crowd cheered.

Peyton held his hand up again. "However, I return empty-handed. I wished to pay you wages for your efforts and give you what you deserve. But I cannot. Not for this year. I am sorry."

Tad rose from his place by the fire. "You let us live in this beautiful valley. For the first time, many of us have homes, regular meals, and safety for our families. We don't need pay and never did."

He turned to the faces illuminated by the firelight. "What say you?"

All of the men stood and gathered around Peyton. They clapped his back and shoulders, agreeing with Tad.

Someone shouted, "Let's dance!" The music started again.

Tad began to chant, and the voices cried in unison, "Dance! Dance! Dance!"

Peyton took Alexina's hand and swung her around until their hips met. Firelight reflected in her perfect eyes. He pressed her body close. She pushed her firm breasts against him. The music stepped up its pace, becoming primal, strong. He spun Alexina around, bent her over backwards, and kissed her passionately. The crowd went wild. He pulled her upright and turned her to the crowd. "My beautiful wife, Mistress of Applewood."

Alexina curtsied and slipped her arm around Peyton's waist. Again, the Wanderers cheered. Peyton beamed with the warmth of camaraderie, support, and the closeness of the woman he loved. They danced until the musicians took their first break and the tray of Jack came their way. After the dancing, Sissy handed Peyton a plate. Alexina begged his pardon, telling him she would like to sit with the women. He needed time alone with the men. He kissed her, and another roar rose from the crowd. She ambled toward the women's circle. He mingled with the men and talked about the equipment he had ordered and how they would use the sweet apples to produce Eden's Joy for the coming year.

The sound of a cart and the whoops of its passengers diverted everyone's attention. The Wagon Girls had arrived, with the exception of one. Men rushed to help them from the cart. Each woman bid Alexina welcome and reminded her of their names. As a group, they ran to Peyton and threw their arms about him. Alexina waved, laughing. He relaxed and allowed the Girls to hug and kiss him with the knowledge that he belonged to her forever.

Another cart arrived without fanfare, carrying Granny and her acolytes.

Molly approached Alexina. "Granny is losing Sophia."

"Why?"

"It's time. Sophia has become the Auntie Doctor, and someone from her tribe is on the way to get her. Granny will ask the Young Master permission to take a new apprentice."

The crowd parted for Granny as she made her way toward the women's circle. Alexina understood her true place in the Valley's hierarchy. She rose and escorted Granny to the seat. Another woman offered her place to Alexina, but she refused, accepted a plate from Sissy, and ate standing. Molly flashed her a well-done wink.

"Tell me about Tom, Molly," Alexina said.

"Do you believe in love at first view?"

"I do."

"Then there's no more to tell. Other than, if the Young Master had not let Tom stay, me and Little Jim would have left with him. And that would have been impossible, dear Mistress, for I have pledged my deepest loyalty to you. Love seems to have bloomed even as the trees lose their leaves, eh, Mistress?"

"Truly, it has, Molly. I have never been so happy."

Molly threw back her head, and her distinctive laugh followed. "Aye! There shall be much happiness tonight! You and the Master, me and my Tom, and the Wagon Girls for them what's left."

Sissy brought several cups of ladies' punch.

"Mmm, as delicious as I remember," Alexina said. Molly's words echoed in her head. *Much happiness tonight…starting with the magic of Applewood's product.*

Chapter Eighty-Six

The days grew shorter and colder. Even though the valley helped trap the sun's warmth to lessen snowfall, the air became chilly. During this time, the men devoted their work to building the small rounded stone houses from the rock piles they made during the year. Mounds of river reed became roofs, allowing more families to move from their wagons and into cozy homes.

Molly smiled constantly and kept company with Tom at every chance.

"Good Mistress," Molly said one morning while making the bed. "I plan to take up with Tom. Aye, you might know he sleeps in the loft of the distilling barn with Seat." She punched the pillows fluffing the down.

"Oh?"

"Being your personal maid, you kindly offered me and Little Jim your guest room, which I most appreciate." Molly smoothed the bed cover with deliberate strokes. "I'm not one for mincing words, Mistress."

"You want to marry Tom and have a place of your own. I understand."

"It's not so easy as that."

"Tell me what you want, Molly. You've helped me ever so much and deserve happiness."

"Tom hasn't been accepted into the tribe. We, the Wanderers, seem coarse and ignorant—"

"Not so, Molly."

"Aye, thank you for that. We have a code, you see. Before I

can say my vows to Tom, the other men must accept him, or I will be outside of the tribe. In order for the tribe men to allow him to join, you and the Young Master must give your consent."

"Peyton and I?"

"Of course. We live in your valley. We've accepted you as our leaders."

Alexina chuckled. "We all know Granny is the undisputed leader."

"Granny only leads us when she thinks we head in the wrong direction. In matters of importance, the men decide together and seek the approval of our good Young Man. If Master Peyton allows Tom to stay in the valley, the men of the Wanderers will accept Tom into our tribe, and we can be joined."

"It should be easy then," Alexina said. "Tom has lived up to his word these past months. His workmanship has exceeded his claims. What should I do to help?"

"Give me your blessing, Mistress."

"You have it."

"Thank you. It is up to the master, then. When me and Tom share our vows, I'll still be your maid and take good care of you like I do now, but not live here. Seat has offered to move from the loft."

"The loft? Won't you want a home?"

"At the right time, Mistress."

"I remember what you said. The men are ranked by their importance. I'd say Tom has a very important job."

"Yes, Mistress. All in the right time."

Within the week, Peyton agreed Tom could stay. The men invited Tom into the Tribe, and the women prepared for a wedding. The couple stood in front of the valley's residents and promised to be true to one another until their death. They kissed to seal the promise. Then Tad put up his hands and said, "Celebrate!"

Like Tasting Day and other festivities held by the Wanderers, the revelers danced, sang, ate, and drank until the bonfire died down to glowing embers, and the paired guests made their way to warm beds, including Alexina and Peyton.

The next day Molly and Little Jim moved from the guest room at Stone House and into the loft of the distilling barn. Life in Applewood Valley hummed along. Winter progressed into spring, and the hours of daylight increased, along with the good cheer in the valley.

One warm spring day, Peyton ran into the kitchen. He wrapped his arms around Alexina's waist. "We have buds on the trees!"

"Is that unusual this time of year?"

"Not at all. What is most exceptional, though, is our grafts have taken hold. We have buds on them too."

"The Sweet Apple tree grafts? The apples to make Eden's Joy?"

"Yes!" Peyton danced Alexina around the kitchen. Sissy, Dutch, and Molly clapped their hands in time to nonexistent music.

Peyton released Alexina and grinned. "We shall have a huge crop of sweet apples. As the trees have no official name, I proclaim them to be Eden Trees. We can make barrels of Eden's Joy! All of our equipment has been delivered and is ready to implement. Because of you," he said and bent Alexina over his arm in a deep kiss. He pointed to the three maids. "And you." He straightened to his tallest and bowed at the waist. "Thank you, all."

Before they had a chance to enjoy the good news, Tad rushed into the kitchen holding two letters. "The man from Turnersfield just brought these."

He handed them to Alexina, who read them to herself. "They're both from Hester. The first one says she will be accompanying a student north and will ask the headmistress for a few extra days to see us at Applewood." She slapped the second one against her palm. "But this one says she has left the school, and after calling on some relatives in Cornwall, she will visit us for an extended period. Oh, Peyton. Hester is coming. Isn't that grand?"

Peyton took the letters. He looked them over and narrow-eyed her. Grasping her elbow, he escorted Alexina into the study and shut the door. With a grim look on his face, he gently pushed her against the wall next to the writing desk. He shook the letters. "Isn't Hester the woman I saw in the park with you when we were in London?"

"Yes, that was Hester."

"Isn't she the woman who offered to help you secure an annulment?"

Blood left her face. "Peyton—"

He laughed. "And the one to whom you proclaimed your love for me?"

Alexina sighed in relief. "The very same, you rascal."

"Rascal?" He brushed his body against her and kissed her neck. "I'll show you a rascal." As he moved kisses up her cheek, he unbuttoned her dress. Within minutes, he had her skirt pulled up around her waist and his own leather breeches puddled at his ankles.

Later, as they restored their clothing, Alexina bit her lip. "Now I have to return to the kitchen and pretend you and I conferred in the study."

"While I stroll triumphantly out to the orchard."

"You are indeed a rascal, husband."

He put her hand to his lips. "You have made many things of this man. One, a rascal. Two, a very happy man." He swatted her behind. "Now go out there and pretend we just talked." He held the door. "Wait. I have a better idea. Come with me."

Alexina looped her arm through Peyton's elbow while they walked toward the orchard. The lake shimmered in the sunlight. Approaching the trees, the fragrance of the blooms filled the air. Pink and white blossoms covered some of the trees, and others showed varying sized nubs of green fruit.

"Our orchard," Peyton said. "Our fortune."

Alexina breathed in the rich scent of the apple blossoms. "How beautiful."

Peyton pulled a flowery branch and encircled her head. "There. What beauty. What perfection. Next year, with our profits, I'll send for an artist to capture your face against the flowers."

"Listen to you," Alexina teased.

Chapter Eighty-Seven

"Indeed," Peyton said. "Words formerly unused by me jostle for position on my tongue to describe my joy. I did not know it was possible to feel this way. I did not know love."

Alexina brushed away a stray petal on his shoulder. "Surely you saw love and affection amongst the Wanderers?"

"I thought of it as a weakness. I now see it as incredible strength. And I say a quick thank you to the Maker each morning when I awaken and see you next to me."

"For a man of quiet nature, I see words have taken you over."

"I understand it, my beloved. Poetry, songs of the heart, love letters. I see the beauty in everyday things. What before was a day of sunshine for my plants has become a radiant day of light that illuminates your beauty."

"I don't know what to say, other than I also understand the glorious feeling."

"Speaking of a glorious feeling, how shall we *confer* when Hester visits?"

"We can't. We'll be forced to confine our conferences to nighttime in our bedchamber."

"Hmm. I'll have Seat take her for tours, to the lake or... something."

"She can give concerts," Alexina suggested.

"You will want to attend," he said with a hint of disappointment.

"True, but...." She brushed another petal from his shoulder. "Maybe I can leave a little early."

They laughed, held hands, and strolled through the trees.

Chapter Eighty-Eight

A few weeks later, Hester arrived on the drayage cart from Turnersfield. By the time her trunk and cases had been unloaded and placed in the front hall, several of the folk had come to Stone House to see the visitor.

Alexina ran to her friend's side. "Hester, dearest girl! A vision for sad eyes you are. I am so pleased to see you!" After an extended hug and a second, she pulled Hester into the kitchen and introduced her to the gathering crowd. "Your second letter said you left Greenfield School. Now I'm doubly glad to see you. Let's have tea."

Hester nodded. "First, if you don't mind, a private word?"

"Of course." Alexina led her friend to the bedchamber and closed the door.

"Remember the red book and the drawings? Do you recall our pact?"

Alexina laughed and sat on the bed. "Sit here. I have much to tell you."

"My ears are quivering. Make haste with your information."

"It's wonderful, and I understand why the teacher before me left with the groundskeeper. You wouldn't believe how your body becomes hot, hungry for what the man possesses. And remember how we couldn't comprehend how the small body part makes its way into the woman? The man's part, like a twig, swells and enlarges to a hardened limb. No stuffing is needed unless he isn't fast enough to please. Then you are in charge of getting it inside you. Peyton says it swells with blood, the portion meant for his brain, which is why men aren't themselves when they are with a woman. Oh, and then when the man and woman's union develop a rhythm, something explosive happens inside you, delivering the most indescribable waves of pleasure, so intense it can produce prodigious yelling. I yell so loud I'm afraid someone will hear me."

Alexina answered all of Hester's questions with the resulting yearning for Peyton. *How many hours until nighttime?*

After giving themselves a few minutes to calm down and end the giggling, Hester and Alexina combed their hair and splashed water on their reddened faces. They returned to the kitchen.

Seat was waiting for directions to stow Hester's luggage and other things. "Should I put the cases into the guest room, Mistress?"

"Yes, thank you. Seaton, meet Miss Hester Langley. Hester, this is Seaton…." Alexina turned to the man. "I don't know your last name."

"O'Quigley, Mistress," he said without taking his eyes from Hester.

With her eyes locked on the man with the reddish hair with a curl clinging to his forehead, Hester pointed at the leather cases. "Do be careful. Those are my instruments. Sabrina, my cello, and Contessa, my viola."

"Yes, miss. If your instruments have names, they must be dear friends to you. I will take the best of care."

"Thank you, sir." Hester smiled.

Seat remained a few minutes longer than he usually did, making Alexina wonder what she should say.

Peyton entered the room and bowed his head. "Hello."

Alexina said, "Please meet Peyton Woodleigh, my husband."

Hester extended her hand. "Ever so pleased. I've heard wondrous things about you." Hester kept a straight face, but Alexina burst out in a raspberry snigger. Alexina pushed Hester's shoulder, which caused peals of laughter between them. Peyton shot Alexina a glare, to which she shrugged. He shook his head. It took a few minutes until both women could regain their proper deportment and go into the dining room, where tea, sandwiches, and sweets waited.

Peyton raised his eyebrows. After he gave his wife a quick kiss on her cheek, he clapped his hand on Seat's shoulder. "Let me help you with the baggage."

Hester watched Seat leave the room. She cast her gaze to her teacup. "This is an interesting place in which you live. I think we have a few more things to talk about."

"I believe we do, my friend."

Sissy brought sweet cakes Dutch had just taken out of the oven.

Hester selected two. "Delicious."

"You will enjoy many of the dishes from our valley."

"Like the menu from Corrinne's Table?"

Alexina looked away, suppressing her smile. "That, as well as food. Oh. I just thought about something. Fish."

"Did I hear you say fish?" Peyton asked, reentering the kitchen with Seat.

"Wouldn't it be nice to have the jumping carp for dinner?"

Hester's forehead puckered. "To what kind do you refer?"

"They jump into the boat," Alexina said.

"I've never heard of such a thing."

"You should see it for yourself," Peyton said. "Perhaps you would like to see the lake. Little Jim and Seat could take the boat out and show you how they catch the fish."

Molly, who had come into the room with Little Jim, nodded. "I know he'd love it," she said, putting her arm around the boy.

"I'd like to see that," Hester said.

Seat, Hester, Molly, and Jim filed out the door. Peyton held Alexina back. "Let them go to the lake, wife." He winked. "I need to confer with you for a few moments."

At suppertime, Alexina invited Seat to join them. He excused himself and returned clean and sweet-smelling.

"How lovely," Hester said as she slid into the chair Seat held. "Your table looks fit for a queen."

Peyton held Alexina's chair. "She is the Queen of Applewood."

Sissy served the fish fried in batter along with thin-sliced root vegetables sauteed until crisp.

"These crusty potatoes are divine," Hester said.

"Dutch is a wondrous cook." Alexina crunched a bite of the thin potato. "What do you think of the fish?"

"I didn't think watching the things being caught in mid-air could be surpassed, but the taste has done that for sure. What a paradise you have here."

"Wait until the apples ripen," Peyton said as he buttered his bread. "It will be a regular Garden of Eden."

Alexina explained how they came to make Eden's Joy and the success they had in interesting buyers for the coming year. When supper concluded, Hester asked to be excused because she had a long day of travel added to several hours of fishing.

In the morning, Peyton ran to the kitchen, where Molly sat with Little Jim, Dutch, and Sissy. His normally controlled demeanor was gone, and a panicked voice took its place. "Send someone to get Granny. Alexina is sick."

Molly bolted out of her seat. "Little Jim, hurry. Find Tad and have him fetch Granny." She turned to Peyton. "What is it, Young Master?"

He ran his hands through his hair. "She's vomiting. The least movement sets her off. Her color…it's so pale."

Dutch wiped her hands on her apron, and marching behind were Sissy, Molly, and Peyton.

Alexina lay on her side, holding a towel to her mouth. She turned her head toward the door. Her pallid face whitened, and she quivered, followed by a round of wrenching. When the sickness subsided, her head flopped back on the pillow. Her eyes pleaded for relief.

Molly put her hand on Alexina's forehead. "No fever." She turned to Peyton. "Don't worry. Granny will put her right."

Sissy poured warm water from the metal ewer onto a cloth and wrung it out. She washed Alexina's face.

Peyton paced the room, returning to the bedside every few minutes.

Molly said, "Why don't you make some mint tea, Dutch? Two cups. Pour a little product in one for the master."

Peyton waved her off. "Nothing until Granny gets here."

Soon they heard the cart. Granny and her new disciple, Martha, approached the bed. Granny peered into Alexina's face and then nodded to Molly.

"Go have breakfast, Young Master," Molly said. "Granny will take care of her. Not to worry."

"But…," he protested.

Molly ushered him to the door. "She's in good hands. Eat and then go out to the orchard. We'll call you if we need you."

"But…."

Molly shoved him gently through the doorway. "Trust Granny."

Granny sat on the bed next to Alexina then spoke to Martha. "Give our mistress some sleep elixir."

"What's wrong with me?" Alexina said.

"Not a thing, Mistress. Right as rain, you are."

"I can't stop vomiting."

"That is normal."

"Normal?" She held a towel to her mouth. "For what?"

"You're expecting."

"A baby? How...?"

Molly laughed. "Why are you surprised?" She glanced at Granny. "They're at it all the time. The Young Master comes back to Stone House most every day with some excuse to get her alone." She mimicked Peyton's voice. "Where is the mistress? I must confer with her."

The women in the room laughed. Alexina pulled the towel over her face.

Hester knocked at the door. "Alexina?"

"Come in. She's fine," Molly explained. "A little nausea. Granny Doctor, this is our mistress's guest, Hester Langley."

Granny looked Hester up and down. "Uh huh," Granny said, with the unmistakable sound of approval.

Martha brought a slim bottle of brown fluid and poured a spoonful. She held it to Alexina's lips. "That will make you sleep for most of the day. You'll feel better later. Plus, ten drops of this," she held another, smaller bottle with clear fluid, "each morning."

Alexina hesitated to take the medicine. "It won't hurt the baby?"

Hester came close to the bed. "Baby?"

Molly stood next to Hester. "She'll be asleep soon. Let's find someone to entertain you for the day. Would you like to see our cooper make barrels? Come, let our mistress take her rest."

Granny pulled the curtains. In the soft darkness, the room became quiet when the women left. Soon Alexina felt calm, then drowsy.

During the rest of the day, Alexina had dreams of whistling, screams, then the soft strains of her favorite Vivaldi. When she fully awoke, women sitting on chairs and the floor filled the room. She sat up.

Granny came to the bedside. "Feeling better?"

"Yes, but...why...?" Violin music played softly from the other room. "Music?"

Molly came to her. "Mercifully, you slept through it." She pulled back the curtains. A tree branch pressed against the cracked windowpanes.

Alexina strained to see the window. "What happened?"

Peyton rushed into the room, sat on the bed next to her, and helped her sit up. "Are you all right?"

"Yes. Why are you bleeding? Peyton?" She ran her hand over the long tear in his sleeve.

Peyton hung his head. "Whirlwind in the valley. The apples...."

Chapter Eighty-Nine

"Our apples? Oh, Peyton...."

He took her hands. "Don't worry. Let me handle this. You are safe, and no one is injured."

Molly stood next to Peyton. "When the hard winds started, the men rounded up the animals into the barn. The women and children came to Stone House. Your friend, Miss Hester, entertained the children with her music. She is wonderful with the young ones."

Alexina nodded, then rested her head on the pillows.

"Is it safe for us to go outside, Young Master?" Molly asked.

"Yes, the wind is gone. It went through the pass and died. Have some of the older children take baskets and gather the fish that the whirlwind plucked from the lake. Some of the fish are still flopping." He smiled at Alexina. "These we shall call Flying Carp."

Alexina saw through his smile. When the people had returned to their homes, she would demand a detailed description of the damage.

Granny shooed the room's occupants away. She offered Alexina another spoonful of her elixir. "I believe you need more sleep. Things will be better tomorrow."

Peyton looked at Granny with relief in his eyes. Alexina took the spoonful, not for herself, but to allow Peyton to do what he needed without worrying about her.

When they were alone, Alexina patted the bed, inviting him to sit next to her. She took his hand and kissed it. "Today is not a total disaster, my love."

"True," he said, and swept the back of his hand against her cheek. "I have you."

"This time next year, you will have me and one other."

He cocked his head. "What does that mean?"

"I'm going to have a child. That is what made me sick. But Granny has fixed that."

"I didn't think I could love you more," Peyton whispered. "But I do."

"Fate is sweet, my love."

The next morning Peyton stayed in the bedchamber long enough to put ten drops of Granny's elixir into a glass of water. The tinge of nausea Alexina felt developing immediately ceased.

"Keep inside Stone House today," Peyton said, and kissed her forehead.

Alexina dressed, went to the front door, and stood in the open doorway. She had never seen anything like the destruction scattered about. Tree parts lay strewn like fall leaves. Several huge oaks had been blown down, with their gnarly roots reaching to the sky. A wooden bowl was wedged into the thatch of the roof. Birds and fish were impaled on stumps of branches in bushes and shrubs. All manner of household items lay about. None of the items brought as much sadness to her as the thousands of green fruits, from walnut to fist size, that withered in the sun.

The sound of hoofbeats took her attention. Peyton rode Dragon in a full gallop. He stopped and slid from the saddle.

"I hoped we'd get this cleaned up before you saw it." He motioned for Seat and Tad to return to their cleaning around Stone House.

"Are all of the apples gone?"

He nodded. "Blown from the branches. We'll have no product this year."

"How could this happen?"

"The warmth we enjoy in the valley turned against us. Cold winds blew into the northern pass and mingled with the warm air. We've had whirlwinds before, but this is the worst I've seen." His eyebrows came together. "I'm going into Kerrstead to ask for a mortgage."

"Peyton, no! I have more jewelry. I could ask Grandfather—"

He put his hand up to stop her. "I've let other people take my responsibility. Boyce, then you. If I had known you were selling your jewelry to fund our venture in London, I wouldn't have allowed it. I can't let you do that again. I need money for taxes and supplies.

"I'll take a mortgage on the valley. Even with that, we may have to grind our grain into flour and sell it." He kissed her. "I might be late coming home. Please…stay inside. I don't want to add your safety to my worries right now."

"I'll stay inside. Please be careful, especially in the pass at night."

Peyton mounted the horse and patted the mane. "Dragon knows the pass. We'll be fine."

Alexina watched until horse and rider entered the narrow path between the stony walls of the ridges. She listened to the echoes of the horse's hoofbeats until they faded, then returned to the house for her morning meal.

Hester joined her at the breakfast table. They dined with little conversation, a fitting demeanor for the mood at Applewood.

Molly came into the kitchen with Little Jim, who ran to Hester. "Sing?"

Hester nodded. Alexina looked to her friend, silently asking her to explain.

"A few of us will be taking the children on a walk to find missing animals. I promised to teach them marching songs as we go along."

"A few of us?"

"Well, that is…. I mean…." Hester sputtered.

Molly brought a cup of tea to the table. "Our Miss Hester has agreed to teach the children some songs while they accompany Tad, Carl—"

Alexina smiled. "And Seat?"

"Aye. Seat will be there, too," Molly said.

Alexina sipped her tea. "Perhaps I will join you."

"Nay, Mistress," Molly said. "Our Good Lad has told everyone you are to stay at Stone House."

"I'm not sick. Granny gave me the most wonderful cure for the nausea."

"Aye, what you have ain't sickness, but you must take cautions. And we did promise Master Peyton we'd look out for you."

Alexina's shoulders sagged. She had promised him, too.

The house became quiet in the afternoon. Alexina kept busy by asking, then begging Dutch to allow her to help with the stew being made from the various meats made available by the whirlwind. All around Applewood, stew pots steamed, making use of the fowl and other meats, plus the young vegetables uprooted up by the winds. The Wanderers, being resourceful and clever, would not let something like weather be a total disaster. Alexina thought that must be one of the beauties of their lifestyle—own little, work and enjoy each day, and don't worry about the future.

As Alexina put the peeled vegetables into the pot, the voices of children echoed from the walls of Stone House. She recognized their song as one that Hester had taught in the Greenfield School. The difference was that these children sang with gusto, enjoying each note and singing to the top of their volume. Alexina laughed to herself. Within a few days, Hester had gathered a following, and not just from the young ones.

By the time dinner had finished cooking, the sounds of hoofbeats gave Alexina a wave of relief. Peyton had returned. *That was fast.* She wondered what he would have to tell her.

He wiped his boots at the back door. He rushed inside and held her.

She couldn't read him. "Bad news?"

"I got the money," he whispered. "But I'm in debt." He tilted her chin upward and kissed her. "Not to worry."

"I don't want *you* to worry, my love."

"We'll be fine," he said with a forced smile.

That she could read, meaning discussion over.

Once again Seat joined them for their meal, him keeping his eye on Hester and Hester keeping her gaze to her plate.

"Master Peyton, you mentioned selling the grain as flour," Seat said.

"We have plenty, so much we feed the animals with it. I've never sold it because it is an unknown grain. Once the townsfolk became aware of it, they would want more, and I don't wish to give them any reason to come into the valley."

At bedtime, Alexina joined Peyton in the shower-bath. He had been quiet since he returned, and she hoped he would tell her about his time in Kerrstead.

When they curled up together in the big four-post bed, he pulled her close. "I had to give them my deed when the bank approved the mortgage."

"At what interest?"

"Five percent"

"Payments or total at the end of the year?"

"Total."

"Compounded interest or—"

"I don't know. And how is it that you know about loans and interests?"

"The headmistress wanted all the girls to understand what their husbands would be doing with *their* fortunes. I think she did those wealthy girls a service. It will only be until next year."

"I know. But I haven't let that deed out of my grasp since I got it when I was sixteen."

He related how he left Harrow and fled to Applewood and what he remembered about his youth and things she didn't know about his life.

"Look what you've done by yourself, with no support from relatives or friends."

"True, but our child will not have to face what I did."

"Our child won't, my love. If something happens to us, these wonderful people, including Hester, will take over."

"That offers me comfort. Just one more thing you have done for me. And for you, I shall rebuild and replant our life here in Applewood."

Chapter Ninety

When Alexina awoke the next morning, she was alone. After dressing, she sat at the table for her morning meal

"Hester?" Alexina asked.

Sissy poured the tea. "Gone already this morning, Mistress. She said she planned to be back this afternoon."

Alexina put two lumps of sugar in her cup. "She has surely taken well to the valley."

Molly sat down at the table. "Sure has. Little Jim's been *singing*. You're looking well, Mistress."

"Ten drops of Granny's elixir. How many elixirs does Granny have?"

"Quite a few. I suspect most of them are the same recipe but have different colors and maybe a few different herbs."

Dutch brought fried cakes still hot from the pan and coated in sugar to the table. "Ya. I thinks mostly what Granny does is touch-healing. The 'lixirs just for show."

"Whatever her method," Alexina said, "it works, for I have had no more problems."

After breakfast, the maids tended to their chores, and Alexina sat by herself. She needed to stay busy, and the large wardrobe in the bedchamber required organization. As she stood peering into its depths, horses stomped outside. She ran to the front door. Rufus Smith's fine carriage had stopped at the front steps. His driver hopped down and opened the door of the white lacquered vehicle.

Rufus tipped his hat. "Good morning, lovely Neighbor Alexina."

"Mr. Smith, such a surprise."

"Yes, I come unannounced...you know why. I trust you are well and have some time to chat."

Alexina closed her eyes, trying to think of a reason to be rid of the man. Being the lady of the house, she did not work at chores, and Smith would know that. Perhaps if she engaged in a short conversation, she could excuse herself and send him on his way. "As you can see, we had a bit of a wind a few days ago."

He turned his head to survey the valley. The workers had taken care of the most important work, but the surroundings were still a mess. The green fruit blown all over had started to rot.

"Indeed," Smith said. "I deem it more than a bit. I didn't have better than a breeze at my home, a home at which you are most welcome to visit, an invitation I've extended frequently. Look around you, dear lady. So out of place are you. I—"

She hoped the workers had been so busy that none of them noticed the carriage, and at this moment, no one was running to tell Peyton of Smith's presence. Peyton surely did not need the aggravation.

"Mr. Smith—"

Alexina didn't have the opportunity to finish her retort. Horse hooves pounded from the direction of the orchard, and within a few seconds, she recognized Dragon, but for the first time, Dragon had a pulling collar around his neck. Peyton rode bareback and held on to the top of the collar. Dragon stopped at the carriage and snorted loudly. The four white horses hitched to the fine carriage, stepped about nervously, and whinnied. Peyton's open shirt showed gleaming sweat between patches of black soil on his chest. He slid from the horse's back and stood between Alexina and Rufus. Pressing his arms against his sides, he balled his fists and glared at Smith.

Instead of backing away in his usual cowardly response, Smith grinned at Peyton with surprising menace. He raised his eyebrows and cocked his head. "While I was in Kerrstead yesterday, I learned from my contact at the bank that you had taken a mortgage on your *farm,*" he sneered.

"What's it to you? Get off my property."

"Actually, Woodleigh, I've come to see the lady of the house."

"You've seen her long enough. Leave," Peyton said through clenched teeth.

"Well, I also had to see for myself why you would take a mortgage and such a small one at that. Enough to cover your taxes, which have not been paid, and a little more is my guess."

"Not your business. Go."

"Oh, but it is my business. I bought that mortgage, and when I decide to call it in.... Figure it out for yourself. It seems like you won't have many apples to make your drink, that is, unless you can make something with green apples...damaged and spoiled. I doubt that even they, the workers so skilled at making liquor, could do that. You know, I have some unwanted plants growing in my grass. Maybe they could do something with the weeds and call it Weed Wine. Oh, I like that. And maybe you could sell enough of that to make your mortgage. Ah, but you can't. How do I know this? Oh, yes! It's because I know when the mortgage will be called in."

Alexina burned at the effect this mockery was having on Peyton. "Neighbor Smith, you said you wished to talk with me?" She shot a look at Peyton, meaning to let her handle the pest.

Peyton sent her a cautioning look. She returned his gaze with a silent *trust me.* He turned and stomped toward the barn.

Smith laughed. "Indeed. May I come in?"

Alexina kept her face blank of expression, even though she did not wish to invite him inside. She nodded, and he followed her to the front door. He opened the heavy oak panel and allowed her to precede him.

As they entered the parlor, he moved his head left and right. "Oh my. What you have done to the place. But I expected no less."

"You wished to speak with me?" she said, not hiding her growing impatience.

He sat, uninvited, on the settee. Patting the other side, he waited for Alexina to join him. "I'll get right to it, then. You know my love for you exceeds all bounds."

Alexina started to rise and protest.

"Tut, tut, hear me out," he said in a serious voice.

She turned her attention to him.

"If you will come with me, I will tear up the mortgage and save this valley farm."

"Are you mad?"

"Obviously, I am. Here's your opportunity to do yourself a good turn and keep the land for them. I know you fancy these Gypsies. I also know Woodleigh is a beast who has mistreated you and denied his affections. An annulment would be no problem to obtain."

Alexina shook her head. "Mr. Smith, I know not how this information came to you, but it is false. My husband is a kind and affectionate man. We love each other very much." She centered her hand over her waist. "Although I wish not to be indelicate, I believe you must be told this to disabuse you of your ideas. I carry his child."

Smith shot up like an arrow. "Oh, say it isn't true!" He pulled at his hair. "I don't care. I'll take you anyway."

Alexina opened the door and fled. He followed, shouting, "Please, dear neighbor. Won't you slow so I can talk to you?"

She turned around in time to see him slip on a rotten apple. His feet airborne, he took a hard fall. His shouting turned to strident calls for help, claiming his back was surely broken.

Chapter Ninety-One

Peyton ran to Smith and got there at the same time as Alexina.

Alexina kneeled beside Smith. "We can't let him suffer."

Peyton made a sound, not unlike a growl, stomped his foot down on an apple, and crushed it into the ground.

Alexina crouched next to Smith, who sobbed piteously. She touched his shoulder. "You'll be all right."

The sounds of the quarrel brought many of the folk about, but no one moved to assist the man except Alexina. She called, "Carl, Tad? Will you please assist Mr. Smith into Stone House?"

Peyton, arms crossed over his chest, stood still while the men picked up the complaining sufferer. He did not follow the men but headed for the barn. Molly opened the door as Alexina led the way into the great room. They placed him on the settee and took two pillows from the armchairs for Smith's head.

Alexina bent over him. "We're sending for Granny now. She'll be here in a few minutes. Try to relax."

Smith's eyes flew open. "Granny? The witch? Don't let her near me."

"Our Granny is a fine medical practitioner. You have nothing to worry about."

"No! No! Alexina, please!"

She didn't scold him for using her first name. His shoulders rose and fell. "It's true? You *love* Woodleigh, and I have no chance?"

"Absolutely. Mr. Smith. You're lonely, but I'm sure there is someone for you." She remembered Seat's comment about crooked asses and seats to fit them.

Smith struggled to a sitting position. "There *is* someone I've seen. She's not as beautiful or cultured as you, but—"

"Wonderful! Where? Do you know her name? Is it someone nearby?"

"She lives in this valley, but *you* wouldn't know her, I'm sure. Her name is Pearl Pink."

He obviously did not recognize Daisy, her former lady's maid, as Pearl Pink. He had not made eye contact with her on the day of their arrival to the valley because of Daisy's lowly status. Even if he had, her appearance was drastically altered. Alexina was at a loss for words, but Molly saved the moment.

"Mistress, you're needed in the kitchen."

"Excuse me, Mr. Smith." Alexina hurried out of his view but stood where she could peek and listen.

Molly knelt beside the settee. "Mr. Smith, I know Pearl Pink. Shall we make a deal? If I bring her to you, will you not demand the mortgage until next year?"

"You know Pearl Pink? You would introduce me?"

"Aye, that I would if you make your promise."

"I promise. Please, talk to Pearl Pink for me." He lay back on the settee, the look of pain fading from his face.

"I can do better than that. I'll bring her to you right now."

"Yes, yes! Fetch the lovely Pearl."

While Molly had a word with a messenger outside, Dutch brought their visitor a glass and a slim bottle, one of Granny's tonics. He sipped the glass, licking his lips. Every so often, he muttered, "Pearl Pink."

Inside a half hour, a cart arrived with Granny and the illustrious blonde Wagon Girl, Pearl Pink. The former maid strolled through the open front door in a queenly fashion, head held high, allowing the satin of her voluminous skirts to brush the floor in an audible swish. Pearl had gained a stone of plumpness and now sported ample cleavage in her low neckline. Long blonde curls cascaded over her shoulders and back. A pearl pendant and dangly earrings representing the color of her name jiggled as she walked.

Pearl stopped in front of the settee. "Someone wishes to see me?"

In the hush of the room, Smith cleared his throat. "It's me. I wish to meet you."

Pearl put her hand to her chin and studied the man. "You're

the rich man who lives in that big house yonder." She pointed in the direction of the pass. "Haven't I seen you at the camp trying to visit Sapphire?"

Smith's face beamed with delight. "You've noticed me then!"

"I know you," she said in a guarded way. "Why have you called me here?"

"I adore you." His arms extended in a gesture of supplication. "I wish you to be mine."

Alexina put her hands on her hips. *That was a fast turn-about from his adoration for me.*

Pearl shifted her heftier weight and cocked her head. Dim-witted Daisy had learned a thing or two from the shrewd bunch with whom she resided. Her expressions changed from wide-eyed incredulity to wrinkled brow calculation. At last, she removed her eyes from Smith and stared at the others in the room. "What's in it for them?"

"If you join me, I won't recall the mortgage I hold on this place. I'll wait until next year."

Pearl's charcoal-enhanced eyebrows united, and her forehead furrowed. "Let me understand. You live in the big house on the huge estate. And if they don't pay you, you can take this property?"

Granny silently moved toward the settee, casually removed a long pin from her hair, and jabbed the pin into Smith's buttocks. He howled, jumped up, and ran around the room holding the spot of attack.

"Cured," Granny said.

Molly laughed loudly. Alexina held her hand to her mouth.

He halted. His face looked like a raincloud ready to storm. Then he straightened his shoulders and extended his hand toward Pearl. "Will you come with me?"

Pearl fisted one hand on her hip. "Is this a matrimonial proposal?"

"Is that what you wish?"

"If we are joined, as your legal wife, does that mean I own what you own?"

"Under certain conditions."

"Very well. I'll marry you."

Molly stepped up close to Pearl. "If you leave the Tribe, you can never come back."

Pearl gave that consideration a moment. "I'll have him and all his goods. Why would I need to come back? The gold I've saved can't possibly match what I would get from him." Then she looked at Alexina. "The Wagon Girls wanted to pool their money to buy that mortgage, but without my part, they didn't have enough. Isn't that amusing? I stood in the way of saving this valley." She put her arm around Smith. "I think you should call your carriage, Dearie."

When they left, Alexina sat hard on the settee. Granny sat next to her and took Alexina's palm. "I see good fortune and happiness."

"Oh, Granny. I hope so."

Everyone departed to complete their chores, leaving Alexina alone with her thoughts.

The sound of horse hooves brought her to the door. A cart pulled up to the front, and Seat hopped from the driver's position. He ran around to the other side to help Hester down from the big-wheeled cart. He held her for a long moment.

Hester turned to Alexina. "Good afternoon."

"Maybe for you," she said.

"Are you all right?"

"I'm fine. You two missed the madness." Alexina explained what had transpired.

"I have some money saved. Let me help."

"Let her help, Mistress," Seat said. "Then she'll have to stay to see her investment prosper."

Hester turned her head to the man. "I have already decided to stay, Seaton. I wish to start a school."

"I'm so glad! You won't be sorry." Alexina frowned. "Oh, Hester, perhaps you will regret your decision. What if we lose Applewood?"

"You will not lose Applewood," Seat and Hester said together.

He smiled. "We can make alcohol out of our rich grain. The townsfolk may miss the Jack, but they can replace it with vodka. We sure got the barrels for it. Give us a month. I have to go now." Seat took Hester's hand and kissed her palm. "This is my people's way of saying goodbye for a short time and a silent promise to see you soon."

"What is it you kiss if you're going to be away for a longer time?"

Seat raised his eyebrows and smiled wide. "Perhaps I can show you that and the vodka later."

Alexina threw her arms around Hester and hugged her. "You are so naughty. Lord, have I missed you!" Her friend offered the diversion she needed. She wished Peyton had a similar distraction from the financial stresses the valley and its people faced. Perhaps the prospect of having vodka to sell to the locals would help alleviate his concerns.

That night in bed, their love-making fell short of the mark. At breakfast the next morning, Peyton sat at the table like a gloomy scarecrow.

Alexina brushed her husband's arm lightly. "I'd like to see the orchard today."

"No. It's not safe. You would suffer despair from the sight. Plus, it stinks from the rotting fruit and dead fish."

"Are there any Eden trees left?"

Peyton's eyes turned to steel. "Not one. The trees grew too tall for the root system. I knew that would be a problem someday. I had a fortune within my grasp, and one wind storm took it away."

Alexina picked up Peyton's hand and traced the lines of his palm. "Something good will happen, my love. Granny said we will have health and good fortune. See? Right here, the wealth line, and here, health. You trust Granny, don't you?"

"All I know is that we have to dig another pit to bury all the rot before the smell drives us out of the valley. I must provide for you and our child. These people depend on me, too."

"Stop."

He kissed her forehead. "Sorry."

"Unacceptable," Alexina said. "I require a proper adieu."

"Indeed," he said. He pulled her from the chair up into his arms, where he kissed her, folding her gently backwards. She needed his support as her spine liquefied. He touched his tongue to hers, and the rest of her body dissolved.

Later that morning, Alexina heard the gravel at the pass. The drayage wagon from Turnersfield that delivered their goods and mail rolled closer. Hester joined her at the front door.

Peyton and Seat came at a run as the cart thudded on the packed dirt of the driveway. When it came to a halt, the passengers stood.

"Grandfather!" Alexina called. "Mother Bertha!"

Peyton opened the wooden tailgate and lifted his mother to the ground. "Hello, Mother."

Bertha put her hand against his cheek. "Hello, Son."

Peyton turned to assist Geoffrey Downing from the cart.

"Here, Seat," the driver called and threw him a bundle of mail. "Sorry, had this for a while."

Bertha shot him a stern look of condemnation. "No doubt with the letter I wrote saying I would be here today."

"Please come inside," Alexina said. "Would you like tea?"

Alexina bid her guests to rest in the living room as Seat and Peyton brought in their luggage. Before they had a chance to speak, they heard the distant sound of the gravel echoing off the sides of the pass again.

Looking out the window, a chill ran up Alexina's spine. Rufus Smith had returned with Pearl Pink by his side. The fancy white carriage stopped. They did not knock but strode through the unlatched door.

Peyton jumped up from the settee to block their entrance.

"Step away," Pearl Pink said.

Alexina spoke through clenched teeth. "You may not enter my home,"

"Maybe that's true, if you had one," Pearl Pink answered with a smirk and wiggled her finger with the gold band. She jerked her new husband by his shoulder, projecting him forward into the parlor. "I just came by to check on them dishes." She turned her gaze to the shelves in the dining room. "You really fixed this place up. I can use a few of these things in *my* house. Too bad you didn't get your carpets." She glared at her husband. "That stupid Boyce. He didn't do right by you, Rufus. He shouldn't have left until she'd finished decorating!"

Pink was the only one amused, for the rest of the assemblage remained quiet, including Rufus. She eyed Bertha, then Geoffrey. "I'm guessing you'd like to know who I am. I'm Pearl Pink, but you can call me Mistress. My husband is the new master of Apple Valley and Stone House."

Bertha left the velvet wing chair. "I know you. You're Rufus Smith, Ignace's son. You used to play with my son when you were young. Alexina was too small to remember."

"It doesn't matter if you know him," Pearl Pink said, stepping around Rufus to face Bertha. "This place has a mortgage, and he holds it. He's calling it today, and if they don't pay it, which they can't, then the place is ours, and all the stuff in it."

Geoffrey rose to his feet and moved to stand in front of Rufus. "One of the Eden's Joy investors visited me, asking about a mortgage his bank recently approved for Peyton Woodleigh. Since I am the financial officer for the product, *I purchased* the debt, not you. So, tell your guttersnipe wife to close her flap. I don't know what kind of a flim-flam you are trying to pull, but neither of you own a thing in this valley."-

Bertha said, "Now that you mention it, who is living in Applewood Estate, the manor house? We passed it on our way into the valley. This is the greenhouse."

Chapter Ninety-Two

Rufus grabbed Pearl Pink by her arm. "Come, Sweet Pea. Didn't you say you had gold back at your wagon for us to retrieve?" They rushed out the door, and soon the sound of a carriage speeding away was heard.

Alexina shook her head. "What is happening?"

Bertha sat next to her. "My dear daughter, it's clear to me. I fired Ignace because I believed he was stealing from us. Your mother wouldn't believe it. I think he wrote letters to each of us saying we were never to see each other. His plan got stronger after my husband's accident."

Geoffrey pulled the wing chair close to the settee. "And I don't believe for a minute the explosion in your father's mine was an accidental collapse. Smith could have easily sent an agent to blow up the mine, and then have the event covered up. After all, it happened in India, which was too far away to be investigated properly by authorities."

"And I'm ashamed to say," Bertha continued, "Ignace used my grief against me. When I sent my boy away to boarding school, I think that man had someone intercept Peyton's letters to me and mine to him."

Peyton spoke for the first time. "Mother, is the manor house truly part of Applewood Estate?"

"It *is* Applewood Estate. This valley had no name that I knew of. It was where your father conducted his experiments. I have brought some papers with me—his notes and the deed."

"When I demanded a copy of the deed, Smith must have

changed it to not include the manor house and told Rufus to occupy the premises. I didn't remember what the estate from my childhood looked like and didn't question the boundary description." He cast a worried glance at Alexina. "Was our marriage contract false also?"

Bertha smiled. "No, it was real. We wrote it as a farce because, as children, the two of you were so fond of one another. I'm glad Ignace saved his copies."

Peyton kissed the top of Alexina's head. "Me too."

Bertha removed her shawl and folded it on her lap. She wore a large turquoise brooch displaying a pink design made with flashing gems.

"I don't remember much of my childhood, Mother, but I remember that brooch."

Alexina peered closely. "It's the fish! You were going to tell me about it."

"I'll tell you now. Your father, a brilliant geologist, had been employed by a company who made oil paints for artists. He traveled to find natural elements for colors. He found a bright yellow deposit, chromium, in India. While he supervised the digging, he noticed the area had gemstones in the stream. He quit his job and bought the land, knowing it would become a great mine, in which we all invested."

Geoffrey nodded. "I was lucky enough to have invested too."

"When he returned to India to start the mining, he noticed the natives grinding up the red roots of a water plant they claimed could make a root system out of any plant. Alex knew Clive would want to play with that, so he asked to bring some of the plant back to England. The natives told him the plant could only survive if a special type of fish lived near it. Alex brought samples of both back and gave them to Clive, who brought them here. I don't know how far he got with experimenting before he died, but I brought his notes if you are interested."

Peyton said. "Yes. I want those notes."

Alexina asked, "How does the brooch figure in?"

"Your father became very wealthy from the gemstones in his mine, and as a hobby, he learned to cut and set jewelry. He made wondrous pieces for your mother. When he saw the fish, he said their ugliness piqued his artistic interest. He made me this brooch with pink sapphires to commemorate the discovery. It was right before the mine collapsed or exploded."

Geoffrey said, "I had Ignace Smith investigated. You didn't

believe me when I said your father and mother had left you a fortune, not to mention what Simon has sent. Well, they did. Ignace has been living on your money since your mother died."

"And his son lived in my house," Peyton said.

"The reason I came with Bertha to Applewood was to inform you Smith has been arrested for theft."

Peyton put his arms around Alexina. "If you had access to your fortune, every bachelor in England would have been after you, and you would not have married me. For that, I thank the man."

"Don't get too generous," Geoffrey said. "I have found some interesting issues. Smith chose to represent certain criminals who had no means to pay attorney fees. Upon acquittal, he pressed them into his service. One of the gentlemen, Albert Bently, and another fellow were paid by Smith to blow up a river bed mine…sixteen years ago in India."

Alexina shook her head. "Albert Bently? Daisy's maiden name is Bently."

"I believe he mentioned a daughter. For the price of a good attorney, Bently and Mason are willing to testify against Smith in court. Whatever happened to that silly thing who accompanied you here as a personal maid?"

"You just saw her. She has two new names—Pearl Pink and Mrs. Rufus Smith."

"I thought there was something familiar about that nasty bit of fluff. There is more to tell about Ignace Smith."

Geoffrey pointed to Bertha. "Smith was afraid you would eventually convince Edwina of his treachery. He sent documents to both of you to cease contact. He knew that when Alexander died in the explosion, Edwina would turn to you. The fact that Clive was killed was an added bonus for him."

Bertha put her hands to her face. Peyton embraced his mother for the first time in many years.

Geoffrey continued his explanation. "Edwina extracted my promise not to interfere with your life in any way. I could not interfere, so he proceeded to steal your fortune."

"Do you mean I did not have to live on a stipend or teach at that horrid school?"

Bertha turned to Alexina. "Your father's mine provided a great wealth, my dear. Smith saw his opportunity to seize it by removing you from anyone who could advise you."

Alexina hung her head. "I am ashamed to admit that Ignace convinced me you were mad, Grandfather."

Geoffrey paced a few steps and stopped. "Well, being separated from you did make me mad for a while. However, Smith's plan backfired when he sent you here where his son Rufus could spy on you."

Bertha nodded. "Rufus has always been a pawn in his father's service after his mother fled Ignace's abuse. Then he had to contend with you, Peyton, besting him in every way, especially in cornering little Alexina's attention."

Peyton made a face. "Rufus loved Alexina when we were small?"

Bertha smiled. "Oh, yes, but she only had a heart for you. It was such agony for him."

Peyton chuckled. "I fear his agony has just begun."

Everyone in the room laughed.

Alexina stood. "Our future has changed, but I don't know what we should do next."

Peyton put his arm around her shoulders. "The first thing we should do is send men to the manor house and see that Rufus doesn't return. Then we'll have to make sleeping arrangements for our guests."

Bertha laughed. "The manor house can accommodate a small army. I suggest we all go there. Ah, it has been so many years since I've seen the place."

Chapter Ninety-Three

Alexina, Hester, Bertha, Molly, Dutch, and Sissy crammed into the old carriage. With Peyton on the driver's perch, Silverton trotted the assemblage out of the valley. Seat drove Geoffrey in the cart.

As they neared the house, Alexina took in an astonished breath. Seeing it from the road only offered a portion of its beauty. A closer view provided awe. Dark boards in horizontal vees between whitewashed stone were spectacular. The huge roof made of slate tiles in the shape of fish scales covered the building, along with turrets on every corner. On foot, the group walked through a garden to get to the carved door, where a large lion's head had a knocker between its nostrils. Two pools, sadly in need of cleaning, flanked the walkway. Untended wisteria with its gnarled vines grew up wooden pillars and over the porch roof. Even through the disarray of the lawn and shrubbery, the beauty was striking. *What will it look like inside?*

Bertha pushed open the unlocked door and gave them a tour of the place, starting on the left in the parlor. A great marble fireplace competed with the many diamond shaped window panes sparkling in the light from the afternoon sun. The wood paneling took Alexina's breath away.

From there, they saw the library, all walls loaded with books in gilt cabinets.

Alexina hurried to the bookcases. "Hester, look. We can use these when we start our school."

Hester moved to the shelves and ran her hand along the spines as she read the titles aloud. "How soon can we start?"

Alexina pulled out a leather volume. "Right away. We can put

Stone House to use as our school. Peyton?"

He nodded. "The Wanderers would welcome a school. Thank you, dear wife, and you, too, Hester."

Next on the tour was the dining room. The long table had been used as a desk at one end, with newspapers and journals crowding the silver candelabra and unused porcelain flower holders. Each of twelve chairs had carvings a little different from each other, but with caning in the back that matched. Bertha pointed out the manor's many attributes, including the artwork she and Clive had selected.

As they walked, Alexina admired the design and details of the exquisite residence. The kitchen was large enough that the staff would not run into each other. Dutch admired the ovens, one exclusively for bread.

Alexina spread her arms and looked up to the carved wooden ceiling. "So many wonderful things. What awaits us in the other rooms?"

When they reached the main bedchamber, Bertha picked up a glass dish resting on the dresser. She removed a delicate chain from the dish. "Isn't this yours, Alexina?"

Alexina took the necklace and ran her finger over the small ruby, sapphire, and diamond pendant. Tears flooded her eyes. "Yes, it's mine." She recalled the recent visit to Ignace Smith's office when the pink velvet box had dropped to the floor. The image of him holding on to the box brought her perfect understanding. "Ignace thought I would bring the jewelry back to Applewood, so he hired bandits to stop us. He wanted to take everything away from me."

"He tried, but instead, he gave you this." Geoffrey spread his arm around the room.

"And he gave me Peyton."

"You are the Applewood Estate mistress now," Bertha said.

Alexina shook her head. "This is the house your husband built for you."

Bertha smiled. "Which now belongs to you, my dear, and I can't imagine anyone better for the position."

Alexina slid her arm around Peyton's waist. "I was happy at Stone House."

Bertha smiled wider. "Precisely why you are so perfect for my son. Your mother and I saw that years ago."

"Thank you for your foresight, Mother Bertha. Will you please help me until I learn how to manage the real Applewood Estate?"

"Of course. May we start with sorting out where we shall rest our heads?"

"And tea afterwards?" Alexina said.

The maids headed for the kitchen. They cleaned the table, putting the papers in a pile in the mudroom. Everyone sat at the table for tea. Alexina thanked Dutch, Sissy, and Molly for their service. "You three will have to learn to deal with this new house, along with me."

Bertha accepted a cup of tea from Molly. "When Bridget returns, she can help set the house in order and work with your servants."

"I don't have servants, Mother Bertha," Alexina said, taking Molly's hand. "I have beloved helpers."

Bertha took a sip. "I see that, and I admire you all the more."

Molly poured tea into Peyton's cup. "That don't mean we won't need training. Aye, this house deserves a well-trained staff. Aye, that's what we be—staff."

"Well," Bertha said. "It might take a few months for thorough training. I don't want to overstay my visit."

"Not a visit, Mother Bertha. Let us consider this a homecoming. This is your home, too. Forever." She patted the small bump concealed by her skirt. "And I would be most obliged if you could be here to welcome our child."

Bertha's eyes watered. "A grandchild. My dear, you can't know what this means to me!"

Geoffrey grinned. "A child! Good work, young man."

"Grandfather!" Alexina glared for a second, then they all laughed.

Peyton cleared his throat for attention. "Speaking of our child, I'd like Granny to move into the house to be closer."

Molly shook her head. "I doubt she'd take a room. But she might be persuaded to move her wagons onto the grounds. If you offer to provide a large garden with all of her herbs and plants in one space, I believe she wouldn't be able to resist."

"I'll speak with her this evening," Peyton said. "We'll have the wagons moved to where she directs."

"Only Granny's wagons," Alexina said in a firm voice. "The Wagon Girls stay where they are."

Peyton rubbed his nose and chuckled. "The Mistress of Applewood has spoken."

Bertha smiled. "It is clear, my dear Alexina, you need no help from me to assume your position as lady of the house."

Days later, with the move from Stone House to the manor house completed, the large dining room in Applewood Estate rang with the conversations of a happy group. Peyton described his plans for rooting the Eden trees, and according to what he had read in his father's notes, in ten years, the newly grown trees would be once again bear their almost magical, sweet fruit.

Months later, on the anniversary of their traditional Tasting Day, the Wanderers, the Woodleighs, and their guests joined the festivities. The music played. Peyton danced a slow, careful reel with a heavily pregnant Alexina. Geoffrey bowed to Bertha as his invitation.

Seat swung Hester from her chair. "Exchange one seat for another."

Tad, Carl, and Tom rolled two huge barrels across the lawn and righted them close to the firelight. Seat escorted Hester toward the barrels. He accepted a spout and a hammer. The final bang started the flow, and Tad was there with a cup. They presented the first taste to Peyton.

He sipped the brew and shuddered.

"Not good?" Seat asked, with a disappointed note.

Peyton threw his head back and laughed. "Good, but not Eden's Joy. We'll have a fine time tonight with vodka."

Seat held his mug up. "I plan to take a wife." He went to where Hester sat with the ladies. "Hear me, friends. I love this woman." He went down on one knee. "How about it?"

Hester blushed so deeply, it showed in the firelight. "Is that a marriage proposal?"

"Of course, it is." He thought for a minute. "Will you be my wife?"

Hester kissed Seat, then held up a cup of ladies' punch. "I will!"

Everyone cheered.

Peyton held his glass high. "To us, the happy people who live in Applewood Valley, and now on Applewood Estate."

<<End>>

Patricia is a former art teacher and high school librarian. She lives in South Florida with her husband and three dogs. She writes short stories, novellas, and novels, mostly Fantasy and Sci-Fi. She has also written three Romances, a Sci-Fi, a Victorian, and a Contemporary. Her stories revolve around action and deep relationships, allowing the reader to watch the scene unfold as if present. Patricia is active in three critique groups and often helps new writers learn the ropes. She is an active member of the Florida Writers Association, Mystery Writers of America, and Romance Writers of America.

When not writing, Patricia enjoys painting watercolors and drawing in several media. Currently, she is learning illustration techniques for future books. Her frequent travel provides opportunities to check off bucket list items and sometimes inspires new stories. She is a voracious reader and loves a good book talk.

Check out her Facebook page at Carpewordum@gate.net.

Made in the USA
Las Vegas, NV
01 October 2021